Praise for
CATHERINE ANDERSON!

"A delightful comedy of errors.... With this
latest, Anderson creates a heartwarming
page-turner while establishing herself as a
major voice in the romance genre."
Publishers Weekly (*Starred Review*) on *Simply Love*

"Seldom have the themes of trust and forgiveness been
so well treated.... Ace Keegan, despite his alpha-male
persona, is a paragon of patience and understanding,
a romantic hero in every way."
Publishers Weekly on *Keegan's Lady*

"Catherine Anderson is one of the best romance writers
today. This book is the definition of a keeper:
moving, touching, with amazing characters who live
with you long after the book is done. A brilliant author
and fabulous not-to-be-missed romance."
Affaire de Coeur on *Annie's Song*

Winner of nine consecutive
KISS Awards for her heroes!

Other Avon Books by
Catherine Anderson

ANNIE'S SONG
FOREVER AFTER
KEEGAN'S LADY
SIMPLY LOVE

CATHERINE ANDERSON

Cherish

AVON BOOKS 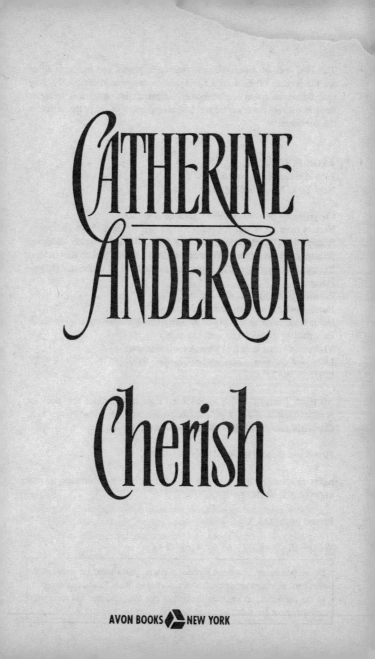 NEW YORK

This is a work of fiction. Names, characters, places, and incidents either are the product of the author's imagination or are used fictitiously. Any resemblance to actual events, locales, organizations, or persons, living or dead, is entirely coincidental and beyond the intent of either the author or the publisher.

AVON BOOKS, INC.
1350 Avenue of the Americas
New York, New York 10019

Front cover art by Paul Stinson
Inside front cover art by Doreen Minuto
Inside back cover author photo by Terry Day's Studio
Published by arrangement with the author
Visit our website at http://www.AvonBooks.com
Library of Congress Catalog Card Number: 98-92774
ISBN: 0-380-79936-7

First Avon Books Printing: November 1998

AVON TRADEMARK REG. U.S. PAT. OFF. AND IN OTHER COUNTRIES, MARCA REGISTRADA, HECHO EN U.S.A.

Printed in the U.S.A.

WCD   10 9 8 7 6 5 4 3 2 1

To my son, Sidney D. Anderson Jr., and his wife, Mary Hamilton, who were joined in holy wedlock in Alice Springs, Australia on July 19, 1997. We hold you both close to our hearts even though you are thousands of miles away. May your days begin and end with a smile for each other, and may the hours that stretch between be filled with love. If you have love, you have everything, so that, dear ones, is my prayer for you.

And also to my brother Tom La May for all the times you have filled our lives with the sound of music. There is no sweeter gift than a song that touches the heart. When I think of you, I will always picture you strumming on your guitar and singing to our mother. Thank you for all the times you made her smile, brother dear. To me you'll always be a superstar, and my favorite song will always be your rendition of The Little Mohee.

Prologue

Pennsylvania, 1868

Moonlight bathed the rolling pastureland, its silvery glow turning the weathered fence posts gray and making the sections of sagging wire look like ribbons of tinsel. Not caring that the hem of her black skirt was growing heavy with evening dew from the tall grass, Rebecca Morgan strolled over the uneven ground, her hands clasped behind her back and her gaze drinking in every detail of the landscape. Everything looked the same as it always had, yet so very different. For one thing, no cows dotted the clearings amongst the trees now. The last of the livestock had been sold yesterday.

The night seemed oddly silent without the constant lowing of cattle all around her. An ache filled Rebecca's chest. She had lived on this church farm all of her twenty-one years, and it wasn't easy for her to say good-bye. A sad smile touched her mouth as she drew up near the fence. Propping her arms atop the post, she studied the old elm in the pasture beyond, her eyes stinging with nostalgic tears. She could scarcely believe that all of this land had been parceled off and sold.

All of her memories had happened here, yet now the earth beneath her feet belonged to other people, and in the morning, she would have to leave, never to return. She couldn't help but recall the happy hours she'd spent climbing on the sturdy branches of that elm as a very young child. Where had the years gone? It seemed to her that time had passed so swiftly, taking her from childhood to adulthood in a twinkling. Now an entirely new chapter of her life was about to unfold.

Turning her gaze westward, Rebecca wished she felt lighter of heart at the prospect. For reasons beyond her, every time she thought about the long journey that she, her parents, and the other ten church members would embark upon in the morning, she was filled with foreboding. *Silliness.* Last year all the other church families had made the trip to Santa Fe without incident. There was absolutely no reason for her to feel so anxious.

The others weren't transporting money, though, and we will be, a little voice whispered at the back of her mind.

For at least the dozenth time, she wished other arrangements could have been made to transport the funds. Once divided into parcels, this community farmland had sold to several different buyers for a great deal of money—far more than was wise for a small, unarmed caravan of travelers to carry. What if something happened? Rebecca's lifelong friend Matthew, who was a bit of a rascal and was forever breaking the rules by reading secular publications, had told her all manner of horrific tales about the west. Between here and Santa Fe, there were men who actually earned their bread by stealing, robbing not only banks and trains but unwary travelers as well. It struck Rebecca as being foolish to take any unnecessary chances. It would have been easier and far safer to send the proceeds from the sale of the church farm to New Mexico by stage under armed guard. If anything happened to that money, their new church farm in New Mexico territory would be doomed. The church members who awaited them there would be unable to buy livestock, farming implements or seed to plant crops next spring.

But, no. Despite all of Matthew's warnings, the brethren had voted against hiring someone else to transport the cash. As Rebecca's papa had so patiently explained to her, the use of weaponry to defend themselves or their property was against their beliefs, and hiring armed guards would be a roundabout way of breaking that rule. The brethren trusted in God, not a Colt .45.

Rebecca understood the brethren's reasoning. Truly, she did. And she believed as they did, completely and with her whole heart. But even so, her friend Matthew's warnings rang in her ears. None of the brethren in her traveling party, her papa included, were equipped to handle trouble. In the event of a robbery, what on earth would become of the church?

Dragging in a breath, Rebecca said a quick but heartfelt prayer for more faith. Her papa and the other five brethren were intelligent men and would take every precaution during the journey west. They even planned to hide the money under a fake floor in one of the covered wagons they would purchase once they reached St. Louis. All would be well. She was just letting all the stories she'd heard about gunmen and hostile Indians unsettle her. The heavenly Father would protect them, just as He always had, and she was being foolish to worry.

It wasn't as if they had a choice about leaving, after all. Relocating to Santa Fe was necessary for the good of all the church members, especially the younger ones. Even she could see that. Philadelphia had been growing by leaps and bounds. With each passing year, this farm's boundaries had been more closely encroached upon by landowners of secular persuasion. While working outdoors, Rebecca frequently glimpsed strangers passing by out on the road, and occasionally their new neighbors were even so bold as to trespass on church property. The elders' concern for the younger church members was legitimate, for even Rebecca had caught herself gazing with longing at the colorful clothing worn by females not of her faith. Worldly temptation was knocking at their door on a regular basis, no question about it, and sooner or later, the younger people might be led astray.

After living all her life in one place, Rebecca supposed her uneasiness about the move was due to the fact that she was more easily unsettled by changes than most people were. She'd grown up here, gone to sleep in the same bed for as long as she could recall, and had believed she

would die here. Now all that seemed familiar and safe
was being stripped from her life, and she was about to
strike out for parts unknown. The farthest afield she had
ever been was to Philadelphia, and then she'd always gone
with her papa or one of the other brethren. Now she was
about to travel nearly two thousand miles. The mere
thought seemed frightening to her.

Once she was happily settled at the farm in New Mexico, she would laugh at all these misgivings, she felt sure,
and before she knew it, she would grow as fond of her
new home as she was of this one. There was much to
anticipate in the near future. She would soon be officially
betrothed to Henry Rusk, and next June she would become his wife. In no time, she would probably have a
brood of children. How foolish of her to cling to the old
when her new life would be so much more exciting.

Releasing a weary sigh, Rebecca took one last look at
the elm tree, then turned to go. Dawn would come early,
and she would have to do a lot of walking beside the
wagon tomorrow. Like everyone else, she needed to get
a good night's sleep. There were probably last minute
things to be done before leaving in the morning as well,
and her mother was undoubtedly wondering what had become of her.

As Rebecca approached the church common, she saw
that golden lantern light illuminated the windows of the
half dozen occupied houses, the warm glow all the more
marked because the other homes looked so dark and
empty. Another wave of nostalgia washed over her. With
only a handful of people still here, there were no voices
or laughter to greet her. It struck her as being even sadder
that the church bell, which had called her to prayer several
times each day for as long as she could remember, would
never be rung here again.

Realizing that she was about to cry, Rebecca straightened her shoulders and raised her chin a notch. Enough
of this. She didn't want her parents to see her with a long
face. In preparing for the trip, they had enough on their
minds without having to worry about her.

Even at a distance, she could see her papa checking the

load on their buckboard, his shoulders jerking as he tugged to check the ropes. For days, he'd been fretting because her mother had insisted on packing so many of their things. A buckboard could bear only so much weight, and they were bound to encounter some rough roads before they could purchase a larger, sturdier conveyance in Missouri.

A smile curved Rebecca's mouth as she surveyed the lofty jumble of possessions piled in the wagon. Even after sorting and tossing out a fair half of their household contents, they still had an incredible amount of stuff to take with them. Her papa was right; Ma was a little pack rat. Just the thought of having to transfer all that stuff into a covered wagon once they reached St. Louis made her feel weary.

As she crossed the common, Rebecca resisted the urge to look over her shoulder at the pastures that stretched almost as far as she could see behind her. The time had come to look forward, not back, and she meant to do so with a glad heart. No more anxiety. If she began thinking about the frightening stories Matthew had told her again, she would give herself a good scolding and pray for serenity. A good Christian had utter confidence in the Almighty. She would do well to follow her parents' example and trust in God to watch over them.

Chapter 1

Southeastern Colorado, 1868

There was nothing quite as distinctive as the scent of human blood, Race Spencer thought grimly. Warm and slightly sweet with a coppery tang, it put him in mind of his childhood and the stolen pennies he'd often clutched in one grubby fist.

All his life, he'd heard men tell of seeing things so terrible it curled their hair. Race, whose wiry, jet-black locks were as straight as a bullet on a windless day, had always believed those tales to be flapdoodle. Until now. Judging by the prickly feeling under his collar, the short hairs at the nape of his neck were curling as tight as the topknot on a bald-faced calf.

Even his horse Dusty was all het up, withers twitching, ears cocked, freshly shod hooves nervously striking partially buried slabs of rock on the sandy rise. Race leaned forward in the saddle to stroke the buckskin's muscular neck. Not that he figured on it doing much good. Dusty knew the smell of death, and like any living thing with a lick of sense, the horse had a hankering to make fast tracks.

"Easy, old son," he murmured to the mount who was also the best trail partner around. "Give me a minute to eyeball this here mess before we decide to hightail it."

In the arroyo below, a half dozen wagons sat in a loose circle around a lone candelabra cactus. The stretch of sun-baked, yellow clay between the wagons was littered with all manner of possessions and so many dead people Race had trouble counting them in a sweeping glance. All were dressed in black clothing, with large, crimson patches staining the yellow earth under their spread-eagle bodies.

Though a few rays of fading sunlight were still visible over the distant peaks of the Rocky Mountains, Race felt chilled to his marrow. A shudder did a do-si-do up his spine, and his skin went as knurly as a plucked goose.

Over a mile back, he had started catching whiffs of the blood. Knowing it was fresh and most probably human, he should have been braced for the sight that greeted him now. But to say these people had died violently was like saying Methuselah was sort of old. This was a massacre, nothing less, the type of thing Apache warriors might do, only as far as Race could see, there hadn't been a single scalp taken.

All totaled, Race counted eleven bodies in the rubble, six middling-aged men and five women. Citified folks, he reckoned, lured west by the promise of free land and wide-open spaces. It was disheartening to think that high hopes for a better life had led them to such a sorry pass.

From the looks of things, they'd traveled a far piece, probably clear from St. Louis, a hell of a journey for both man and beast. A fellow lying in the foreground wore boots with patched soles, indicating that he'd walked many a mile, and the canvas on the rattletrap wagons was tattered and sported so many holes, it reminded Race of the punctured Arbuckle can that his biscuit roller, Cookie Grigsley, used as a strainer.

The poor damned fools. What craziness had led them to leave the main wagon train? And after doing that, why in the hell had they ventured off the Santa Fe Trail? He supposed they might have taken a wrong turn. The Mountain Branch of the Santa Fe Trail meandered in a north-westerly direction for quite a spell before it dove south toward New Mexico, and sometimes inexperienced travelers got to thinking they were headed the wrong way. When they tried to correct their course, they often got lost.

He heaved a weary sigh, knowing even as the questions

circled darkly in his mind that he'd come up with no answers. None that made sense, anyhow. After hiring out his gun to Santa Fe Trail wagon masters for ten long years, Race knew that all westward-bound travelers were warned repeatedly that it was dangerous to light out on their own. Unfortunately, in almost every caravan, there were those men whose high opinions of themselves outflanked their common sense. For whatever reason, these folks had broken off from the main group.

It would be their last mistake.

In his thirty years of living, Race had seen more things to turn his stomach than he cared to recollect, but this beat all. Even most of the oxen had been slaughtered, only two of the creatures still standing. Whoever had done this was plumb loco.

The ticklish sensation at the back of Race's neck suddenly became more pronounced. He scanned the surrounding terrain. He wasn't alone in this place.

Another man might have pooh-poohed the notion, but Race had learned when he was knee high to a tall grasshopper never to question his hunches. Maybe it was the dash of Apache flowing in his veins, but he had always possessed keen senses. Like his being able to smell blood from well over a mile off. No how, no way could he explain that, yet to him the ability was second nature.

Putting all else from his mind, he pricked his ears to listen, his body motionless, his breathing slowed almost to a stop. What he saw and heard—or in this case, what he didn't see and hear—was mighty worrisome. On a prairie grassland at this time of evening, the horned larks and prairie chickens usually twittered to beat the band, and small creatures always darted to and fro through the foxtail barley and blue grama grass. Not so in this place. An eerie quiet lay over everything. Even the wind seemed to be holding its breath. Not so much as a twig moved in the tall stands of saltbush that dotted the sand hill at the opposite side of the arroyo.

Shifting in the saddle, Race slowly reached back to loosen the strap that secured his Henry in the rifle boot. At close range, his pearl-handled Colts were his weapons of choice, but they were as useless as teats on a boar hog for long-distance shooting. The two-legged animals responsible for this piece of work wouldn't be the kind to face him. They'd stay under cover and try to pick him off with their rifles.

Race wanted to kick himself for not bringing a few of his hired hands along. But he really hadn't anticipated trouble. A half hour or so back, when he'd heard all the gunfire, the shots had been so close together and similar in pitch that he figured it was someone target practicing. He had decided to circle out from his cattle herd to have a look-see only because rapid, evenly spaced gunshots could be a distress signal. Granted, the usual way to signal for help was to fire only three shots, then pause for a spell before shooting again. But who was to say a greenhorn would know that?

Still scouring the opposite hillside, Race could almost feel eyeballs staring back at him. He had a good mind to get the Sam Hill out of there. The poor souls in the camp below were beyond his help, and if he hung around to bury them, he'd be as easy to pick off as a bottle on a post. A smart man would go back to the herd, recruit some men for a burial detail, and return here tomorrow.

But since when had he ever claimed to be smart? The smell of blood would draw predators, and by morning, there wouldn't be much left of the bodies. There were womenfolk down there amongst the dead, and by the looks of them, they'd suffered shame enough already. He couldn't just ride off and leave them to become carrion for the coyotes or vultures. There were also the two surviving oxen to consider. Still trapped in the traces, the beasts would wander off before morning in search of water, pulling what was left of a sorry-looking wagon behind them. Sooner or later, a wheel would get hung up, stopping the wagon as surely as if it were hitched to a Mormon brake, and they'd die a slow death. If he turned them loose, at least they'd have a fighting chance.

Race saw a black-tailed prairie dog frozen stock still in front of its burrow, tiny hands held to its mouth like a nervous woman biting her fingernails. Prairie dogs had a knack for sensing danger. This one's paralytic terror wasn't an encouraging sign.

Setting his mouth in a grim line, Race touched his boot heels to Dusty's flanks. The horse sidestepped and chuffed nervously, reluctant to descend the slope.

"It's okay, pardner," Race said in a voice gone oddly thick.

As Race nudged Dusty down the embankment, the muscles across his shoulders snapped taut. If the no-account skunks were out there somewhere, they were taking their own sweet time to say how-de-do.

Even as he scoured the brush, Race kept jerking his gaze back to the ruined wagons. His strongest feeling of a presence seemed to be coming at him from that direction. Could it be that someone was still alive down there? Not likely. Leastwise not anyone in his range of vision. He knew dead when he saw it.

Still, there were six men in the clearing and only five women. That left an odd man out. Maybe the sixth man's wife had hidden and was now afraid to show herself.

As he drew closer, Race saw that all but one wagon had been nearly dismantled, the tops ripped off the driver seats, attached tool chests and storage bins pried loose from the beds and torn completely apart. Shifting his gaze to the one wagon still intact, he wondered why it hadn't received the same treatment. Not enough time, maybe? Judging by the way his hair was standing up, Race decided his arrival might have surprised the killers. They could have spotted him in the distance and skedaddled only a few minutes before Race got there.

He scanned the opposite slope for any sign of stirred up dust. At one point along the ridge, the air looked a mite murky, the way it would if a group of men had fled over on horseback. Whirlwinds were common out here, though.

He returned his gaze to the encampment. Going by the havoc wreaked on those wagons, the killers had been searching for something. Only what in blazes might it have been? Folks like these wouldn't have been carrying cash or valuables. Mixed in with the stuff thrown from their wagons were farming implements, telling Race that the dead men had probably been clod busters. He had yet to meet a rich clod buster.

Keeping one eye on the hillside, Race guided Dusty to the center of camp. As he swung from the saddle, one of the oxen began to bawl, the forlorn sound slicing through the silence. Glancing down, he saw that the heel of his riding boot was planted on the spine of a small black book with gold lettering. Several other books exactly like it lay scattered around, the covers of a few closed, some open, their ribbon markers and pages fluttering forlornly in a sudden gust of wind. Race couldn't be sure because he'd never learned to read, but it looked to him as if the sky had clouded up and rained Bibles.

Had these folks been religious zealots? That would explain all the black clothing and why none of the dead men had a weapon on or near his body. *Cheek turners.* Race had run across a few in his day—men who allowed others to spit on them, praising the Lord while they were at it. If he lived to be a hundred, he'd never get his lasso tossed over that kind of thinking.

What in tarnation had happened here? Armed with nothing but courage and those little black books, had these poor fools walked out to meet their killers, never lifting a finger to defend themselves? Race had a feeling that was exactly what had happened. No wonder it had sounded as if someone were target practicing. These people hadn't even tried to hide.

Letting Dusty's reins dangle free, Race slipped his Henry from the rifle boot, then turned and nearly tripped over a dead woman. Since entering the camp, he'd been trying not to look closely at the bodies, but that became difficult when he was damned near nose-to-nose with one.

Middling-aged and plump, the woman had light blue eyes and gray hair, worn in a braided coronet at the crown of her head. She looked like somebody's granny. Not exactly the type to drive a man wild with lust. But the torn state of her clothing along with the nasty red marks on her wrists and exposed thighs told a different story. She also had caked blood under her fingernails, a telltale sign that this particular cheek-turner had fought for her life toward the last.

A trickle of crimson, only now beginning to congeal, ran in a jagged line from the corner of the woman's lax mouth down the crease of her chin. She hadn't been dead too long. Thirty minutes, maybe forty. If only he had heard the gunfire sooner, he might have gotten here in time to save her. He switched his rifle to his left hand and tightened his grip over the stock, his fingertips pressing hard against cool gunmetal. A choking sensation grabbed hold of his throat as he bent to close her sightless eyes and straighten her torn clothing. *Too little, too late.* But it made him feel better to restore what little he could of her dignity.

What kind of animals did things like this? Race guessed he was fixing to find out. If he didn't get shot in the back while digging these graves, he would have to go after them. He couldn't let crimes like this go unpunished. Not if he hoped to sleep at night.

A fatalistic calm settled over him. The long and short of it was, a man had to do what he had to do. Race's conscience wouldn't let him leave, and if he ended up dead for his trouble—well, maybe it was meant to be. Besides, he could just as easily get shot in the back trying to ride away.

That being the case, he set his uneasiness aside, determined to take things as they came. Before disturbing the ground, he searched the area for any clues that might help him track the killers later.

Assuming, of course, that he lived to see another sunrise.

The hoofprints he found near the wagons indicated that the group was sixteen strong and riding shod horses. That ruled out Indians and comancheros. Indians rode only barefoot ponies, and a band of comancheros would have left a mishmash of tracks, some of their mounts shod and some not.

Walking slowly, Race circled the area. Then he retraced his path and bent to examine the footprints of the men themselves. They had been wearing low-heeled riding boots like his own, and the spur cuts were shallow. The ornate Californio spurs preferred by Mexican vaqueros left deeper cuts than these, the shank marks curved and blurred by the drag of instep chains. Plainer, more practical spurs—the kind usually worn by Anglos—had left these marks.

White men had done this. Race had been hoping to find evidence to the contrary, not because the atrocities committed here would have been any less horrible, but because it seemed particularly obscene when men did things like this to members of their own race, not out of hatred or to avenge, but for the sheer joy of killing.

Following the hoofprints to the edge of the clearing, Race determined that the killers had indeed headed north over the rise after doing their dirty work. He stared in that direction for a moment, recalling the traces of dust he had seen there earlier. All the signs pointed to his having surprised them, curtailing their search before they could rip apart that last wagon.

He burned to follow them. Right now, though, he had a more immediate concern—giving the dead a proper burial.

To do that, he'd need a shovel. In hopes of finding one, he headed toward the closest wagon, which was lacking a wheel. Looking around, Race spotted it leaning against a nearby boulder. Two of the spokes were broken, and it appeared that the men had been trying to do repairs and had probably been interrupted by the killers. The broken wheel answered one question, at least, why the travelers had set up camp in a dry creek bed so far from water.

As he drew up near the wagon's front axle, he noticed a rifle in the boot at the opposite side of the dismantled driver's seat. He stared at the well-varnished butt of the gun for a long, hard second. Why he felt surprised, he didn't know. Even cheek turners would have to carry firearms in order to hunt for fresh meat along the trail. He just found it difficult to believe these people had made no attempt to save themselves when they'd had weapons within easy reach. These men could have fought back— could have defended their women—but they hadn't.

Cheek turners. He'd never been able to understand them, and he sure as hell hadn't admired them. In fact, until now, he'd always considered them cowards. Now he realized he couldn't have been more wrong. It took a rare kind of courage to die for your convictions, especially when you had a gun handy.

The next wagon in the circle had been parked at an angle almost perpendicular to the one in front of and behind it. As Race circled a pair of oxen that lay dead in the traces, he came upon an open, camel-back trunk, the lid blocking his view of what lay on the other side. As he stepped around it, he caught a glimpse of someone in his side vision. Not a dead someone either.

Instincts honed to a sharp edge by years of guarding his back, he whirled, dropped into a half-crouch, and jacked a cartridge into the chamber of his Henry, ready to shoot the first thing that moved. *A girl?* She knelt only a few feet away from him, looking for all the world as if she were praying.

Incredulous, Race stared at her. Golden hair that shone like a ten dollar gold piece. Sky-blue eyes. A face so perfect that a man expected to see its equal only in dreams. He blinked, convinced he was conjuring her up. But when his vision cleared, she was still there.

Over the past years, Race had covered nearly every trail in this godforsaken territory, and seeing a pretty female was an uncommon occurrence. So uncommon, in fact, that one step up from ugly started to look damned good to a man after a few months. This girl looked a whole lot better than damned good.

And she was definitely real, he decided. He had a vivid imagination, but not this vivid. He sometimes dreamed of women with golden tresses. What man who saw mostly black-haired, dark-skinned females didn't? But the images he conjured were always perfect in every way—golden hair falling in a cloud of curls over a naked body, with pink-tipped breasts peeking out at him through the silken strands. This girl's hair was so curly it bordered on unruly. It was also badly mussed, with stubborn corkscrew tendrils popping loose from the braided coronet atop her head, the wisps catching what remained of the sunlight and shimmering like gold filigree. Race had never yet dreamed up a woman whose hair needed combing.

Then there was her dress, a relentless black and so modestly fashioned, it covered her from chin to toe. When he dreamed up a female, he dreamed her up naked—or damned close to it—and what little he did let her wear wasn't funereal black, no how, no way. And—no small point, this—he liked females with some meat on their bones. This girl was slightly built—fragile, almost—with a skinny little neck, narrow shoulders, and breasts on the smallish side.

Oh, she was beautiful. No question about that. But she was too pure and sweet-looking for his taste, not to mention way too young. Some men might cotton to robbing the cradle, but Race Spencer wasn't one of them.

She was staring fixedly at the sprawled body of an older woman who lay near her. "Miss?"

She didn't turn at the sound of his voice or acknowledge his presence in any way. Did she even realize he was there? Her stillness was starting to alarm him. Tension clawed his backbone. Was she deaf? Gone loco? She looked it, all stiff the way she was, her head tipped slightly to one side, as if she'd been about to ask a question and lost her train of thought sort of sudden-like. Even the set of her soft mouth hinted at that—lips slightly parted, as if she were about to speak. He had to look sharp to even be certain she was breathing.

"Miss?" he said again, this time more loudly.

Again, no response. Race stepped toward her, his heart catching at the mix of emotions he saw reflected in her unchanging expression—stunned disbelief, dawning horror, and an awful, paralyzing fear. It was as if she were caught in the throes of a bad dream—frozen stiff by the terror. Only this was no nightmare, and there would be no shaking her awake. Like a fist plowing into his midriff, realization struck.

This girl was in shock.

Race scanned the clearing again, his guts clenching. None of these poor people had met with easy deaths, especially not the women, and judging by the state this girl was in, she must have seen it all happen. *Sweet Jesus*. His first impulse was to gather her into his arms and try to reassure her. Anything to take that look out of her eyes. But he knew better. No sudden moves. A soothing tone of voice. If she was aware of him on any level, she'd be scared to death.

The breeze ruffled the golden curls that had escaped her braid. Studying her, Race noticed scratches on her chin, a bruise along her cheekbone, and a scrape at her temple. Had she taken a tumble? There were streaks of dirt on her skirt and a rent in the shoulder seam of her dress, all of which could have happened in a fall.

Race just hoped she wasn't badly hurt. Draped from chin to toe in multiple layers of cloth as she was, it was difficult for him to tell if she'd sustained any injuries from the neck down. He sank to one knee in front of her. Slowly—very slowly—he set his Henry aside, just in case seeing it might frighten her.

"Sweetheart, are you bad hurt anyplace?"

No response. As he gazed into her eyes, the naked pain he saw reflected there got to him as nothing else ever had. *Shattered innocence.* Until today, this girl had probably never seen the dark side of humanity.

Gently he cupped a hand to her cheek. Considering the warmth of the evening, her skin felt awfully cool. Almost chilled. That worried him. Was this type of shock similar to the shock men suffered from a serious physical injury?

Tracing her cheekbone with his thumb, he whispered, "It'll be all right now, honey." His throat felt as though he'd swallowed flour paste. Anger surged through him. An awful, helpless anger. If he ever got his hands on those bastards, he'd kill them. "You don't gotta be afraid of me. You hear? I heard the shootin', and I came to help. Ain't nobody gonna hurt you now. Understand?"

If she heard him, she gave no sign of it. But he felt better for having said it.

Her skin felt like satin. And that face. Like the rest of her, it was small and delicately made, every angle and plane perfect. She was older than he'd first thought. Nineteen, maybe twenty. Not a girl, after all, but a woman fully grown. It was the sweetness of her countenance that had made him think she was younger. His experience with women ran more to prostitutes, and no matter how young they were, none ever looked sweet. Hard as nails, more like, with eyes gone glassy from too much drink and a contempt for men that ran bone-deep.

By contrast, this girl put him in mind of the angels he'd seen painted on church ceilings down in Mexico. *A wounded angel.* The thought came from out of nowhere. He didn't even believe in angels, and if, by chance, they did exist and one of them tumbled from heaven, he felt pretty damned sure God wouldn't choose Race Spencer to rescue her.

"If this ain't a hell of a note, I don't know what is," he said softly.

The dark gold of aged honey and tipped with platinum, her eyelashes fluttered, making him wonder if she was reacting to the sound of his voice. Maybe she was starting to come out of it. Almost afraid to breathe, he watched her, alert for the slightest change in her expression. Then she resumed staring again, apparently unaware of him and everything else around her.

He shifted his gaze to the corpse lying beside her. Like the other women, this one had been sorely abused before she died, the only difference being that her throat had been slit, an Arkansas grin curving from ear to ear under her small chin. Her black dress and gray underclothing were torn, her sprawled legs exposed, caked with dry blood, and bearing the marks of a man's brutal grip.

It took Race a moment to notice that the dead woman's gray hair was streaked with gold, the sheen dulled by the passage of years, but not so much he couldn't tell that she'd once been a blonde. He threw a startled glance at the girl. There was no mistaking the resemblance—the same fragile build, the same delicate features and ivory skin. Mother and daughter?

Jesus-God, no.

A strange feeling came over Race in that moment—an almost frightening sense that powers beyond his under-

standing had led him here to this arroyo. *Loco*. He didn't
normally let foolish notions overtake him, and thinking
that he'd been destined to find this girl was about as foolish as a notion could get. It was like saying that fine silk
and burlap went well together.

"Honey?" he whispered, gently taking hold of her
hand. "I'm gonna go get a wagon ready to roll so I can
get you out of here. I'll only be a few feet away, so don't
go gettin' scared at bein' left all alone. I'll keep an eye
on you the whole time, and you'll be all right. Understand? Nobody's gonna hurt you."

That was a promise Race meant to keep. If the killers
returned, he'd keep back one bullet with her name on it.
He wouldn't let those loco sons of bitches get their filthy
paws on her.

He started to push to his feet, but then he thought better
of it. Judging by the tear in her dress and the scratches
on her face, she had taken a nasty tumble. Blood might
not show through the heavy black muslin. Wouldn't that
be a fine kettle of fish, leaving her here to bleed to death
while he went off to fix a wagon?

Grayness. Rebecca was trapped in a thick blanket of
it—a warm, fluffy grayness that closed in around her like
goose down. She kept hearing a voice—the deep, silken
voice of a man. It didn't sound like Papa, yet he kept
calling her "honey" and "sweetheart" as if he were a
close relative. Uncle Luke, perhaps?

Rebecca strained to see him. He was there—right on
the other side of the grayness. *"You know, darlin', it just
struck me. You could be bad hurt under that dress you
got on, and I'd never know,"* he said softly. *"I swear on
one of them there Bibles that I ain't fixin' to do nothin'
out of the way. I just gotta make sure you're all right.
You understand?"*

No, she decided. It wasn't Uncle Luke. This man spoke
like an uneducated cracker. She felt big, hard hands settle
on her shoulders. Panic welled as bold fingertips traced
her collarbone. *Oh, God.* He was making free with her
person. She attempted to move. Couldn't. Wanted to

scream, but was unable to make her voice work. A dizzying, falling sensation came over her. Then she felt the cold earth against her back. She realized he had laid her on the ground. The next instant she felt him reaching under her skirts.

One of the strangers? Oh, dear Lord in heaven! *Just like Ma. He's going to do me just like they did Ma.* Horror filled her. She couldn't move, couldn't fight back. She felt big, searing palms sliding up her leg.

Suddenly a tiny pinprick of light appeared in the wall of gray. As though looking the length of a narrow tunnel, she peered through it and saw her tormentor's face, burnished and chiseled, his jaw sporting black stubble. *The devil himself.* His dark eyes glittered as he looked down at her. She felt his touch nudge at the apex of her thighs. Renewed horror washed over her in an icy, flattening wave, the reflux catching and carrying her like flotsam, deeper into the grayness. Tumbling, lost to sensation, she surrendered to the darkness, plunging farther and farther into it, glad to escape awareness.

Scowling, eyes slitted, ears attuned, Race made fast work of examining the girl's second leg, unable to shake the feeling that she might snap awake at any moment. He was heartily glad when he found no sign of a serious injury. A few scratches and scrapes was all, and only a little bleeding from those. Otherwise, she seemed to be all right.

He wasn't certain he could say the same for himself. If just feeling his way up her skirt had his heart drumming a war dance, he hated to think how he'd have felt, fitting her with a splint. He might have died of the excitement.

"Well, darlin', it looks to me like you're gonna live," he announced, his voice ringing with relief.

Pushing to his feet, Race went to fetch a quilt that had been tossed from a wagon, then returned to lay it over her. Her expression remained frozen, like one of those porcelain dolls he'd seen in a shop window in Santa Fe when he'd been a bare-faced kid.

Damn.

As he rocked back on his boot heels, it occurred to Race that somebody would have to care for this girl until she recovered. *Not him. No, sir.* Just the possibility made sweat bead on his forehead again. But if not him, who? He had several young hired hands who'd probably jump at the chance. But he'd have to be out of his mind to let a single one of those randy whippersnappers get within ten feet of her.

There was Cookie, his biscuit roller. Cookie had snow on his roof—where he wasn't plumb bald—and not much of a fire still burning in his grate. An older, grandfatherly type with a heart of gold, that was Cookie. His worst vices were chewing tobacco and telling whoppers about the amazing things he used to do in his younger days. He still liked to talk about the ladies, of course. But Race figured it had been at least a decade since the old fart's pistol had cleared leather. No question about it, Cookie would be the perfect person to play nursemaid to a pretty young woman.

Convincing Cookie of that might prove to be a problem, though. Somehow, Race couldn't see it happening, and Cookie was just ornery enough to collect his pay rather than get pressed into service.

Ideally this young lady should be settled in with relatives until she got well. An aunt, maybe. Hell, even a distant cousin would be a leg up on the present situation. She surely had family somewhere, people who loved her and would take her in. She'd probably get well a lot faster if she had familiar faces around her. With any luck, maybe she and her folks had been journeying west to join relatives who had already settled out here. Only where?

Retrieving his Henry, Race pushed to his feet. Someplace in all this rubble, there'd be a journal that could tell him where she harkened from and where she and her parents had been headed. All caravans kept a roster and daily record. Unfortunately, even if Race found a journal, he wouldn't know it. He couldn't read a lick, and none of his men could, either. He recognized only a few letters of the alphabet, mainly those used in cattle brands, the Rocking Y and the Circle D and the Triple M, to name a few. A lot of good that did him.

What in the hell was he going to do with her? It wasn't that he resented the inconvenience. In this country, a man got used to helping folks, his hope being that the favor would be returned if he ever got in a fix himself. It was just that a pretty young female didn't mix well with a bunch of lonesome cowboys. Sort of like dynamite and a lighted lucifer.

Not only that, but it was Race's observation that messing with an unmarried woman, no matter how good the reasons, was a damned good way for a man to end up married whether he wanted to be or not.

Galvanized by the thought, he turned a full circle, searching the horizon in all directions. There had to be another woman somewhere in these parts. But try as he might, he couldn't think of a single one. Between here and his ranch, a two-week ride to the north, it was mostly open country, the only dwellings along the way a few lean-to cabins belonging to trappers. Pretty much the same held true along the trail from Arkansas that he had just traveled, the only exceptions a couple of trail stops operated by bachelors. Four days ago, he and his men had passed a cabin with a dress hung out to dry on the front porch, but that was the only sign of a woman Race could recollect seeing in nearly a week.

Four days back? *Hell's bells.* Before he could get the girl to that cabin, he'd have every freckle on her fanny memorized. And after riding all those miles to find her a nurse, it would be just his luck that she'd recover her senses about the time he got her there. Where would be the point? No matter how he circled it, he would have to care for her between here and there, anyway. So he might just as well keep heading for home and save himself a lot of aggravation.

Not one to fret long over things he couldn't change, Race took a deep breath, mentally jerked himself up by his boot straps, and turned to survey the group of nearly destroyed wagons, one of which he would have to commandeer to transport the girl back to his herd, and from there to his ranch. *His ranch?* That was a highfalutin term, now that he came to think on it. Next spring, he planned to start construction on a house. But for now, all he had was a one room cabin, a bunkhouse for his men, a rickety old barn and some outbuildings, with a few horse corrals and cattle chutes mixed in.

He made a quick tour of the encampment, examining the wagons. *Buckets of junk.* The only one still held together with more than a hope, a prayer, and precious few rusty rivets was the wagon the killers hadn't had time to rip apart, and even it was in sorry shape. By the time he got a decent means of transportation assembled and had hitched the two surviving oxen into the traces, he was flat tuckered, it was damned near dark, and the girl felt as cold as death when he went to get her. The quilt hadn't provided her with enough protection. Some caretaker he was proving to be.

Resting his Henry against a wagon wheel, he went to search through the rubble again, his boots slapping the parched earth in impatience as he collected every stitch of bedding he could find. After fashioning a pallet in the wagon bed, he returned to get the girl, drawing the quilt off of her and carrying her quickly across the clearing.

Just as he planted his boot on the backboard of the wagon, a section of the tailgate exploded, splinters of rotten wood pelting him in the face. Almost simultaneously, the report of a rifle exploded in the twilight. Reacting instinctively, he dropped like a felled tree. Catching his weight with his forearms, he landed in a sprawl over the girl, using his body to shield her. Another bullet zinged past his jaw, coming so close he felt his whiskers stir. Dirt shot up.

Tears streaming, he balled a fist and rubbed frantically at his eyes, horribly aware that bullets were striking the earth all around him, chunks of clay stinging him through his shirt. *Christ on crutches.* He felt like a bale of hay at a shooting match.

Stupid, so stupid. He'd had a feeling from the first that the killers were still in the area. Then he'd found the girl and relaxed his guard, thinking hers was the presence he'd sensed. He *knew* better than to ignore his hunches. Why hadn't he taken more precautions? He'd even left his rifle leaning against the wagon, a good five feet away.

Clasping the girl tightly in his arms, he rolled under the wagon and crawled like a panicked crayfish to the far side, dragging her limp body with him. Even with the wagon bed to provide cover, slugs of lead still plowed into the dirt around them.

Crab walking and rolling, he drew the girl into the clearing, then leaped up and pulled three trunks to where she lay, forming a barricade to protect her. That done, he ran a loop around the clearing, dodging bullets as he jerked the dead farmers' rifles from the wagon boots. En route back to the barricade, he detoured to retrieve his Henry as well. All totaled, he had six rifles hugged to his chest when he dove for cover behind the storage trunks, yet another indication that he had surprised the killers. No one would have left all these rifles behind on purpose. Weapons of any kind cost dearly, and a person of shady character could make a tidy profit selling them to Indians.

Only three of the confiscated weapons were repeaters, two fully loaded. The others were single-action, and God only knew where the cartridges for them might be. Luckily, he had plenty of extra ammo for the Henry in his saddlebags. He whistled shrilly through his teeth, and Dusty, trained from a colt to come at the signal, galloped across the enclosure.

As the horse slid to a stop near Race, the twilight exploded with more rifle shots, bullets thudding into the trunks and raising clouds of dust. Coughing and squinting against the burn, Race grabbed the buckskin's reins and jerked the animal to his knees.

"Down!" he cried.

All the hours that Race had invested in training his horse paid off now. Dusty nickered in fear but obeyed the command, folding his back legs and rolling onto his belly. Race could only hope the trunks would shield the horse's huge body. Exposing himself to the rifle fire, Race straddled the buckskin and dug through the saddlebags for his extra ammunition. When he'd gathered all the cartridges he could find, he dove for cover again, then belly-crawled from one trunk to another until he found the most comfortable rifle rest.

Sighting in on the hillside above the clearing, Race finally had a few seconds to ponder the situation, and with the opportunity cane a question. Why had the bastards waited so long to start shooting at him? Race could only guess at an answer, the most likely being that the killers had hoped he knew the victims and that if they watched him long enough, he would eventually reveal the whereabouts of whatever it was they had been trying to find.

He cast a thoughtful glance over the clearing, noting the wagon contents that had been scattered everywhere, an indication that his first suspicion had been right on target. The men on the hillside had been searching for something. To back that up, there was also the condition of the women's bodies, which bore signs that they'd been tormented before they died. When Race had first come upon the carnage, he had assumed the no-good polecats had tortured the women out of sheer meanness, but now another possibility came to mind. If the killers had come here hoping to get their hands on something, maybe they had prolonged the women's agony in an attempt to make them or their husbands talk. If that were the case, though, why in the world had they killed everyone before getting the information they sought?

A chill crept up Race's spine, for he knew the answer to that question the moment it entered his mind. *The girl.* The killers had probably been following this small group of wagons for a spell, waiting for the right moment to ambush the travelers. If they had, then they'd known of the girl's existence and that they were leaving one person alive who could tell them what they wanted to know. By a twist of Fate or sheer luck, the girl must have been absent from camp when the attack occurred. Then Race had arrived, forcing the killers to hide. They'd obviously been watching him and the girl ever since, hoping Race knew the whereabouts of whatever it was they wanted. Now they realized he didn't, and they meant to kill him so they could torture the girl for information.

Crazy, so crazy. What in the hell were they after? Race found it difficult to believe these poor dirt farmers had anything of value in their wagons. As for the girl, those murdering skunks would get their hands on her over Race's dead body.

He recalled his vow to keep one bullet in reserve for the girl. He hoped it wouldn't come to that, but realistically, he knew the odds were against him. By his calculations, there were sixteen men up there, maybe more. He was a damned good marksman—one of the best, even if he did say so himself—but no man was that good.

He glanced at his charge, who lay so deathlike beside him, her face a pale oval in the deepening twilight. If those men circled around him in the darkness, they could sneak up on him from behind. If they did, they would probably rush him, and he might have time to fire only one bullet.

For her sake, he had to make that one bullet count.

Chapter 2

Race didn't have enough hands. While firing one Colt in the general direction of the hillside, he worked frantically to reload his other .45 and the Henry. He didn't care if he hit anything. At this point, keeping the enemy busy dodging bullets while he replenished the rounds in his other two weapons was his main concern. The second he backed off, the bastards would be on top of him.

Since the shooting started, he'd lost track of time. The sun had slid behind the mountains, darkness had closed in, and one by one the stars had come out. Judging by their position, the actual time that had passed was probably closer to forty minutes, maybe an hour. If so, it had been the longest hour of his life. Trying to keep the girl safe, shooting almost ceaselessly, reloading with only one hand, and constantly searching the darkness for movement already had him drained. His back ached, and his arms trembled with exhaustion.

So far, he had hit only three men for sure. That left thirteen still out there, and the lulls between fire were few, which provided him with his only opportunities to reload.

A blessing though they were, the lulls worried him, one thought pounding away at him in the sudden silence. What were they up to? In their shoes, he'd be circling the encampment.

Race was in serious trouble, and he knew it. One against thirteen was damned rotten odds, even for a man used to fighting for what he got. When the enemy advanced from two directions at once, he wouldn't be able to cover himself from both the front and the rear.

Glancing over at the girl, Race grimly accepted the fact that he not only didn't have enough hands, but that the two he did have were tied. Normally he wouldn't remain behind a barricade, vulnerable to attack. He'd attempt to turn the tables. They would never expect a lone man to sneak up on them from behind, and with a little luck, he could take them out, one at a time, using his knife.

Only he didn't dare leave the girl. If something happened to him, her fate would be sealed. He couldn't allow that, knowing as he did what those animals would do to her.

The possibility that he might have to take her life hadn't been far from Race's mind since the shooting started, and with each passing second, it loomed as a bigger threat. God help him, he only hoped he had the guts to do it.

After reloading the Henry, Race resumed his firing position. The metal edge of the trunk was sharp and had creased his forearm, making his wrist numb. He kept seeking a more comfortable rest, but then the first thing he knew, he had his arm back in the same spot again. If he lost the feeling in his fingers, it would be a hell of a note.

A glint of metal in the moonlight caught his eye, and he swung the nose of his rifle to the right, sighting in on the spot and lightly touching his finger to the trigger. *Patience.* The best marksman in the world could pull a shot if he became too eager, and in a battle, there were seldom second chances. He peered at the spot where he'd seen metal flash, his eyes aching with the strain as he took a deep breath, exhaled, and went absolutely still.

After several seconds, his patience was rewarded by another mirrorlike flash. *Slow and smooth, easy does it.* He pulled the trigger, and the bark of his Henry exploded into the night. A man cried out in startlement and pain. Silence followed—a silence so thick that Race felt as if he could damned near sink his teeth into it.

That's four. And he'd gotten them all because their guns flashed in the moonlight. Race blackened the metal on his own weapons. Reflective gun barrels had been the death of too many men. Granted, a nickel-plated Colt .45 in a silver-studded, hand-tooled holster was an attention getter, and a rifle with a carved, high-gloss stock and butt looked real fancy. But fancy wasn't what separated a man from the boys. What counted was who walked away when the smoke cleared.

He would have bet his last gold eagle that those fellows on the hillside went in for fancy weapons. Lots of flash and short on brains. Looking mean was the only edge some men had.

Just as that thought went through his mind, Race heard the snick of a gun hammer behind him and slightly to the right. With the lightning-fast reflexes of a man who'd been slapping leather most of his life, he dove sideways and brought his Henry around. *Damn.* Just as he had feared, they had circled around behind him. All hell was gonna break loose in short order, with bullets coming at him from both directions. If he wasn't Johnny-on-the-spot with a slug every time a man showed himself, he and the girl would be eating lead for supper.

Race jacked another cartridge into the chamber. Then, never taking his gaze off the wagons, he shoved forward on his belly to slap Dusty on the rump. "Hee-yaw!" he yelled.

To save the girl's life, Race would have sacrificed the animal without a qualm. But with men firing at them from a standing position at such close range, the angle was all wrong for the horse to provide protection. That being the case, Race saw no reason to let the loyal buckskin be caught in the crossfire.

With a plaintive nicker, Dusty finally managed to lurch to his feet. Race sent the buckskin on his way with another slap on the rump, then sank back to the ground and drew the butt of the Henry snugly to his shoulder.

For the next few minutes, the explosive sound of gunfire became Race's only reality, the reports of his weapons imploding against his eardrums. The enemy had come in behind him with a vengeance, and they were deliberately drawing his fire. At one point, Race felt sure he wasted three bullets on a jacket and hat they draped over a tree limb. *The bastards.* There were so many of them, he had to react instantaneously to movement, and in the darkness, it was impossible to tell if his target was a man or a decoy. He emptied his Henry and one of his Colts, knowing as he began using the second handgun that time for him and the girl was about to run out. The thought made him feel sick, not so much for himself but for her.

From out of the darkness came a sudden burst of orange flame, and a bullet whizzed past Race's shoulder, hitting the trunk behind him. He returned the fire, cracking off two shots in quick succession at the indistinct outline of a man's torso. He never heard the first bullet hit. The second struck wood, making a solid *kerthunk* that echoed in the darkness. *Damn.* At this distance, how could he possibly miss?

Race fired three more times, and again he never heard the slugs hit their mark. The muted thud of a bullet embedding itself in flesh had an unmistakable sound, and he always knew when he'd hit a man.

Trickles of sweat ran from his forehead into his eyes. He blinked at the burn and swiped his shirt sleeve over his face. He had only one bullet left in the Colt, and no way in hell were the bastards going to give him a chance to reload. The minute they realized he was no longer returning their fire, they'd advance on him. The trunks and saddlebags would provide no protection when the sons of bitches were standing right on top of him. He'd be as defenseless as a duck in a barrel.

The rapid spat of a six-shooter suddenly broke the quiet, a spray of slugs coming so close that Race ducked his head. Then a sudden volley of shooting erupted from the opposite direction. Bullets spattered into the trunks and *pinged* on the brass strapping.

He cast a glance at the girl, knowing what he had to do. Blessed release, people called it. Race had heard tell of it all his life. In this country, sometimes a man had no choice but to kill a woman to spare her a worse horror. Until now, Race had always considered it a man's duty to pull the trigger, if and when it became necessary. Only it didn't seem so cut-and-dried when you were the poor son of a bitch elected to do the honors. He had killed more men than he wanted to remember, but only because he'd had no choice. Afterward, no matter how deserving his victim, he'd always felt sick to his stomach.

How was he going to feel after taking the life of a golden-haired girl who looked more like an angel than a flesh-and-blood person?

The rushing sound of footsteps brought Race's head back around. He saw the shadowy figure of a man running toward him. Reacting instinctively, Race took quick aim. But, no. If he wasted his last round on that sorry excuse for a human, the girl would be the one who paid for it.

He had only seconds left. Everything that was decent within him rebelled at the thought of what he had to do.

The strangest sensation came over him. On the one hand, he felt as if the seconds were flying by in a dizzying rush, but on the other, he felt like an ant crawling through sorghum, every move he made taking an eternity. As he turned toward the girl, the killer's movements seemed sharp and clear and separate, like sketches on the slowly turned pages of a picture book: *bending his knee, pushing forward on the ball of his foot, thrusting out his opposite leg*. The man dipped his head to sight in on Race, his jowls shaking with each footfall, his hat bouncing and then resettling on his head.

Race could hear every beat of his own heart, every swish of his blood echoing against his eardrums like a loud whisper bouncing off canyon walls. He grabbed the girl. Her head lolled as he lifted her, the loosened strands of her golden hair gleaming like quicksilver in the moonlight and catching on his sleeve. Cupping his left hand over the side of her face, he drew her cheek to his chest. His hand started to shake as he pressed the barrel of the Colt to the underside of her chin.

Never had she looked more like an angel. That perfect face, sweetness and purity in every line. When he'd first seen her that afternoon, he'd thought she was too beautiful to draw breath. And now she no longer would.

Race hooked a thumb over the hammer spur, drew

back, and curled his finger over the trigger.

Do it, he ordered himself. But his hand refused to obey. His arm began to tremble as he strained to pull back on the trigger.

Then another shot rang out. In his side vision, Race saw the man stumble and pitch forward in a sprawl. His hat, knocked from his head by the impact, rolled on its brim and landed just short of Race's knees.

Dead? Race couldn't stop staring at the blood on the back of the man's shirt. Who had shot him? Race hadn't done it. *No bullets. No time to reload.* His thoughts dangled in his mind like snipped strands of wire, going every which way and curling back on themselves. Guns seemed to be going off all around him. But no one seemed to be shooting in his direction now.

Bewildered, he glanced first at one side of the arroyo, then at the other. In the darkness, he glimpsed the flare of gunfire on both slopes. Crossfire? Hallelujah! His men? They had heard the shooting and come to help him.

Race couldn't believe it. Was afraid to believe it. In his experience, that was never the way life worked. Maybe he was dead. A bullet to the brain, so quick and painless, he hadn't felt the hit, and now he was floating somewhere between heaven and hell, caught up in a crazy dream. That made sense. Sort of. Only the girl felt too real, her slight body soft and sweet where it pressed against him, her hair tickling his fingers like scissor-curled strands of silk ribbon, her breath forming a warm, moist spot on his shirt. Not only that, but his oversize vest had twisted around her, and one of her breasts thrust through the front opening, her chilled nipple as sharp-tipped as a screw shank under the layers of her clothing.

This was *real*. His men were truly up there.

Still dazed, Race stared down at the girl's face, deciding then and there that maybe she really was an angel.

With the arrival of Race's men, the killers ceased fire almost immediately and hightailed it, the tattoo of their horses' hooves thunderous at first and then fading into the blackness. After their departure, the arroyo was cloaked in silence—the same absolute silence that had so unsettled Race upon his arrival. No night birds. No crickets chirping. Not even the wind seemed to blow. But then, after the almost ceaseless percussions of gunshots exploding in the air all around him for so long, Race wasn't sure he would be able to hear the raucous cry of a hawk directly above him.

A rushing noise moved through his head, sort of like a creek sounded from a distance, a high-pitched ringing filled his ears, and intersticed with all of that was the frantic repetition of one, singsong thought: *Don't let her be dead . . . please, don't let her be dead.*

Tossing aside his rifle, Race knelt beside the girl to make sure she hadn't been hit since he'd laid her back down. He trembled like a palsied old man, dying a little with every sweep of his hands over her slender body, terrified that he might find a wet, sticky splotch of blood on her clothing. He was so relieved when he felt no trace of blood on her clothes that his breath stuttered from him, the sound ragged, partly a laugh and partly a sob.

In the wake of his relief came a crushing exhaustion, the weight of it making his arms feel leaden. Resting limp hands on his bent knees, he hung his head, his lungs grabbing for breath with tremulous rasps, his body quaking with shudders. *Okay. Both of them, okay. Thank God, thank God.* Tomorrow would come, after all, for him and for her. Another sunrise, another meal. *Life.* A man tended to take things like breathing for granted until he nearly died, and then the simplest things seemed wondrous.

The stupidest thoughts circled in Race's mind—like how great johnnycake, burned on the bottom and raw on top, was going to taste for breakfast. Thinking of that—and, oh, yeah, of fresh-boiled coffee, poured from a sooty Arbuckle can, with grounds floating all through it—made him want to shout. No more complaining about the hardships of being on the trail. He'd shave without water, and be damned glad of the nicks because he could still bleed. And he'd bathe in muddy river water, no problem. And when his ass ached from saddle rub, he'd thank God he could still feel pain. He was *alive*. In one piece. Safe. And so was she.

After assigning several men to burial detail, Race and his foreman, Pete Standish, returned to the cattle herd. Pete drove the wagon while Race rode inside with the girl. Half the time, the going was so rough that it was all Race could do to keep his charge from bouncing off the pallet. At one point, when the going smoothed out for a bit, he tried to get some water down her. Just as he tipped the mouth of the canteen to her lips, one of the wheels hit a hole. He sloshed water all over her, soaking her hair and the front of her dress.

By the time Pete finally drew the oxen to a halt behind the trail-camp chuck wagon, Race was wishing there were a way he might weasel out of caring for her. She couldn't be left in wet clothes all night or she'd take a chill. That meant someone needed to get her into a dry nightdress. The thought brought Race surging to his feet, and the next second, he was scrambling out the back of the wagon to go find Cookie.

The cantankerous but good-hearted cook didn't take kindly to Race's suggestion that he assume responsibility of caring for the girl. "Hah!" he cried. "You gotta be jokin'. No how, no way. I ain't gettin' wrangled into doin' no such thing!"

"Now, Cookie," Race replied, putting as much sternness into his voice as he could muster, "this ain't a matter of choice. None of them prune-faced Bible thumpers in Cutter Gulch is gonna come huntin' for you with a preacher in tow. Plus, I have a herd to get moved. I need to be supervisin' my men."

"Well, now, that sounds like quite a wrinkle." As Cookie spoke, he clanked the ladle on the edge of the pot to rid it of sauce, his green eyes flashing in the flickering amber light of the lantern suspended above him. The lamp hanger, a rusty iron rod with a hooked arm at the top, hadn't been driven far enough into the sun-baked earth and wobbled a bit with every gust of wind. "A real bad wrinkle, sure enough. But it's yours to iron, not mine. I'm a cook, not a nurse, and a danged good cook at that!"

A short, stocky little fellow with long, grizzled hair as coarse as fence wire and a matching beard that billowed over his chest, Cookie put Race in mind of a stump that had sprouted new growth at the top. The tattered gray Stetson he constantly wore, even while sleeping, only added to the effect. Foot-long, corkscrew strands of grizzled hair poked out from under the hat brim like gnarly twigs going in all directions. Unfortunately, Cookie could also be as immovable as a stump when the mood struck.

"I realize you're a fine cook," Race conceded, "and I know that cookin' is all you wanna do. But this is—"

"If'n you got ideas about me doin' somethin' else, you can find yourself another man to keep your boys' bellies filled. Put that in your pipe and smoke on it!"

Cookie always threatened to quit his job when the least little thing didn't go his way. If any of the other men had dared to speak to Race this way, he would have cut him his pay and told him to ride out. But good cooks were hard to find, and Race couldn't keep men on the payroll without one.

"You're the senior man, Cookie, and you know more about nursin' sick folks than all the rest of us put together. The girl'd be better off with you tendin' her than someone like—well, a young pup like Johnny Graves, for instance. Nobody'll raise their eyebrows over you takin' care of her."

"Johnny?" Cookie's mouth fell open, his toothless gums gleaming in the lantern light. "You ain't actually considerin' *him* for the job!"

"Not unless I don't got a choice. I was just tryin' to point out that of all of us, you're the"—Race frantically searched his mind for a tactful way of putting it—"most seasoned." At the expression that came over Cookie's face, he rushed to add, "And the most trustworthy."

"Another words, too old to be needin' a poke." Cookie huffed with indignation. "And the rest of you yahoos ain't?"

"No, that isn't what I meant at all."

"Too old to be a threat, then? Let me tell you somethin', son. I need me a poke now and ag'in, same as the next man. And I ain't *trustworthy*. You got no call to be insultin'!"

Race could see he was losing this argument fast. "Come on, Cookie. Sayin' you're trustworthy ain't no insult! I meant it as a high recommend. Think of the girl, why don't you? Poor thing, seein' all her folks get killed that way. Don't you got it in your heart to feel a little bit sorry for her?"

"Of course, I feel sorry. I just ain't so sorry I plumb lost my mind, that's all." Cookie dipped a finger in the chili he was fixing for tomorrow, then popped the sauce-coated appendage into his mouth. The sucking sound he emitted reminded Race of a froth-nosed calf rooting for the teat. Cookie gummed the chili particles and smacked his lips, nodding decisively. "If that ain't a fine chili, I'll eat my winter drawers. Same goes if I let you hoodwink me into tendin' that girl!"

Given the fact that Cookie stitched himself into his longhandles with the first snow and wore the same garments until the following spring, that was saying something. Race bit back a curse and tried again. "You wouldn't be saddled with her for very long."

"*Saddled!* Now there's a word." Cookie jabbed the spoon at Race's nose. "Pete says her folks was a bunch of them there fan attics! Them there people that quake."

"People that what?"

"Quake!" When Cookie became agitated, he had a way of squinting one eye closed and bugging the other one that made Race worry he was about to rupture a vessel. "You know, shiverin' and shakin'."

"Quakers, you mean?"

"There you go, Quakers! He said they was all wearin' black, that they was the thee-and-thou type who talk so peculiar a man can't figure out what in tarnation they're sayin'. Call 'em whatever name suits you. Toss folks like that in a gunnysack, give 'em a stir, and you can't tell one from another. They're all crazy. That's how come they's called fan attics, 'cause they're drafty atwixt their ears!"

Race had to admit, as a general rule, people like that

did seem a little strange. But by the same token, white folks had felt the same way about his mother, and her only crime had been the color of her skin. "Now, Cookie, there's nothing wrong with folks bein' different. Some of them Quaker types is probably right nice people."

"Holy and high-minded, more like. Them kinda women got so much starch in their drawers, they crackle when they sit! Last year I seen a bunch of 'em in town— in mid-August, mind—and ever' last one of 'em was wearin' black gloves, I reckon to keep their hands hid. Kept their heads down, like as if they'd go straight to perdition if they looked me in the eye. If that ain't crazy, what is?"

That was pretty damned crazy, no two ways around it.

"You take a girl who's been reared by glove-wearin' fan attics, and you got yourself a girl who ain't gonna be happy when she wakes up and finds out some man's been takin' care of her private needs," Cookie predicted. "She's gonna be a handful, mark my words! And I want no part of it. You decided to bring her along." He jabbed with the ladle again for emphasis. "So *you* take care of her."

Race had never been one to fight for a lost cause. No matter what he said, Cookie wasn't about to change his mind. That was plain.

Dusting his black Stetson on his pant leg, Race returned to the other wagon, a loud *whack* of the hat brim against denim enunciating every thud of his boot heels on the packed dirt.

Crouched on a bent knee beside the girl's pallet, Race gazed at the black dress he held clenched in his fists. Not a scrap of lace, even at the collar, and the bodice was plain with none of the tucks and pleats currently in fashion. A girl like her probably *did* wear gloves in August. He'd seen her kind. They even tacked skirting around a piano to hide its legs and wouldn't say the word "breast" while naming chicken parts. And here he was, about to lay hers bare.

No two ways about it, she'd be fit to be tied when she

woke up and would probably hate him until her dying day. Why that bothered him so much, he didn't know. He was doing the best he could. At least he had thought to gather some clothing for her from the arroyo, and she had garments to wear.

A horrible thought hit him. He wasn't entertaining silly notions about her, was he? Like, maybe, that this situation would backfire, forcing her to marry him to restore her reputation? Hell, thinking along those lines was worse than silly. Plumb stupid said it better. He didn't even know her name. And what man in his right mind wanted to be stuck with a woman who'd look down her nose at him for the rest of his born days? Race Spencer, the un-educated, rough-mannered, has-been gunslinger, wasn't exactly the stuff a beautiful girl's dreams were made of, particularly not a religious one like her.

Granted, he no longer hired out his gun. But in reality, he was only a half-rung up the ladder from that—a strug-gling cattle rancher who'd won a worn-out parcel of land from a hapless drunk in a poker game. This girl wouldn't give him a second look, and if he was entertaining notions to the contrary, he needed to thump his fool head against a rock.

In his younger years, he'd hoped he might marry him-self a sweet-natured woman someday—one of those high-falutin types with lace on her drawers, who'd set a fancy supper table, trim all the pillowcases with eyelet, and teach his children how to talk educated and have good manners. In short, he'd wanted his young'uns to be every-thing he wasn't and had never had a chance to be.

Oh, yeah, he'd hoped. But hoping was just a fancy handle for wishing. Any fool knew that. And Race had learned a long time ago that wishes rarely came true. That one sure hadn't, leastwise. He'd never met a proper lady yet who'd let him get close enough to say howdy-do, let alone ask her to marry him. And until two years ago, he wouldn't have been able to offer her much, even if he had.

A cramp in his bent knee jerked Race from his musings, and he realized he'd been crouched by the girl's pallet for

God only knew how long, letting his mind wander off every which way. The truth of it was, he dreaded shucking those underclothes off her, and any excuse to put it off was good enough. Meanwhile, she wore nothing but a threadbare gray chemise and ankle-length drawers to shield her from the cool night air.

The lantern, suspended from one of the hickory bows that supported the wagon canvas, emitted a flickering brightness that played over her slender form like liquid gold, highlighting the thrust of her small breasts under the chemise and defining the curve of her waist and hips in shadow. Damn, but she was nice to look at. And wasn't that just the problem? A homely girl wouldn't have had his tail tied in such a knot.

Through the insubstantial walls of canvas, Race could hear the rise and fall of male voices and an occasional burst of laughter. The crackling of the fire drifted to him through the night, as did the smell of boiling coffee. Out on the trail like this, the men worked the hours of darkness in short shifts so everyone could get some sleep. From dusk to dawn, weary cowboys gathered at the campfire, their aching hands wound around tin cups of steaming coffee. Right then, Race would have given his last dollar to be out there with them.

Hauling in a deep, bracing breath and exhaling through loosely pursed lips, he settled his gaze on the chemise again. Aside from being an ugly gray, far more modest in cut, and snugger in fit than what he was accustomed to, the coarse muslin undergarment was pretty much like any other he'd come across, stretching to mid-thigh and laced up the front. He rubbed his palms on his pant legs, then leaned over her and began tugging on the cording.

As the muslin parted to expose the beginning swells of her cleavage, his heart started to pound against his ribs like a water-powered triphammer on an anvil. Sweat popped out on his brow. *Son of a bitch*. What in the world was the matter with him? Nothing in Race's past gave him a basis of comparison to help him answer that question. He only knew he felt as if he were invading sacred territory. Kind of like when he accidentally wandered into an Indian burial ground, only then he never had to worry about any of the dead people coming suddenly awake.

What was he going to say if she suddenly opened her eyes? Howdy? How did he get himself into fixes like this?

The chemise parted, and her breasts spilled out, plumper and more well-rounded than he expected. She wore the chemise way too tight, undoubtedly to flatten her chest and conceal the curves God had given her. Damned fool girl. As if she could hide the fact that she was female? He wasn't used to a bosom jumping out at him. It was enough to make a man's heart stop.

He averted his gaze and groped for a quilt, dragging it up to cover her chest before he proceeded with undressing her.

So far, so good. He'd just pretend she was a man, keep all of her covered that he possibly could, and think on what he had to do next. He'd get through this. And later, after she woke up, he'd be able to look her in the eye without a trace of guilt, knowing he'd barely even noticed anything he shouldn't have. Well—almost barely, anyhow.

As he tugged to remove her bloomers, one slender leg slipped out from under the quilt, exposing an expanse of milk-white thigh. Race noticed some scrapes on her skin that needed to be tended as he tucked the cover back around her.

No problem. He'd just bare one part of her at a time to clean her cuts with whiskey, leaving the upper portion of her chest and her nether regions covered. If she had any hurts in those places, they'd just have to heal on their own.

He grabbed the jug of Mon'gehela on the floor beside him, popped the cork, and was in the process of moistening a square of cloth when it occurred to him that he needed a dose worse than she did. He took a hearty gulp. As the warmth spread through him, lending him courage, he bent to lift the quilt and peek under the edge at her belly, which made his own clench like a tight fist. He spied a cut on her midriff and reached under the cover to dab at it with the whiskey-moistened cloth. Once finished,

he took another long pull from the bottle. For purely medicinal purposes, mind. A man needed some fortification
in a situation like this.

Gulp, dab. Gulp, dab. Once he got a rhythm going, he
relaxed a little.

She'd definitely taken a nasty tumble and had a number
of abrasions on her torso and legs. After doctoring them,
he sat back on his heel and did a peel-and-peek body
check to make sure he hadn't missed any spots. Thus convinced that he'd dabbed them all, he blew like a badly
winded buffalo. Taking care of a woman was a hell of a
lot different from taking care of a man.

Almost as if she sensed the liberties he'd just taken with
her person, the girl began to toss her head, her fair brows
pleating in a frown. Race almost jumped out of his skin,
thinking she was about to wake up.

He grabbed the fresh nightgown he'd laid out and
started stuffing her into it. Getting her limp arms down
the sleeves was like trying to thread wet leather laces
through boot eyelets. When he tried to reach up the sleeve
to get hold of her hand, his fist got stuck in the cuff. He
shook his wrist and jerked. If she woke up right now, half
in and half out of her nightgown, with a strange man's
arm shoved up the front and one hand stuck in her sleeve,
she'd fly into raving hysterics, for sure.

He finally got his hand out of the cuff by pulling with
such force that he nearly toppled backward. She continued
talking out as he finished wrestling her into the nightgown. Nothing she said made much sense. *Nightmares.*
Race hurried to fasten the buttons that ran from her chin
to her waist. Fifty of them, at least. It seemed like that
many, anyhow; all of them so little, he had trouble getting
hold of them.

When he finally got her completely dressed and tucked
back under the quilts, he was worn to a frazzle. She
thrashed her legs, her lips moving as she whispered things
he couldn't make out, her small face twisted with what
could only be anguish. Race's heart caught at her expression. She was obviously reliving the events of the day.

"Whoa, sweetheart." He lightly stroked her golden

hair, fascinated by the flyaway tendrils that caught at his fingertips. The only time his own hair had ever gone that kinky was when he'd bent too close to the cooking fire and singed the ends. "You're just havin' a bad dream, that's all. You're safe. Ain't nobody gonna hurt you. I swear it."

She quietened and turned her cheek against the inside of his wrist. A defeated whimper came from her, shrill and broken.

The sound cut through Race like a dull-edged knife. He'd walked through that encampment, and he'd seen enough to know that her papa hadn't done much of anything—hadn't gone for a rifle or lifted a hand. He'd just stood there and let the unthinkable happen.

Now, in her mind's eye, she was seeing it all unfold again, and as before, an able-bodied man was standing aside, doing nothing. Every instinct Race possessed bridled at the thought. He wanted to crash through the barriers between dream and reality—to take her in his arms and press her face to his shoulder so she wouldn't see, if nothing else. Anything to take the pain away. But she was trapped in a world he couldn't reach.

Race had no idea how long he sat there, stroking her hair and trying to call her back from her troubled dreams. Minutes? Hours? He only knew he sat in one position for so long that pain knifed through his legs and zigzagged up his spine. When she finally quieted and drifted into a deep sleep, he was so weary he could scarcely keep his eyes open, and his head felt as if someone were driving a spike through it. He stretched out beside her on top of the blankets, using the crook of his arm as a pillow. As he let his eyes drift closed, he promised himself he'd only lie there long enough to get rid of his headache. It wouldn't do for her to wake up and find a strange man in her bed.

That wouldn't do at all.

Chapter 3

Eyes closed and feeling oddly disembodied, Rebecca came slowly awake. First she became aware of the familiar sounds of early morning that drifted to her from outside the wagon—the muted shuffle of footsteps on loose dirt, the clank of cooking pots and utensils, the sporadic snap and crackle of campfires, the indistinct clucking of chickens, and another noise coming from directly behind her that reminded her of someone snoring. Strange, that. Papa had never been one to snore. Then she heard a dog bark, which struck her as even stranger. No one in their caravan even owned a dog.

On the tail of that thought, Rebecca began to notice other noises that didn't fit. In the distance, there was a monotonous droning sound, like the lowing of cattle. And somewhere close to the wagon, a gruff male voice muttered a profane expletive.

She frowned in bewilderment. Was that tobacco smoke she smelled? And what on earth was making that persistent jingling noise? It reminded her of the sound riding spurs made as the rowels dragged in the dirt or stuttered across the planks of a boardwalk, a distinctive *chuhchink—chuhchink—chuhchink.*

Something wasn't right. None of the brethren used profanities or wore spurs on their boots, and worldly indulgences, such as the use of tobacco, were strictly forbidden. Vaguely alarmed, Rebecca struggled to open her eyes, a feat that proved to be beyond her. *Tired. So awfully, hor-*

ribly tired. Her arms and legs felt as if they were anchored to the bed with iron weights.

No need to worry, she thought drowsily. Papa was out there, and so were Ma and all the others. Perhaps another caravan had left the main trail and camped near them last night, and this morning, the strangers had walked over to introduce themselves. The Brothers in Christ seldom mingled with outsiders, but when people did make friendly overtures, they felt it their Christian duty to reciprocate.

Rebecca nuzzled her cheek against the coarse linen pillowcase, luxuriating in the wonderful softness of the down-filled ticking. The lure of sleep seemed irresistible, and she drifted in the hazy mists between dreams and awareness, too exhausted to force herself totally awake. She had no idea how long she lay there, blanketed in dimness. She was simply too weary to care. But then, from just outside the wagon, a loud clanking noise startled her back into renewed awareness.

"Damn it, Blue!" a male voice barked. "Keep your nosy self outta my cookin' fire, you no-account, addle-pated hound!"

That definitely was *not* a voice Rebecca knew. With supreme effort, she managed to crack open her eyes. Through the spikes of her lashes, she stared blearily at what appeared to be the interior wall of their wagon, which meant she must be lying on the floor. How she had come to be there, she had no inkling. With little or no surplus space inside the cram-packed wagon, she and her parents slept on top of the cargo, three to four feet above the floor.

She ached all over, she realized, as if her whole body had been pummeled with a club. Even the strands of hair that hung free from her braid seemed to hurt. Had she been ill? She batted her lashes, struggling to keep her eyes open and clear away the fogginess inside her head. Yes, she must have been ill, possibly even delirious with a fever. That would explain why she felt so awful and had no recollection of making her pallet on the floor. Little wonder she ached and felt too weak to move.

It was past sunup. A brisk morning breeze buffeted the

wagon canvas, carrying with it the scent of a plains grassland, a not unpleasant mix of sage, saltbush, and dust.
Straining under the bucking tarp, the hickory support
beams creaked above her.

As her awareness sharpened, the clucking noise she'd
heard earlier resumed, and with a growing sense of alarm,
she realized it wasn't chickens, after all, but men talking
softly and cackling with laughter. She tried to make out
what they were saying, but the words were so indistinct
they were nearly drowned out by the snoring sound,
which seemed to be coming from somewhere near her ear.
So near, in fact, that the sputtering huffs of breath were
stirring a lock of hair at her temple.

What man, besides her papa, would be sleeping in their
wagon? The question wove in and out of her thoughts like
a strand of yarn through the warp of a loom. In some
distant part of her mind, she sensed that she should feel
alarmed, but she was too befuddled and dizzy to grab hold
of the feeling.

Instead she studied the vertical wooden stud only inches
from her nose, struggling to impose clarity of thought
over the haze of vague and disturbing impressions. Was
she having a dream? An especially vivid one?

She felt as if she were drifting on a cloud. No. She was
definitely inside the wagon. Only where had all their
trunks gotten off to? Since their departure from Philadelphia, Papa had never once completely unloaded their
cargo. The closest he'd come was to rearrange some of
the trunks to distribute the weight more evenly. Yet now
the wagon was empty.

The gauzy pink of early morning shone through the
canvas, lending a rosy glow to the shadowy interior of
the wagon. Through the tatters in the heavy cloth, shafts
of sunlight formed pearlescent motes that caressed her
face with warmth. She smelled eggs and bacon frying,
which made her stomach pang with hunger. Lands, she
felt as if she hadn't eaten in days or had a drink of water
either, for that matter. Thick and cottony, her tongue was
stuck to the roof of her mouth.

She tried to push up on an elbow, realizing with no

small amount of alarm that it wasn't exhaustion alone that made her arms and legs difficult to move. Something actually was holding her down—something heavy and warm.

Just below her hip, a weight rested over her legs. Her searching fingertips traced its shape, which felt very like a muscular thigh sheathed in worn denim. Following the tapered length, she curled her fingers over a bony knee. A very *large* bony knee, so square and sturdily made it could only belong to a man.

Her heart skittered. That couldn't be. She pressed more firmly with her fingers to better explore the shape. If not a knee, what on earth was it? She reached to see what lay over her waist. Her fingertips met with a finer weave of cloth, lying in bunched folds at the bend of someone's elbow. A shirt sleeve? Venturing farther down, she traced the shape of a corded forearm. A hysterical urge to giggle came over her. This wasn't happening. She was still asleep and having a strange dream, after all. Lord save her, there couldn't actually be a man's arm and leg in her bed. Unless, of course, there was a man attached to them.

Her heart leaped when she came to a broad, thick wrist and the back of a leathery hand nearly as big as a supper plate. Her father had coarse, curly hair on his arms, while this man's was short, straight, and lay close to his skin like a silken veil.

She circled the realization cautiously, for if this wasn't Papa's arm, it meant that some other man was lying on the pallet with her. A man with long, sturdy fingers that were loosely cupping her breast.

Her breast? With a jolt, Rebecca came fully awake, her breath trapped in her chest, her body frozen, horror mushrooming within her. *Oh, dear God!*

Memories flashed through her mind in a vivid rush. She had gone out to gather buffalo chips for the cooking fires, heard screams, and run back to the wagons. As she drew close, she'd seen strange men in the encampment. Sweat beaded on her face as she recalled the horrible things those men had been doing to the people she loved.

Oh, sweet Father in heaven. Those men had come back, and somehow she'd been taken captive.

She let loose with an ear-splitting shriek.

"Jesus H.—Washington—Adams—Jefferson—Christ!" Race shot up from the pallet as if a hot brand had been laid to his backside, his sleeping partner scrambling in the opposite direction. Landing on his knees at the edge of the quilt, he stared incredulously at her cotton-draped bottom as she crawled frantically on all fours toward the front of the wagon. The headache that had plagued him so mercilessly last night recommenced, exploding behind his eyes like gunpowder touched off by a lighted lucifer. *The girl?* How in tarnation had he ended up in bed with her? His last clear recollection was of stretching out beside her to shut his eyes for a minute. *Damn it!* He had done exactly what he'd cautioned himself not to do—he'd fallen asleep.

Her flight aborted by the end of the wagon bed, she huddled on her knees in the left front corner, her well-rounded fanny uppermost, her pointy elbows resting on the plank floor in front of her, her forearms folded protectively over her head. She was scared half to death, and who could blame her? In his sleep, he'd been hugged up to her like a pair of rain-soaked buckskins.

The inside of the wagon had grown so quiet that the air seemed to crackle. He needed to explain everything to her—the faster, the better. Only where should he start?

"This ain't how it looks, darlin'." His voice still gruff with sleep, he sounded like a bullfrog croaking. He worked his mouth for spit he didn't seem to have. "I— uh—" His brain went as blank as unlined paper. What could he say to her? That he was real sorry for cozying up? "I—uh—*damn!* I know how this looks. Real bad, that's how! But I never meant to get in bed with you, I swear. Not under the covers, leastwise."

The words seemed to hang there, echoing like the blast of a shotgun. How come, he wondered, at times like this, the God's honest truth always came out sounding like a lie?

"I had a real bad headache, is all," he rushed to add, "and I just laid down to try and get shut of it. I reckon I fell asleep."

Race wasn't sure what he expected. Some kind of re-action, at least. For her to look at him, maybe? Instead, she just continued to huddle there, arms shielding her head. He had a bad feeling she was so scared that she wasn't hearing a word he said.

And wasn't that a fine kettle of fish. On his best day, he wasn't exactly gifted at putting a shine on words.

"I must've got chilled during the night," he said, as much to himself as to her. "In this country, it can get colder than a well digger's ass along about dawn. In my sleep, I reckon I went burrowin' for warmth under the quilts."

Nothin'. Just that terrible shaking. Frustrated, he raked his fingers through his hair, encountered tangles, and damned near jerked the strands out by the roots. The sting brought tears to his eyes. He blinked and sighed, pinching the bridge of his nose.

In his mind's eye, he pictured her waking up this morn-ing and realizing a man was in bed with her. He doubted she had any recollection of what had happened yesterday after the attack on her traveling party, which meant she had no idea who he was or how she'd come to be in his company.

The thought brought his head up. No recollection? If she remembered nothing save for the killings, she prob-ably thought he'd been involved.

Even when he was scrubbed up, clean-shaven, and wearing a fresh shirt, Race knew he had a look about him that made strangers leery. He had always laid it off on his coloring, the dark skin and eyes, the high cheekbones, and the blue-black hair that marked him as a breed. There was also the distinctive way he wore his guns so low on his hips, the stamp of a gunslinger. In this country, folks had a healthy fear of both Indians and gunmen, especially la-dies, and this girl had more reason than most.

Of all the dumb things he'd ever done—and he'd pulled some good ones—falling asleep beside her took the prize.

Race pushed to his feet. At his movement, the wagon jounced slightly. The girl gave a startled squeak, pushed off on all fours like a frog in a hopping contest, and grabbed hold of the rough half-wall behind the driver's seat. When she threw up a leg to crawl out, Race nearly leaped after her. But then he thought better of it. That would only frighten her more.

Even if she got outside, she wouldn't go far. The surrounding area was crawling with his men, for one thing, and she wore no shoes to protect her feet. The grassland that stretched forever in all directions was chock-full of burrs and stickers. There was also the fact that he had longer legs, which made the outcome of any footraces between them a sure bet in his favor.

As he anticipated, she poked her golden head out the front opening of the canvas, saw all the men milling about, and froze with one knee hitched up over the seat, the hem of her nightgown riding high in back to reveal her calf and ankle. He'd never seen a leg so daintily made. Her ankle bone looked about a third the size of his.

For some reason, seeing that leg drove home to him what a hell of a fix she must think she was in, outnumbered and outflanked everywhere she turned, by men she thought were cold-blooded killers.

"Sweetheart, don't be afraid. You got no call to be. You're safe here. Me and my men won't harm a hair on your head, I swear it. As for the killin' of your people, I didn't have nothin' to do with it, and neither did they."

Her breath coming in shaky rasps, she turned to look at him. Her expression caught at his heart. Fear. Hopelessness. Defeat. She slid off the wagon seat and sank to the floor, her back pressed to the wall, her slender body once again drawn into a protective huddle, arms locked around her bent knees. Her small face was so bloodless that he could scarcely tell where her white cotton nightgown left off and her skin began. Under her blue eyes, dark circles stood out in stark relief against her pale cheeks, and her soft, full lips were tinged with purple.

He searched his mind for some way—any way at all— to reassure her. The way she looked at him made him feel too big for his skin. Six-three in his bare feet, he stood a head taller than most men. To someone of her slight stature, he knew he had to seem huge. There had been countless times in Race's lifetime when he'd had cause to wish his legs weren't so long or his shoulders so wide, but never more so than now.

Barely aware of his movements or the thoughts that ran through his mind to prompt them, he folded a leg under himself to sit down, hoping he might seem less intimidating that way. Then, very slowly so as not to startle her, Race unbuckled his gun belt. Bless her heart, she was shaking so hard, she looked incapable of standing, let alone making a run for it. As she followed the movements of his hands, a look of stunned disbelief crossed her face.

Never taking his gaze off her, he folded the ends of the gun belt around the holsters, then leaned sideways to lay the weapons on the pallet, putting them as close to her as his arm would stretch. He followed the guns with his sheathed knife. Then he scooted away, the seat of his britches rasping on the floorboards, until his back met with the wall.

She stared at the weapons for a moment, then looked back at him, her expression indicating that she thought he'd gone plumb loco. And maybe he had.

He smiled slightly. "I got only one request," he said in the gentlest tone he could muster. "If you decide to shoot me, aim true. Gettin' gut shot ain't real high on my list."

Her gaze darted back to the guns, and she stared at them for several long seconds, as if she couldn't quite believe he'd laid them there, unguarded and within her reach. That made two of them. He couldn't quite credit it either. At this close range, she wouldn't have to aim; just pointing the gun in his general direction and pulling the trigger would get the job done. And wouldn't that be a hell of a note? Race Spencer, shot dead by a slip of a woman who'd probably never touched a sidearm in her life. Folks would talk about it for years to come.

Not that he was all that worried. If he was guessing right and she was a cheek turner, killing went against her religion. Besides, he seriously doubted she had what it took to shoot someone. Three things had kept Race alive to see the ripe old age of thirty: being able to draw a gun faster than a man could spit and holler howdy, having the sense to choose his battles, and being a good judge of character. There was a gentleness in this young woman that ran bone-deep. He couldn't say for certain what it was about her that led him to believe that, only that he did. Enough that he was willing to bet his life on it.

"Like I said, you got no call to feel afraid." He inclined his head at the weapons. "You'll notice I put 'em closer to you than to me. In these parts, it's what we call a show of good faith, a layin' down of arms so folks can feel safe while they parley." At her blank expression, he quickly added, "Parley means to talk things out. And I reckon I got a heap of talkin' to do. Now that I ain't wearin' my guns, I'm hopin' you'll feel a mite more inclined to listen. You reckon?"

A fair hand at reading people's eyes, Race was starting to get a little worried. There was nothing in her expression to indicate she was getting the gist of what he was saying. Not a good sign. It occurred to him that maybe she didn't understand English.

"You ain't one of them Dutch folks, are you?" While riding shotgun on the Santa Fe Trail, Race had, on two different occasions, escorted an all-Dutch caravan from Missouri to New Mexico, never understanding a word said to him the entire trip. "Please, darlin', tell me anything but that. An expert at dealin' with babblers, I definitely ain't."

Still looking bewildered, she continued to stare at him. He leaned slightly forward over his knees, touched two fingers to his lips, and then swept his hand outward, making the Indian sign for talking. "English. *Comprende?*" Her blank look told him she didn't know any cowpen Spanish either, which was the only other language he knew, save for a smattering of Apache and Cheyenne. *Damn.* "Come on, darlin'. Don't tell me you don't know English. 'Cause, I'm tellin' ya, if you don't, we're eyebrow deep in a fine fix!"

With a suddenness that startled him, she lunged for his guns, her long nightgown hanging up under her knees as she scrambled across the floor in a frenzied crawl. Race made no move to stop her. If he was misjudging the girl, then he'd die for his mistake. But he honestly didn't believe she had what it took to shoot him.

As a safety precaution, he kept a chamber in each Colt empty and the cylinder latch locked. It was a damned good thing. Otherwise, she might have hurt somebody, who being anybody's guess. Never had he seen anyone handle a weapon so back-ass-wards. First off, she frantically tried to jerk one of the Colts from its holster without unfastening the strap, pointing the gun every which way in the process.

Under her breath, he heard her whispering, "Oh, God—oh, God—oh, God!"

Unless he was hearing wrong, she was calling on the Almighty in good, old-fashioned English. Just to be sure, he narrowed one eye and said, "It clears leather easier if you undo the strap."

She threw him a startled look, then renewed her attempts to withdraw the weapon, fumbling at the strap with frantic fingers. She had understood him; that much was plain.

After jerking the Colt from the holster, she clutched it in both hands, the force of her grip on the pearl butt turning her knuckles white. Then, still hampered by the nightgown, she hobbled about on her knees to face him and take aim. Sort of, anyhow. She was shaking so badly, the barrel weaved, not only from side to side, but up and down, which damned near made him dizzy trying to keep track of it.

His gaze colliding with hers midway along the gun barrel, Race relaxed against the wall, drawing up one knee to support his arm. "Can I offer you a couple of friendly pointers?" He inclined his head at her unsteady aim. "Find yourself a firing rest. Weavin' like that, you couldn't hit a bull in the ass with a handful of banjos. Sit cross-legged with your elbows propped on your knees."

Her lips drew back from her teeth, her lungs rasping as

she took rapid, shallow breaths. "I-I'll shoot you, mister."

Even spouting threats, she had a sweet voice, soft and distinctly feminine. He smiled slightly.

Evidently misinterpreting the reason for his smile, she rushed to add, "If you're under the gross misconception that I won't, you have another think coming. I shall, and without any compunction whatsoever."

Race had never heard anyone spit out so many high-falutin words. He was surprised she didn't get her tongue tied into knots around them. *Compunction?* He rolled that one around in his head for a minute, trying to figure the meaning. Given the gist of all else she'd said, he decided it must be a fancy word for "error."

"That's heartenin'. Like I said, I got a dread of bein' gut shot." Knowing as he did that the gun wasn't even cocked, he struggled not to smile. "I'll tell you what. How's about you sittin' back and keepin' a bead on me while you hear what I got to say. Then, if you still wanna shoot me, you can empty the gun tryin', and if I ain't dead enough to suit you by then, I'll help you reload."

"I have no interest in hearing your pathetic fabrications!" she cried, her voice going even shriller. "You're a horrible, conscienceless creature who doesn't deserve to be called a man. A black-hearted, lowlife *scoundrel!*"

A sob caught in her chest. He searched her gaze. She was trying to summon the courage to kill him. He'd seen murder in the eyes of too many men to mistake it now. Confident the gun wouldn't fire, he watched her in a detached sort of way, wondering if he'd misjudged her, after all. She was mighty scared, and panic could push even a gentle person to violence.

He'd thought never to see anyone tremble more violently than she had been a minute ago. But as she tried to tighten her finger over the trigger, her arms began jerking as though she'd been taken with fits. Fresh tears welled in her eyes.

Those eyes. Looking into them, Race felt his heart break a little. Shattered. That was the only word to describe the expression in them. Like pretty blue glass, broken into a thousand fragments and washed with raindrops. Ruined dreams, destroyed innocence, desperation, and a growing terror as she realized she couldn't bring herself to kill him.

"Ah, honey, don't . . ." His voice rasped like a fingernail over the backside of silk. "I told you, I ain't gonna harm you. Just put down the gun."

She didn't believe that he meant her no harm. He could read that in her eyes as well.

Before Race could anticipate what she meant to do or try to stop her, she turned the gun on herself. He couldn't believe his eyes. Point-blank at her temple, the barrel snug to the side of her head. Pulling the most awful face he'd ever seen, she hunched her shoulders, closed her eyes, and tried to draw back on the trigger. When the curved metal refused to budge, her eyes fluttered open, the expression that moved over her face a mix of startlement, bitter disappointment, and panic. She glanced at the gun, evidently realized it had to be cocked, and hooked her thumb over the hammer spur. Fortunately, the cylinder latch was still locked, which prevented the mechanism from working.

Race launched himself at her, seizing her slender wrist just as she reached with her other hand to feel for the latch. Fortunately for her—and also for him because he would have carried the guilt of her death to his grave— he was able to twist her arm and aim the gun at the floor as he tackled her.

Nonetheless, it had been close. Too damned close. Fear robbing him of caution, he wrestled her none too gently to the pallet, his longer and more powerful body pinning her to the quilts, his hands vised on her wrists. Pressing on the nerve below the heel of her hand, he paralyzed her fingers, enabling him to shake the revolver from her grasp.

She sobbed, bucking and twisting as she fought to escape his hold, but Race was having none of that. He'd learned his lesson, and a bitter one it was. The girl might not have it in her to kill him, but she wouldn't hesitate to kill herself. He had laid the sheathed knife on the pallet as well, had no idea where it might have gotten kicked during their tussle, and wasn't about to turn loose of her to find out. Not when she was in this frame of mind.

She had more staying power than he would have guessed, straining against his greater strength until her face went shiny with sweat. And long after he felt her muscles begin quivering with exhaustion, she refused to give it up. Finally, though, utter exhaustion claimed its victory, and she went limp beneath him, her surrender followed by an ear-piercing shriek that startled him so, he damned near turned loose of her.

The cry made his blood run cold, reverberating in the air and cutting clear through him. It was laced with pain that went too deep for tears, and as it trailed away into silence, she screamed again, and then again, each burst of sound weaker than the last, until the cries gave way to gut-wrenching sobs.

Race moved the gun beyond her reach, then caught her wrists in the grip of one hand, gathered her close, and sat up. Still sobbing, she hid her face against his shoulder and tried to escape his hold.

"Sweetheart," he whispered, "it's okay. It's gonna be okay."

He kept seeing her, coming around on her knees to face him, a gun almost bigger than she could handle clutched in her fists, her arms quivering as she waged war with her conscience. He hated using his strength to hold her against her will, but he was afraid she might hurt herself if he turned her loose.

"You need any help in there?" Pete called from just outside the wagon.

Hell, yes, he needed help. But he doubted any of his men could provide it. What the girl needed was a woman to tend her, someone she could trust. Only there wasn't another woman for well over a hundred miles. He tucked his boot heels under his rump to sit cross-legged and positioned her more comfortably on his lap.

"I got it under control," he called back to Pete.

"You sure?"

Taking measure of the situation, Race touched his free hand lightly to her hair. "Positive. Thanks, anyhow."

Her exhausted sobs caught at his heart. He knew by

their sound that she was remembering things best forgotten. Her mother, her father . . . He wished he could wipe what had happened from her mind. But that wasn't the way life worked.

To his amazement, she continued to strain against his hold, even though he could tell she was weary. Deciding to use a favorite horse-gentling tactic, he kept his arms braced against her just enough to restrict her movements, playing her out and whispering to her all the while. He was only dimly aware of what he said. Comforting reassurances, mostly, which soon began to sound like nonsense because he repeated them so many times.

Explaining how he'd come to be in the arroyo yesterday evening. Telling her what had occurred afterward, about the killers returning, the ensuing gun battle, and his men arriving in the nick of time to save their hides. Promising her that he'd never hurt her. That she was safe. Assuring her that he was sorry—for not reaching the arroyo in time to stop the killing, for not knowing how to help her afterward, and for doing a damned fool thing like falling asleep beside her and scaring her half to death.

At some point—Race wasn't sure exactly when—she stopped resisting his hold on her, and once she did, he let go. She sank against him then, her face buried in the hollow of his shoulder, one of her fine-boned hands curled in a loose fist over the front of his shirt. Still beset by residual sobs, she jerked slightly every few seconds, soft huffs of breath snagging in her throat.

For an instant, the years fell away in Race's mind, and he remembered how good it had felt to be rocked in his mother's arms when he'd been a small child—surrounded by her warmth, knowing he could fall asleep and that she would keep him safe. His throat tightened at the memory. He had lost his mother when he was only seven, and after that, there'd been no one who gave a damn. There still wasn't, and it was a mighty lonely feeling.

He looped his arms around the girl and rested his cheek on her hair. He liked the way her curls caught on his whiskers, the ends so soft they reminded him of frayed silk. He also liked the way she felt in his arms— as if she'd been measured to fit. He closed his eyes, cautiously circling the feeling of aching warmth that spread through him. He had felt it before in the arroyo, wasn't sure he wanted to feel it now, but didn't seem able to push it away.

"You got a name, sweet face?" he asked huskily.

Her breath caught and she stiffened, her fist knotting on his shirt. "Becca," she said with a wet-sounding catch.

"Ah . . . Becca." Race moved his cheek, more to feel the texture of her curls against his bewhiskered jaw than to seek a more comfortable resting spot. *Becca.* He liked the ring of that. It suited her, somehow.

"*Re*becca," she repeated, her voice muffled against his shoulder.

He liked Becca better. "I'm Race Spencer." As he spoke, he cracked open one eye. "And just in case you've heard the name and the tall tales that go with it, don't believe most of 'em. I ain't but half-mean and only a quarter ornery. The rest of me is a damned fine fellow."

He moved his hand up her slender back and curled it over her shoulder. She shrank into herself, trying to escape his touch. She moved her head, her cheek coming to rest on his shirt as she fastened a swimming blue gaze on him—bruised, distrusting eyes, the pupils large, the frost-tipped lashes that lined them spiked with wetness from her tears.

"Please, Mr. Spencer," she whispered tremulously, "don't toy with me. I'm begging you, please, just—end it."

A smile tugged at the corner of his mouth. "You ain't heard but about half of what I said, have you? And you've decided not to believe that part."

The shifting shadows in her eyes answered that question for him.

"I'm tellin' you, I had nothin' to do with the killin' yesterday. I wasn't nowhere around."

"Give me one reason why I should believe you," she demanded shakily.

"Why would I lie?"

"We both know the answer to that!" Fresh tears

flooded into her eyes, sparkling like morning dew shot through with sunlight. "Well, think again. I'm not *that* lacking in intelligence. You hope to trick me—pretend to be my friend, gain my confidence. Well, it won't work. I refuse to cooperate. Not in any fashion. If you hope to lay hands on it, you'll do so with no help from me. I'll go to my grave first."

If she was talking about what he thought she was talking about, it'd be a cold day in hell when he needed help to get the job done. Her cooperation was another matter entirely, but that was one of those things that a man said best with his actions. "I ain't got no plans, immediate or otherwise, to lay my hands on nothin'," he assured her, "so rest easy in your mind."

"If only I could. But I was there. I saw what went on, *heard* what went on. I know very well what you want from me, and what you'll do to me if I give it to you." Her voice quavered, and she paused to gulp, the sound making a hollow *plunk* at the base of her throat. "My mother chose to *die* rather than surrender, and I can do no less!"

Race glanced around, located his knife, and moved her off his lap onto the tangle of quilts. "You don't happen to harken from Missouri, do you?" At her blank look, he chuckled. "To convince a Missourian of anything, you gotta show 'em. I reckon that's what I'm gonna have to do with you. Sooner or later, you'll start to see I'm tellin' the truth."

He could see that she wanted to believe him, perhaps desperately, but for reasons he couldn't figure, she refused to let herself. He holstered his Colt and returned the gun belt to his waist, buckling the leather with practiced ease. As he lifted each knee to tie the thongs that anchored the holsters to his thighs, she watched him with blatant wariness. He smiled as he threaded the knife scabbard onto his trouser belt. Retrieving his Stetson from where it rested on the floor, he settled it on his head.

"I don't know about you, but I'm hungry enough to eat the south end of a northbound mule, and that coffee out there on the fire is callin' my name." He pushed to his feet, pretending not to notice the way she shrank back. "I'm gonna go eat, then I'll bring you a plate." Nodding toward an empty Arbuckle can on the floor, he said, "That's the best I got to offer by way of a chamber pot. If you need anything else, don't be shy about hollerin'." He fell silent for a moment, then rubbed beside his nose, a habit of his when he felt tense. "While I'm gone, I've got a thought for you to ponder."

She looked up at him expectantly, her luminous eyes making him feel guilty as hell for what he was about to say. He could see no way around it, though.

"That thought is this. Why would I go to so much fuss tryin' to make you trust me, if all I had in mind was to do you meanness?" Leaving that question hanging, he moved to the rear of the wagon in two easy steps. As he swung a leg out over the gate, he hesitated to look back at her. "Just you think about that. All else aside, and whether you believe what I told you or not, you gotta see that me tryin' to trick you just plain don't make sense. I ain't pointin' this out as a threat—don't think that for a minute—but however which way you look at it, darlin', I don't need tricks." He slowly took her measure. "If I had it in mind to do what you're thinkin', I'd just do it. In case you ain't noticed, I got you outflanked, nine ways to hell."

Chapter 4

Back to the wall, Rebecca sat with her knees drawn to her chest, her arms locked around her shins. *Outflanked, nine ways to hell.* The words circled endlessly in her mind. And they were true. So horribly true. Race Spencer did have her outflanked. She was powerless against him, and whether he wanted to admit it or not, his trying to trick her made perfect sense. He wanted the church money, and he needed her to trust him so she would lead him to it.

Money, the root of all evil, the Bible proclaimed, one of the few things the Good Book said that she could testify was true. Terribly true, Rebecca thought, swallowing the sob that tore at her throat. That church money was the reason her parents and everyone else she loved had been slaughtered.

Did Race Spencer truly believe she was that naive? All those honeyed words and his deceitful air of concern. Playing tricks with those ugly six-shooters while he mouthed lies. He'd known all along that the stupid gun wouldn't work.

He obviously hoped to make her believe he was her friend so she would tell him where the cash was hidden. Well, he could think again. She knew very well what he and his cohorts would do to her once they got the information they needed. Oh, yes, she knew. She'd seen them execute their handiwork with her own eyes.

Hugging her bent knees, she struggled to stop shaking,

but much as she had upon first awakening, she felt oddly separated from her body, its functions defying her control. Her teeth chattered maddeningly, the jarring clacks sending vibrations through the roof of her mouth and into her sinus cavities with so much force her face actually ached. There was also a squeaky noise trailing up her throat, part moan, part whimper, and try as she might, she couldn't squelch it. A pathetic, weak sound, like that of a mewling child in the clutches of unreasoning terror.

Only she wasn't unreasoning. Nor was she a child. And it was infuriating to feel that she was behaving like one. Quivering and whimpering. All her life, she'd prided herself on being a strong person. What had happened to her? Overnight, it seemed, her usually stable personality had fallen apart. It made her aware that she was far more vulnerable than she wanted to be, or had ever believed she might be.

Irritation flared within her when she felt tears streaming down her cheeks. She swiped at her eyes with hands so tremulous she could barely direct her fingers. The invested effort proved futile. A fresh onslaught spilled over her lashes, making icy trails on her skin and gathering in chilly pools in the creases at each side of her mouth. She bunched her hands into tight fists, infuriated with herself. She had to do something. Anything but just huddle there, cowering and shaking.

First of all, she needed to formulate a plan. An escape was the first thing that sprang to her mind. Getting out of there, and putting as much distance as possible between herself and those men. But first she had to clothe herself. Only in what? She ran her gaze over the wagon.

To her surprise, she spotted a heap of what looked like clothing in one corner, black dresses and gray undergarments. There was even a hairbrush lying on top of the pile. Race Spencer must have collected some of the clothing that had been tossed from the trunks in the arroyo, things that had once belonged to other women in her caravan. Though it seemed unfeeling to borrow clothing from the dead, she couldn't very well parade around in a nightgown. Needs must, Mama used to say. And she desperately needed a dress and shoes. Never yet having borne a babe, she wasn't as full-figured as most of the women in her party had been, but considering the company she was presently keeping, a loose garment would be a godsend.

The thought brought her to her feet. Being held here against her will was nightmare enough without having to face those animals half-clothed.

The instant Rebecca stood, her legs, so suddenly released from the tight circle of her arms, began to jerk, the spasms so violent she couldn't direct her steps. Once, a long time ago, she'd seen a man similarly afflicted. He had been walking along a city street, his arms and legs going every which way, like a loosely jointed marionette controlled by a prankster.

Merciful heaven, what's wrong with me?

Feeling as if she might fly apart unless she curled back into a ball, Rebecca sank to the floor next to the pile of clothing, hugged her waist, and bent forward over her knees. As she clutched herself, a horrible thought occurred to her. What if this never stopped? Her memory of the killings had ended in blackness. Could she have fallen, possibly striking her head? Had she somehow sustained a brain injury?

Even as the thought settled in, the spasmodic jerking abated a bit, becoming instead a convulsive shivering. She rocked back and forth on her knees, her eyes tightly closed, her jaws clenched to stop the chattering of her teeth. Disjointed prayers formed in her mind, coming to her unbidden, the result of a lifetime of training and habit.

An awful hopelessness filled her, for the solace she'd found in prayer as recently as yesterday evaded her now. Never once in her memory had she doubted the Almighty's existence. But now, in a twinkling, her faith was gone, stripped from her, like paint from a wall. The only conviction left to her was a haunting disbelief.

After all, if there was a God, where had He been when her parents called His name and begged Him to deliver them? Busy having high tea with His angels, perhaps?

In a terribly vivid tableau, she kept seeing her father, his Bible held before him as if it were a holy shield. That image, stamped indelibly upon her mind, now seemed representative to her of nothing but a clever hoax that dated back nearly two thousand years. Papa had believed in God with his whole heart, and he'd rigidly patterned his life after the tenets of his faith, placing utter trust in the heavenly Father to protect him and his loved ones. But in the end, his God had proved to be a monstrous chimera, a being created by and born in the needful imaginings of men.

And where did that leave her? Her mother and father were dead. The only people she knew and loved who were still alive were in New Mexico. Perhaps in actual physical distance, Santa Fe wasn't all that far away, but between here and there stretched a brutal, hostile land, over which she would never be able to travel alone.

Forcing her eyes open, Rebecca stared at the clothing. The uppermost dress resembled one that had been her mother's. With quivering fingers, she lifted the garment to examine the bodice, and sure enough, the tiny rent her mother had so carefully mended was there on the front placket, between the second and third button.

Pain lanced through Rebecca. *Ma.* Pressing the dress to her face, she breathed of her mother's lingering scent. For an instant, she could almost imagine that her mother's arms were around her. Only, of course, they weren't and never would be again. With the acceptance of that came the reality of her loss and a sense of loneliness that cut so deep it seemed to settle in her very bones.

Contrary to Race's assumption, the men in camp were not busy with morning chores when he emerged from the wagon. Instead, several of them were milling around the girl's wagon like spectators hoping to buy tickets to a curtained-off circus act. Others were hunkered around the fire in a loose circle, some smoking roll-your-owns or sipping coffee from dented tin cups, others enjoying chews of tobacco and spitting with incredibly accurate aim at respective spots in the fire pit.

Not wishing to speak with any of them right then or deal with their questions about Rebecca, Race decided to forgo a cup of coffee and struck off across the rolling grassland. The morning wind plastered his shirt to his body and whipped under the brim of his Stetson to trail his hair into his eyes. He ignored the sting, concentrating instead on the scents that wafted up to him from the sun-kissed earth. Grass, sage, saltbush. He dragged in several deep breaths to clear his head and calm down.

Please, Mr. Spencer, don't toy with me. Just end it. Those words kept circling in his mind. He could almost hear the girl's voice, quavery with terror, and each time, he felt sick. To be that frightened . . . Fear in any measure was never fun. He'd been there a few times. But to feel so vulnerable and defenseless that you actually pleaded for it to end? He couldn't imagine that.

On a rise not far from camp, Race drew to a stop. Booted feet braced wide apart, he rested his hands on his hips as he contemplated the horizon. *Please, Mr. Spencer.* An awful, choking sensation grabbed him by the throat. He'd done all he could to reassure her. Yet, somehow, it didn't seem like enough, and he felt badly for walking off and leaving her when she was so afraid. There had to be something more he could do—something he might say. But what? Convinced as she was that he and his men had been involved in the killings yesterday, she was so terri-fied in his presence that he doubted she could think straight.

Sighing, Race turned to gaze back toward camp. Whether he wanted to admit it or not, there was one more way he might try to ease her fears. The wind buffeted the canvas of her wagon. He pictured her, flinching each time the cloth snapped, fearful that he or one of his men was about to enter her wagon. It was anyone's guess what she imagined they might do to her, the only certainty being that her thoughts weren't pretty. After the horrors she'd witnessed in the arroyo yesterday, how could they be?

He couldn't leave things as they were. Granted, she would eventually come to realize he and his men were innocent of any wrongdoing and that they would never harm her. But what of the time between now and then? For Rebecca, it would seem like an eternity.

Scarcely aware that he had reached a decision, Race headed back toward camp.

After getting dressed with the slapdash speed of an actress changing costumes backstage, Rebecca huddled at the front left corner of the wagon bed, her shoulders wedged tight against the walls. She didn't really feel safe there, but at least the barrier of wood guarded her back and no one could sneak up on her.

Arms hugging her ankles, the folds of her mother's skirt carefully arranged to cover all but the toes of her black shoes, she sat with her chin resting on her raised knees, her gaze fixed on the back opening of the wagon. What in heaven's name was she going to do? The memories from yesterday that flashed through her mind were too awful to contemplate. She would never submit to a monster of Race Spencer's ilk. Never. She would die first.

In her mind's eye, she pictured every lethal, dangerous inch of him. Incredibly tall, with a loose-jointed, muscular build. Broad shoulders that rippled with strength, stretching the black cloth of his shirt taut. Arms that had locked around her like tempered steel and powerful thighs sheathed in black denim so snug it hugged them like a second skin.

Outflanked, nine ways to hell. He'd smirked when he told her that. She'd never forget how she'd felt while looking into his eyes, impenetrable yet piercing, and so dark a coffee-brown they were nearly black. When he'd skimmed his gaze over her before leaving the wagon, she had felt naked and vulnerable, her skin burning as if he'd actually touched her.

Panic rushed at her. She pressed her mouth hard against her knee to stifle any sound that might slip up her throat. Had it been Race Spencer who had so brutally abused her mother and shot her father yesterday? She'd thought never to forget the face of that man, but for reasons beyond her, she was unable to call it up. Strange, that. Everything else that had happened in the arroyo was tormenting in its vividness. But the faces of the outlaws were a blur. It could have been Spencer . . . or any one of a hundred other filthy, unshaven individuals. She simply couldn't say. It seemed to her the man had been wearing tan clothing, not black. But Spencer might have been wearing a tan duster or, for that matter, could have changed outfits.

She knew one thing; he had the look of a killer. Those dark eyes, slicing into her, yet seeming to twinkle with laughter, as if her terror of him was amusing. Those sun-burnished features, every plane and angle so harshly cut that they might have been chiseled from granite. That full yet firm mouth that never quite curved into a complete smile, tugging up at only one corner, the twist of his lips pressing a deep crease into one leathery cheek.

Oh, yes. He had a merciless look about him, make no mistake. The kind of man who knew what he wanted and could be brutal in the taking.

Unfortunately for her, what Race Spencer wanted now was that money.

The wagon gave a sudden lurch. Rebecca nearly parted company with her skin when Spencer's dark face suddenly appeared above the tailgate. Using only one hand, he swung up on the backboard and climbed inside.

To her frightened eyes, he seemed a yard wide at the shoulders as he moved toward her, his back slightly hunched to avoid bumping his head on the canvas roof. Relaxed at his sides, his fists looked leathery, rock-solid, and capable of concussing a full-grown bull. There wasn't a doubt in her mind that he could strangle her with the grip of one hand. Suddenly the bane of her existence was Race Spencer, dressed head to toe in satanic black, his Stetson cocked at an angle over his eyes.

Why black clothing seemed satanic on him, she hadn't a clue. It made no sense, now that she came to think of it. Everyone in her church community wore relentless black, and none of them looked evil. Yet Race Spencer did? She decided he would probably look dangerous no matter what he wore. Those sharply carved features, his burnished skin, the blue-black glint of his hair, the raw power that seemed to emanate from every pore of his skin. There was an untamed, lethal aura about him that couldn't be denied.

"Howdy," he said in that deep, silky voice she was already coming to detest.

Rebecca didn't return the greeting. She couldn't have spoken if she tried. Why had he come back so soon? He'd brought her no food. He wasn't holding a coffee cup. And there was no mistaking the purposeful glint in his brown eyes as he sat down across from her. Gauging the distance he'd left between them, a scant two feet, she knew he could be on her before she could blink.

Extending one long leg, he drew up his other knee to rest his arm, his large, brown hand dangling. His gaze never left her. Her heart was pounding so violently it felt as if it were going to crack her ribs.

He started to speak, then seemed to think better of it, closing his eyes and pinching the bridge of his nose. After a moment, he raised his black lashes and settled his gaze on her again. Smiling slightly, he rasped his fingertips on the whiskery stubble that shadowed his jaw.

"I must look like hell," he said. "No wonder you don't trust me." As he lowered his hand, he heaved a weary sigh. "We gotta talk this out, Rebecca. I can't leave this go, knowin' how afraid you are."

Talk it out? She just wanted him to go away and leave her alone.

He nudged the brim of his hat back, his gaze trailing slowly over her face. "I reckon the first thing I wanna do is lay all the cards out on the table. We can't deal with this by tryin' to talk around it."

She didn't want to be dealt with, she thought frantically, especially not by him.

"First off, I'm gonna say plain out what I think you're afraid of, beggin' your pardon before I start, because I reckon it's gonna offend you. I know you're a proper lady, and a religious one, to boot. You probably got some pretty fixed ideas about what's fittin' and what ain't." He gestured limply with his hand. "I guess you could say I'm just the opposite. Proper ain't exactly my middle name. In short, I'm no gentleman and don't got an inklin' how to go about pretendin' I am."

Rebecca was beginning to wonder what on earth it was that he meant to say.

His firm mouth tipped up at one corner in a self-deprecating grin. "That bein' the case, I'll offer you a thought to hold on to while I'm talkin'. In my experience, an overpolite man is usually hidin' some mighty unpolite ideas. With me, what you see is what I am, rough edges and all. I don't keep much under my hat."

Oh, how she wished she could believe that.

He swiped at his mouth with his shirt sleeve and shifted his gaze from her to a floor plank that lay between them. The expression on his face conveyed that he felt extremely hesitant and uncomfortable about what he intended to say.

"Plain out, I think one of the things you're scared to death of is that I'm gonna rape you," he said, his voice turning gravelly. "I know that ain't a word for polite company, and I'm sorry for . . ." He looked up, his gaze lingering on her burning cheeks. He swallowed, his larynx bobbing. "I'm sorry for usin' it. There's probably a high-falutin way of puttin' it, but I ain't got no idea what it is."

He went back to staring at the floor again. Rebecca pressed a hand to the base of her throat, feeling as if she might faint. This man had to be the most diabolical schemer and accomplished actor she'd ever met. But despite the warnings that whispered in her mind, she felt herself beginning to waver. He looked so sincere—as if he truly did feel ill at ease and regretted using a word that she found abhorrent.

"I ain't gonna straddle the fence on that issue," he informed her gruffly. "I've been the bulldogger on enough brandin' crews to know I can throw and hogtie a calf twice your size in record time. I ain't never raped me a woman, but there ain't a question in my mind that I got the wherewithal, especially with a little gal like you." He flicked another glance at her before resuming his intent regard of the floor plank. "You ain't much bigger than a minute. If I was of a mind to rape you, I could do it, lickety-split, and we both know it."

No question about it; she *was* going to faint. A breathless, light-headed feeling stole over her.

"By me sayin' that, please don't think I'm plannin' on doin' it," he quickly added. "Or that I'm threatenin' you. I'm just tryin' to clear the air. It's one of the things you're scared of, and without it bein' in the open, I can't very well deny it."

He settled his back against the wall and lifted his dark gaze to hers. His mouth twitched at one corner in a suppressed smile as he studied her. After a long moment, he said, "I'm scarin' the livin' hell right outta you, ain't I?" The smile moved slowly over his mouth, deepening the crease in his lean cheek. "I'm sorry. Gifted at talkin', I definitely ain't. I wear a size twelve boot, and most of the time, I got it shoved in my mouth crosswise. So let me move on real fast to the denyin' part. I ain't got it in me to rape you, darlin'. Not you or anybody." The diffused light coming through the canvas shimmered on his mobile lips. "I know you don't believe that, but I'm gonna do my damnedest to convince you, so bear with me. All right?"

It was Rebecca's turn to avert her gaze. When she allowed him to look into her eyes, she got the unsettling feeling that he saw far more than she wished to reveal.

"The other thing I think you're scared of is that I'm gonna kill you," he went on. "I ain't gonna lie and say I haven't never taken a life. I have, and if it comes down to defendin' myself, I most likely will again. But I never took joy in it, and I never killed a woman. I've never even laid a hand on one, and I sure as hell don't plan to start with you.

"I know you don't believe that either. But there you have it. I know I look like a mean hombre, and I reckon if I'm honest, I gotta admit to doin' my share of wrong things. But I ain't a murderin', rapin' polecat. No how, no way. And neither is my hired hands. They'd be more apt to die for you than lift a hand against you, and that's an honest-to-God fact."

He shifted his shoulders and drew up his extended leg. Releasing a weary breath, he said, "Now we come to the convincin' part. I'm gonna tell you right up front, this ain't gonna come easy for me. It's somethin' I ain't never talked about, not to anybody. But I feel like I oughta tell you. Maybe I'm dead wrong and it won't matter a whit to you, and maybe it won't do a thing to ease your mind. But it won't be for lack of me tryin'."

He cleared his throat, sighed, and then straightened out his leg again. "You ain't the only one to see your ma get raped. Or to watch her die. It's been a lot of years, but I lost my mother the same way. Sort of, anyhow. The bastards didn't slit her throat. They was just so brutal in the takin' of her that she was tore up inside after they finished, and she bled to death."

Taken off-guard, Rebecca stiffened. Her gaze flew to his like bits of metal to a magnet. That was the very last thing she had expected him to say. What she read in his dark eyes caught at her heart. *Pain.* An awful, aching pain that seemed to reflect the hurting within herself. For several long moments, they simply stared at each other, a weighty silence hovering between them that seemed to magnify the sound of their breathing. Rebecca imagined she could even hear herself sweating—a sticky, clammy sweat that was suddenly popping out all over her body. She dug her nails into the muslin of her skirt, her muscles knotted so tightly they ached.

"I was seven," he told her huskily. "My pa—he was an Easterner who come out this way to prospect for gold. My mother . . . she was a half-breed Apache. To her way of thinkin', he married her, but to him, he traded for her with a few blankets and some trinkets, so she was just a bought thing, like a horse. Except most men treat their horses better. He drug her to his minin' claim, gave her a tent to call home, used her for his pleasure, and worked her like a slave. When I come along, he thought no more of me than her 'cause I was a breed, and in his eyes, that meant we wasn't quite human."

Rebecca closed her eyes, feeling sick. He couldn't be lying about this. Just the tone of his voice told her that, every word he spoke coming hard and laced with heartache. That he would do this—for her, just so she wouldn't feel afraid. Oh, God. It made her feel ashamed for not trusting him in the first place.

"Anyhow, he wearied of prospectin' and took us south to Santa Fe for a spell. Then he all of a sudden hightailed it back east, leavin' us to fend for ourselves when I was six. My ma—she wasn't much more'n a kid herself. Bein' female and Injun, there wasn't no decent way for her to earn us a livin'. She took to beggin' on street corners to feed me. Most times we went hungry. When there was food, she didn't take much for herself, and she got real frail."

Rebecca found herself staring at him again. He was gazing at something above her head, a distant expression in his eyes. A muscle along his jaw ticked, indicating that he was clenching his teeth.

"Right before she died, we went through a lean spell. No food, period, for three days." He shifted his gaze to look at her. "I don't reckon you've ever been on the streets and starvin'. You get to a point that you'll eat damned near anything. We dug through garbage in the alleys to stay alive quite a lot, but for that three days, we couldn't find nothin' in there to eat. She got real frantic, worryin' about me dyin' on her. So she stole some roses outta some rich man's walled-off garden. She tried to sell 'em for a penny each on a street corner, me sittin' there watchin' and prayin' she'd sell enough of 'em for us to buy some eats. The men who passed—they didn't want her roses, and they wasn't inclined to throw coin away on no Apache squaw and her brat. So they just kept walkin', some ignorin' her, some shovin' her outta their way."

He fell silent for a moment, his gaze locked on hers.

"Then along come two drunks from a saloon up the street." His throat convulsed as he swallowed. His gaze wavered, and he directed it at the floor again. "They was real interested in a rose," he said tautly. "Just not the garden type. Somehow, even bein' so young, I knew when I saw 'em that they meant trouble." He smiled slightly. "My ma—she used to say I was born with a real old soul. I reckon in a way she was right, 'cause I was leerious of lots of things she wasn't, and most times it turned out I was right to be. She had a pure heart, my ma. You know what I'm sayin'?''

He repositioned his arms on his bent knees and lifted his shoulders as if to work out a muscle cramp.

"She didn't have no ugliness in her, so she didn't see ugliness in other folks." He scratched beside his nose. "Me—I guess I got a ugly streak. I ain't never had a problem knowin' ugly when I see it." He hauled in a deep breath, as though to brace himself, then slowly exhaled. "Anyhow, them fellas laughed and throwed her roses down and tromped on 'em. And then they dragged her off into the alley. I tried to stop 'em, but I was smallish from lack of grub and only seven, so they just knocked me away and—" He closed his eyes and just sat there for a moment, his face unnaturally still. "And they just went on about their business," he said hoarsely, "havin' themselves a real fine time."

The images that flashed in Rebecca's mind made her stomach lurch and her blood run cold. The very air seemed suddenly thin, and she grabbed a little frantically for breath, feeling dizzy.

"When they finished, they just left her lay, like as if she was a dog they'd kicked senseless. She was bleedin'. Bleedin' real bad. I knew she was gonna die if I didn't get help so I ran up the street, poundin' on doors. But it was a Sunday and the shops was all closed. I wound up at the saloon, but the men in there was too busy playin' poker to bother with a snot-nosed Injun brat, and they didn't give a shit about some Apache squaw who was dyin' out in the alley. So I went back to her without no help, and there wasn't a damned thing I could do but kneel there beside her and watch her life bleed outta her into the dirt." His mouth twisted with bitterness, and his black lashes lifted to reveal eyes gone glittery with anger. "A fittin' end for an Injun squaw. Right? Dirt to dirt. It was a full day before the law even saw to it she got carried away, and I never got told what they done with her. I figure they buried her, but I don't know where."

Rebecca felt a ticklish sensation on her cheek and realized it was a tear. She said nothing. What was there to say? That she was sorry? She knew firsthand how pathetically inadequate a response that was.

"Anyhow," he said, running his palms over his pant legs, "I got that memory in my head, as clear as yesterday. It's one of them things you don't never forget, I reckon. At least, I haven't. It's always there at the back of my mind and visitin' me in my nightmares. My ma . . ." His voice trailed away, and she saw his larynx bob again as he tried to swallow. She knew the feeling— emotion becoming a knot in your throat that made it nearly impossible to speak. "She was the only pretty thing in my world—the only good thing. After losin' her, I was alone, without nobody who gave a care. There ain't no worse feelin' in the whole world, I don't think. So I kinda know how you're feelin' right now, like as if you been hollowed out with a sharp knife."

He removed his hat and ran long, thick fingers through his black hair. As he settled the Stetson back on his head, he flashed her a crooked grin that didn't reach his eyes.

"I reckon you could say me seein' that happen to my ma has given me a real strong dislike for men that ride roughshod over women, for any reason. And that's how come I ain't got it in me to do you any meanness." He ran his gaze slowly over her. "You're a real pretty little swatch of muslin, darlin'. I ain't sayin' that the wantin' ain't there when I look at you because it'd be a lie. But for me, wantin' and doin' don't ride double. You got nothin' to fear from me—or from my men. And as long as we're around, you ain't got a whole lot to fear from nobody else, either. If anyone lays a hand on you, it'll be over my dead body, and I got me a knack for bein' the fella who's still standin' when the smoke clears, so there ain't much chance of that either."

Tears burned in Rebecca's eyes. She tried to speak, but her chest felt as if a steel band was being tightened around it.

He pushed slowly to his feet, a towering specter, his guns riding his hips like portents of death. Yet looking up at him now, she felt no fear. Just an aching sadness for the little boy he had once been and the man he had become. Since hearing his story, her opinion of him had altered drastically, becoming the very antithesis of what it had been earlier. No one would fabricate a tale like that, especially not a hard-edged man like Race Spencer. And if she believed that much of what he had told her, she had to believe all else as well.

Finally finding her voice, she whispered shakily, "Thank you for telling me, Mr. Spencer."

He settled his hands at his lean hips, the smile on his mouth at last warming his eyes. "Can I take that to mean you feel some better?"

"Yes. Thank you. I, um . . . know it wasn't easy for you to talk about that, and I appreciate your sharing it with me." She caught the inside of her cheek between her teeth, feeling she should say something more. Only she couldn't think what. "Thank you," she ended up saying again. "It means more to me than I can say."

He stood there for a moment, searching her gaze. This time, she didn't let herself look away. No one had forced him to share something so painful with her, and in doing so, he had stripped his emotions bare. Because he had, she no longer felt inclined to try to hide hers from him.

"It's gonna get easier as time wears on," he told her softly. "You probably don't believe that right now, but I promise you, it does. I wish I could say it'll happen quick, but the truth is, you're probably still kinda numb and could feel a good deal worse before you feel better."

She nodded, knowing he was probably right.

"It'll hit you hard sometimes—when you ain't expectin' it. Like a fist in your gut, hurtin' so bad it takes your breath. If you need to talk, I ain't a stranger to the feelin', so don't hesitate." He hauled in another deep breath, this time exhaling on a sigh of relief. "I'm glad that's behind me," he said with a chuckle. "Now I'm hungry. If I bring you a plate of breakfast, you reckon you could try to choke down a few bites? I don't want you takin' sick."

Rebecca was having enough trouble swallowing her own saliva, let alone food. But the concern in his expression prompted her to nod. "I'll try," she said faintly.

He turned and moved to the rear of the wagon. As he swung a leg out over the tailgate, it occurred to Rebecca that it was no longer necessary or even wise to keep secrets from him. If he and his men hadn't committed those atrocities in the arroyo yesterday, then other men had. That meant the actual killers were out there somewhere, still bent on getting their hands on the church money.

"Mr. Spencer?"

He paused to glance back over his shoulder, a dark eyebrow lifted in question.

"I, um . . . about what happened in the arroyo. There are things I need to tell you. Things you should know."

"How's about I get us each a plate, and we can talk over breakfast?"

"All right."

He flashed her a slow grin. "I'll be right back."

Chapter 5

Race stood near the drop-down work station at the rear of the wagon, waiting for Cookie to stop rummaging in a crate and dish Rebecca up a plate. Serving yourself wasn't allowed, not in Cookie's grub line. *"I do the fixin' and I do the dishin',"* was the cook's motto, and he stood ready with a wooden spoon to thump any offenders on the head if they dared to help themselves.

"I'd like to feed her sometime before Christmas, Cookie," Race groused.

"I'll be right there!" the little man replied. "I swow, you boys want ever' darned thing done yesterday!"

"Mornin', boss!" a youthful voice rang out in the clear morning air.

Race turned to see his youngest employee, Tag Jones, loping across camp toward him, his footfalls impacting the parched clay like uneven drumbeats. His thin body a tangle of uncoordinated long legs and arms, the twelve-year-old looked like a scarecrow with his denim jeans and blue chambray shirt flapping loosely on his thin frame. He skidded to a stop a scant two feet away, the soles of his oversize riding boots, which had once been his father's, digging sidelong trenches in the clay. Below the brim of his Stetson, Tag's ears poked out like teacup handles.

"Dang it to hell!" Cookie cried. "Don't be raisin' dust around my cookin' fire, boy. You think you gotta do ever' darned thing at full gallop, or what?"

"I didn't stir up that much dust!" Tag cried, his large gray eyes dancing with mischief. He turned a worshipful gaze on Race. "I heard all about how you gave them rotters what for last night! Johnny says you must've been shooting and reloading at the same time. One man, holding off a small army!"

Race waved a hand to clear away the dust. "Johnny's exaggeratin'. What're you doin' back in camp? I thought Pete had you ridin' flank with Johnny this mornin'."

"I am!" Tag ran over to the bedroll wagon, swung up on the backboard to lean over the gate, and jumped back to the ground an instant later, clutching his rifle. "Johnny says he'll take me off somewhere away from the herd to do target practicin' after our shift, so I came to get my gun." Tag beamed an excited grin. "I figure if I keep at it, someday I'll be as good a shot as you."

God forbid. Race considered himself the last person on earth that the boy should try to copy. But no matter what he said or did, he couldn't seem to get the crazy notion out of Tag's head. If Race slurped his coffee, Tag did. If Race belched, Tag did. It was like carrying a mirror everywhere he went that reflected the worst of him. Race laid it off on the fact that the boy had lost his pa less than a year ago. Mac Jones had died chopping wood when the ax bounced back and nailed him between the eyes. In a twinkling, he'd been snatched away, leaving the boy without a father. Tag had adopted Race as a surrogate.

"You just be sure you go off somewhere to do your shootin' this time," Race called as the youth ran from camp. "You fire that rifle near my herd one more time, and I'll hang your hide on a post to dry."

"And I'll help him!" Cookie inserted, wagging a finger. "No more nonsense with that gun, boy, or it's gonna come up missin', be it your pa's or not! I mean it!"

"I learned my lesson," Tag called over his shoulder. "Geez. You fellas think I'm addlepated or something?"

"Addlepated!" Cookie said with a snort. To Race, he observed, "You're the one that's addlepated, bringin' a boy still wet behind the ears on a cattle drive."

Race stabbed his fingers through his hair. "I couldn't

very well leave him at the ranch alone. Now could I?''

"You coulda not hired him to start with. When that kid ain't actually in trouble, he's dreamin' up some kind of devilment to try next."

Watching the boy's awkward, gangly stride as he hurried back to his horse, Race smiled to himself. Tag reminded him of a rambunctious pup, more trouble than he was worth, but so cute you couldn't stay angry with him for long. "Leave off, Cookie. I can't send him home, and you know it. Since Mac died, Tag's ma can't feed six young'uns on her own. Tag's monthly wages is keepin' the wolves from their door."

"And bein' a rich cuss like you, it's your job to feed 'em?" Cookie snorted again. Then he chuckled. "I gotta admit, he's a cute'n, ain't he? Ornery as sin, though. Some days, I feel like snubbin' him to my wagon gate with a short rope."

After watching Tag ride from sight, Race turned just in time to catch Cookie spitting on a tin plate he'd found. The cook began shining the metal with his sleeve as best he could before spooning up some food for the girl.

"That's disgustin'," Race said.

Cookie stopped rubbing. "What is?"

Race snatched the plate away from him. "Spittin' on her plate like that. I swear, Cookie, we can't be that hard up for water!"

"Bitch, bitch, bitch! Here I was tryin' to be nice and clean it up special." Cookie huffed and bent to stir the contents of the pot on the cooking fire. "And get it straight outta your head. You ain't touchin' none of my water! You don't like the way I cleaned it? Well, then, go scrub it with sand. I keep tellin' all of you it works real slick. But do you listen? Heck, no. You just gripe. I swear, it's worse than a bunch of ol' women!" Cookie shoved his finger into the chili and popped the coated digit into his mouth. After smacking his lips, he shoved his finger back in the pot. "I can't spare water for ever' little thing!"

Race jabbed a thumb over his shoulder. "There ain't a speck of sand out there. The sand hills is south of here.

All we got is dirt, and it don't clean nothin' worth a darn. Seems to me you could spare some water for the girl, at least. It ain't sanitary, spittin' on someone's plate. Or stickin' your finger in our dinner pot. Haven't you ever heard of germs?''

"Of course I have. And I ain't got none." Cookie squinted one eye to peer up at Race. "You sayin' I got one of them communicatin' diseases? Well, I don't."

"It ain't 'communicatin',' it's communicable, and how do you know you don't?''

"Because I ain't feelin' puny. And they are so called communicatin' diseases." He wagged the spoon under Race's nose. "Passed amongst folks when they're talkin'. That's how come they's called communicatin' diseases! Ain't you ever noticed how folks spit in your face when they talk? Pert' near everybody does it, some worse than others."

Cookie was one of the latter. The only reason Race didn't go hunting for a towel was that the old codger's beard caught most of the spray. " 'Course I've noticed," Race said, rubbing even harder at the plate. He held it up to the sun, gave it a close inspection, and then turned it toward Cookie. "You reckon I got all your germs off?''

Squinting, Cookie leaned closer to look with one buggedy eye. After a moment, he snorted. "How'n' hell am I s'posed to tell? I'm long sighted. I think. What's it called when you can't see nothin' unless it's sittin' on your nose?''

"Blind."

The cook snorted and bent back over the pot, dipping his finger in the chili up to his second knuckle again. "Just what I always wanted, a boss that's a smart ass."

"I reckon I ain't too smart," Race retorted. "If I was, I'd wring some water outta you instead of puttin' up with your nonsense."

"We finally agree on somethin'." Cookie shook his head. "There's days when I find it purely amazin' that I work and take orders from such a dumb son'buck."

Race lowered the plate to his side. "Well, this dumb son'buck is gonna wash this plate."

"You're the boss. When we run outta water, don't let the boys complain to me 'cause they ain't got coffee!"

The report of a high-powered rifle exploded in the morning air. Simultaneously the plate jerked out of Race's hand, spun past Cookie, and struck the chili pot, knocking it off the fire and spilling it sideways.

"Balls on biscuits!" Cookie cried, and dropped to the ground like a felled oak.

Race hit the dirt beside him. "Jesus!"

Cookie shinnied under the wagon. Race raised up on one knee. Across camp he saw McNaught and Jesperson inching their heads back up as well. Race heard more gunfire over near the herd, which set the beasts to bawling. "What the hell?"

"That kid again, mark my words!" Jesperson yelled. "Probably shootin' at a rabbit. Boss, you're gonna have to take him in hand. He's gonna keep on, and one of these times he'll stampede the herd!"

"Take him in hand?" McNaught said with disgust. "If he was my boy, I'd take him apart. This is about the fourth time! It isn't like he hasn't been warned, and more than once."

Race pushed to his feet. The bullet that had come through camp could have killed someone. This time, he had no choice but to punish Tag. If he didn't, the kid was going to seriously hurt someone.

"I tell ya," Cookie cried as he started to crawl back out from under the chuck wagon, "somebody oughta wrap that rifle of his around his scrawny neck!"

Race dusted off his pants. "Well, I guess I'd better go find him."

Cookie suddenly let loose with curses to singe chicken feathers and began digging into the dirt with elbows and knees to get out from under the wagon. Race knew trouble in large measure must be headed their way. The cook didn't even bother to detour around the spilled chili, which was still hot enough to send up steam. Instead he slithered right out to the center of the puddle, then flapped his short arms and legs like an overturned turtle, trying to find purchase in the grease and smashed beans to gain his feet.

"Christ A'mighty!" he cried. "Run, everybody. Run for your life!"

Race looked up and saw a wave of red and white fur coming toward them. A stampede. McNaught and Jesperson both swore and raced for their horses.

"Them steers is comin' right for us! Run! Run for your life!" Cookie cried as he headed for a tall pile of rocks some forty yards east, his short legs churning with amazing speed.

Race headed for the girl's wagon. "Rebecca!"

Just as he was about to swing up on the backboard, the cattle veered, completely changing directions, as often happened.

Gripping the wagon gate, Rebecca leaned out, the morning sunlight glancing off her golden hair. "A stampede?" she cried, obviously frightened, whether by the gunfire, which undoubtedly had recalled bad memories of yesterday, or the thunderous pounding of hooves, he didn't know.

"A kid who works for me fired off a rifle!"

"And that's all it took to spook them like that?" She gazed after the panicked cows. "Just a couple of gunshots?"

"Nobody but cattle know how come they stampede, and they ain't talkin'," Race told her. "Them are all boogers, straight off open range."

"Boogers?"

"Easy cattle to spook."

"It's a miracle they turned like that."

Race nodded. "That's what makes stampedes so dangerous; you can't never predict what a bunch of scared cows might do."

In the dust that rose all around the cattle, Race could see his men, darting their mounts in and out at the edge of the charging herd, the Stetsons they waved above their heads cutting through the yellowish cloud. They were doing their level best to head the animals off. Race just prayed one of the horses didn't lose its footing. More than one skilled cow pusher had gone to meet his Maker under the hooves of frenzied cattle. *Damn.* He had to get out there and help them get those steers under control.

After watching a moment longer, Race determined that the cattle weren't likely to double back. Rebecca would be safe where she was. "I have to go help my men, honey. If you just stay put, you won't be in any danger. And Cookie should be back shortly."

"I'll be fine," she assured him. "Go!" As he turned to leave, she called, "Do be careful, Mr. Spencer. That looks like dangerous business."

That wasn't saying it by half. "Just stay right where you are, honey."

Race ran for his horse. Luckily Dusty was a trusty mount, saddled or barebacked, which saved Race the trouble of bothering with tack. Several feet from the tether line, he took a flying leap onto the stallion, then leaned forward along the animal's neck to jerk the halter rope loose. With a nudge of his heels against Dusty's flanks, he spurred the horse into a full-out gallop.

Ten minutes later, Race found himself at the opposite side of the panicked herd and as helpless to stop the crazed animals as his men had been. Before his very eyes, the profit he'd hoped to make by buying and reselling these beefs before winter was dwindling away to nothing. In a stampede, a rancher lost countless cattle, some to plunges off embankments, some to chuckholes that broke their legs. Race had even heard of a rancher who'd lost an entire herd to drowning when the stupid animals charged straight into the swift, churning white water of a river.

For Race, who'd owned his own spread for only two years and was just now beginning to operate in the black, a sizable loss would be financially devastating. He wouldn't lose his land, thank God, because he owed no mortgage payments. But a catastrophe like this would still set him back—way back—and with hurtful results not only for Race, but every man in his employ. To survive, he'd have to trim expenditures, and that meant laying off some of his crew. In turn, they would face winter without jobs, and without jobs, they would have no income. For those without families to support, it wouldn't be so bad. But for the husbands and sons who put food on the table, this damned stampede would cause a world of grief.

Furious, Race guided Dusty around the perimeters of the charging bovines and brought the horse to a skidding stop alongside Johnny Graves. Startled, the skinny, sandy-haired young cowboy spun in the saddle. Upon seeing Race, an expression of relief washed over his dust-streaked face.

"Where's Tag?" Race roared to be heard over the deafening din sent up by the bawling cows. "I swear to God, he won't sit down for a week after I'm done with him!"

Johnny's horse threw its head and sidestepped, whinnying shrilly. Graves jerked hard on the reins, dug a heel into the animal's haunch, and wheeled it back around. Yelling to be heard, half his words drowned out by the noise, he cried, "Damn if—know! It—Tag, though! He—with me!" He shrugged and shook his head. "Don't know—did it!"

"You're sure it wasn't Tag? How in hell could it not be?" Race roared to be heard over the thundering of twelve hundred hooves. "A quiet herd one minute, and fireworks the next? Somebody was shooting, and you know damned well no one else would!"

Johnny shook his head. "It wasn't him! Tag was ri—front—me! Everything—quiet, then—hell—loose! Rifle—and every—went crazy!" He hooked a thumb over his shoulder. "It came—up there—hind me! From some—on—rise."

Race turned to look, and there was indeed a rise in the distance, although the cattle had run a goodly distance from it in the time since the first shot had been fired. "And you're sure it wasn't one of our men who fired the shots?" he yelled.

Johnny shook his head. "Wha—think? That—a bunch—damned fools?"

Hauling back on the halter rope and throwing his weight, Race spun Dusty in place on his back hooves. He gazed at the distant rise, all thought of financial loss fading from his mind as a new fear took root. If Tag hadn't fired those rifle shots, that meant an outsider had done it in a deliberate attempt to stampede the herd.

Race needed no detailed pictures sketched in the dirt to tell him the rest of the story. Like a goddamned fool, he'd ridden off to save his cattle, leaving Rebecca alone back at camp, believing she'd be safe there. Now, he was a good five minutes away—if he pushed Dusty to his limit and went back as a crow flew—and that wasn't counting the ten minutes he'd already been away from her to get here.

That added up to fifteen minutes. His stomach dropped to somewhere in the region of his boot heels. Sweet God Almighty. He'd let himself be lured away, leaving her there with no one to look after her. Even Cookie had run for high ground.

The bastards who had slaughtered all those people in the arroyo yesterday could do untold damage to a defenseless slip of a girl in fifteen minutes. And damn his own worthless hide, he'd be the one who had let it happen.

Chapter 6

Hands locked on the wagon gate, Rebecca stared after the horse and rider racing away from camp, her admiration for Race Spencer growing with each powerful stride of the buckskin's long legs. The man was a magnificent horseman, his well-muscled body flowing with the movements of his mount, making stallion and rider seem like one entity.

As she watched the dust billowing behind the horse's flashing hooves, Rebecca decided she should probably get out of the wagon to better monitor the stampede. Just in case the cattle turned back toward her, she didn't want to be caught unprepared. Mr. Spencer had said that someone named Cookie would be back in camp shortly, but otherwise it appeared that all the other men were gone, chasing after the cattle. That meant she'd have to manage on her own if the panicked herd reversed its direction.

Except for clumps of brush, a large pile of rock in the distance, and the peaks of the mountains far to the west, nothing but rolling grasslands stretched for as far as she could see. After having traveled over this sort of terrain for weeks on end, Rebecca knew all too well that the dips between hills could conceal an approaching wagon train until it was nearly on top of you. She could only assume the same might hold true for a herd of cattle. She would be wise to watch in the direction they had gone for any sign of dust, for that might be the only warning she got that the cows were headed back her way. Not a pleasant thought.

Gathering up her skirts, which were inches too long, she swung a leg out over the gate, searched with her toe for a foothold, and then lowered herself to the ground. A quick peek around the corner of the wagon told her that no one had remained behind. Not far away, she saw a length of rope stretched between two sturdy wooden stakes driven deeply into the ground. That was undoubtedly where Mr. Spencer and his men tethered their mounts. Since all the horses were gone, it followed that all the men were gone as well.

Just beyond camp, twelve wagon-team mules were staked out to graze with two oxen, which she assumed were from her caravan and had been used to pull her wagon from the arroyo. In the event that the stampeding cattle turned back, she supposed she might ride one of the mules to safety, the only problem being that mules were often difficult to handle, their stubbornness compounded greatly if they'd never been broken to ride. But unlike practically everything else she had encountered thus far in this godforsaken territory, at least mules were something she knew about and could confidently handle, even if it meant having to ride one that bucked with far more enthusiasm than it walked. Papa and the other brethren had always used mules in the fields, so she had dealt with the creatures all of her life. The secret of handling them successfully was simply to be as stubborn and cantankerous as they were.

Hugging her waist and keeping her gaze fixed in the direction that Race Spencer had been heading, Rebecca took a few tentative steps away from her wagon to provide herself with a better view. Her legs still felt weak, she realized, whether from the ordeal she'd just endured or from not eating for so long, she wasn't sure. Her line of vision blocked by another wagon, she angled right, craning her neck to watch for any sign of a new dust cloud. The only one she saw was receding, which told her the herd was most likely still heading away from camp.

A thumping sound drew her attention. She glanced over

her shoulder to see a large, mottled brown hound standing next to a low-burning fire at the rear of what she surmised was the chuck wagon. An incurable dog lover, Rebecca turned and pressed cautiously closer, watching the creature for any sign of viciousness. The hound was so intent on whatever it was devouring that it scarcely seemed aware of her.

When she got within a few feet, the dog finally looked up, affording her a glimpse of what had to be the homeliest hound face she'd ever seen, the skin loose and wrinkled with drooling jowls that hung in long flaps at each side of its muzzle. Its sad-looking eyes were badly bloodshot, the lower lids sagging so that the red, inside tissue was exposed.

"Nice dog," she said, bending forward and extending a hand. "You don't bite, do you?"

The animal gave her a bored look and resumed eating, nudging an overturned pot with its nose, then thrusting its head inside. Hollow-sounding slurps and tinny thumps followed. Dropping to a crouch, Rebecca smiled slightly. It was silly of her, she supposed, but somehow, seeing the dog lent her a sense of continuity and well-being. Life did go on. Mr. Spencer was right; the sadness inside her wouldn't remain an unbearable ache forever. The morning sunlight felt deliciously warm on her face and shoulders. Watching the hound reminded her that there were still sweet, wondrous things in the world to anticipate—newborn puppies, frolicking kittens, the perfume of spring wildflowers. Someday when the sadness lessened, she would laugh again and feel at peace.

Hugging her knees, Rebecca closed her eyes and took a deep breath, visions of her parents moving softly through her mind, her father's kindly smile, her mother's lovely blue eyes. That was how she should try to remember them, she realized—as they'd been in life, not as they'd been in those last few terrible moments. They would never have wanted her to dwell on that sort of ugliness, for it was contrary to all that they had believed and upheld. *Violence.* Rebecca's father had never even disciplined her physically, nor had she ever seen him lift a hand to her mother. After living her whole life never seeing any sort of violence, then witnessing a rash of it at its very worst, she felt horribly vulnerable and afraid. If she let herself continue to think about it, she had no doubt the memories might drive her mad.

Lifting her lashes, Rebecca glanced over her shoulder to be sure no dust cloud had appeared on the horizon. Then she returned her gaze to the dog. It appeared to be eating chili, which had somehow gotten knocked from the fire and spilled. Her stomach, which hadn't seen a morsel of food in over twenty-four hours, protested with hunger sounds at the smell of the meat sauce.

Evidently unsettled by her presence, the hound lifted its head, which now sported smears of chili sauce and beans, even on the long ears. Under other circumstances, Rebecca would have laughed, for the animal was nothing if not comical looking, a smashed bean at the center of its forehead adding a special touch.

Still feeling a bit shaky, she sighed and pushed to her feet. At her movement, the hound startled her with a low growl, hovering protectively over the chili pot, sauce smearing its muzzle.

"As hungry as I am, I don't care to eat dirt with my dinner, so you can rest easy," she told the dog, clucking her tongue. "Selfish thing. If I was of a mind to take some, you've more than enough to share. How much can one dog possibly eat?"

Jowls dripping foamy slobber flecked with chili sauce, the dog growled again. Afraid that the animal might be vicious after all, she decided the best course of action was to keep her gaze on the ground, ignoring him as she moved away. Silly creature. As if she were inclined to crawl about, rooting in the dirt for her dinner.

Just as she started to turn and leave, the dog surpassed its previous growls with a deep, rumbling snarl that raised the hair on her arms. A crawling sensation moved up the back of Rebecca's neck, and she got the awful feeling that someone was staring at her. Her pulse skittered as she whirled to look behind her. Almost as if the hound sensed her sudden fear, it let loose with another blood-chilling growl and moved away from the fire to stand abreast of her.

No more than fifteen feet away stood four men, though to include them in the male gender was, in her estimation, an affront to the human race. They walked on two legs and wore the trappings of men, but there all comparison ended. The breeze shifted directions, carrying the smell of body filth to her, so malodorous and thick she could almost taste it.

"Well, now," one said, cupping his crotch with a grimy hand to scratch himself as he spoke. "Ain't you a fine swatch of calico?"

Rebecca's feet felt rooted to the ground, and all she could do was stare. She'd never seen such filthy, evil-looking creatures in all her life. Shifty, bloodshot eyes. All of them sported long stubble on their jaws and chins, the coverage oddly thin and patchy, as if, like the plant life in this parched country, their beards had suffered for lack of nutrients and water. They put her in mind of mangy porcupines. Not that she'd ever seen any. But that was the best she could do to describe them.

Until Rebecca and the others in her caravan had departed from the Santa Fe Trail two days ago, they had traveled with a much larger wagon train, and during the journey, they had been told stories about men of this caliber. Desperadoes or border ruffians, they were sometimes called, bold and reckless outlaws who marauded, far and wide, killing anyone who dared to get in their way. Many of them from New Mexico, the desperadoes generally rode in large, ragtag gangs, she'd been told, most of the members of white descent, their main strength lying in sheer numbers rather than skill with weaponry. They were reputedly men without feeling or common decency, who knew no limits and revered nothing, be it secular or holy.

She saw that they'd left their horses at the edge of camp, a fair distance away, undoubtedly the better to sneak up on her. For what purpose, she had yet to determine, her only certainty being that it couldn't be good.

Snarling again, the dog crouched slightly, its shoulder on a level with her knee. The fellow who had scratched himself moved his hand to his holstered revolver, his fingers curling loosely over the butt. Judging by his wary watchfulness, he meant to shoot the hound if it made a move toward them.

Realizing now that the animal hadn't been growling at her, after all, but trying to alert her to danger, Rebecca touched a shaky hand to the top of its bony head, her gaze never leaving the men. They wore tan leather shirts and pants, the leg and arm seams trimmed with long fringe and silver conchae that flashed in the sunlight like mirrors.

Pictures moved through her head, and an awful dizzy sensation washed over her. Their clothing was the kind one might expect Indians to wear, only these garments bore a distinct Spanish influence. Their pants fit snugly in the legs but flared widely at the ankle over ornately hand-tooled boots. Their close-fitting shirts, cut similar to jackets, had standing collars, epaulets, front shields and cuffs decorated with beaded trefoil and silver brads, which matched those on the bands of their tan hats. The overall effect was one of overdone flashiness, the motto of these men evidently being, the more garish the better.

Her dizziness increased as she studied their garments. *Tan.* She jerked her gaze back up to their faces, her legs going watery as snatches of memory returned to her and realization slowly dawned.

As if he sensed her mounting horror, the man who stood to the far left smiled at her. It was a cruel smile, calculated to terrify, his lips drawing back in a snarl to reveal dirty, yellow teeth with a nasty, dark brown substance caked between them. Greasy strings of collar-length, wavy blond hair framed his face—a face that she knew, in that moment, would haunt her for the rest of her life. Close-set, beady eyes, so pale a blue they were almost colorless. A beaklike nose and sharply cut, sun-baked features.

Fear slammed through her brain like a fist through glass. These men had taken part in the bloodbath at the arroyo. She knew it as surely as she breathed, even though she couldn't recall their faces. She gasped and fell back a step, pressing a hand to her throat.

*Tell me where the money is, old man, and I'll leave
your worn-out old woman alone*!

The words rang in her mind, recalling images so awful
that Rebecca couldn't breathe for a moment. Fear washed
over her in icy waves. More pictures flashed. Of a faceless
monster, brutalizing her mother and laughing at her cries
of pain. Of her father, holding up his Bible as though for
protection and pleading for mercy. And then the blood.
Everywhere, the blood.

Feeling as if a red haze filmed her vision, she could
only stare as they slowly advanced toward her. The dog
growled another warning, which they ignored. Of the four,
the face of the leering blond drew her gaze most strongly.
Had he been the man who killed her mother? She didn't
know, couldn't remember. But it didn't matter. He'd been
there. That was enough.

"You!" she whispered, her voice throbbing. *"You!"*

She'd no sooner spoken than someone hollered, "Run,
honey! Run for your life!"

Startled by the shout, she glanced past the desperadoes
to see a funny-looking little man with short legs racing
into camp, one hand clamped to the top of his head to
hold his gray hat in place.

"You, there!" he cried, his voice breaking with each
jarring step he took. "You got no business here! Clear
out! Ever' last one of you. Go on, get!"

For a short person, the little man covered ground with
amazing speed, his stubby legs pumping like well-oiled
pistons. As he drew closer, she could make out his features. Those that weren't covered with the wild, gray
beard, anyway. He had a huge hawk nose, which seemed
to be the largest thing about him, that jutted from between
deep-set green eyes capped by thick, grizzled brows that
reminded her of squirrel tails. He wore a green plaid shirt
and oversize blue dungarees held up by scarlet suspenders, and it looked as if he had chili beans smashed all over
his front. The floppy legs of the dungarees had been
hacked off just below the knee, exposing faded red long
handles from the frayed edges of denim down to his dusty
boot tops.

Much as she had stared at the desperadoes, Rebecca gaped at him as he drew closer. Born and raised in a religious cloister where black, conservatively fashioned garments were mandatory, she'd not only never seen men like these, but could not have imagined they existed.

Skidding on his boot heels, the little man stopped directly in front of Rebecca and turned his back on her to shake his fist at the outlaws. "Go on, I said! Get while the gettin's good. The boss and the others is comin', and if you ain't cleared out afore he gets here, he'll fix your wagons for sure!"

"Hoo-ee!" a man with long black hair cried. "I'm so scared!"

His cohorts elbowed each other and laughed, the sound straight out of Rebecca's nightmares. They obviously didn't believe other men were coming, and quite honestly, neither did she. Her gaze darted from the strange little man to the ruffians, her fear steadily mounting, only now not so much for herself as for her self-appointed rescuer, who'd begun to bounce around in front of her like a crazed pugilist with no opponent. The desperadoes, who loomed head and shoulders above him, regarded him much as they might have a flea, vaguely surprised at his temerity, but ready to swat him dead if he hopped too close.

She stared dumbly at the red crisscross of the little man's suspender straps, frantically trying to think of some way she might make him stop this lunacy. Didn't he realize these four men were cold-blooded killers? That for no reason at all, they had slaughtered twelve people yesterday? Now this fellow was challenging them? It was madness.

"Well?" the little man cried. The crisscross of his red suspender straps bounced past, blurring in Rebecca's vision against his green plaid shirt. "What are you fellas, yeller from nape to bum?" Still pumping his fists, the little man licked the end of his thumb and touched it to his nose before taking another swing at empty air. "You was brave enough with a girl half your size. What'cha waitin' on now?"

Evidently growing winded from the spurt of activity, the little man finally ceased bouncing. He stood with his back to Rebecca, about four feet away. Boots set wide apart, stout legs braced, he rested his knotted hands on his hips. "It figgers! Two-pistol bullies!"

"Ain't he cute, Orv?" a man with oily sable hair said with a laugh. "A little fightin' rooster." So quickly Rebecca barely saw him move, he snaked out a hand and knocked the little man's sweat-stained hat from his head. "I knowed it! Bald as an onion on top!"

It was true. A round patch at the crown of the little man's head was completely hairless and shiny pink. Free from confinement, the rest of his hair lifted in the breeze, the long, kinky strands poking wildly in all directions like overstretched wire springs.

"Don't take a full head o' hair to make a man!" Pumping his fists again, the little man resumed bouncing. He rocked to and fro, then sideways, balancing on the balls of his feet, his stout upper body flowing with the movements. "You'll think I'm a rooster 'bout the time I knock you into a cocked hat!"

The blond man flashed another of those bestial smiles. "Well, now, I'm flat quakin' in my boots," he said, and then, in a blur of motion, drew back a fist and struck the smaller man squarely on the nose.

Reeling back with the force of the blow, Red Suspenders fell against Rebecca, nearly knocking her down. As she staggered backward, she grabbed the little man's arms to keep him from falling. Beneath the grip of her clutching fingers, she felt him shaking.

He was afraid, she realized incredulously. So afraid he was trembling. Yet he stood between her and the other men, clearly prepared to die in defense of her. "Don't do this!" she cried. "Please, it won't do any good. They'll only hurt—"

The hound, no longer held back by Rebecca's touch, let loose with a feral snarl and leaped at the blond, its mottled brown body arcing through the air like a well-aimed, furry cannonball. The animal struck the man with such force that the two went flying, the blond landing on his back in a rise of dust, the dog on top of him. Chaos erupted, the other three desperadoes shouting, the blond crying out in startlement and pain, the dog emitting frenzied yelps, and the little man yelling, trying to call the canine off.

Rebecca, having already seen one of the men reach for his gun when the dog behaved aggressively, knew what was going to transpire and added her screams to the din, frantically trying to make the dog abort its attack. It was useless. Over all the shouting and yelling, her voice was scarcely audible.

As if in a dream, she saw the crotch scratcher draw his revolver. "No! Please, don't! He's just—!"

Kaboom! The blast of the gun imploded against her eardrums. The dog yelped only once and then went limp atop the squirming blond. Rebecca saw crimson spreading over the hound's mottled brown fur near its shoulder. *Oh, God.* Her fault. All her fault. Every single word from Race Spencer's mouth had been the absolute truth. He'd had *nothing* to do with the killings in the arroyo, nor had any of his men.

If only she had believed him sooner, she might have warned him of possible trouble, and he might have been able to prevent this.

Now the dog was dead. *Dead!* And by her hand, as surely as if she had fired the gun that killed it. And the stampede? What of that? Had these horrible men been responsible for the rifle shots that spooked the cattle? *Dear God.*

The blond shoved the dead dog off him and rolled to his feet, checking himself for injury. Rebecca sank to her knees beside the hound. *Newborn puppies, frolicking kittens, and the perfume of spring wildflowers?* With the blast of the gun, her feeling of hope shattered. The world was a horrible place, filled with evil. And she was trapped, square in the middle of it. The hound had done nothing but try to defend her and Red Suspenders. Now it was dead.

The pain that knifed through her made little sense. She'd only just seen the dog for the first time a few minutes ago and could bear it no affection. But it had growled to warn her of danger! And now it had sacrificed its life, trying to protect her. Kneeling there, she hugged her waist, staring down at the animal, its death undeniably her handiwork. A foggy grayness gathered inside of her head.

She remembered having this same feeling yesterday— fog creeping over her, then utter blackness. *Yes.* She wanted to sink into it. The little man was going to be killed, that was a given. She would be killed as well. Why remain aware, when she knew what was in store for her?

"Blue!" Red Suspenders cried hoarsely. "You rotten son'bitch! You shot ol' Blue!"

The raw pain in the little man's voice jerked Rebecca back to reality. Still hugging herself, she looked up, wanting to tell him that fighting these horrible men was pointless, that he'd only be killed for his trouble. But her voice wouldn't work.

He gave his grizzled head a shake, as if to clear away muzziness. "You no-account, lowdown bastards! You kilt ol' Blue!"

Green eyes sparking with anger, his hawk nose streaming blood, Red Suspenders started to bounce about on the balls of his feet again, his hair flying, his elbows pumping, his bald pate barely clearing the shoulders of the outlaws when his feet left the ground. "Ain't nobody gonna git away with barrelin' into this camp, frightenin' a lady and killin' ol' Blue. Not when Bartholomew Lincoln Grigsley's around!" He danced back and forth, jutting his bearded chin at the blond who had punched him. "Come on, you greasy, no-account son'bitch! You got in a lucky punch, is all. Now come take your medicine!"

The blond struck the little man again. This time the blow knocked Red Suspenders to the ground. He sprawled like a limp scarecrow beside Rebecca and the dead dog. Before she could quite register what had occurred, the blond sprang forward, grabbed Red Suspenders by the front of his shirt, and began to pummel his face. Knuckles smashing against flesh and bone was one of the most horrible sounds Rebecca had ever heard, and she flinched with each blow.

The other three filthy heathens stood there, watching and laughing.

She scrambled to her feet. "Stop it!" she cried. "Oh, dear God! Don't do this, I beg of you! Don't."

The words she spoke, so reminiscent of those she'd heard her father cry yesterday, seemed to hang in her brain like icicles. *Please, I beg of you. Have mercy. Don't do this terrible thing!* These men had ignored her Papa's petitions, just as they ignored hers now.

Again and again, the blond smashed his fist into the little man's face, the sickening thuds making Rebecca feel sick. Above his gray beard, Red Suspenders's features were besmeared with blood, his green eyes glazed with pain. Then, as if that weren't enough, the younger man let go of the poor old fellow's shirt, reared back, and started kicking him.

Rebecca clamped her hands to her cheeks, staring in disbelief, so frightened she could scarcely think. Then, almost as if she grew separate from her own body, she saw herself. Just standing there. Again. Wanting nothing more than to run and hide. Again. Too terrified to move. *Again.* Her papa had done the same, never lifting a hand to help Ma, just standing there, Bible uplifted, imploring her tormentor to stop. And the other brethren? She remembered the looks on their faces when her father had been shot—horror mingled with disbelief, their Bibles clutched over their hearts. None of them had offered to do a single thing.

Nay! she could almost hear her papa saying. *Not an eye for an eye, Rebecca. Live by violence and forever be damned. Let my brother smite me, that I may turn the other cheek! So saith the Lord.*

Was this not damnation? To be brutalized by vicious men, doing nothing to defend oneself or others, her reward to be haunted by the memories and guilt of it for the rest of her life?

The blond kicked the little man again, and in that heartbeat of time, something inside her snapped. Her sanity, maybe? Or perhaps the constraints drilled into her by a lifetime of training. She only knew that the tight band of fear that seemed to be squeezing the breath from her chest suddenly went lax, replaced by a rage so intense it made her blind to nearly everything else.

It was as if she were seeing everything through a telescope, her vision tunnellike and black at the edges. She threw herself at the blond.

The impact of her body sent him staggering backward. Pressing a frontal attack, Rebecca went after him, pummeling his face, scratching at his eyes, biting him.

"Murderer! You murdering *animal*!"

Sweat ran into Race's eyes as he sighted in along the barrel of his rifle. Damn it, he didn't dare shoot. If he chanced it, he could accidentally hit the girl. The crazy little fool. He'd been just about to pick the ruffians off when she suddenly flew into a frenzy, attacking the blond fellow like a she-cat defending her cub.

Now the bastards were playing with her, dodging her blows, tossing her back and forth, and putting their filthy hands all over her in the process. Every time he almost got a clear shot at one of the no-good worms, she moved in front of his target.

Finally Race gave up and lowered the gun. It didn't look as if he had a choice. He would have to move in closer and take on all four of them, hopefully with the element of surprise in his favor. He preferred picking them off at a distance—less risky that way—but it just wasn't going to happen.

Henry clasped in one hand, Race slithered forward on his belly, keeping his head down as much as possible. Only tall clumps of grass springing up here and there from the mat of green provided him with cover, and not much, at that. Cookie looked to be unconscious now, his stout body sprawled in the dirt. Race couldn't tell at this distance how seriously the old codger might be hurt. Poor old Blue, though, he was most probably dead. Race couldn't fault the hound for leaping to Cookie and the girl's defense. But for all the good it had done, he wished the wrinkled mongrel had just stayed out of it.

Shoving his thoughts aside, Race kept his gaze fixed on the men as he made his way closer. Time enough later to worry about Cookie and mourn old Blue. The same went for trying to make sense of this situation. What had Rebecca and her people been carrying that the bastards wanted so badly? Money? It was the only explanation that Race could think of.

No matter. He'd get answers later. Right now, he had more important fish to fry, namely dispatching those murderous devils straight back to hell and saving that fool girl's pretty little neck.

Chapter 7

Race crawled to within forty feet of Rebecca, but even then, he couldn't get a clear shot at any of the plug-uglies. Evidently bored with tossing her back and forth, they began grabbing her by the shoulders to spin and shove her, their laughter vicious and mocking when they released her and she staggered like a child fresh off a swiftly turning merry-go-round. Looking dazed and terrified, she just managed to catch her balance before one of them would grab her again. *The bastards.* Each man took full advantage of having her in his clutches, clamping his hands over her breasts or gyrating his hips against her, before he twirled her roughly into the embrace of the next man in line.

Fury rolled through Race in searing waves. Never had he wanted so badly to spill blood. Animals like that weren't fit to draw breath. Only, damn it, he didn't dare shoot. Not unless the situation got completely out of hand and he had no choice. Even with his lever-action Henry, which could jack out rounds at a mighty good clip, he feared he wouldn't be able to drop all four men before one of them had time to hurt the girl.

Ending the game they'd been playing, the blond fellow grabbed Rebecca from behind, clamped one arm under her breasts, and pressed the gleaming blade of a knife to the underside of her chin. For an instant, Race thought the bastard meant to slit her throat, and he damned near died on the spot. At the same time, the plug-ugly bent his head and began whispering something to Rebecca, his sun-darkened face twisting in a cruel smile. The breeze was a bit too brisk and Race too far away to hear what the man said. Spine arched, Rebecca held herself absolutely still, her head thrown back, the tendons at each side of her slender neck distended.

"I don't know what you're talking about!" she cried, the shrill terror in her voice shivering down Race's spine.

The blond said something else, pressing the blade more firmly against her skin, the enthralled expression that came over his face making Race's skin crawl. Christ, he had to get her away from the loco son of a bitch, the sooner, the better. The question was how to do it without getting her killed in the process.

"I'm not lying!" she insisted, her voice catching on a sob. "There's nothing *in* the wagon. I keep telling you that. Why won't you believe me?"

Where the knife dug in below her chin, a thin trickle of crimson appeared and coursed slowly down her neck. Race scrubbed sweat from his eyes, his heart pounding so hard, he could have sworn the ground was shaking.

No longer feeling he had a choice, Race nestled the butt of his Henry against his shoulder, drew a bead on the man, and curled his finger snugly over the trigger. His ears rang with the sound of the blood rushing through his veins. *Damn.* He could shoot the blond in the head, no problem. But if the bastard's hand jerked? Then, what? Race knew the answer to that one. With that damned Arkansas toothpick held so firmly to Rebecca's throat, one twitch of the ruffian's hand might kill her. Race hated to take that chance. Yet how could he not? From the looks of it, the blond was going to kill her, either way. At least if Race shot him, Rebecca might have a fifty-fifty chance. *If* the ruffian didn't jerk when the slug hit him. *If* she kept her head and took advantage of the confusion to run. *If* the other three men hesitated. Maybe, then, she could come through this alive.

Race had done his share of gambling, and high-stake games had never rattled his nerves. But goddamn it, he'd never gambled with another person's life, which was essentially what he'd be doing when he pulled the trigger.

Time had run out, though—and so had his options.

With the Henry braced against his shoulder, Race put slow pressure on the trigger, squeezing, squeezing—then suddenly the blond ruffian shifted, moving his head, which had been Race's target, from one side of Rebecca's to the other. Relaxing his trigger finger, Race watched, waiting and hoping the son of a bitch would move back into his line of fire. Instead the man drew the knife from Rebecca's throat and grabbed her roughly by the hair. Jerking her clear off her feet, he proceeded to drag her behind him toward the cheek turners' wagon, Rebecca's body shielding him every step of the way.

"You'll by God tell me!" he yelled. "Easy or hard. It's your choice, sweet thing! I'd just as soon do it the hard way. I ain't played with a pretty young gal like you in a good, long spell, and I'm gonna have a real fine time."

She'd tell him *what*? Race wondered. The crazy bastards. There was nothing in that damned wagon but a bunch of quilts and some clothing.

"No, listen to me! Please, you have to listen!" Rebecca cried, struggling to keep her feet as she was jerked along behind him. "I'm telling you, it's not in there!"

Race glanced at the wagon, his bewilderment increasing. Any fool could see that the damned thing was as empty as a mudsill's pocket.

"Let me go! You're making a mistake. Please, just let me go!" Rebecca clutched the blond's wrist and tried to loosen his hand from her braid. "How can I tell you what I don't know?"

"You say that now. But there's no other place it can be. Plain and simple, it's gotta be in this wagon! You know it, and I know it. And you're gonna save us the trouble of tearin' the damned thing apart to find it. You hear?"

"You're crazy!" Rebecca cried. "Crazy, do you hear? Do you think I wouldn't tell you if it was in there? I don't want to die!"

With her hands now clamped to the top of her head to

ease the pull on her hair and the hem of her skirt catching under her feet each time she stepped, Rebecca half-ran, half-scrambled behind him, her cries shrill and laced with panic.

"Of course you don't wanna die, darlin'. And that's exactly why you're gonna be a good girl and talk to me. Your hotshot cowboy won't come back to save you, if that's what you're thinkin'. Those steers of his ran every which way, and we got men out there to make sure they keep on runnin'. Some of those cows are probably half-way to Oregon by now."

At the rear of the wagon, which partially blocked Race's line of fire and made taking a shot risky, the blond turned to grab her around the waist. Rebecca fought him, flailing her arms, striking at his face with her fists. But the man was by far the stronger, and he easily over-powered her, lifting her and shoving her roughly over the wagon gate, then leaping up to go inside after her.

Race heard a thud and saw the wagon rock. He clenched his teeth, imagining the man throwing her to the floor. Rebecca screamed. The sound of a slap rang out, and Race winced. He couldn't take much more of this without going in to get her like all possessed. Even an open-handed blow could do a lot of damage to a woman's face, and Rebecca was more delicately made than most. Race remembered how small and birdlike her bones had felt to him when he'd checked her for fractures yesterday, how easily he'd borne her weight as he carried her. And now that lunatic was knocking her around.

He forced himself to block out the sounds. If he meant to help her, he couldn't afford to think about anything else, especially not about what might be happening in there. He wasn't likely to get any second chances if he made a stupid mistake.

Now that the blond had disappeared into the wagon with Rebecca, Race decided that using the rifle might not be his best option. The three men who'd remained outside were powwowing about something beside the wagon, completely unaware of his presence. From what little he could hear of their conversation, he decided they were arguing about where they could hide the wagon, which meant they planned to take it somewhere. He could only assume they meant to abscond with Rebecca as well.

Race hoped he was reading them right. If the three were busy getting the wagon ready to go, fetching and hitching the oxen team, they would relax their guard, which might allow him to sneak in and quietly drop them, one at a time, without alerting the others. A knife wasn't his choice of weapon, but that didn't mean he wasn't handy with one.

A dangerous half-smile settled on Race's mouth when two of the men left the wagon and walked toward the grazing area where the mules and oxen were tethered. He set aside his rifle, slipped his knife from its sheath, and went after them.

Like a satanic incantation, the desperado's voice droned on and on, holding Rebecca fast in the clutches of terror. *Insanity*. It was a word people used offhandedly, giving little thought to its true meaning, a word Rebecca had once used lightly herself. Now, she realized that most people had no idea what real insanity was.

This man was insane—the mad as a hatter kind of insane that made her skin crawl when she looked into his eyes. There would be no way to save herself from him. She had accepted that. He gave every appearance of being relaxed and unguarded, but she could sense his watchfulness and knew he was only playing with her—like a cat toying with its prey, hoping she might try to bolt so he could swat her senseless and drag her back. Nevertheless, stark terror swirled in her head, urging her to run. Only the certainty that he would catch her kept her from throwing herself away from him.

He sat slumped against the wagon wall, with her sitting between his bent knees, the base of her spine drawn firmly against the crotch of his leather britches. In a soft, sing-song voice, he threatened her, giving explicit descriptions of the things he would do to her if she didn't give him the information he sought. The stink of him—of old sweat and foul breath—filled the confines of the wagon with mugginess.

Rebecca had already come to realize she was a sniveling coward. After yesterday, how could she not know that? But it still made her feel sick when she found herself wanting to yield to his demands. Anything to save herself, she kept thinking. What did it matter if he took the church money, as long as he spared her? Human life was priceless. Worldly treasures meant nothing in the end, so wherein lay the sense in dying for them?

Oh, yes. She could come up with a dozen valid reasons why she should tell him what he wanted to know, and, almost mindless with fear, she nearly convinced herself to do it. *Give in,* a voice whispered in her mind. *Don't be a fool. Relent and save yourself.*

Only she knew it would do no good. Nothing in her life had prepared her to deal with a man like this. But instinctively she knew that even if she told him where the money was, even if, heaven help her, she led him to it and tore up the fake floor in the Petersens' wagon herself, he would still kill her. This sort of man didn't honor his word or keep to a bargain. He would just avail himself of her body, as had happened to her mother, making her yearn for death, perhaps even beg for it before he was finished with her. And then, without a moment's hesitation or a shred of remorse, he would end her life, either by cutting her throat or putting a bullet in her brain. And afterward? The answer to that was simple. He would gather up the money and ride away, pleased as punch with himself.

The very same money her parents had sacrificed their lives to protect . . .

Since there was naught to be gained by surrendering, Rebecca sat with her spine ruler straight, enduring his taunts, which seemed all the more diabolical because he whispered them so sweetly, all the while taunting her with his knife. Tracing her features. Catching flyaway strands of her hair on the blade's edge. Leaning forward to trail the razor-sharp point down the row of buttons on her bodice.

"Do you know what I've always wanted to do?" he asked in a throaty whisper, running his tongue along the edge of her ear as he spoke. "All my life, I've wanted to find me a real fine swatch of calico—someone just like you—and make her all mine. You know what I mean?"

Rebecca couldn't have formed a reply if she tried. Her throat felt as if a noose was cinched around it. He licked the side of her neck, laughing under his breath. The hot, wet rasp of his tongue, combined with his fetid breath, made her want to retch.

He touched the blade tip to the pulse point below her ear. "Some men—they marry a woman. Put a ring on her finger. They figure that makes her theirs. But, you know, it doesn't. Not really. Me? I wanna put my brand on a woman—sort of like that hotshot cowboy of yours does his cows." He pricked her with the knife, not hard enough to cut, but with enough pressure to sting. "Only instead of a branding iron, I'll just carve my initials all over her. You wanna be my lady, sweet thing?"

Rebecca licked her lips with a tongue as dry as dust. "I—no, I think not," she managed to say in a thin voice.

"Ah, you break my heart. Here I'm wantin' to do you the honor of wearin' my initials all over your pretty little self, and you're turnin' me down?" He ran the blade along her cheekbone. "They'd look right fine on that pretty face." Trailing the knife to her bodice, he rasped the sharp edge of the blade over the tip of one breast, his breathing growing rapid when the hardening peak thrust visibly against the muslin. "Ah, now, would you look there?"

Rebecca closed her eyes, wanting to die. Then she felt a tugging on the front of her dress and cool air washed over her upper chest. She looked down and saw that he'd severed the threads of several buttons. Her panicked pulse began to drum in her ears.

"Uncover that little beauty for me," he said.

She made a fist over the gaping front placket of her dress. "No," she replied stonily. And she meant it. No matter what he did to her, no matter how terrified she became, she would never accommodate him. Let him kill her. Death would be preferable.

He touched the knife to her chin. "Do it, sweet thing. Right now. I'm gonna have me a taste of that little beauty."

"No." She despised herself for the way her voice sounded, so weak and quavery.

"You ain't never done it, have you?" He gave a low chuckle. "I'll be damned. You mean to say none of those old men ever got you off alone? You ain't never in all your life been honeysuckled?"

"Been wh-what?"

He seemed to find the question hysterically funny and barked with laughter. "Good God, you don't know nothin', do you?" His smile faded, and his eyes took on a feverish shine. "I say it's high time you learn. For a Bible-thumpin' female, you sure ain't got a clear notion of what God made you for." He slipped the blade tip under another button and cut the threads with a flick of his wrist. "It's like this, see. God made men strong and smart, then gave them leave to rule the earth. You read that in the Bible, didn't you? Then God, he got to thinkin', decided men needed mates, and made females, all of them weak and dumb so men wouldn't have no trouble bossin' them and teachin' them manners. Ain't that the way it is with you church folks, the men bossin' the women?"

That had been the way of it, Rebecca thought, only not. The women of her faith were subservient, deferring to the men in all things, but they were also loved, and respected, and cherished. She doubted this creature understood the meaning of love, let alone respect or devotion.

"Anyhow," the man went on, "that's how come, on top of bein' weak and dumb, that females are mostly pretty and all soft and sweet, so's men can enjoy them the way God meant, without the females givin' them a lick of trouble." He leaned forward to peer at her face. "How come else would you have those pretty little darlin's, if they wasn't for men to honeysuckle. They ain't no use, otherwise. Name me one other thing they're good for."

Rebecca fixed a yearning gaze on the rear opening of the wagon. She wanted out of here. *Out.* His wickedness was like slime in the air. She was breathing it, tasting it. Almost gagging on it. Recalling her papa's kindly face, gentle manner, and unfailing love for her ma, she could scarcely believe the filth that came from this man's mouth. None of the brethren touched a woman in that way. Rebecca was certain of it because her mother had told her as much while defining a woman's wifely duties.

"So, sweet thing, now that I got you set straight, you gonna give me some honey?"

She threw him a horrified glance, saw by the glint in his eyes that he meant to force her, and jerked sideways, escaping the tip of the knife just long enough to throw herself forward and scramble away from him. He was on her in an instant, his weight crashing down on her back and slamming her face to the floor. Stunned, all Rebecca could do was lie there, blinking and rasping for breath.

He reared back, sitting on her rump to anchor her as he grasped her by one arm, then withdrawing a bit of his weight as he rolled her over. It felt as if he jerked her shoulder out of its socket in the process.

Tossing aside the knife, he said, "I told you, sweet thing. Easy or hard. Since you're choosin' hard, the least I'm gonna get for my trouble is a little honey."

She caught him alongside the jaw with her fist, landing the blow with all her might, but he only flinched, then smiled, as if it were little more than a tap. Catching both her wrists in the grip of one hand, he relaxed his legs, dropping hard onto her middle. The breath rushed from Rebecca's lungs once more. He laughed and bounced again. Then again. Black spots began to dance before her eyes and she feared she might pass out. Knowing she would be defenseless if she did, she struggled to stay conscious, fighting frantically to draw breath. *Oh, God.* Her ribs. He'd broken her ribs.

Dimly aware of his hand jerking at the front of her dress, she tried to scream, but all that came out was a squeak. She shrank against the floor planks in an attempt to evade his vile touch, but the hard surface allowed for scant retreat. She heard cloth rip and knew he would touch her bare skin at any moment, that there was little she could do to stop him.

He wasn't all that large a man, really. Not much bigger than her papa. But her strength was no match for his, and his insanity gave him the power of the biblical Legion. Horror gripped her. She strained to free her hands, ignored the knifing pain in her midriff, and tried to buck him off. Pictures of what had been done to her mother flashed in her mind. She gulped back a sob.

"That's it, darlin', fight me," he whispered. "I like it best that way. Scream if you want. I like that, too. Scream real loud." He gave an insane-sounding laugh. "Ain't nobody gonna hear you, anyhow! Except for my friends, of course. And all they'll do is come in to take their turn."

Not willing to give him the satisfaction of hearing her scream, she averted her face and tried to stifle the whimpers crawling up her throat. She felt his fingertips gain access to her chemise and begin to fumble with the lacings. She had expected him to simply tear the undergarment off her.

But, no. That would be too quick. He wanted to prolong this, make it as humiliating and endlessly unbearable as possible in hopes that she would tell him where the money was. She closed her eyes, another sob welling within her, then slicing and tearing its way up from her belly as if she were vomiting glass.

Clammy knuckles grazed her skin as he loosened her lacings. She couldn't endure this. Dear God in heaven, she couldn't. Would no one come to help her? Were she and this man with his weaselly followers the last people on earth? In that instant, even though his weight still crushed the breath from her, she screamed. Not a squeak this time, but an ear-splitting scream. She put all she had into it.

"Oh, yeah, darlin'. That's how I like it."

In a panicked frenzy, Rebecca saw fleeting pictures of Race Spencer's dark face, remembering that morning when he had pinned her beneath him and how she had screamed in much the same way. That was the only similarity.

Though Race Spencer's hands were much larger and harder than this man's, he hadn't bruised her wrists in a punishing grip. Nor had he crushed her with his far greater weight. At the time, as she had struggled with him, she'd believed he was being rough and using all his strength against her. Only now did she understand how much restraint he must have employed, holding most of his weight off her and gentling his grip. Granted, he had pinned her to the pallet like an insect to a board. But for all of that, he hadn't hurt her. Not even once.

And his voice. She could almost hear his whispered reassurances, trailing through her mind like wisps of warm smoke. Telling her he wouldn't harm her. That she was safe. That she had no call to be afraid. That he would protect her with his life. She wished with all her heart that he were here right now to keep that promise.

Her mind spinning dizzily with pictures of him, Rebecca prayed to him instead of the God she had yesterday forsaken. *Please, please, please!* Half-formed pleas spiraled through her head, fleetingly there, then gone, to be replaced by another. That Race Spencer would return to camp. That he would suddenly appear and, like an avenging angel, save her.

By concentrating on that, Rebecca was halfway successful in separating herself from what this animal was doing to her, only vaguely aware of his awkward, feverish fumbling. *Race Spencer, her hotshot cowboy.* If only he'd come. He would enter the wagon in a killing rage, drag the ruffian off of her, and pound his face until it was a bloody mess.

Rebecca became so focused on that hope and so separated from reality that when the blond's weight was suddenly jerked off her, she thought she was imagining it. For a moment, she just lay there, startled and blinking, her vision still impaired by black spots. Only she wasn't imagining it. Her wrists were no longer manacled by cruel fingers. And she could breathe. It was as if a fierce wind had swept through, knocking the ruffian off of her.

Her oxygen-starved lungs grabbing desperately for breath, she hugged her battered midsection and twisted to her knees. In a spinning blur, she saw four boots that came slowly into focus, two of ornate, hand-tooled leather with spurs at the heels, two a plain, dull black. Lifting her gaze, she stared, uncomprehending, at a like number of legs, one pair sheathed in black denim, the other in buckskin. Race. He had come back. By some miracle, he'd come back. The thud of a fist impacting with flesh and bone rang in her ears.

Keeping one arm curled at her waist, Rebecca clawed with her free hand at the rough upper rail of the wagon wall to get out of their way, pulling herself along in a crawl to the front of the enclosure. Once in the corner, she struggled erect, grabbing a hickory support beam to keep her rubbery legs from buckling under her weight. Even empty as this one was, wagons weren't very roomy inside. With two men fighting, the scant space seemed minuscule. Rebecca pressed her back against the canvas, half-afraid they would stumble and fall on top of her.

Race pummeled the ruffian with his huge fists, every bit the avenging angel, just as she had envisioned. As lethal and quick as lightning, he struck and withdrew, the jolt of his well-placed blows so forceful that they nearly knocked her attacker off his feet.

Never had Rebecca been so glad to see anyone.

He dealt the blond punch after punch to the belly, burying his fist just above the man's belt and angling upward to lift the man's feet off the floor. A rush of expelled breath accompanied every blow. "How does it feel, you rotten son of a bitch?" Race buried his fist in the man's stomach again. "Hurts like hell at the receivin' end, don't it?"

The blond staggered sideways, his knees nearly folding as he fought to keep his balance. Race jerked the other man's guns from the holsters, then tossed them onto the rumpled pile of quilts along the opposite wall. Then he grabbed the ruffian by his jacket and roughly shoved him toward the opening at the back of the wagon.

"Outside, you bastard!"

His back toward Race, the blond tripped and fell to his knees, shaking his head as if he were so dazed he could scarcely see. Looking at him from an angle, however, Rebecca was able to see his washed-out gaze dart to where he'd tossed his knife.

"Look out!" she cried.

The ruffian lunged sideways, hitting the floor with a deafening crash and grabbing the knife as he rolled to his feet. Rebecca screamed when she saw the long blade flash through the air, glinting like hammered lightning, Race Spencer's broad chest its target.

Chapter 8

Oh, dear God! *Race Spencer was going to die, right* before her very eyes!

Rebecca knew she had to do something. Only what? Legs still so weak she could scarcely stand, she clung with one hand to the hickory support beam above her head. With every shift of the struggling men's weight, the wagon pitched so violently it threatened to throw her off her feet.

She glanced frantically around the cramped enclosure, searching for something, anything she might use as a weapon. There was nothing in the wagon but the quilts she'd slept on last night and the lantern that hung from a center beam, which at the moment was working against Race rather than for him. He was so tall that the top of his head skimmed the apex of the canvas roof. With each pitch of the wagon, the lamp swung wildly back and forth, its heavy metal base narrowly missing his shoulder. As she lowered her gaze from the lantern, Rebecca's attention fell on the piled quilts, and suddenly she remembered Race disarming the other man. *The guns.* If she could just reach them.

Hugging an arm to her middle to ease the pain in her ribs, she let go of the hickory beam and scrambled to the pallet. The guns! Where were they? During their struggle, the two men had rolled, kicking the quilts every which way. Oh, God! The guns. She couldn't find them.

Race. He was going to be killed. Her breath came in

shrill little gasps, pain lancing over her ribs with each inhalation.

Then something hit her shoulder, knocking her sideways—away from the quilts—away from the guns. She landed on her belly, and a weight crashed down on her back. Stunning her. Slamming what little breath she had from her lungs. Pinpricks of light danced before her eyes. Pushing with her toes and groping blindly at the rough planks beneath her, she tried desperately to move.

Someone grabbed her by the braid. Fire exploded over her scalp. Her head snapped back. Pain stabbed in at the small of her back and the base of her skull. The vertebrae in her neck popped, hollow little sounds, one so close upon the other that they reverberated through her head like firecrackers going off under a box.

"I'll slit her throat!"

Rebecca flailed with her arms, dimly registering that her body was being lifted and jerked backward. The back of her head slapped against wood. Above her, a blur of images swirled, like reflections on water being stirred with a whisk. Daylight, canvas, hickory beams. And Race Spencer, his dark face there one second, then gone—there, then gone. Something hard dug into her lower belly, feeling as if it smashed her spine against the floor.

"Back away! I'll kill the bitch, I swear to God!"

Kaboom!

The blast exploded in the small enclosure, bursting against her eardrums, deafening her. Something fell on her. Leather-coated, slimy with grease. Suffocating, desperate for air, she struggled wildly, shoving with her hands, tossing her head from side to side, blinking furiously to clear her vision. She felt something wet on her cheek, trickling into her ear, down her neck. Her vision cleared a bit, only something—hair—greasy, smelly hair—was over her eyes, getting in her mouth. Yellow-brown strings of it, tangling in her eyelashes, slithering between her parted teeth like worms.

She sputtered and pushed, gagging, trying to squirm free, to shove the weight away, but barely managing to move it. Then a face. Nose to nose with a face. Dirty blond eyebrows, arching like vulture's wings, one at each side of a blackish-red hole that seeped jagged streams of crimson around staring, pale blue eyes.

Blood?

It *was* blood.

Blood, everywhere.

Oh, God—oh, God—oh, God—oh, God—that man— He was *dead!*—he was *bleeding!*—On her—all over— blood *everywhere!*

"No—oh, *no*—not—*no-oo-o!*" She shoved with all her strength again, trying to get him off of her, and this time, he went. *Thunk!* His head hit the floor like a dropped squash, his body sprawling. "Oh, God! Oh, *God!*"

She jackknifed upright, digging at the floor with her heels and pushing with her hands to scoot backward, forgetting her tortured ribs, forgetting the pain that racked her neck and back. Forgetting everything but the need to get away. Away.

Rebecca! a faint voice called.

She threw a horrified look at the dead man. Oh, dear, sweet Lord! He was *dead!* How could he be calling her? Was he alive? He had to be alive! Oh, dear God, he was going to kill her.

Run. She had to run. Escape. Before he got up. *Run now.* Far, far away. Fast.

Her shoulders thudded against the wall. Not far enough. She kept digging in with her heels, slamming her back into the wood.

Rebecca?

No farther. Couldn't go any farther. She stared at that face, at the hole between the staring eyes. At the blood.

Blood—blood—blood. It was everywhere. She was swimming in it. Blood on her hands. Red polka dots, wide smears, splatters. Blood on her dress, shiny and blackish. Oh, dear God. Off, off, *off!* Had to get it off. *Blood.* On her face! Oh, *God!* Not in her *mouth.* Please—please— please. It was everywhere, all over her. In her ears, in her hair.

Rebecca, darlin'.

Calling her? *Him?* Still there. Not gone. All over her.

On her tongue, the roof of her mouth, between her *teeth.*
Rebecca!

It was him. Back from the dead. Coming to kill her.
She twisted onto her knees. Away. Toward light. Out.
Help. Someone. Please.

"Race! Race!" she screamed. No sound. Voice gone.
No God. No Race. No help. Going to kill her. Slit her
throat. Hurry. Run—run—run! He would catch her.
"Race! Help me-ee-e! Help me-he-ee-ee!"

She collided with something so solid, it felt like a rock.
She reeled back. Strong arms caught her from falling.
Race? She threw herself at him, clutching his shoulders,
grabbing handfuls of his shirt. He lifted her against him.
Wonderful, strong, hard arms. So warm and tight, all
around her, holding her close. A wide chest radiant with
heat. *In.* She wanted in. She could hide there. Safe. *Race.*
He felt so wonderful. She was safe now. No one could
get her. He was there, and she was safe.

Uh-thump—uh-thump—uh-thump. His heart. Pounding.
Uh-thump. Such a wonderful feeling, the sturdy thuds vi-
brating out past bone, through a deep wall of flesh and
thick pads of steely muscle, to go *uh-thump* against her
cheek.

And the feel of his body against hers, like a boulder
carved to fit her shape and warmed by the sun, only cush-
ioned on the surface. His shirt, the weave slightly coarse
against her face. His smell—clean sweat, leather, grass,
sunshine, wind, and horses.

Race. Close, press close. Melt into him. Safe there . . .
safe . . . No more Rebecca. She'd just melt down into him
and disappear. Never come out. He wouldn't let them hurt
her. Nobody. Not ever.

She felt his large, hard hands moving over her.

Are you cut?

His hands on her hair, lifting her chin.

Rebecca? Are you hurt, honey?

Strong fingers lightly tracing her ribs, his touch soothing away the pain. On her back, around to her side, then
to center front. Hard knuckles under her breasts, pushing
up against their weight, grazing bare skin through loos-

ened laces. It was okay. These were Race's hands. So different from those others. Big, gentle, radiating warmth into her skin.

Talk to me, darlin'. Sweetheart—so much blood. Can't tell if you're hurt. Can you talk to me?

No. Couldn't talk. She could hear, now . . . a little. Didn't want to talk. So tired. Heavy all over. He felt so nice and warm. She'd just stay like this. Let his hands find the hurt places with light touches. She wanted to stay just like this, always, surrounded by vibrant muscle, protected, not afraid—with his hands soothing away the hurting.

"Dad-*blame* it!" Cookie hollered, his voice so clear that Race could hear every inflection from where he sat in the bedroll wagon, cradling Rebecca in his arms. "Stop that, I said! You're makin' it worse instead of better! That stuff stings like a son'bi—like the very *devil!*"

"Well, shit! It's only a little salve," Johnny Graves retorted. "The way you're carrying on, a body would think I'm killing you!"

"Johnny, I'm tellin' you for the last time, watch your mouth!" Cookie sputtered with indignation. "We got us a *lady* present, in case you ain't noticed! We can't be usin' obscurities!"

"Obscurities?" Johnny chuckled. "You mean obscenities?"

"I said what I meant!" Cookie gave one of his loud snorts. "Sometimes I flat can't believe I'm rubbin' elbows with such *dumb* son'bucks! I swow, I don't know why I bother talkin' about nothin' to nobody around here."

"You like to hear yourself, that's why. Your tongue's tied in the middle and loose at both ends! Goddamn it, Cookie, sit still, why don't you? I almost got it in your eye!"

Shifting ever so slightly on the folded wool blanket he used for a seat, Race smiled to himself, though more with relief than amusement. If Cookie could yell that loud and raise so much sand, he wasn't seriously injured. Mighty banged up, for sure, but he'd mend and probably be back to his old self before the salve was washed away.

Race just thanked his lucky stars that Johnny was there to take care of the old codger. As it was, Race had his hands plenty full trying to soothe Rebecca. If he'd been the only man in camp, he wasn't sure what he would have done.

There was hope for Johnny Graves, after all, he guessed. And wasn't that a wonder? Sometimes Race despaired of the kid ever growing up, and more times than not, he felt like throttling him. But just about the time Race ran completely out of patience, Johnny would do something unexpected to redeem himself, as he had today.

Alarmed by Race's behavior when he'd left the stampeding herd and headed back for camp, Johnny had guessed there might be trouble afoot. So, all on his own, the kid had notified Pete of his suspicion, then rounded up two other men to ride back to camp with him and see if Race needed help. And, boy, howdy, did Race ever. With four dead men, a dead dog, an unconscious cook, a hysterical girl, and the possibility of more trouble on his hands, he'd been in a hell of a mess. Thanks to Johnny's quick thinking, he and two other men had shown up to relieve Race of the load.

"Jesus H. Christ! Would you stop batting at my hands?" Johnny groused. "It's your own damned fault I'm hurting you, old man. How can I be careful with you thumping me?"

"You need thumpin'! Watch your mouth, I said!" Cookie snorted again. "Mark my words, if the boss hears you talkin' filth around that girl, you're gonna think thumped. He'll make like you're a puddle he's stompin' dry. Unlike you, he knows what's gentleman-like and what ain't. He also knows a lady when he sees one. She's a fine bit of lace, that'n."

Race raised an eyebrow. Granted, he recognized a lady when he saw one, but nobody could claim he was real clear on what constituted gentlemanly behavior. He glanced down at the "fine bit of lace" in his arms. Somehow, the description fit, even though he knew for a fact she didn't have a scrap of lace on her anywhere, not even on her drawers. Some gals just seemed lacy. All soft and frilly and fine, no matter what they wore. With her face pressed to the hollow of his shoulder, all he could see was golden curls and the dainty shell of her ear, which was ivory smooth and etched in pink, reminding him of strawberry juice trickled over cream.

"You sure have had a change of mind," Johnny pointed out to Cookie. "Way I remember it, you ran the other way last night. Told the boss she'd be nothing but trouble. A crazy fanatic, you said. Threatened to quit if you had to take care of her."

"*Ouch!* Dad-blame it, be *careful.* I need that nose hole to blow out of, you know! As for me quittin', that was afore I see'd her! I'll tell you somethin' else, too, boyo. On top of bein' a lady, that there girl's got more pluck in her little toe than you got in your whole body."

"Now, Cookie, that's not nice. You're bruising my tender feelings."

"You ain't got no feelin's. If'n you did, you wouldn't be rubbin' my nose plumb off!" Snort, snort. "You know what that little gal done today? Jumped right into the thick of it, takin' up for me, a fella she don't even know. A little thing like her, bellyin' up to four growed men. Ain't that somethin'?"

"Took up for you, did she?" Johnny laughed. "Why, Cookie, I never thought I'd see the day. I do believe you're sweet on her."

Race smiled again, wondering how much of that nonsense Rebecca was hearing. Maybe she was just blocking it all out, an example he decided he should follow. Cookie and Johnny seemed to take pleasure from going on at each other like that, but no one else enjoyed it much.

Turning a deaf ear to their bickering, Race rubbed his jaw back and forth over her braid, thinking for at least the dozenth time that he'd never felt the like. He'd gotten his hair from his ma, thick, straight, and Apache black, without a curlicue in the lot. Hers squiggled in all directions, silky little curls poking up from her braid and everywhere else. When he touched them, they coiled around his finger and tried to hold on.

He pressed his mouth to the wisps, pleasuring himself with the ticklish sensation and the nice way she smelled, a mixture of scents, vanilla, feminine sweetness, and lingering traces of bath soap. As he breathed in, he sensed a difference come over her—a subtle tension in her slender body—that told him she was more aware of him and all he did than she was letting on. He recalled all the times he'd thumped poor old Blue for sniffing of ladies, and heat crept up his neck. He quickly drew away. Too quickly. The back of his head connected with a nail in the hickory bow behind him.

"Ouch!" Loosing an arm from around her, he clamped his hand over the smarting spot. "Damn that Cookie and his infernal nails!"

He felt Rebecca move, and from the corner of his eye, he glimpsed a startled blue gaze looking up at him. He stopped rubbing to glance down, but by then, she had hidden her face against his shoulder again. At least now he knew for sure that she knew what was going on around her. That was a relief.

Since he'd brought her to the bedroll wagon, she'd shown no inclination to speak, and until this instant, he hadn't been sure if she was registering anything. She'd just been huddling on his lap and clinging to him, her slender arms locked around his neck, her face buried against his shirt. It was as if she were about to plunge off a cliff and he was all that could keep her from falling.

Wedged between the lard bucket and a tin full of cracklings, he sat with his back to the wagon wall, one leg folded under him, the other extended and propped on a meal sack. According to Cookie, the chuck wagon was full, so he was using this wagon to store their extra food supplies. It wasn't exactly an ideal place to have brought Rebecca, but with a dead man in her wagon, his only other choice had been to clear out a spot in Cookie's gear wagon, which looked as if a tornado had gone through it.

He wasn't sure how long he'd been sitting there now. An hour, maybe? He only knew that being in the same position for so long was beginning to tell on him. The leg he sat on had fallen asleep, the other one was starting to cramp, and something sharp, probably another of Cookie's nails, was jabbing him between the shoulder blades. In addition to that, now he had an extra hole in his head, compliments of the nail in the hickory bow.

For fear of startling Rebecca, he hated to move much, not even to get more comfortable. Nevertheless, he was starting to wonder how much longer she might need him to hold her like this. Considering how terrified of him she'd been upon awakening that morning, she sure had taken a mighty fast shine to him.

Not that he was complaining. Hell, it wasn't every day a beautiful girl glued her sweet curves so tightly to a man's body that he couldn't pry her loose. There was also the inescapable fact that it was his fault she was in this shape. *Damn.* He felt bad about that. Shooting the man right in front of her had not been his intention, not to mention letting the bastard fall directly on top of her. If there had been a last thing she needed, that was it.

Given all she'd been through yesterday at the arroyo, Race had decided before entering the wagon to rescue her that he should take the ruffian outside to finish him, if there was any way he possibly could. But things had gone wrong, and in the end, sparing her the ugliness of it just hadn't been in the cards.

Race closed his eyes and tightened his arms around her, wishing with all his heart that it had happened differently. If he lived to be a hundred, he'd never forget how she'd reacted to seeing the bastard's blood all over her. Slapping at herself and trying to rub it off, like someone being attacked by red ants. Panting shrilly for breath. Scrambling to get away from it. Before he could get to her, she'd been hysterical.

"Boss?" Corey Halloway called from just outside the wagon. "Yo, boss, you still in there?"

"Of *course* he's still in there!" Cookie groused. "Where you think he coulda went?"

Rebecca jumped as if someone had poked her. Splaying a hand over her back, Race gave her a quick squeeze. "It's okay, honey. That's just Corey, one of my hired hands," he whispered. "He ain't gonna hurt you."

She made a sound at the back of her throat, a soft *"Mmm,"* that didn't tell him much of anything, except that she'd heard him. Race angled his head forward to peer around the flour and cornmeal sacks. Corey Halloway stood at the rear of the wagon, peering into the dim enclosure, his white-blond hair gleaming in the sunlight, one hand balancing a five-gallon bucket that he'd propped on the gate.

"Yo, Corey," Race greeted him softly.

"Brought the hot water you wanted." Raising his free hand, Corey dangled a red neckerchief for Race's inspection. "This do for a washing stick? I couldn't find nothing else without looking in the gear wagon, and you know how Cookie is."

Race felt the girl's body grow more tense and cupped a hand over her shoulder, lightly massaging with his fingertips to reassure her. "That'll do fine, Corey. You mind bringin' it in here to me?"

"No, sir." Corey lowered the bucket over the gate, then climbed inside himself, moving with the limber agility of youth. As he carried the bucket to where Race sat, his light blue eyes remained fixed on the girl in his boss's arms. "How's she doin'?"

"A lot better," Race replied confidently, even though he felt none too certain of it. In his experience, it was always best to be positive about things. Gloomy words made for a gray day. As Corey deposited the bucket next to his right leg, Race said, "I thank you kindly, Corey. I know you fellows have had your hands full out there."

"No problem. I'm glad to help." Glancing over his shoulder and shaking his head at all of Cookie's carrying-on outside, Corey chuckled, then turned back to hand the neckerchief down to Race. "We about have all the digging done. That'll be the worst of it, I'm thinking." He glanced at the girl again. "I, um, did that cleaning up you asked me to do, first thing. Used a brush and sprinkled down some lye. It bleached out of the wood pretty fair."

Race realized the youth was referring to the bloodstains on the floor of Rebecca's wagon. "That's good. And the other?" he asked, meaning the ruined quilts, but not wanting to be specific, for her sake. "You get 'em washed up, or what?"

"Chucked them in the fire. They were past help." The youth scratched behind his ear. "McNaught rode out to the herd and gave Pete your message. Pete sent three men back to pull the bobtail, like you ordered. Trevor and me and Johnny'll be finished up here in camp pretty soon, so we'll pull the second shift. By then, everyone else should be back."

Race didn't try to disguise his relief at hearing that. Just in case those bastards came back, and he suspected they would, he didn't want to get caught by surprise again. With three men riding guard at all times, it was unlikely anyone would be able to sneak up on the camp again or even get close enough to snipe with a rifle.

"Pete circled back to camp a bit ago. Said for us to tell you he took your message to heart." Apparently fearful of speaking too plainly and upsetting Rebecca, Corey glanced down at her. "They're ready to handle whatever comes up, he said, and they've got the herd settled down, so you don't need to fret. He was in a hurry to get back, I reckon, or he would have talked to you himself."

"Anybody get hurt in the stampede?"

"A lot of cows. But all the men are hale and hearty," Corey assured him.

"Losses?"

Corey shrugged. "I hate to bear bad tidings, boss. But I'd say the news isn't good. Pete didn't give an exact number, but he didn't look too chirp."

Race's heart sank. If they'd lost a substantial number of cattle, it would take him a year to recoup. Financially, he'd be sunk, and all his men along with him.

"I'm real sorry, boss. The herd bolted so unexpected, like. We did our best."

"I know you did, Corey."

Race hauled in a deep breath and slowly expelled it, imagining Pete out there, not only having to guard his back against attack, but putting down injured steers and having no choice but to leave the meat lay. Little wonder the foreman hadn't looked very happy. Unable to risk firing a gun, Pete would be forced to use his knife, slitting the steers' throats to put them out of their misery. That was risky business, not to mention sickening enough to make a strong man want to puke up his boot heels.

"Well, let's not cry over milk we ain't sure got spilt," Race said, injecting optimism into his voice that he was far from feeling. "Maybe, all told, it ain't as bad as it looks. You reckon?"

"I sure hope." Corey's tone implied that he had his doubts.

A sharp yearning cut through Race to be out there with his men, trying to save what he could of the life he'd worked so damned hard to build for himself. But then he ran his hand over the girl's back, felt how delicately made she was, and started to feel ashamed. Even if she hadn't been so upset, he would have needed to stay in camp to watch over her. There were more of those sons of bitches still out there, a fact he knew by his own count and tally, taken that night in the arroyo, and now verified by what he'd heard the blond ruffian say today. *We got more men out there to make sure those cattle keep on runnin'.*

At any other time, Race would have been riding the grasslands until midnight or longer, trying to round up strays and minimize his losses as best he could. But he'd lose every cow and every last dollar to his name rather than leave this girl alone again and risk her being harmed. A man could always get more cattle. Or do without the headache of the loco beasts entirely and go back to what he did best, hiring out his gun.

"Fate'll win out in the end," Race muttered, more for his own benefit than Corey's. Old Blue was gone, and now it looked as if his ranch might go under, or damned close to it. Hell, next he might lose his shirt. "Things turn out the way they're s'posed to, I reckon." And maybe he wasn't supposed to be a cattle rancher. Some men were born to be no-accounts, and if they tried to change that, Fate slapped them down. "No point in pullin' long faces over what can't be fixed."

"No, sir. I reckon not." Corey scuffed his boot heel on the wooden floor, then sighed. "Well, I'd best get back out there to spell McNaught. Digging for five is a trying job, and he's been at it alone for nigh on to twenty minutes.'' By way of farewell, he inclined his head toward the girl and said, ''Ma'am.''

If Rebecca heard him, she gave no sign of it.

Race waited until the youth had exited the wagon, then he wet the cloth and wrung it out, intending to wash the blood off her. He decided to start with one of her hands, that being fairly safe territory. Maybe by the time he worked his way up to her face, neck, and chest, she would feel easier about the familiarities he was taking.

''Rebecca, honey? Now don't you be gettin' alarmed or nothin', but I need to get you cleaned up a mite.'' He held up the neckerchief for her to see, then went on in the best whispery voice he could manage. ''Corey brought some warm water, and it'll feel real nice, okay?''

He waited, but she simply stared at him with those deep blue eyes he found so fascinating. Taking that for assent, he gave her his best smile, then got to it. Still, it was no simple task, drawing her left arm from around his neck.

''Let go, honey, so's I can help you.''

Instead of obeying, she pressed her face to his shoulder and clung to him almost desperately, as if all the demons of hell might be loosed on her if she wasn't close against him. Fingers locked around her wrist, he had to force her arm down, and she resisted every inch of the way, trembling with the effort she expended.

''Sugar, I'm not gonna hurt you, okay? But we got to get this done.'' She was no match for him, of course, just as she'd been no match for the ruffian earlier. Bully for him, the uncontested winner, and wasn't he just some pumpkins? He tucked her hand against his chest. The instant she felt his shirt, she latched on with her fist, holding so tight her knuckles went white.

He stared down at those knuckles, which didn't look much bigger than peas, the ridges narrow and sharp, the skin creamy and edged with a delicate pink, the color reminding him of a fragile white rose petal. Just below, where his fingers encircled her wrist, his own knuckles looked huge by comparison, their broad, flat surfaces baked brown by exposure to the sun and rock-hard with calluses. The contrast was stark and impossible to ignore—symbolic of everything she was—and all that she was not and could never hope to be—and also of her destiny, which might be inescapable unless someone stepped in to alter it.

Rose-petal soft . . . that was Rebecca, too sweet and delicate to survive the brutalities of the men in this territory. Unless someone stronger and tougher became her shield, she would be used, and walked on, and left lying in the dirt, like a rose petal crushed under a man's boot.

The image hung there in his mind. He tried to shove it away, to laugh at himself for being mawkish. He was a gunpowder-and-leather man, not one of those Nancy-boy fellows with slicked-back hair who wore checkered suits and wrote poems. The only way women were like roses was that most of them had thorns, and beware to the man who got too close. That was his motto, drilled into him since boyhood by the haughty bitches themselves. He'd stopped believing in romantic nonsense years ago. Liked it that way. Didn't want to change and, by God, wouldn't.

But it was there in his head, nonetheless. *Rose-petal soft.* Since telling Rebecca about his mother's death, memories of her had been resurfacing from a black corner of his mind to haunt him. He could almost see her, trying to hawk those roses on that Santa Fe street corner. *Christ.* He had managed to keep that memory tucked neatly away for so many years, facing it only when unexpectedly reminded or in his dreams.

His failure to do so now was due in part, he felt sure, to the feeling that had assailed him yesterday in the arroyo when he'd found Rebecca and realized she had probably witnessed her mother's rape and murder. A sense that maybe their footsteps had been carrying them toward the arroyo and that moment all their lives, that in some strange way, it had been meant for him to be the one to find her. Not just any man, but *him*. It had been the similarities, he guessed, between his past and her present, a feeling that they were kindred souls. He'd looked at the shocked expression on her small face and into her beautiful, unseeing eyes, and he'd glimpsed not only her pain, but his own. A pain too deep for tears. Pain that he'd carried with him for years in a secret place, hidden from the world and most times from himself, but always, always there, just waiting to be resurrected by some small reminder.

A reminder like Rebecca's hand—slender, soft, and rose-petal dainty. He could crush it in his grip, he knew. Just bear down, harder and harder, until the bones snapped. That's what happened to sweet, delicate things in this old world; they got crushed, like rose petals under a man's boot, just as her mother had been.

He could still remember that summer evening as if it had been yesterday, how he'd sat obediently on the walkway with his back to a post, his gut gnawing at his spine, his head filled with visions of food. All kinds, any kind. Hopeful, he'd watched his mother approach the men who passed, imploring them in her broken English to buy a *"bee-yoo-tee-fool"* rose. Just one penny, she had said, over and over. *"A bee-yoo-tee-fool rose, mee-ster? For your bee-yoo-tee-fool lady? Just one penny!"* But the men hadn't wanted her roses. And then along had come the two men who raped her.

After searching vainly for help, Race had run back to his mother, stopping along the way to gather up some of the dropped roses, a crazy, desperate hope within him that, by returning those roses to her, he might somehow make her better. A few minutes later, she had died with them clutched in her hand, the bedraggled and crushed blossoms pressed to her cheek.

With a dizzying mix of past and present swirling in his mind, Race gazed down at Rebecca's hand, the laughter of heartless men, from out of his past and from that very day, ringing in his ears—the sound of it the same—the cruelty in it the same—the faces of the men much the same.

It had been so long . . . so many years . . . since Race had allowed himself to feel anything deeply. As a half-starved, quarter-breed orphan struggling to survive on the streets of Santa Fe, he'd been forced to develop a tough hide early on, learning the hard way that the strong ruled and the weak groveled. By age sixteen, he'd been damned tired of groveling and had developed a high regard for gunslingers, for when it came to commanding respect and inspiring fear in others, he'd noted that they were without equal. For nearly four months he'd hoarded his stolen coins and gone without food a good deal of the time, saving to buy a Colt revolver and enough ammunition to practice.

By the end of his seventeenth year, word had spread throughout Santa Fe that Race Spencer, the Apache breed, was lightning-fast and deadly accurate at the draw, a reputation that was soon challenged by the reigning fast guns in town. That fateful day when Race had first faced another man on the street, knowing one of them was going to die, he had buried his more tender emotions, and as he pulled the trigger, he'd stepped over the line, leaving childhood behind and becoming a hard-edged man who seldom let anything touch him.

And, goddamn it, he didn't want to feel anything now. Feeling things deeply, caring about someone . . . a man who fell into that trap left himself open and vulnerable. But how could he hold Rebecca like this, feeling the frantic clutching of her hands and the trembling in her body, and not care? Or look into her beautiful, endlessly blue eyes and not care?

He did. Whether he wanted to or not. Whether it made sense or not. He cared. It had hit him the instant he saw her—kneeling in the dirt, looking like a church-ceiling angel. He'd tried to shove it away, but it had sneaked past his guard several times since, each time hitting him a little harder. Then he'd caught her in his arms after shooting the ruffian, felt her frantically hugging his neck, and it had plowed into him with devastating force, dead center in the chest, like a 420-grain slug backed by 90 grains of black powder. That was it. He cared about her, and there'd be no more pretending he didn't.

And, *Jesus, God*, it hurt. Seeing her like this, knowing he might have stopped it, if he'd only just counted her safety as more important than a bunch of stupid cows.

And, even worse, knowing it could and probably would happen again unless he took it upon himself to be her protector. That was a responsibility he didn't want and didn't need. What was more, he knew Rebecca wouldn't want that, either, for even as she clung to him, he sensed her wariness of him as well.

That was the most heartbreaking part of it for Race, knowing how awful her situation must seem to her. A naive, religious young woman, sheltered all her life from every kind of evil, suddenly alone in a world where her only chance of survival was to seek sanctuary in the arms of a gunslinger, the very epitome of all she deplored.

Chapter 9

Race wasn't sure how long he might have sat there, star-ing at Rebecca's hand, if water from the neckerchief hadn't dribbled over his other wrist. He tightened his fin-gers on the cloth, squeezing out droplets of moisture that in turn soaked through the black denim of his jeans and ran in icy rivulets over his thigh. The chill of it snapped him to his senses, reminding him that the water Corey had heated wouldn't stay warm much longer.

"Rebecca," he said softly. "We need to get you cleaned up, darlin'."

She tensed and pressed closer to him, as if by burying her face against his shirt and blocking out the world around her, she could stay hidden.

"Rebecca?" He released a weary breath. "Corey, the fellow who brought the bucket, heated this water for you to wash with, and I hate to ask him to heat it all over again. You need to sit up, honey."

To his surprise, she loosened her right arm from around his neck and pushed with the heel of her other hand, lev-ering herself erect. As she moved, she winced and grabbed her waist with one arm. An increase in pallor left her skin alarmingly white, the only touches of color the spatters of dry blood, the pinkish-purple bruise beginning to show on her left cheekbone, and the dark smudges of exhaustion under her eyes.

Those eyes. They seemed as big as cactus flowers, lu-minous and silvery in the dimness.

"The ribs hurtin' pretty bad?" he asked as he dipped the cloth back in the warm water.

She glanced at the bucket, then around the wagon, as if trying to orient herself. When her gaze came back to his face, he felt a jolt of raw pain. She looked so lost. An innocent caught in a nightmare. He wanted to wrap her in his arms and promise her the stars and the moon and a life with never another bad moment. Instead all he could offer her were words—and damn it, he was damn lousy with them. Still, he had to try.

"This here's the bedroll wagon." Gesturing at the sacks, he said, "Hard to tell it by lookin', I know. Cookie brought so much food, I think we got half of it in here."

She lowered her gaze to her skirt, giving Race cause to remember the story Cookie had told him about the female Bible-thumpers he'd seen in town who kept their heads down and seldom looked a man in the eye. After giving the cloth a hard squeeze to wring it out, he offered it to her.

"I reckon you probably wanna wash yourself."

With tremulous fingers, she accepted the wet neckerchief, started to lift it to her face, and then pressed it over her heart instead, making him think of the Mexican women he'd seen down south who lightly tapped their breasts with a fist as they prayed. Only Rebecca didn't tap. She just sat there with her head bent, staring at her lap. He wondered if her ribs were hurting so badly that she couldn't manage to wash herself. He was about to ask when she made an odd little sound and bent her head farther forward, completely hiding her face.

Race expected her to start sobbing, even found himself hoping she might. It helped, sometimes, to get it all out. Being a man, he'd never been one to cry, though he'd felt like it a few times. But when things got really bad, he did pitch temper fits sometimes, cursing to turn the air blue and throwing things. He always felt a world better afterward.

Most women didn't cuss, and pitching temper fits was usually frowned upon by their fathers or husbands. So they wept instead, which, for reasons beyond him, most men found preferable to screaming and yelling. Race would have rather had a woman take after him with a cast-iron skillet.

"Do you wanna talk about it, honey?"

She shook her head. And then, to his surprise, she straightened and lifted the cloth to her face. No tears. Just a stony, rigid control that made him ache for her. She rubbed at her cheek, her hand shaking so badly that all she managed was to make quivery little dabs, missing most of the spatters, smearing those she hit.

Race had hoped she might be able to do this herself. It would have been a hell of a lot easier, not necessarily for him, but for her. But he couldn't stand this. He grasped her wrist, plucked the neckerchief from her hand, and gently went to work. Keeping her eyes downcast, she lifted her face for him, the expressions she pulled reminding him of a child enduring a mother's fussing and fiddling. Pursing her lips, wrinkling her nose, blinking her eyes, and then drawing her face into a god-awful grimace as he scrubbed her ears. He found himself biting back a smile, and that quivery, achy warmth moved through him again, a feeling as inexplicable to him as it was foreign.

"I ain't real good at this," he said, by way of apology. "Not much practice. It's kind of awkward washin' somebody else."

He turned to rinse the cloth, then set to work on her hair. "If you feel up to it this evenin', I'll heat you some water," he offered. "Your hair ain't gonna come total clean until you scrub it, I don't think."

He rubbed at a place near her temple, stirring up more curls, which made her look as if she had a little more fertilizer in that one spot to send up sprouts. He bit back another smile, dipped the cloth again, and moved down to her neck, taking care to be gentle at the underside of her chin where she'd been cut by the plug-ugly's knife. Luckily the wound wasn't deep and wouldn't require stitching.

When he reached the base of her throat and started to go lower, she looked startled and clamped a hand to her chest, as if she'd only just now remembered that her dress was hanging open. "Oh, my . . ." she whispered. "I'm— my dress—it's—" She broke off and closed her eyes. "He—he c-cut away th-the buttons."

Race could see she was embarrassed beyond bearing. To his way of thinking, her chemise covered her damned near as well as some of the dresses he'd seen other women wear. But, then, he also knew that it was sometimes a lot more uncomfortable to be at the receiving end of a look than to be the one giving it.

He slung the rag over the edge of the bucket and started unfastening his shirt. "There's more clothes for you over in your wagon. Here shortly, we'll go get 'em." He jostled her on his leg as he shifted to tug one arm from his sleeve, then jostled her again as he drew out his other arm and jerked the shirt from between his back and the wagon wall. "Meantime, you can wear this." He touched the back of the hand she held over her waist. "Can you let go of them ribs long enough to stuff an arm down this sleeve, darlin'?"

He ran the shirt through his hands to find the left arm-hole, then held it up. As she thrust her arm inside, he smiled and said, "Bull's-eye." He quickly drew the garment behind her, doing a juggling act to get it tugged around and over her other shoulder. Then, holding the second armhole up for her, he used his other hand to draw a shirt placket over her gaping bodice. "I'll keep you covered while you aim and shove. How's that for team-work?"

Wincing as she moved, she worked her hand down the other sleeve. Race made fast work of getting her battened down, wondering, as he fumbled like an idiot with ten thumbs, why his buttons were so stubborn when the shirt was on her, but went into the holes slick as greased owl shit when he was wearing it.

"There," he said as he fastened the last one, uncertain who was more relieved, him or her. "You can't get much more covered than that." He gave a low chuckle as he rolled up the sleeves, which dangled past the tips of her fingers by nearly a foot. "Jesus, darlin', you ain't packin' much ballast, are you?"

Evidently something he said took her by surprise, for she forgot to keep her eyes downcast and threw him a startled look—a look that went from startled to downright horrified when she saw his bare chest. She gaped at it for a long moment, giving him the feeling she'd never seen a man without his shirt. *Nah.* That was plumb crazy. She'd surely seen her father and others strip their shirts off in the heat of summer when they were outside working.

Making an obvious effort not to gawk at him, she kept jerking her gaze away, then seemed unable to help herself and began to stare again. Her cheeks turned a pretty pink, and her eyes went as blue as the base of a flame. Race revised his opinion about the shirt business. Maybe, where she came from, men never went around bare-chested. What seemed crazy to him might be everyday right to Bible thumpers.

Feeling suddenly self-conscious, he rubbed a palm over his pectorals and was surprised, not to mention slightly discomfited, to find that his nipples had turned hard and were standing up like the exposed heads of six-penny nails.

"It's all right, honey," he assured her, giving his chest another fast rub, halting his palm over the spike closest to her nose. "As you can see, I ain't got much by way of bubbies that I need to keep covered."

At that, her whole face went pink, and then moved on to bright red. As dark as he was, and never having been around any fair-skinned ladies, Race was fascinated. She reminded him of one of those color-changing lizards, like he'd seen one time down in Mexico. Only, of course, she was a far sight prettier, not to mention more colorful. He half-expected her hair to turn pink. Her scalp had.

"You all right?" he asked, not entirely sure she was. He'd seen light-complected men turn red in the face, but only when they were choking or sunburned to a fare-thee-well.

She dropped her gaze back to her lap and nodded. He turned to retrieve the rag, gave it a fast dip and squeeze, then resumed washing her, unbuttoning the collar of the shirt as he worked his way down. It was difficult to tell if he got all the blood off her upper chest, but he figured what he had missed wouldn't hurt her.

Seconds later, as he washed her slender hands, he verified the fact that her knuckles were about the size of peas, maybe a hair bigger, and her fingers were so little around they felt squishy when he squeezed on them. There were also tiny bones that stood up on the backs of her hands and were crisscrossed with blue veins that showed through her fair skin. He couldn't help but wonder if she had little blue lines like that all over her. They reminded him of the squiggles on a trail map.

Sure enough, as he turned her palm up, he saw faint blue lines going up the inside of her wrist to disappear under the rolled shirt sleeve. *Damn.* A man could flat look forward to long winter evenings with a woman like her in his arms. Each night, he could blaze one of those trails with kisses, never knowing until he arrived where it might take him. Not that he'd care. Anyplace on her was bound to be sweet.

He was relieved when he'd cleaned the last of the blood away. He tossed the rag in the bucket, angry with himself for thinking such things about her. If the girl had trails to paradise all over her, it would be some other fellow's pleasure to blaze them, not his. She was too fine for the likes of him, and if he let himself forget that, it'd be no one's fault but his own if he got kicked in the teeth.

The same went for that mawkish rose-petal business. He'd keep her safe until he could get her off his hands, bearing in mind the whole while that having her with him was only temporary. If the good weather held, he'd take her north to Denver as soon as possible. There were plenty of respectable types up that way—the kind of men a girl like her always went for—fancy-mannered, highfalutin talkers. As pretty as she was, she could have her pick, and she'd find herself a husband, lickety-split. Years from now on long winter evenings, maybe she'd tell her children of the gunslinger who once saved her life, and they'd all laugh at her word pictures of him, a man who couldn't read, had no manners, and was an all-around dumb cluck.

"Boss! Hey, boss! Come quick!"

Race glanced up just in time to see Corey appear at the wagon gate. The younger man's blue eyes were wide with alarm. "What's wrong?" Race asked.

"It's old Blue! We finished getting his hole dug, and I carried him out there a minute ago. When I tossed him in, he yelped and kicked up a fuss. Scared me so bad, I damned near wet my britches! He isn't dead."

Race's heart stuttered. *Blue.* So far, he hadn't let many thoughts of his dog slip into his mind. Rebecca had needed him, and he'd postponed his grieving for later. But the loss had been there at the back of his mind, a sadness waiting to be dealt with.

"He ain't dead?" Race could scarcely believe his ears. He set Rebecca off his lap and sprang to his feet. "You sure?"

"Of course, I'm sure! Hurry. He's in a bad way."

Race started from the wagon, then hesitated to glance back at Rebecca. "I'll be just over yonder, honey, not more'n a holler away. You'll be safe here."

Those words had an echo, and he remembered saying the exact same thing to her that morning, right before he left her to chase after the stampede. This was different, though. He *would* be within shouting distance. All the same, he felt bad about leaving her.

Evidently she saw his hesitation. "Go," she said. "I'll be all right."

Taking her at her word, Race vaulted from the wagon and broke into a run.

I'm going to freeze in this position, Rebecca thought, *with my arms hugging my knees. Like those children who go cross-eyed from pulling silly faces.*

Even so, she remained as she was, huddled at the far end of the bedroll wagon, her back wedged into the corner. She felt safer that way. Not safe, but safer. At least she had something to guard her back sitting there, plus she could watch the wagon gate and front opening in the canvas for intruders.

The lowing of cattle drifted to her on the afternoon

breeze—and the sound seemed to be coming steadily closer. *We got more men out there to make sure they keep on runnin'*, the ruffian had told her. Oh, God. Were those other desperadoes still following the herd? If so, they were coming steadily closer to camp. Right this minute, they might even be watching the goings-on, trying to determine where she was. Or, God forbid, maybe they'd already guessed where she was and were *in* the camp, slithering on their bellies like deadly snakes to avoid being seen, coming closer and closer to the wagon where she was hiding. She closed her eyes and swallowed, not wanting to even think about it. But it was there, in the foreground of her thoughts, impossible to ignore.

If those men were anywhere around, they would find her. Even as quiet and still as she was being, they would find her. Oh, lands. Who *were* they? Her papa and the other brethren had been so very careful. Yet somehow those men had found out they were carrying money. How? That was the question. And when? Along the trail somewhere, surely, undoubtedly in one of the towns where they'd stopped to replenish supplies. Somehow, some way, the Petersens or someone else in her caravan had let the secret out.

That money. It had become a curse—causing the deaths of all who'd touched it. Until those ruffians got possession of it, they weren't going to give up. They would dog her footsteps wherever she went, and eventually, no matter how careful she might be, they would catch her by surprise.

Knowing they would kill her was the least of it. What terrified her was what they would do to her first. Playing vicious games with her, cutting on her with those big knives, until she told them whatever they wanted to know. And then . . . oh, God, even then—it wouldn't be over.

A fine film of sweat covered Rebecca's body, turning icy. The breeze caught the wagon canvas, making it snap like a sheet drying on the line. The sudden shift of weight caused the hickory bows to creak and groan. At each sound, she leaped, her sudden movements sending shafts of pain over her ribs. But she couldn't help herself, visions of the ruffian's huge knife dancing in her head. How easy it would be for a man to slash the wagon canvas, she thought frantically. He'd make scarcely any sound, possibly not even enough for her to hear. Then, in he would come, to leap on her before she could even scream for help.

She could hear the cattle—moving ever closer—bringing with them those horrible men who would stop at nothing. Men whose sole driving force at this moment was to force information out of her and then kill her. And to reach her, how many other people might they kill?

You have to tell Mr. Spencer about the money, Rebecca. You have to! And soon, before anything more happens.

The thought made her heart slam. Spencer was going to be *furious* when he learned the truth. He might have been able to prevent that stampede this morning if only she'd told him about the money straightaway. It wouldn't matter a whit to him that she'd had every reason to believe he and his men had been involved in the massacre at the arroyo yesterday. All he would be able to think about were his losses, which, judging by what that man Corey had said, were substantial.

He was going to blame her. No matter how she approached telling him—no matter how many excuses for herself she might make—he was going to place the responsibility for everything that had happened on her head.

Race Spencer, in a rage . . . The very thought made her throat close off with fright. *By the way, Mr. Spencer, remember my mentioning right before the stampede this morning that there were things I needed to tell you? Well, guess what! My not telling you those things may have cost you your cattle herd.*

If only she had warned him, he could have had men riding guard around the herd to run off the shooters before they spooked the cattle. So far, he'd been kindness and patience itself with her. But he hadn't had any reason to be furious with her either. That would no longer be true once she spoke with him. He would want to wring her neck for sure, and to be perfectly honest, she wasn't certain she would be able to blame him.

She wanted to run. Where, she had no idea. Just away. Anything but to have to look into those penetrating, coffee-brown eyes that seemed to miss nothing and tell him all of his misfortune could be laid at her door. His cows, his dog. Since the foreman's last report, maybe even some of his men. If the desperadoes had been following the herd ever since the stampede, what horrid things might they have done out there? Oh, God, oh, God. The loss of animals was terrible enough, but if he lost men? He'd *never* forgive her. What was worse, how could she ever forgive herself?

She had to warn him. And she had to do it now. Did she want someone's death on her conscience?

A little voice at the edge of her mind said, *Now? You mean to go tell him right now? Are you out of your ever-loving mind? This very second, he's out there trying to save his dog, which was shot because of you! If the animal's not already dead, he may have to put it down. Do you really think right now is a good time to incite his anger?*

But she had no choice. The next person who died might be that funny little man, Mr. Grigsley. Or that Johnny fellow who was out there taking care of him. If she kept silent, as surely as she breathed, someone else would eventually die.

Clamping an arm around her waist, Rebecca struggled to her feet and walked to the wagon gate, a distance of only a few feet. But it seemed like the longest walk of her life.

Crouched beside the freshly dug grave, Race watched Cookie examine the hound's wound. Poor old Blue. He touched a hand to his faithful canine friend's head, thinking of all the nights when he'd fallen asleep scratching his ears. Loose skin and wrinkles. That silly, sad-looking face. Funny how he'd come to love such a homely dog so deeply. But there was no denying that he did.

Then again, maybe it wasn't so strange. Except for Blue, he was pretty much alone in the world. Oh, he had his men. And there was Dusty, his horse. But at night, when the day was done, he was always alone in the cabin with only Blue to share the evening fire and supper with him, only Blue to talk to, only Blue to sleep with.

He would be mighty lonesome without his dog. Damned lonesome.

Glancing from the hound to Cookie, whose face was so battered and grotesquely swollen above the frizzy gray beard that he was barely recognizable, Race said, "You sure you're up to this, Cookie? You're lookin' kind of shaky."

"I'm here, ain't I? I reckon I'm up to it."

The truth was, Cookie probably would have dragged himself out here from his deathbed. When it came to cooking or tending to wounds, the old codger was as territorial as a grizzly bear. Since Race had little experience at doctoring dogs, he was glad to have a second opinion.

"Well, do you think the bullet shattered the shoulder?" he asked.

Holding his belly with one arm, the old man leaned closer to peer at the wound. "I don't know, boss." He shook his head. "It's a bad'n, no question about it."

If the bone was shattered, Blue would be crippled even if they managed to save him. Race didn't want that, not for Blue, who lived to chase squirrels and rabbits, baying as if he were on the scent of bear. When life became a painful trial, what was the point? Maybe men had to go on living, in agony with every breath, but that didn't mean Race meant to let it happen to his dog.

This definitely was not a good time to talk to him, Rebecca thought as she approached the group of men at the grave. Race Spencer was hunkered over his dog, clearly intent on the animal's plight, his hired hands milling around him, the only one she recognized being Mr. Grigsley, who knelt beside him, his swollen and discolored profile a glaring reminder to her of why she had come.

Glancing worriedly around, she wondered if the desperadoes were out there someplace. They wouldn't shoot her. She felt confident of that, not until they had pried the information they needed out of her. But there would be nothing to stop them from opening fire on these men.

The thought knotted her stomach.

Her footsteps faltered as she drew close enough to clearly make out each of the men's features. With their filthy clothing and bewhiskered faces, they were a rough-looking lot, all of them wearing dusty, sweat-stained Stetsons, guns strapped to their hips, and knives on their belts. They were the sort of men who would give you a bad turn if you encountered them after dark on a deserted street—the sort of men her ma and the other women in her traveling party had cautioned her to avoid when they'd stopped in cattle towns to replenish their supplies.

Just behind Mr. Spencer, a tall, lanky young man paced back and forth. His thin legs, clad in faded denim turned silvery by wear and too many washings, looked like well-oiled scissor blades cutting through the sunlight. When he spotted Rebecca, he turned toward her, his tan hat, dangling by its bonnet strings, forming a half-moon at the back of his sandy-colored head, the width of the brim nearly as broad as his shoulders. He swept his blue gaze slowly over her, his attention lingering on the top buttons of the shirt she wore, as if he were trying to make out the curve of her bosom beneath the loose folds of cloth. A chill of revulsion washed over her skin.

At the opposite side of the grave, a stockier, older man stood with his feet braced apart, his hands on his hips, his green gaze drilling holes through her. Beside him was a younger fellow with white-blond hair that fell past his shoulders, his body padded generously with muscle.

Rebecca felt her courage dwindling a bit more with each thunderous beat of her heart. She tried to tell herself she was being foolish to feel afraid, that they were just cattlemen, not outlaws, and were probably harmless. But they didn't look harmless. The young man gaping at her chest was nearly as tall as Spencer, his posture conveying a swaggering insolence.

Struggling to his feet, Mr. Grigsley finally broke the tension when he turned and saw her. "Well, now! You're lookin' better'n the last time I seen you." He bobbed his gray head, flashing his bald pate at her, and hooked his thumbs under the wide straps of his suspenders, the shirt beneath them a washed-out blue instead of the green plaid he'd worn earlier in the day. "Howdy-do, missy!"

Race Spencer glanced over his shoulder, spied Rebecca, and pushed to his feet with a fluid grace. As he turned, she revised her assessment of the three strangers. The thin young man whom she'd guessed to be nearly as tall as Spencer was at least half a head shorter, the fellow with the white hair, for all his musculature, looked lanky by comparison, and the older man no longer seemed very big.

Race Spencer gave new definition to the phrase "big and tall," for he was half again as broad through the shoulders as the others and seemed to tower over them. As for muscle? Even without his shirt to lend his torso the illusion of extra bulk, his shoulders, arms, and chest bulged with strength, his abdomen striated, his skin gleaming in the sunlight like polished teak. Standing with one black-sheathed leg slightly bent and his hands curled loosely at his sides, he looked ready to go for his Colts, as if living by the gun for so long had made the firing stance inherent to his nature.

Whipped by the breeze, his hair wisped to his bronze shoulders like strands of blue-black silk. When she met his sharp, impenetrable coffee-brown gaze, she felt an almost overwhelming need to move closer to him. Only a fool sought safety in the arms of danger itself. Even so, she couldn't deny her yearning—an almost frantic need—to fling herself into his arms again, where she might feel protected.

This is madness, Rebecca. Sheer madness. What kind of cowardly, sniveling creature have you become? Get control of yourself.

She dug her nails into her palms, shaking with the attempt. But the confident, levelheaded young woman she'd been three days ago no longer seemed to exist.

"Rebecca," he said, his voice pitched low, his dark eyes aglitter in the sunlight. "What're you doin' out here, darlin'?"

Darlin'. The endearment curled around her like a smoky tendril of heat from an open fire on a freezing

night—the sensation wonderfully reassuring and warming, and, God help her, beckoning her closer. She remembered the heaviness of his big hands on her back and
shoulders, how he'd held her so tenderly after her ordeal
with the ruffian. For all his feral traits, there was a gentleness in this man. She'd felt it in his touch, heard it in
his voice. In the endless nightmare of the last two days,
he'd been and still was the only hope she had to survive.
Her voice of reason cautioned her not to say anything that
would alienate him, which her imminent admission of
guilt might surely do. But unfortunately, her own welfare
was no longer the only concern.

"Mr. Spencer, I—I had hoped to speak with you about
a matter of great importance," she said. Then, gesturing
at the dog, she added, "I can see you're very busy right
now. But do you suppose you could spare me a brief
moment?"

"Now really ain't a good time, darlin'."

Spencer glanced at the bosom gawker. No words passed
between them, but the younger fellow nodded, as if an
order had been issued. As he moved toward Rebecca, her
legs went watery.

Spencer's dark gaze sliced back to her. "Go back to
camp with Johnny, honey. The minute I finish up here,
I'll spare you all the moments you want."

She glanced at the dog, unable to forget that if not for
her, the poor thing might not be lying there with its life
hanging by a thread. She needed to warn Race Spencer
that it could be a man who got shot next, and that it could
happen at any moment.

If that meant blurting out the truth to him in front of
all these men, so be it.

Horribly aware that the lowing of the cattle was getting
louder by the moment, she cast a frantic glance at the
grassland that seemed to stretch forever in every direction.
How could such a wide-open expanse make her feel as if
she were suffocating in a bottle? She tried to take a deep
breath, but pain in her ribs prevented her.

"There are more of those desperadoes," she said, her
voice coming out so faint and shaky that it barely sounded

on the brisk breeze. She swallowed, tensed her shoulders, and in a louder tone, repeated herself. "I'm not sure how many, but I've reason to believe they've been following your herd, which means they aren't far away from here right now."

The words seemed to hang there like icicles, touching the air with frigidity. Spencer stared down at her. She could feel the others staring at her as well.

"You haven't time right now to lend me an ear, so I shan't go into detail," she continued. "Suffice it to say that there is something those men want very badly, and I know where it is. My people in the arroyo refused to divulge the whereabouts of it. Now I'm the only person alive who knows. They aren't going to rest until they can force the information from me, and to that end, they will stop at nothing, including murder."

Rebecca's stomach lurched, and for a horrible instant, she feared she might vomit. "You should guard against an attack," she managed to add, her throat crawling. "And you should get word to your men who are out there with the herd that they should do so as well." She glanced down at the dog again, and tears burned at the backs of her eyes. "I should have told you about it this morning. I'm sorry I didn't. This is—this is all my fault."

While she stood there, feeling like a criminal who awaited sentencing, she kept her gaze fixed on the bullet wound in the hound's shoulder, a means of reminding herself that she deserved whatever punishment befell her.

Finally she could bear the suspense no longer and she drew gaze back to Spencer, expecting to see his expression seething with anger. Instead he was gazing at her with what appeared to be understanding and compassion, and perhaps even a trace of admiration as well.

"I already sent word to my foreman to be watchin' his back out there," he said, his mouth tugging up at one corner. "And I got three men ridin' bobtail guard around our camp. They ain't gonna catch us by surprise again, so you can rest easy, darlin'. You're safe and so are we."

He'd already known? Rebecca stared up at him, her gaze held captive by his. That was why he was looking

at her as he was—with understanding and compassion—
because he'd somehow deduced before she opened her
mouth that she was to blame for everything, that she'd
held back information that might have enabled him to
prevent it all from happening. And that expression in his
eyes—the aching warmth—told her he also knew what it
had cost her to blurt out the truth, not only to him, but in
front of all his men.

Admiration.

The tears that had been burning at the backs of her eyes
welled into the foreground, and she gazed up at him
through a swimming blur. Only minutes ago, she'd been
castigating herself for becoming a pathetic, cowardly creature, and she'd been convinced that traits like pride and
honor and integrity might be forever lost to her. Now the
look in Race Spencer's eyes gave each of those things
back to her in some small measure, not because she could
find them within herself, but because he evidently saw
them in her.

He flicked a glance at Johnny. "Walk her back to
camp." Then, to her, he said, "I'll be along soon. We'll
talk more then."

No wrath. No punishment raining down upon her head.
Just that wonderful warmth in his eyes. Rebecca bent her
head and brushed at her cheeks. From the corner of her
downcast eyes, she saw the younger man's boots approaching from her right. Then his hand gently grasped
her arm.

"Ma'am?"

She wanted to jerk away. Instead she swiped the last
traces of wetness from her cheeks and said, "I've a bit
of experience in treating animals." She glanced back up
at Race Spencer's dark face. "May I lend assistance?"

Her heart caught when she saw the hound looking at
her with woeful eyes. *Her doing.* The poor thing was obviously suffering horribly.

"Please, I'd really like to help."

Spencer raised a dark eyebrow, his expression slightly
bemused. "You know anything about bullet wounds?"

Rebecca stepped closer and bent to look. "No, but my

ma was the closest thing we had to a doctor at the church farm. She treated both people and animals, and I trained at her elbow. I've had experience with other types of wounds.''

He waved her forward. ''If you want to take a look, I'd be glad of your opinion. I'm worried the shoulder's shattered, and I'd rather put him down than have him be crippled.''

Rebecca knelt beside the canine to examine the wound. With a gentle touch, she palpitated the hound's joint. ''Judging by the angle of the bullet hole, Mr. Spencer, I believe the greatest danger would have been in the lead's hitting his heart or nicking a lung. The first would have caused immediate death.'' She glanced up. ''Have you seen any bleeding from his nose or mouth?''

''No.''

She sat back on her heels and sighed. ''Well, then. I can see no reason why he shouldn't recover quite nicely if he receives proper treatment. I can't make any guarantees, of course.'' She lightly touched her fingertips to Blue's bony head. ''I shall certainly give it my best if you'll allow me to try. This fellow proved himself to be a loyal friend to me this afternoon.''

As she spoke, Rebecca remembered how heartened she had felt that morning when she had first seen the hound. In some way she couldn't define, the dog had become representative to her of all the simple things in life that had always brought her pleasure. It made no sense, but she couldn't help but feel that by saving him, she would also be saving a part of herself.

Chapter 10

In truth Race figured he'd had a hell of a lot more experience in treating wounds than Rebecca did. Judging by the way she had blushed at seeing him without a shirt, he doubted she had attended the injuries of many men, at any rate, and it was his observation that, as a general rule, women sustained fewer serious injuries.

Nevertheless he stepped aside and let her take over. He wasn't exactly sure why, only that he sensed she needed to feel she was helping. After carrying Blue back to camp and placing him on a pallet beside her wagon, Race stood ready to assist her in any way he could, boiling water, fetching whiskey and bandages, and then observing as she probed for the bullet in Blue's shoulder, fully prepared to take over if she grew faint. Digging for a bullet was a nasty, stomach-turning job, and he doubted she had the constitution for it.

Rebecca surprised him, though. Despite her fragile, delicate appearance, there was a lot of steel in the girl's spine. She turned pale a couple of times, but her hands remained steady, and she exhibited a skill with the knife that rivaled a qualified physician's. He was also impressed by the way she handled Blue. Under the circumstances, the hound was amazingly cooperative for a dog, but even so, he was a far more difficult patient than any man Race had ever worked on. He had to hold the hound down while Rebecca removed the bullet, for it was a painful process, and even then, Blue jerked and yelped, making what would have been a trying ordeal under the best of circumstances all the more exhausting.

The tension alone would have gotten to most people, making them impatient and short-tempered. Not so with Rebecca. When the hound grew frantic to escape Race's grip, she simply stopped working for a bit, staunching the bleeding with a compress while she soothed the dog with comforting words and caresses. Each time, Blue quieted and surrendered to her ministrations again, almost as if he understood she was trying to help him. Race could see why. Rebecca had a way about her—a gentle goodness. While watching her, he felt that strange, achy warmth move through him again, not just once but several times, until he finally gave up on fighting it. He was drawn to this girl—drawn to her in a way he didn't understand but was helpless to resist.

At one point when Blue's cries became particularly heart-wrenching, Rebecca got tears in her eyes. Watching her, Race felt his own throat tighten. He'd never met anyone whose feelings were so transparent. From the first instant when he'd found her in the arroyo, he'd felt as if he were seeing clear to her soul when he looked into her eyes. Now he understood why. There was no ugliness inside her to block his view. That radiance about her— the angelic sweetness—was absolutely genuine.

"You love animals, don't you?"

Lightly stroking the hound's head and ruff to calm him, she smiled sadly. "I'm fond of them, yes."

Race had a feeling that wasn't saying it by half. In unguarded moments, he had noticed an almost desperate look on her small face. As much as he loved his dog, he began to worry that she might be even more devastated than he if Blue died. She kept whispering, "Oh, Blue, I'm so sorry," her voice throbbing with regret.

At some point, Race began to suspect that Rebecca blamed herself for the dog's injury. On the one hand, he could see how she might. But at the same time, he felt very strongly that she bore no responsibility for what had happened, and it bothered him to think that she was lashing herself with guilt. The girl had enough to deal with.

He had an uneasy feeling that her desperation to save the dog stemmed from something else as well, only he couldn't put his finger on what, exactly. It was almost as if she believed that, by saving the dog, she might vanquish the nightmare that had overtaken her life.

Studying her expression, Race found himself spinning back through the years to the evening his mother had died. After pleading in vain for help from the men in the saloon, he had rushed back to the alley. En route, he had stopped to pick up the roses the two men had thrown on the boardwalk and crushed. He could remember as clearly as if it were yesterday how he had tried to make the flowers pretty again before taking them to his mother, as if by saving them he might also save her. The beautiful roses had been damaged beyond repair, of course, just as his mother had been. But he had frantically tried to fix them, anyway. His mother had smiled when he gave them to her, pressing the crushed blossoms to her cheek. She'd still been holding them when she died.

In retrospect, Race knew that his trying to salvage the roses had been a desperate, futile act—stemming from shock and crushing grief. It occurred to him now, as he watched Rebecca, that perhaps everyone found a rose, or its equivalent, and tried to save it when their life was being destroyed. Something beautiful and sweet that wasn't yet lost. Maybe, to Rebecca, Blue was a beautiful rose, the one little touch of magic left to her in a world turned topsy-turvy.

"Rebecca, you ain't entertainin' the notion that it's your fault Blue got shot, are you?" he asked shortly after she had removed the bullet.

At the question, her face lost color, and she caught her bottom lip between her teeth, biting down with such force that he winced. Though she said nothing, that alone answered his question. She blamed herself, all right. Not just for what had happened to the dog, but for everything else as well.

His heart twisted at the pain he saw reflected in her luminous blue eyes, and he found himself journeying backward through time yet again, recalling the guilt he had felt over his mother's death. He had complained of hunger, and in an attempt to feed him, she had died. Looking back on it, Race knew his feelings of guilt had been ridiculous. He'd been a little, seven-year-old boy, and he'd been starving. But after her death, he had remembered the times he'd cried in her arms, asking for something to eat, and he had blamed himself because she'd been standing on that street corner, trying to earn pennies enough to feed him. *His fault*. At least, he had believed that then.

Maybe everyone lashed themselves with guilt after losing someone they loved, he decided. If so, he could only wonder what sin Rebecca imagined that she had committed. From his standpoint, he couldn't envision her doing anything that was very wrong. But, then, neither could a seven-year-old boy. Whatever the imagined sin, she'd evidently chosen trying to save Blue as a way to atone. And if the dog didn't make it? What then? Would she blame herself for that as well?

Not wishing to distract her while she was working on the dog, Race let the subject drop, but he resolved to broach it again later, possibly that evening after things calmed down. Unless he missed his guess, they hadn't seen the last of those plug-uglies, which meant there was bound to be more trouble. Every time something went wrong, he didn't want Rebecca to berate herself or feel in any way to blame.

Every muscle in Rebecca's body ached—her back, her shoulders, the tendons in her neck. After kneeling on the ground for so many hours with only a thin wool blanket as padding, even her kneecaps hurt. She wanted nothing more than to take a walk and stretch out the kinks. That would mean leaving camp by herself, though, and the mere thought terrified her. Those ruffians were out there somewhere, of that she had no doubt. All evening long, the realization had been at the back of her mind, a constant worry that could quickly turn to terror if she let herself dwell on it. Over the course of the evening, the few times Race Spencer had ventured out of her sight, she'd felt frantic.

Usually a calm, self-sufficient person, she found her need to be near him disturbing. In her recollection, she had never been so fraught with anxiety or tension, and her sudden dependency on him struck her as being irrational. He was essentially a stranger, after all, and the small amount of time they'd spent together scarcely warranted the feelings for him that she was developing. Earlier while she'd been in the wagon bathing, she'd found herself listening for his voice out by the fire, and several times when she'd failed to hear it for a short while, she had grown panicky. It had been the most awful feeling—her heart slamming, her lungs grabbing frantically for breath, sweat filming her body. The complaints had vanished the second she heard him speak again.

Now, as the hour grew late, she was starting to dread the moment when she'd have to retire for the night. Just the thought of going to bed in that wagon all alone made her pulse quicken and her head start to ache. She had never been afraid of the dark or easily spooked. As an only child, she'd slept alone for as long as she could remember. What on earth was wrong with her, that she should suddenly have night terrors? Race Spencer had men riding guard around the camp. Some of his wranglers would undoubtedly be asleep in their bedrolls only a few feet from her wagon for most of the night. She had absolutely nothing to be afraid of. But no matter how many times she told herself that, the disquiet within her didn't abate.

Rebecca lightly rested her hand on Blue's head. In the faint glow of the firelight, his mottled brown ears looked as though they were fashioned from velvet and were nearly as soft. She ran the tip of her thumb along the indentation between his closed eyes and listened to the rhythmic huff of his breathing. *Fast asleep.* Touching a fingertip to the underside of a loose jowl, she checked for fever. Though warmer than a human's, his body temperature felt to her as if it were within normal range for a dog, which was a good sign. As long as she didn't lose him to infection—which she'd done everything she could to guard against—he would live to chase more rabbits, an ability that Race Spencer had stressed as being of utmost importance. The man clearly loved his dog.

She smiled slightly, recalling how Race had hovered over her all evening while she worked on Blue. He had assisted her in every way possible, trying to anticipate her needs. Each time her coffee had grown cold, he had refilled the battered tin cup he'd washed out especially for her, despite Mr. Grigsley's grumbling about his wasting water. Then he had brought her a supper plate of beans and cornbread and spelled her so she might eat.

In all honesty, Rebecca felt he was treating her far more nicely than she deserved. Because of her, his very livelihood was in jeopardy, and she wouldn't have blamed him a bit for feeling resentful or bitterly angry. In fact, she found it rather incredible that he wasn't. All evening long, he'd been receiving nothing but bad news, the tally of lost cattle climbing sharply with each report. How much more could he take without wanting to take the losses out of her hide?

Gazing out into the endless darkness that lay beyond camp, Rebecca allowed herself to wonder what she would do without Race Spencer's protection. She'd lived her whole life on the farm in Pennsylvania, her excursions into town rare and in the company of church members or relatives who had always looked after her. She'd never driven a team of horses; one of the brethren had always done that. She'd never had to find her way anyplace; that, too, had always fallen to one of the brethren. She'd simply followed along, like a duckling in a queue, never paying much attention to how she got where she was going. And if she'd had to find her way? In Pennsylvania there were well-traveled roads to follow, with signs to indicate which turns to take.

Now here she was in the middle of nowhere without a road or a sign anywhere. No neighboring farms. No general store. No friends. No family. She'd never felt so horribly alone or so helpless. Out here, one couldn't collect a hen from the chicken yard for supper. No cow with full udders was out in the barn. There was no smokehouse a few paces away. No dried vegetables. No garden. No cool cellar where potatoes were stored in abundance. Just mile after mile of nothing. If left to her own devices in this place, she would die out here. It was as simple as that.

Race Spencer was her salvation. If he abandoned her, she would be helpless.

A rustling sound came from her right. For at least the hundredth time since darkness had fallen, she turned to peer through the shadows, her heart slamming. A black shape moved. It wasn't her imagination this time. There was actually someone coming around the rear corner of the wagon.

Clamping an arm over her bruised ribs, she tensed to spring to her feet. But then the shape moved into the flickering light cast by the dying fire and took on the outline of a man, a tall man who moved with fluid strength. She went limp with relief. *Race.*

He'd evidently left camp to gather wood for the fire, though where he might have found it, she hadn't a clue. More amazing, he had a full armload. He must have walked some distance, for she'd seen no firewood or anything close to it in this desolate area.

The pain behind her eyes seemed to explode, knifing to the back of her skull. He'd left camp? She threw a glance at the shadows, so black and impenetrable, that closed in on her from nearly every direction, some of them seeming to move with each flicker of light. She had poor eyesight at night. If there were a man crouched in one of those puddles of darkness, she'd never see him. And Race Spencer had left her alone?

Panic welled. *Calm down, Rebecca. He's back now. Nothing happened. You're overreacting!* But it was easier said than done. Mr. Grigsley was sleeping in the bedroll wagon only a few feet away, she reminded herself. It wasn't as if he'd left her entirely alone. He also had men riding guard. With them circling camp, it was highly unlikely that any of those ruffians would be able to slip past them.

Hugging her ribs, she dragged in a deep breath and

forced herself to slowly exhale. *Calm.* She had to stop this. Nothing had happened during his absence, after all. Only now she was afraid to take her eyes off of him.

An almost overpowering urge came over her to join him at the fire. She stared at his trouser belt, imagining her hand curled over the leather. He couldn't very well leave her if she attached herself to him.

She closed her eyes and forced herself to breathe again. In and out. Lands, her thoughts were making no sense, even to her. Quailing with trepidation one moment because she feared he might become angry with her, then wanting to hold on to the poor man and never let go of him.

In an attempt to laugh at the absurdity of it all, she envisioned herself hanging on to his belt—eating with him, following him everywhere he went, even sleeping with him. A hysterical bubble of laughter worked its way up her throat. *Mr. Spencer, would you mind holding my hand while you do your business behind the bush? I realize it may seem a bit unconventional, but bear with me. I do, of course, promise not to look.*

She lifted her lashes, watching as he reached the circle of rocks and crouched, dumping the armload of branches onto the ground beside him. In the combined light from the moon and the low-burning fire, she could see a constant play of muscle stretching the back of his shirt taut as he fed the scrawny pieces of wood to the eagerly reaching flames. Saltbush branches, she realized. He'd gone out into the darkness and collected wood from the thickets that grew all around there. He wouldn't have had to go far to do that. Twenty feet, possibly thirty? He hadn't left her alone, after all.

Unable to help herself, she clung to him with her gaze as she longed to do physically. The only time she'd felt really safe since this nightmare had begun was today in the bedroll wagon, when he'd held her. And no wonder. Even covered by black denim, the powerful lines of his upper torso were evident.

The only other man she'd ever seen without his shirt was her father, and that had been only a glimpse, for Papa had quickly ducked into the bedroom to cover himself properly. Going by what she recalled, though, her father had been pale-skinned and thin, his arms not much bigger around than hers.

Race Spencer's arms were thrice that size, his forearms thick and ridged with sinew, his upper arms and shoulders bulging with pads of muscle. She remembered how, just beneath his bronze skin, distended veins marbled the otherwise glossy smoothness. She also recalled how perfectly she had fit against him when he'd held her, her round places filling his hollows, and his filling hers. She wished his arms were locked around her now, that he'd hold her like that again, stroke her hair, make the jumpy, electrified feeling inside her go away. By the fire, maybe, with a blanket drawn over her. So she could forget. Maybe even sleep for a bit.

Madness. Until yesterday, she'd never been alone with a man. Not even with Henry, to whom she would soon have been officially betrothed. Once they'd slipped away into the front parlor, with her parents right there in the adjoining room, and Papa had pitched a fit when he found them. An unmarried woman didn't keep company with a man without a chaperone, Papa had informed her later. Never. No matter how innocent the situation, it simply was not done. Now here she sat, wanting Race Spencer to hold her while she slept.

Appalled at herself for thinking such things, she averted her gaze, her cheeks as warm as if she were standing near the fire. It was wrong to stare at the man, especially when she kept remembering how he'd looked half-naked.

The slender pieces of green wood he fed to the fire finally caught, snapping and crackling as they sent up a spray of orange sparks. The sudden flare of light cast flickering patterns of amber into the darkness, illuminating the figures of two men approaching. Their voices rose and fell, interspersed with laughter, as they made their way into camp.

"Got any coffin varnish?" one called.

"It's even fresh," Race replied.

As the men drew closer, Rebecca recognized them as

Corey Halloway and Johnny Graves. Over the course of the evening, Rebecca had revised her opinion of them both. Johnny, the bosom gawker, reminded her a little of Samuel Stevens, a young church brother of hers whom she'd known all of her life. Incurably mischievous and irreverent, Samuel kept his parents and many of the elders in a constant dither, making them despair of his ever growing up. Secretly, Rebecca had always enjoyed Samuel's pranks, his lively wit, and his penchant for laughter, and she hoped he never changed. Everyone had a special gift to give others, and Samuel's was the ability to make people smile. Johnny Graves was like that, his blue eyes dancing, his attitude about most things flippant and devil-may-care.

After joining their boss at the fire and pouring themselves some coffee, Corey and Johnny hunkered near the flames to warm themselves and rest. Their positions didn't strike Rebecca as being very comfortable. Her own legs would have soon grown weary of the strain. But these cattlemen seemed content to rock back on a boot heel for hours, one knee uplifted to rest their arms, their gazes fixed on the fire.

"We just saw Preach and Madison down at the tether line, rubbing down their horses," Johnny said, nudging his hat brim up to look at Race.

"How many head did they bring in?" Race asked.

That had been an oft-repeated question tonight, the counts ranging from zero to only a few, and with each report, Race's expression became a little more grim.

No longer convinced that prayer was a magic cure for every ill, nor even certain, at this point, if there was a heavenly Father to whom she might appeal, Rebecca found herself crossing her fingers and holding her breath, something she hadn't done in years. *Please, let it be better news this time!*

"Nine," Johnny replied.

"That's a help."

Johnny nodded and took a slow sip of coffee. "Yeah. Maybe things are starting to look up."

Race lifted a battered tin cup from where it had been

sitting on one of the rocks. After gazing into it for a moment, he tossed away the contents with a flick of his broad wrist.

Corey crouched with his head bent, curtains of white-blond hair falling forward to hide his expression. "You need us to spell you tonight, watchin' after Blue?" He glanced up. "I imagine you and Miss Rebecca would like to get a little rest."

Race took his time answering. "If you wouldn't mind watchin' him for the next little bit, it'd be much appreciated. I got some business to take care of."

Johnny drew his cup from his lips, swallowing and swiping at his mouth with his shirt sleeve. "Not a problem. We aren't going anywhere for a spell. Not until I've had at least two more cups of coffee, anyway."

"Great. I never did get a chance to talk with Rebecca, and after that, I should probably get her settled for the night. I imagine she's tuckered."

Rebecca's stomach dropped. Talk? She thought back to what she'd said out by the graves and recalled having told him that she would give him more details later. And she would, of course. He had every right to know. It was just—oh, lands, she hated to get into that right now. After all the bad news he'd been getting all evening? Why risk angering him by confessing that someone else's money was at the root of all his troubles? Especially since, because of it, he apparently had lost a great deal of his own.

Race pushed to his feet and brushed his palms clean on his pants. As he turned in her direction, his sharp gaze routed through the shadows to give her a long perusal. Illuminated by firelight and cast against the darkness behind him, he looked more like a wood carving than a flesh-and-blood man, the open collar of his shirt revealing a swatch of molten bronze chest, his black trousers reflective with muted gold. Amber flickered over his face, etching his chiseled features in shadow.

With a catlike fluidity he moved toward her, his boots touching the ground so lightly that his footfalls could scarcely be heard. With each stride his massive shoulders shifted, his powerfully roped arms swinging loosely at his sides, his broad hands curled slightly and always hovering near the dull-finish handles of his Colts. His expression told her nothing as he drew up before her. Neither did his brown eyes, which glittered with reflected light as he locked gazes with her.

"You feel like takin' a little walk before you turn in?" he asked. "I need to stretch my legs."

A walk? She glanced at the darkness beyond the firelight. It had to be well after midnight. Then it hit her. A *walk*.

She imagined peering at him over the top of a short bush. Somehow the picture no longer struck her as being very funny. Horribly embarrassing was more like it. At home, such things were never discussed or alluded to. She couldn't imagine having a man accompany her to do her necessary business. On the other hand, the thought of his leaving her behind in camp made her feel panicky.

"I, um—yes. A walk would be nice."

He reached down and took her arm. He had a grip like a steel vise, yet it was also oddly gently, the pressure of his fingers firm but not bruising. Once she'd gained her feet, he led her from camp. The moment they moved beyond the firelight, Rebecca couldn't see. She peered into the blackness, her footsteps faltering.

"You night blind?"

"A bit."

She no sooner spoke than she caught the toe of her shoe on a rock and nearly fell. Abandoning his hold on her arm, he caught her from pitching forward, then slipped an arm around her waist, his large hand splayed over her side, his thumb and forefinger resting perilously close to the underside of her breast. Rebecca's breath snagged. No man had ever dared to touch her so familiarly, not even her father. She wondered if the fact that Race Spencer had cared for her last night and then again today made him feel that he could take liberties with her person.

"A bit?" His tone was laced with amusement. He steered her around something in their path that she was unable to see, his hand shifting slightly on her side as he pulled her to follow him. Reacting instinctively, Rebecca grabbed hold of his fingers. He glanced down. "You feelin' nervous about my hand bein' there, honey?"

Her mouth had gone suddenly dry. "I, um . . . a little."

He flashed her a crooked grin, his teeth gleaming white in the moonlight. Looking up at him, she was heartened by the fact that she could at least see the shadowy cast of his features now. "Well, I'd say we got ourselves a problem then. I'm gonna be a whole lot nervous if I turn loose of you. I'm afraid you'll trip."

Since she'd already nearly done so, she couldn't very well argue the point. "My eyes are beginning to adjust now, I think."

He looked ahead. "Can you see that rock?"

Rebecca peered into the gloom. "What rock?"

He veered sharply to the left. "That rock." He chuckled, the sound deep and vibrant. "I don't think you can see quite good enough to do your own navigatin', if it's all the same to you." He glanced back down at her. "As for the hand, it ain't gonna go nowhere. You got my word on it."

In her estimation, his hand wouldn't have to go very far. His thumb already grazed the beginning swell at the side of her breast, the heat of his touch making her skin tingle even through the layers of cloth. In all fairness, however, she doubted the touch was deliberate. With his fingers splayed, the spread of his hand could have encompassed a supper plate. Nevertheless, she couldn't quite bring herself to release her hold on his fingers.

"Is them church fellas the gropey type?" he asked.

"Pardon?"

"You know—gropers." He wiggled a captured finger. "Judgin' by the way you're squeezin', I'd wager that you kept company with some fellas who was given to coppin' touches without askin' you first."

Without asking her first? Rebecca gaped at him for a moment, so appalled to think there might actually be women who would grant a man permission that she couldn't think what to say. When at last she found her voice, she said, "I've never kept company with any gentlemen."

He arched a dark eyebrow. "Never?"

"Only when my parents were present. Unmarried men and women aren't allowed to be alone in our church community, and Ma and Papa strictly observed the rule." A wave of sadness hit her at the thought of them. Her voice going taut, she added, "I guess those times are forever behind me. My life will probably be quite different from now on." She laughed softly, the sound without humor. "I guess it already is. Here I am, taking a walk late at night with a man, and without a chaperone."

He drew her around another obstacle. Squinting, Rebecca tried in vain to see where he might be taking her.

As if he guessed her thoughts, he said, "There's a big pile of rocks up ahead. I thought we could find a place to sit and talk for a spell. You needin' to stop before we get there? I reckon your eyeteeth must be floatin'. I can find you some bushes if you want."

Rebecca felt the heat of a blush spread from her cheeks to her hairline. "No, I, um . . . I'm fine, thank you."

"You sure? Don't be bashful. Privies is few and far between out here. I can turn my back and roll myself a smoke while you're doin' your business."

That morning, Rebecca had used the Arbuckle can in her wagon, and she fully intended to continue to do so, the only problem being how she might empty it. "No, thank you." Hoping to distract him, she added, "I didn't realize you smoked."

"I don't much. Does smokin' offend you?"

"I, um . . . don't know, actually. I've never known anyone who indulged."

Both of his eyebrows went up at that revelation. "My God, darlin'. What do you church folks do for fun?" Even in the moonlight, she saw a twinkle enter his eyes. "No courtin', no coppin' touches, no smokin'. I don't suppose drinkin's allowed either."

"Spirits, you mean?" She smiled at his appalled expression. "No, I'm afraid not."

He shook his head. "You got some rough trail ahead, sweetheart. The real world ain't quite so right and proper."

Out of the darkness, the pile of rocks suddenly loomed before them. Rebecca gave a startled squeak when Race grasped her at the waist and swung her up to sit on a boulder. Leaning forward, she peered at the blackness below her dangling feet. "Are there jagged rocks down there?"

"I won't let you fall," he said huskily.

Resting a hand on each side of her, he stepped close, pressing his wide chest against her knees. His advance brought his face to within a scant inch of hers, and she straightened, feeling unaccountably unsettled. In the pit of her stomach, she had a fluttery sensation that intensified every time she looked at him. She glanced over her shoulder.

"Are you sure it's safe to be here?"

He followed her nervous gaze. "You think I woulda brought you here if I thought it wasn't?"

She knew he wouldn't have. In the space of a day, she'd come to trust this man in a way she really couldn't justify. How many times had her ma cautioned her never to place herself in compromising situations with men? According to Ma, the male of the species, no matter how pious, was cursed with powerful physical yearnings that could overcome his good sense. Race Spencer was far from pious, yet as she gazed into his dark eyes, she felt no fear of him.

"What?" he asked softly.

"Nothing."

His mouth quirked at one corner. "There's somethin'. Whenever you're feelin' upset or worried, it's plain on your face."

It was rather unsettling to have him verify her suspicion that he could read her so well. "It's just that my ma would have conniptions if she could see me now. She maintained that it was perilous for a young lady to be alone with a gentleman."

The grin that flirted with his lips took hold, deepening the slash in his lean cheek. Rebecca stared at it, wondering if it had been a dimple in his younger years that had become more deeply chiseled by time and harsh exposure to the elements.

"And what, exactly, are you afraid I'm gonna do?"

"I'm not sure," she admitted. "Ma just said gentlemen have powerful yearnings that can get the best of them sometimes. And that I shouldn't trust them."

He startled her by reaching up to grasp her chin. He traced the shape of her mouth with the pad of his thumb, his gaze holding hers. "Your ma was a smart lady," he admitted in a gravelly voice. "You shouldn't trust a man too far, darlin'. You're too pretty by half, and it could get you into trouble."

Rebecca's heart skittered. Not that she believed for a moment that she was all that pretty. But there was a strange heat in the look he gave her that she found rather disconcerting. "Are—are you saying I can't trust you?"

She realized he'd been staring at her mouth as she spoke. As her question trailed away, he lightly dragged his thumb across her lips again. After a long moment, he said, "No, I ain't sayin' that." He smiled and lowered his hand back down to rest it on the rock. "You can trust me, darlin'. I give you my word."

He seemed almost reluctant to make that promise, which she found even more alarming. Her lips tingled where he'd touched them. Regarding him with a concerned frown, she scratched with her teeth to make the sensation abate. "I'm glad," she blurted. "If I couldn't trust you, I don't know what I'd do."

At her admission, Race's smile faded. An ache spread through him as he studied her small face. She truly would be in a pickle without him. That went a long way toward explaining the frantic expression he had glimpsed in her eyes several times.

"Well, don't worry on it," he told her. "You can trust me, honey." Race meant to live up to that promise if it killed him. She desperately needed a friend, and he wanted to be that for her. Any overpowering urges that came over him would have to be set aside. It was just that simple. He offered her his handshake. "Friends?"

Almost pathetically eager, she crossed his palm with her fingers. "I hope so," she whispered.

He enfolded her slender hand in his. There was an unmistakable note of doubt in those words. "Can I take that to mean you're thinkin' somethin' could happen to make us not be friends?"

She averted her gaze to stare off into the darkness. "Are you certain we're safe from the ruffians out here?"

Sensing that she needed to circle the question for a bit before she answered, he allowed her to change the subject. "I got men ridin' guard. Six of 'em, now that it's full dark. On top of that, we're both wearin' black, which don't show up good at night, so we ain't makin' targets of ourselves. And if trouble comes callin', I figure I'm handy enough with a gun to hold it off until my men out there can reach us."

She sighed and began worrying the buttons of her bodice with tense fingertips. "That's good to know."

He caught her chin with the crook of his finger, forcing her to look at him. "Rebecca, what is it that's troublin' you?"

By her expression, he knew she dreaded telling him. She lifted her gaze to the star-studded sky above them, managing to avoid his gaze after all. "I, um . . ." She gulped. "I just don't want to make you angry with me."

"Why would I get angry with you?"

"Because of your cows. Losing so many, I mean. My being here has visited misfortune upon you, and I'm afraid that—" She broke off and looked back down at him, her eyes shimmering in the moonlight. "When you find out what those ruffians are after, I'm afraid you'll detest me."

Race could see that the possibility frightened her, and he supposed, if he were in her shoes, he'd feel the same way. "Because they're after money?" he asked gently.

She looked mildly horrified. "I never—how did you find out about the money?"

He released her chin to scratch beside his nose. "Well, now, there's a question. I reckon I just figured it out." He allowed a smile to touch his mouth. "It seems clear as rain in March that they're hellbent to get their hands on somethin'. If it ain't money, what could it be?" He let that hang there for a moment. "Maybe now'd be a good time for you to tell me about it, honey. Then you won't be worryin' no more about me gettin' mad when I find out."

She nodded, albeit without much enthusiasm. Then she slowly told him the story, beginning with the brethren's decision to leave the Philadelphia area and their subsequent search for a suitable parcel of land on which to resettle, which they found outside Santa Fe, New Mexico. "We were being encroached upon by people of secular persuasion on all sides, you see." She shrugged. "The elders felt the membership should be farther removed from such influences, and they voted unanimously to relocate."

"What the hell is people of secular persuasion?"

Her eyes widened at the question, and for a moment, she looked flustered. "They, um . . . are worldly people. Ordinary people, I suppose you could say."

"Like me?"

Even in the moonlight he saw her cheeks grow pink. "Yes," she admitted faintly. "Please don't be offended, Mr. Spencer. There's nothing wrong with you . . . or anything. It's simply that we lived in a religious cloister."

"A what?"

"A cloister—in seclusion—insulated from the outside world so we might practice our beliefs without interference. To someone like you, we would probably seem quite peculiar."

Studying her sweet countenance, Race thought it more accurate to say he found her angelic and precious, and now that he was getting a better grasp of how she'd been raised, he was beginning to understand why. She had been sheltered all of her life, kept apart from any kind of bad influence, her daily focus, from dawn to dark, on her religion. She gave a whole new meaning to the word "innocent."

"Anyway," she went on, "we had enough money in our coffers to purchase the land in New Mexico, construct the homes, and have some left over for living expenses until the parcels in Pennsylvania were sold. The main body of the church made the move a year ago this spring.''

"But you and your folks didn't go?''

She shook her head. "Six couples were chosen to remain behind, my parents amongst them, to sell the parcels of land outside of Philadelphia. They were to transport the sale proceeds to Santa Fe. If all had gone well, we would have arrived there in a few more weeks, just in time to settle in before the harsh winter weather.'' She began wringing her hands. "I don't know what the brethren in Santa Fe will do now. Without the money we were taking to them, they won't be able to buy farming implements, work animals, or the seed to plant their crops next spring. Nor will they have the necessary funds to make a mortgage payment to the bank. The church will go under.''

"Where's the money? Do you know?''

"My papa and the other brethren installed a false floor in the Petersens' wagon, and they hid the money underneath it. As far as I know, it's still there.'' She dragged in a shaky breath and lifted her hands in a gesture of bewilderment. "I've no idea how the ruffians learned we were transporting a large amount of cash. Papa and the brethren went to great lengths to keep it a secret, even going so far as to install the fake floor in the wagon by dark of night. Yet somehow those ruffians got wind of it. Along the trail, somewhere, I presume. Perhaps when we stopped in one of the towns to purchase more supplies. Someone in our party must have let it slip.''

"I don't reckon the how of it matters much,'' he told her. "Somehow they found out.'' He searched her gaze. "Forgive me for sayin' it, darlin', but it strikes me as plumb foolish, all them folks choosin' to die rather than hand over that money.''

A stricken look came over her face. "Yes,'' she whispered. "Foolish, for in the end, the money may never reach Santa Fe anyway.'' Her mouth trembled and she gazed off into the darkness for a long while. When she looked back at him, she said, "In their defense, however,

I must point out that in their minds, the money wasn't theirs to surrender. It belonged to God. And my papa and the other brethren also counted rather heavily on the heavenly Father to protect them, which He failed to do." Her eyes went sparkly with tears. "Those of my faith believe that love is stronger than hate, and that if we love our enemy, he will be touched by God's goodness and respond in kind."

In Race's opinion, that belief went straight past foolish to plumb stupid. "Out west, there's some mighty evil men on the loose," he told her. "A smart man loves his enemy, but keeps his gun well oiled. Ain't you never heard the sayin' that God helps them that helps themselves?"

She bent her head. "I'm not defending their beliefs, Mr. Spencer. Since the arroyo, my faith has been badly shaken, and I'm no longer sure I believe in much of anything."

She sounded so forlorn and lost that he touched a hand to her hair. "That'll pass, honey. You're just bleedin' inside right now. In time, you'll heal, and your thinkin' will all come right again."

"I'm not so sure."

"I am. But for right now, that ain't the most important thing we need to talk about."

She looked up, her eyes so big and appealing he felt the tug on his heart.

"I wanna discuss you bein' afraid I'm gonna get mad at you. Can you explain that to me?"

She closed her eyes and sent tears spilling down her cheeks. He caught a glistening droplet with the backs of his fingers. "You've been financially devastated because of me," she whispered. "I feared that you'd be furious when you learned it was over someone else's money, and even more furious because I might have warned you early this morning so you could have guarded against trouble."

Race took his time in forming a reply. A glib talker, he wasn't. What he said to her and how he said it might make all the difference in how she felt from now on. "I'm gonna take the last point first, about you warnin' me. To start with, last night you was in a bad way, so deep in shock you wasn't aware of nothin' happenin' around you. Then, when you come right this mornin', it was to find me in bed with you. You was scared, and rightly so. I didn't blame you for that then, and I don't now. On top of that, I think you tried to tell me about the money. Right before I left to go get us our breakfast. Am I wrong?''

"No. I did mean to tell you, but you left, and then the herd stampeded, and then those men—"

"Whoa, whoa!" Race flashed her a grin. "You don't gotta convince me, honey. I know things got crazy after that and you never got a chance to tell me."

She looked at him incredulously. "You truly aren't angry?"

"Why would I be? You want the truth? I think you're a mighty brave lady, comin' out there to the graves and tellin' me in front of my men. I never once felt you had a chance to tell me sooner, and I ain't the least bit angry, I promise."

"But if not for me, none of this would have happened to you!"

"Rebecca, when I found you in the arroyo, I figured them plug-uglies must've been after somethin'. The wagons was ripped apart, all the trunks had been rifled. Judgin' by the things they done, I also knew they was mean-hearted bastards. But I went ahead and brought you here. That was my decision, not yours."

"What choice did you have? If you'd left me, I would have perished."

Perished? Race decided to let that one pass. He could more or less figure out what the word meant from the rest of the sentence. It made him want to smile, nonetheless. The girl sure knew a passel of strange words. "It's true. I didn't have no choice," he admitted. "The same goes for you. You didn't choose for any of this to happen to you. Sometimes, darlin', bad things just happen. It ain't by nobody's choice, and it ain't because of anything they done. I don't want you blamin' yourself. You hear? I should have taken extra precautions to protect the herd. It ain't your fault that I didn't."

"I feel as if it is."

He framed her face between his hands. "Well, I want you to stop feelin' that way. If anything'll make me mad, that will. Them stampedin' the herd and shootin' Blue. What happened to Cookie. If you go blamin' yourself, I'll tan your hide and hang it on a post to dry. You understand? It's like blamin' yourself if it rains."

She drew away to wipe her cheeks. "You're a very kind man, Mr. Spencer. I wouldn't blame you at all for feeling resentful. I am so very sorry. You'll never know how—"

He cut her off by touching a finger to her lips. "You're apologizin', and you've done nothin' to apologize for."

She averted her face to free her mouth. "Perhaps you should go get the church money from the Petersens' wagon. The brethren would want to recompense you for the damages, I feel certain."

He sighed, feeling at a loss. Despite all he had just said, she seemed bent on holding herself responsible. He understood why. But he wished with all his heart that she didn't. "I thought you said the church'll go under without that money, and now you're offerin' some of it to me?"

"I'm sure they could spare that much. We could send the remainder to them in Santa Fe."

"I'll think about it," he conceded. "But if there's another way, I'd rather not. Like you said, it's God's money. Not only that, but a lot of fine folks died tryin' to protect it. I'd feel funny about helpin' myself to it."

For what seemed to him an interminably long while, she gazed up at him. Then, taking him totally by surprise, she slipped her arms around his neck and gave him a fierce hug. Race was so startled that for a moment he couldn't think how to react. Then instinct took over. He encircled her in his embrace and drew her close, pressing his face to her hair. He had received some heartfelt thankyous in his day, but this one was by far the sweetest. It also occurred to him as he registered the softness of her body against his that it was undoubtedly the most dangerous. He needed to get her back to camp before one of those powerful male yearnings her ma had warned her about got the best of both of them.

Chapter 11

The last thing Rebecca wanted to do was go to bed, but Race insisted she looked tired and that she needed to get a good night's rest. She attempted to use caring for Blue as an excuse to stay up, but he would have none of that.

"I'll watch over Blue," he assured her as he led her to the back of the wagon.

The next instant, her feet parted company with the ground, startling her half out of her wits. She clutched his shirt sleeves, her heart skittering as he swung her up into the wagon. Once she'd gotten her footing, he placed a hand on the wagon gate and vaulted inside after her.

With the canvas filtering out the moon and the fire burning low, the wagon's interior was as black as smut. Rebecca groped blindly for a handhold when the conveyance rocked with Race's weight. Judging by the sound of his boots on the floor planks, he was moving away from her. She strained to pick him out from the shadows, her eyes feeling like grapes being popped from their skins. Glass and metal went *ka-chink*. Something rasped.

She blinked at a sudden flare of orange. A lucifer. The scent of sulphur drifted to her. She watched him cup the match with his palm, then touch it to the lamp wick. As he waved out the flame, he carefully adjusted the feed knob until a golden wash of light fell over them. Then he replaced the glass globe. Sticking the match between his teeth, he turned to regard the pallet.

Rebecca's stomach lurched as she followed his gaze

and recalled the blood-soaked quilts. As if he guessed her thoughts, he said, "Corey cleaned up in here a mite. He threw the soiled quilts on the fire. I hope they wasn't special to you."

As it happened, two of the remaining quilts, a wedding ring and a drunkard's path pattern, had been made by her mother. "The ones he took had no sentimental meaning to me," she assured him. "And I greatly appreciate the thoughtfulness."

He bent to straighten the rumpled covers. "You gonna be all right in here?"

Judging by his tone, he realized how nervous she was about sleeping alone. Heat crept up her neck, and for a long moment, she stood there, caught between stung pride and mounting anxiety, not entirely certain which emotion would win out. It was so childish to feel afraid to sleep alone, and practically speaking, she knew that asking him to stay with her was highly inappropriate, not to mention perilous. Though he had promised her that she was safe with him, he was still a man, and Ma had warned her countless times to beware.

She threw a frightened glance at the wagon canvas, thinking it would provide scant barrier against a ruffian with a knife. "I'll be fine."

"I'll sleep under the wagon hitch," he informed her, his dark gaze fixed on her as he straightened. "If you so much as wiggle, I oughta hear you. You'll be safe enough. I just wanna make sure you can get some rest. If you want, I can bunk in here with you."

Rebecca stared up at him, battling against her yearning to say yes. Had she moved past irrational to completely insane? A woman didn't invite a man to share her sleeping quarters. The wagon was narrow, the space so confined they wouldn't be able to roll over without bumping into each other. Yet it was all she could do not to plead with him to stay with her.

"N-no—I-I'll be fine," she said, not sounding very convincing, even to herself.

He searched her gaze, which was unsettling. Each time he directed those dark eyes her way, she invariably got the feeling this man could see far more than she wished to reveal. "You sure? If you're feelin' froggy, don't feel embarrassed. God knows you got plenty of call."

Froggy? Yes, that described it, all right. The moment he left, she'd be jumping out of her skin at every little sound. "No, truly, Mr. Spencer. I, um . . ." She waved a limp hand. "After all, what on earth is there to feel nervous about?"

"Nothin'." He glanced around the wagon, stepping to the front to make sure the flap was tied down before he turned back to her. "It's been my experience, though, that a rash of bad can get a person all dithered up to the point that there's a damned thin line atwixt threat and fancy."

She hugged herself, rubbing her upper arms and thinking how absolutely true that was. Race Spencer might be the most ill-spoken individual she'd ever met, but he had a way with words, nonetheless.

"You cold, sweetheart?"

She stopped chafing her arms. "Oh!" Nervous little laugh. "Heavens, no. Just nerve—well, maybe a bit chilled. I'm sure I'll be fine once I get under the quilts." She glanced at the pallet. "Have you and your men plenty of covers? I surely won't need more than one."

"Nah. We all got our bedrolls." He stepped around her to the wagon gate. Before vaulting to the ground, he glanced back. "If you have trouble sleepin', just sing out. The floor in here ain't no harder than the ground, and I can get the fellas to watch after Blue till mornin'."

"Thank you, Mr. Spencer. But I'm sure I shall sleep like the dea—" She broke off and rubbed her arms again, her gaze sweeping the floor for bloodstains. "Like a baby. Thank you for your concern, however. It's greatly appreciated."

"Speakin' of Blue, that reminds me. I meant to ask if there's somethin' special I oughta do for him durin' the night."

"Make sure he stays warm, and if he wakes up, offer him water." She shrugged. "And you shouldn't let him walk."

Swinging a leg over the gate, he sat astraddle the partition and eyed her with undisguised concern. "Honey, are you sure you feel all right about sleepin' in here alone?"

Rebecca wanted to break eye contact with him but couldn't. She tried to moisten her lips only to find that her tongue was a dry lump in her mouth.

"If I have a problem sleeping, I'll call you," she finally managed to say.

"I'm used to gettin' woke up at night. I can go straight back to sleep, no problem. So don't hesitate if you need me. All right?"

"I won't."

He nodded as if that satisfied him. "Well, g'night then." He jumped over the gate to the ground and disappeared into the shadows.

Rebecca wasted no time in securing the canvas flap. Then she turned to regard the enclosure, feeling as though it had become her torture chamber for the night. Her gaze kept cutting back to the floor, where only the faintest hint of bloodstain remained. Nonetheless, her skin crawled.

At the right front corner of the wagon, she was relieved to see the empty Arbuckle can, which she could use as her chamber pot for the night. Beside it was the stack of clothing. Atop the assortment of gray and black garments were two white cotton nightgowns. She had no inkling which of the women in her party had owned them, and at this point, she couldn't allow herself to care.

After traveling so far in a wagon very like this one, Rebecca knew better than to undress before she turned down the lamp. The light threw one's silhouette against the canvas. The first few days on the trail, Papa had scolded her and Ma numerous times for forgetting and putting on a scandalous display. She quickly grabbed a nightgown and moved the can over next to the pallet where she might easily reach it. Then she doused the light.

Blackness. It swooped over her like a blanket. Her skin crawled. Pictures of the ruffian spiraled through her head. She could almost hear his oily voice in her ear, feel his stinking breath against her cheek.

Dead. He's dead. Put him out of your mind. With shaking hands, she quickly divested herself of her clothing and drew on the nightgown. Then she all but dove under the covers, jerking them over her head and huddling. She hadn't done anything so ridiculous since early childhood. *Hiding from monsters, Rebecca?* She wanted to give herself a good shake, but even as she chided herself for being absurd, she shivered and burrowed deeper under the quilts.

Oh, lands! What was that? She went still and held her breath to listen. A creak. She'd definitely heard a creak. *The wind, Rebecca Ann. Nothing but the wind. Don't be any sillier than you must!* But the lecture to herself did little to soothe her frazzled nerves.

Race's deep voice drifted to her through the darkness, the smoky warmth of it curling around her. He was standing only a few feet away by the fire, close enough to hear if her stomach growled, for pity's sake. And he'd assured her he meant to sleep under the wagon. The chances were slim that anyone might sneak past him during the night. What had she to be afraid of?

What if he leaves camp?

The thought made her feel as if a steel band were tightening around her chest, making it difficult to breathe. She lay there, stiff with fear that had no basis in reason, and even worse, knowing it didn't. But the fear didn't abate. It was like a living thing with a vitality apart from her, its icy tentacles wrapping around her, the relentless grip impossible to break.

Rebecca had no idea how long she lay there. Minutes? Hours? Exhaustion made her thoughts fuzzy, and there was terror even in that, for she was afraid to sleep. She struggled to keep her eyes open, her mind forming horrible pictures of jerking awake to find a knife at her throat. She had to stay alert. Be ready. They were out there, even now.

And if they reached her, they would kill her . . .

Race had no idea how long he'd been crouched beside the fire alone. Two hours, possibly three? A number of the men were bedded down for the night, Corey, Johnny,

and Tag among them, their reclining bodies forming dark
lumps on the ground near the bedroll wagon. Race almost
wished Johnny were still hunkered by the fire with him,
chattering ceaselessly.

Instead Race was alone with his thoughts. He stared at
the base of the dancing flames where blue heat shimmered, the brilliant hue reminding him of Rebecca's eyes.
The delicate rose had her share of thorns, after all, he
thought with self-derision. Not that he blamed her for it.
It wasn't her fault that he felt so drawn to her. Prim and
proper, buttoned clear to her chin. She wasn't exactly a
temptress. And yet she tempted him in a way no other
woman ever had.

If that wasn't a hell of a note, he didn't know what
was. The one time in his life that he was responsible for
the welfare of a young woman, every time he looked into
her big blue eyes, he wanted to kiss her senseless and
loosen her braid so he could run his hands into her hair.
Christ. He kept trying to douse his feelings, but it was
impossible. He kept remembering how he'd felt while
holding her earlier that day—the tenderness, the ache in
his chest. In his recollection, no female he'd ever run
across had had this kind of effect on him. In short, he
wanted her, not only in a sexual way, but simply in his
arms as well, so he could hold her and protect her.

Craziness . . . He barely knew the girl, and if ever a female had been too fine for him, she was. Earlier when she'd
hugged him, he had damned near gotten tears in his eyes.
What in the hell was happening to him? No woman had
ever tugged on his heart as she did. He couldn't understand
it, let alone find an explanation for it. The feelings were just
there, and he seemed unable to set them aside.

In an attempt to stop thinking about her, Race turned
his thoughts to his cattle herd. Time after time tonight,
his men had walked into camp, their shoulders slumped
with defeat, to deliver more bad news. Bad news that
spelled Race's ruin, not to mention that of all his hired
hands. *That* was what he needed to be thinking about—
the ruination of his life and the fact that he would be
taking a lot of other men down with him.

A shuffle of footsteps coming toward camp brought Race's head up. Shifting his weight slightly so he could easily reach for his gun, he squinted to see into the shadows. A moment later, he saw Pete Standish entering camp, the butt of his rifle grasped in one hand, the barrel resting against his shoulder. A leather-faced, bow-legged little man, the ranch foreman had always reminded Race of a strip of beef jerky; small, dried up, and not much to look at, but more than a mouthful and too tough to chew if a man decided to take a bite.

As he moved toward the fire, Race took in the foreman's haggard face and filthy clothing, stark evidence of grueling hours spent in the saddle.

"Howdy." Pete drew to a stop next to the circle of stone, his wiry body taut to combat the weight of exhaustion. "That coffin varnish fresh?"

Race ran his gaze over Pete's bloodstained shirt and chaps, then brought it to rest on the man's arms. From the tips of Pete's leathery fingers to the rolled-up shirt sleeves at his elbows, his skin was caked with dry blood. Race knew the man had been slitting steers' throats— putting the animals down to end their suffering. Broken legs, usually. The bovines panicked in a stampede and ran blind, into gullies, pitching off banks into arroyos, stepping into gopher holes.

"You won't get coffee much fresher than this. I just made it," Race replied in a gravelly voice. Tugging a glove from his belt, he bent forward on one knee to lift the Arbuckle can. Pete met Race's reach midway over the flames, a tin cup clutched in his bloody fingers. "It'll burn the hair off your tongue, so watch it," Race warned.

"So long as it's hot. Mite nippy out there at this hour." Pete straightened, the battered tin cup cradled between his callused palms, his sun-baked, wrinkled face hovering scant inches away to catch the steam. "Boy, howdy, it do smell good."

Race didn't need Pete to tell him that he was so exhausted he could barely stand. He could see it in every line of the foreman's compact body. He returned the coffee can to the bed of coals. "What's the tally, Pete? How bad did we get hit?"

Pete pursed his mouth, deep lines fanning over his brown cheeks. His bleached-out blue eyes glittered like chips of ice as he met Race's gaze. "Over half."

Race's guts knotted, and a sinking sensation came into his chest. He had tried to prepare himself for the worst. But over half of his herd? Pete and all the men stood to lose money as well. Race had promised each of them a percentage of the profit if they were able to get the animals back to his ranch in time for the fall cattle auction on the first of October. Race knew Pete had to be feeling frustrated and deeply disappointed, but not a trace of that was evident in his voice or expression.

Not much say, but a lot of do, that was Pete, a trait apparent not only in his speech, but in his appearance. His faded chambray shirt and saddle-rubbed jeans had seen better days, his Colt .45 had a black, dull-finish grip, and the best that could be said for his gun belt, bat-wing chaps, and kip boots was that they were serviceable, the leather of all three dark with age and worn by hard use. Nothing about the man looked impressive. Yet he was one of the best horsemen Race had ever seen, a damned fine marksman, and, without question, the hardest working man in the outfit.

"I done my best," Pete said hollowly. "So did all the men." He grew quiet for a moment, his head cocked to listen to the constant lowing of the cattle. "Can't be much of a surprise. A body can tell by their bawlin' that their numbers is down considerable."

That was true, and Race had expected bad news. He just hadn't been thinking in terms of over half. "Yeah," he agreed. "I could tell." He recalled the decision he'd made earlier that day to forsake the cattle and stay with Rebecca, telling himself that to protect her life he would happily sacrifice his own. Well, he had sacrificed it, sure as God's favorite color was green. "Son of a bitch."

"You gonna go tits up?" Pete asked quietly.

"No go to it," Race bit out. "This finishes me. We only stood to make thirty percent profit after payin' off the bank loan that I got to buy the herd. If we lost over fifty percent of them, I'll be shy just tryin' to plank down on the debt.''

Pete nudged one of the rocks encircling the fire with the toe of his boot. ''Well, shee-it.''

''To settle with the bank, I'll have to dip into my savin's. And for a considerable amount. I'll have to lay off my men.'' He looked up at Pete. ''We'll tell 'em come mornin'. I got maybe enough to pay 'em until December, and that'll be it. Wouldn't be right, keepin' 'em on until then and lettin' 'em go in the dead of winter. Jobs are kinda scarce when the snow's hip-deep.''

Pete stared into his coffee cup. ''I sure hate like hell to see it.'' His jaw muscle ticked. ''The *bastards!* I swear, every time we'd get them critters soothed down, one of them sons of bitches would fire off a rifle ag'in. Twenty-nine head run themselves to death. Poor dumb things.''

Race closed his eyes. There were few things more horrible than to see a steer that had run until its heart burst. ''I'm real sorry I ain't been out there helpin' you, old son. Must have been one terrible day.''

Pete released a weary sigh. ''You had your work cut out for ya here. And you're right. I seen some bad'uns in my time. But today took the prize, I think.'' The foreman took a loud slurp of coffee. ''How's the girl holdin' up? I hear she come damned close to bein' raped and gettin' her throat slit. Must've been tough on her, comin' so fast on the heels of that slaughter in the arroyo.''

Race bit down hard on his back teeth for a moment. ''It was rough on her, no question. I didn't help matters.''

About to take another sip of coffee, Pete hesitated, his washed-out blue eyes cutting Race a questioning look over the rim of the cup. ''What's that mean?''

Race locked gazes with him. ''When I shot the bastard, he fell right on top of her. Blood all over her. Scared the devil out of me, thinkin' I'd sent her back into shock.''

The words hung in the predawn quiet. Pete's hollowed cheeks seemed to become more sunken, the facial muscles under his weathered skin stretching tight over the bones. ''How's she doin' now?''

"Better. Pretty froggy, I think. But she don't seem willin' to admit it."

"What do you think them bastards is after?"

"Money. What else?" As briefly as he could, Race recounted the story Rebecca had told him. "Somehow the plug-uglies found out they were transporting cash."

"And you figure they'll be back."

Race sighed. "Knowin' that kinda trash, they'll keep on until they get their hands on it or until they're dead."

Pete slowly dropped into a hunker to be at Race's eye level. "Dead's my vote. I reckon that means we'll have to be on our toes. Unless she's made of steel, that girl can't take much more. We gotta make sure they don't get to her again."

"They won't," Race said in a dangerously silken voice. "I guarant-ass-tee it." He smiled slightly. "She offered to cover my losses if I'd go get the money."

"What'd you say?"

Race shrugged. "I wouldn't feel right about takin' it. A lot of folks died for it, for one thing, and then it belongin' to a church, to boot."

Pete chewed on that for several seconds. "I reckon I'd feel the same way." He dug in his back pocket for his plug. After tearing a chunk of tobacco off with his teeth, he returned the plug to his pocket, one cheek puffed as he worked his mouth for spit. "Well, let's just be glad we only lost cows. Coulda been worse. Might still be yet. I bet you've a good mind to go huntin' plug-uglies with blood in your eye."

"If it wasn't for the girl, I would. But I don't wanna leave her."

Pete nodded. "After today, I can't say I blame you." A speculative look came over his face. "You're uncommon fond of her, ain't you?"

Race bent his head and pinched the bridge of his nose. "Yeah, I reckon I am. Don't ask me why. I can't explain it." He glanced up. "She's a sweet little thing. And you can tell straightaway that she ain't puttin' on. She truly is what she seems to be."

Pete winked. "You been hit hard. Way you're lookin',

maybe you oughta take your losses out in trade.''

Race chuckled. ''With Rebecca?'' He shook his head. ''She ain't that kind. Couldn't touch it for no amount of money. The only man who'll ever lay a hand on that girl will be her husband.''

Pete arched an eyebrow. ''You best watch your step, boss. You got a look in your eye I don't recollect ever seein' afore.''

''Yeah?'' Race thought that over for a second. ''Well, I'm feelin' like I ain't never felt. There's somethin' real special about her.''

''All the more reason to watch your step with her.''

''Watch his step with who?''

Both Race and Pete glanced up to see a sleepy-eyed Tag stepping up to the fire. The boy's face was streaked with dirt, his hair stiff with dust and standing on end. He fastened curious, big gray eyes on Pete. ''You fellas talking about females?'' Tag said ''females'' as if it were a dirty word. ''Seems to me that's all any of you talk about. Johnny and Corey, now you and the boss. I think it's a waste of time. What's so special about girls? All they do is fuss.''

Pete winked. ''As you git older, son, they start to kinda grow on ya.''

''I didn't think you liked them none too well,'' Tag observed.

Pete chuckled. ''Well, now, I reckon I don't, truth to tell. Not where's I wanna rub elbows with one over long. But I don't mind the occasional handshake.''

Tag wrinkled his nose.

''What're you doin' up, tyke?'' Race asked.

''I'm not a tyke.''

''Sorry. Old man, then.''

Tag scratched under his arm. ''I swear, them dead steers got fleas on me.''

''We'll head out come mornin','' Race assured him. ''You can bathe when we hit the river.''

''Sounds good.'' Tag yawned and turned from the fire. ''I gotta go see a man about a dog.''

''Stay close,'' Race called. ''Wearin' that light-colored

shirt, I don't want you wanderin' off from camp.''

"I won't."

Race gazed after the boy for a long moment, his smile fading. ''I'm gonna hate like hell havin' to lay him off,'' he told Pete. ''Don't know what his mama will do without his pay comin' in each month.''

Pete sighed. ''We'll work it out. A good number of the men'll probably volunteer to stay on without pay till you get back on your feet. You're a fair man, and good jobs is hard to come by in this line of work.''

Pete had no sooner finished speaking than the blast of a rifle rent the air. Both he and Race dove for the dirt. When Race sprang back into a crouch, he'd already drawn his guns. He swung his gaze over the camp. His men were leaping to their feet over by the bedroll wagon and scrambling for their weapons.

''It came in close,'' Pete whispered as he duck-walked toward Race, his gun arm swinging first right, then left to cover his boss's back. ''Don't think it was aimed at us, though.''

Race's heart caught. ''Jesus!'' He pushed to his feet. ''Oh, sweet Jesus, no!'' He broke into a run. ''Tag? Tag!''

No answer. Just an awful silence stretching beyond the wagons where the boy had disappeared. Race felt as if he were slogging hip-deep through cold mush, his every stride agonizingly slow, the short distance stretching before him like a thousand miles. To the edge of camp. Past the wagons. Out into the darkness.

Where? He cut left, then veered back to the right, his gaze scanning the grass and bushes. ''Tag! Answer me, damn it! Where are you? Tag? Sing out, son, so I can—''

Race reeled to a stop, barely preventing himself from stepping on the boy's arm. Tag lay sprawled on the grass, face in the dirt. Race dropped as if someone had dealt a blow to the backs of his legs.

Hiding, he thought dazedly. That was it. Tag had been scared by the rifle shot, that was all. And he was just hiding.

Race grasped a thin shoulder to turn the boy over. "Hey, Tag. It's all right. You can get up now and come back to—"

Even in the darkness, Race could see the splash of shiny wetness on the front of the kid's shirt. He grabbed the boy's other arm to sit him up. "No. Tag?" Tag's sleep-tousled head flopped sideways. Race found himself staring into unseeing big gray eyes that had been filled with life and intelligence only minutes before. Blood trickled from the boy's lax mouth. "Oh, Jesus, no," Race whispered. "Oh, God, no. No!"

And then he screamed it. *"No—oo-o!"*

Chapter 12

Wind whistled across the grasslands, blowing particles of dirt into Rebecca's eyes as the men filled Tag's grave. She blinked, seeing everything through a stinging blur of tears, but didn't bother to rub away the burn. Pain seemed real, at least. Nothing else did. A gust caught her skirts, whipping them high to reveal her petticoats. If the men around her had the presence of mind to look, let them. What did it matter? Nothing seemed to matter anymore.

Numb. No arms, no legs, no feet. The one thing she could feel was the huge aching emptiness where her chest should have been, a vacuum that compressed her lungs, making it difficult to breathe.

Her mother . . . her father . . . Uncle Luke and Aunt Hester . . . and all of the others. Now an innocent twelve-year-old boy. Was this land that had held so much promise in faraway Pennsylvania just a place haunted by death and failure?

She would never forget the look on Race Spencer's face last night when he'd come back to camp, carrying that skinny, half-grown body in his arms. Twelve years old. Rebecca hadn't known Tag, had never even seen him until that horrible moment when she had rushed across the encampment as Race laid him by the fire. Yet she felt as if her heart had been ripped out.

Race had refused to let her touch the boy. Refused to let anyone touch him. He just kept saying, over and over, "I promised. Dear God, I promised." Later Mr. Grigsley had whispered to Rebecca that Race was referring to Tag's mother—that Race had promised her that he would look after Tag and keep him safe.

God help him, he'd tried. They'd all tried—all of those hard-bitten, hard-riding, well-meaning men. And then along had come Rebecca Morgan, as devastating as any plague. Without meaning to, she had brought nothing but grief to Race Spencer and his men. Financially, he was ruined because of her. His men were out of jobs, or soon would be—because of her. From what she'd been able to gather, he would be letting all of them go as soon as they reached his ranch with the pathetic remnants of his herd. His dog, the pet he so clearly loved, was clinging to life by a thread, which was all her fault. His cook was so battered that he could scarcely walk—because the feisty old man had tried to defend her. And now . . . now a young boy, who'd never done anything to anyone, had been shot down in cold blood. That was the worst of all. The very worst.

Rebecca bit her lip and dashed her trembling fingers over her wet cheeks. Somehow a ruffian had slipped past the guards who'd been riding in a circle around camp since early yesterday. Even more horrible, all the men had been so frantic to save the child that the killer had slipped away before anyone thought to go look for him.

Now here they were . . . gathered at a grave in this endless expanse of nothingness, their faces haggard, their eyes rimmed with red, either from exhaustion, or from the endless grit blowing around, or from tears they'd secretly shed. Broken promises and broken hearts. A bright-eyed, full-of-life boy struck down before he'd even had a chance to experience life. And it seemed to Rebecca that the nightmare would never end.

She wished she could speak to Race Spencer, perhaps console him as he had her. Inside, where no one could see, she ached to tell him how very, very sorry she was. But most of all, she wished she could assure him he wasn't to blame for any of this.

It was her fault. All her fault. Only hers. Her mind stuttered over the pain. And the guilt. If only Race would shout at her. Or treat her with the scorn she deserved.

It amazed her that none of these men had pointed a finger at her yet. Were they all blind? They still watched over her, still treated her courteously. Even Race Spencer, who looked ravaged and hollowed out, whose eyes had become burning orbs of pain in his dark face, still guarded her safety, assigning another man to stay near her if he couldn't remain with her himself.

All of them . . . poor, ignorant fools that they were . . . guarding and protecting the evil that had come among them.

Since Tag's death, Rebecca had been able to think of little else. Last night after everything had quieted down, she'd sat by the fire for hours, agonizing over what she should do.

Death was all around her. The air itself seemed thick with it. So thick she could scarcely breathe. On her skin. Clinging to her hair. The taste of it on the back of her tongue. *Death.* Nearly a hundred and fifty steers, *dead.* Seventeen human beings, counting the ruffians, *dead.* Possibly more. She had no idea how many other ruffians might have died in the arroyo. Then there was poor old Blue, who might die yet.

Death . . . all around her. Hovering, stalking, like a ravening beast.

At some point during the night, the truth had finally come to her. It was so clear to her now—so horribly clear. This wasn't going to stop. Death could not be cheated, and it had come here to collect its due.

She could scarcely believe that none of these men had figured it out. Rebecca Morgan, the sniveling coward. She had fled and hidden in the brush, covering her ears, closing her eyes, ignoring the screams of everyone she loved, her one concern to save herself. She should have died in the arroyo with everyone else. If not for her unforgivable cowardice, she *would* have died with everyone else. It was obvious. Wasn't it? Why would one person out of so many be spared? One lone survivor? She had lived, and everyone else had died.

She was marked. That was the truth of it. She had escaped death, slipped out of its clutches. And now it was following her. A skeletal specter like she'd seen in picture books Elder Ames had shown her once, trying to claim its own, determined to claim its own. And she was still hiding, managing to slip from its clutches, letting others be sacrificed in her place. This wouldn't stop until she surrendered. It was as simple and terrifying as that, the most horrible part being that she was such a coward, she couldn't bring herself to do it.

Every time the shovel rasped as it was plunged into the dirt, she felt as if it cut through her chest. The blade driving in. The fall of dirt. Then the rasp again. The sounds whispered in her mind. *Rebecca.* Then the fall of dirt. *Rebecca.* And another fall of dirt. She stared down into the grave, her vision blurred with tears, glad she couldn't see clearly, for to see was to feel shame that ran so deep she could scarcely bear it.

She wanted to throw herself on the ground and beg that boy for his forgiveness.

Vaguely aware of sudden movement around her, Rebecca blinked and tried to focus. The grave had been filled in and the men were gathering closer. She struggled to concentrate on what they were saying and realized they were attempting to pray in their clumsy, illiterate way. The echo of their voices penetrated the blur of unreality, and an hysterical urge to laugh struck her. They knew not a single prayer in its entirety.

"*Our Father who art in heaven.*" That voice trailed away. Another chimed in with, "*Give us our daily bread.*" Someone else said, "*Jesus, McNaught, ask for more'n just bread. Beans, maybe.*"

Rebecca blinked and rubbed her eyes. Blinked again. As the figures around her came into focus, she gaped at them. *Beans?* A joke, surely. Only none of them was smiling. Drawn faces, haunted eyes. All of them were staring helplessly at the mound of dirt.

She looked at Race Spencer, who seemed unaware of what was being said around him. He stood at the opposite side of the grave, his legs braced wide apart, and for the first time since she'd known him, his arms hung limply at his sides, his hands nowhere near his guns.

The wind sucked his black shirt to his torso and whipped his midnight hair across his face, the strands catching on his lips, drifting into his eyes. He stared down at the grave almost sightlessly, a man alone, cast against a backdrop of parched green and sun-baked yellow, his grief stark in his expression.

"My ma used to say the Hell Mary," Johnny offered. "I can recollect some of it."

Mr. Grigsley sniffed. "That's a good'un."

The only man present, aside from Race, who had removed his hat, Johnny stepped up to the foot of the grave, his mouth quivering and tears filling his eyes. He made what Rebecca surmised was supposed to be a sign of the cross, his fingertips touching his forehead, bypassing his shoulders, and dropping directly to his chest. Then he stood, turning his hat in his hands, his throat muscles convulsing. "Hell Mary," he said in a taut voice. "Filled with grace and better than all other women. And blessed is your baby, Jesus. Pray for us sinners. Amen."

"That's a good'un," Mr. Grigsley said again. One eye still swollen shut, his face a mass of purple and blue bruises above his gray beard, he brushed a tear from his battered cheek. "I don't recollect no prayers, and I feel right bad that I don't, Lord, 'cause this here boy was a good'un and oughta be sent off right." He sniffed. "But I reckon you know that. About how good he was, and all. So I don't need to be tellin' you. I'd just ask that you treat him real fine up there, and don't let no highfalutin folks be holdin' the poor sendoff ag'in him. It ain't his fault he rubbed elbows with such dumb son'bucks. Amen."

Corey pushed his white-blond hair from his eyes. "I know a supper blessing. I could take out the food part."

Rebecca's eyes filled with tears again, only this time not from dirt. She had resolutely refused to pray these last two days. Just the thought of trying made her feel nauseated. If there was a God, He had betrayed her and everyone she loved. Her parents had entrusted their lives to Him, had counted on Him to protect them. Every time she remembered how her father had held his Bible up before him as if it were a shield, she burned with anger.

But that was her. These men wanted to pray, *needed* to pray. It was important to them to say the right words over this boy whom they had loved. If she could give them that, it seemed the least she could do, even if she had to force out every word.

"Would you like me to say the Lord's Prayer?" she offered.

Johnny turned aching blue eyes on her. After staring at her for several seconds, he said, "Would you do that for us, ma'am? We'd all be right appreciative."

Rebecca folded her hands, her gaze fixed on the mound of dirt. "Let us pray."

She flicked a glance at her companions. Everyone except Race Spencer, who seemed off in a world of his own, was staring at her. Not a bowed head in the bunch. Rebecca nearly commenced, convinced the outward postures weren't really important. But then it occurred to her that what these poor souls craved was some ceremony.

She felt sure her legs would refuse to bend. But she would kneel. For them. What she felt in her heart didn't matter. All that counted were the words, the pretense.

She dropped clumsily to her knees. Johnny, who stood closest to her right, made a grab for her, as if he thought she were falling. At the last second, he jerked his hand back and muttered, "Oh, yeah."

Coughs. Throat clearing. Boots shuffling. Joints cracking. She scanned the group. Everyone but Race Spencer had gone to his knees.

"Don't pay no mind to the boss," Mr. Grigsley told her in a half-whisper. "He's doin' his own prayin'."

For a moment, Rebecca gazed at the man at the opposite side of the grave, searching his expression. All she could see was pain—the kind that went too deep for prayers or tears. She wondered if he was going to be all right.

She gulped, then drew her gaze back to her audience. "Your hats, gentlemen."

Blank gazes. The insides of her cheeks were stuck to her teeth.

"You need to remove your hats." Bewilderment. "As a sign of respect," she expounded. "Much as you might remove your hat in the presence of a lady." Judging by the looks they gave her, none of them had ever done that, either. "It's customary," she assured them.

Mr. Grigsley jerked his hat off and shot Johnny a glare. "How come you didn't remind me! I don't know how we coulda forgot that part."

Hats came off. Grimy fingers combed through sweat-dampened hair, stirring up cowlicks of every conceivable color. Rebecca made a show of bowing her head. "Shall we pray?"

"Yes'm," chorused several deep voices.

Rebecca stared down at her folded hands. Clenched her fingers, then relaxed them. "Holy Father, we gather here this morning to say our final farewells to Tag—" She glanced up.

"Jones," Mr. Grigsley inserted.

"To say our final farewells to Tag Jones," Rebecca continued, "a young boy who was friend to most of us, a stranger to me, but whose passing greatly grieves us all." A lump rose in her throat. She had to gulp it down to go on. "To lose a loved one is never easy, Lord."

"It sure as hell ain't," someone muttered in a choked voice.

She could do this. Rebecca swallowed then grabbed for breath. "It's especially difficult when it's someone so young."

Mr. Grigsley said, "I'd switch places with him in a blink. Ain't fair. It just ain't fair."

It *wasn't* fair, Rebecca thought. Why this boy, when it should have been her?

"As sometimes happens," she went on shakily, "Tag Jones was struck down by a violent hand, an innocent who fell prey to the vagaries of Fate. Human as we are and of limited"—she skimmed the down-turned faces all around her—"and of limited knowledge, it is so very difficult to accept that which we cannot understand and to find peace with that beyond our comprehension. So it is, heavenly Father, that we come to you as little children ourselves to commend the soul of this child, Tag Jones, into your gentle and loving hands.

"In keeping with the teachings of your son, Jesus Christ, our prayer to you in behalf of our dearly departed, Tag Jones, shall be expressed with the words He taught us." Rebecca then began to recite the words of the Lord's Prayer. When she came to, "Give us this day, our daily bread," she looked up to find expectant gazes fixed on her. For the sake of easing hearts, she ad-libbed, tacking on, "plenty of beans, fresh lean meat, and all manner of other good things to eat."

"He truly loved his peppermint sticks," Corey informed her helpfully.

"And an unending supply of peppermint sticks," she added before finishing the prayer. "Amen."

Mr. McNaught grasped Rebecca's arm to assist her to her feet. She rubbed her palms on her skirt.

"That was right fine," Mr. Grigsley said. "Ain't nobody ever gonna get a nicer sendoff than that."

Rebecca couldn't speak. It was as if the prayer had sucked her empty. She touched McNaught's sleeve to thank him for his gentlemanly assistance, then turned and struck off for camp, too tormented to care that she would be alone and defenseless once she got there. Indeed, she wished the ruffians would be there, that all of this could simply end, saving her the agony of having to bring an end to it herself.

"I've heard of some lowdown, rotten things," Pete cried as he approached the grave. "But this beats all!"

Jerked from his misery by the fury in Pete's voice, Race looked up to see who the foreman was angry with. He was surprised to find that Pete's glinting, pale blue eyes were fixed, not on any of the other men, but directly on him. "For God's sake, Pete, whatever's eatin' you, now ain't the time. I'm not finished here."

Pete jabbed a finger in Race's direction, fairly sputtering, he was so mad. "It ain't like she meant to bring this to our door, goddamn it! I know it ain't easy on you, losin' the boy like this, and I can see you feelin' sorta grizzly bearish. But, by God, sendin' her off like that is just plain *lowdown*."

"Sendin' her off?"

Pete doubled his hand into a fist. Race half expected the wiry little man to come over the grave after him. "They'll kill her, sure as I breathe, you stupid son of a bitch!"

"Rebecca, you mean?"

Pete jammed his hands on his hips. "Who'n hell you think? Of course, Rebecca! I tried to talk sense to her. But she ain't hearin' a word of it. Got her orders from the head man, she said, and off she went! If you don't step fancy, we'll be diggin' another grave this day, mark my words! And her blood'll be on your hands!"

Race's stomach dropped. "Went?" he said hoarsely. He cast a frightened glance toward camp. "Went where?"

"God knows! She's just goin'. I don't think she knows where herself. Not talkin' good sense! But who can blame her. Losin' everybody like that, and then bein' sent off by the only folks she's got left. I wouldn't be thinkin' clear, either."

Race took off at a run, Pete trailing behind him and yelling every step of the way. "It's a damned good thing I followed her when she left the grave." Huff, huff. "Knowed as soon as I got to camp that her deck was all shuffled. Talkin' loco." Huff, huff. "Tearin' hell outta the chuck wagon. Emptied the salt bag and writ somethin' on it with a burnt stick! Me tryin' to talk sense to her the whole time." Pant, pant. "I just plain can't believe you sent her off thataway!"

Race staggered to a stop when he reached the center of camp, his gaze darting in all directions. "I didn't send her off!"

Pete planted his hands on his knees and struggled to catch his breath. "You sure as shit must've! Got her send-off from the head man, she said."

"That's not true. She actually said that?"

"Well, not in them exact words. Goin' on about that

money too. Yours to do with whichever way you want, she said. Writ it all down for ya on the salt sack.''

"Which way?" Race demanded. "Which direction did she go, Pete?"

Pete pointed, and Race took off running again.

It took Race twenty minutes to find her, and when he finally did, he wasn't sure whether he wanted to hug the breath out of her or tan her backside. Of all the times for her to get a maggot in her brain and go wandering off. Tag not cold in his grave. Killers possibly behind every bush.

She sat at the top of a slope, the brisk morning wind whipping the hem of her skirt and tossing the curls that had escaped her braid. As Race approached her from behind, he said, "What in *hell* do you think you're doin'!"

He expected her to jump out of her skin, which would have at least given him some sense of satisfaction. Instead she glanced calmly over her shoulder, scanned him with a flick of her blue eyes, and resumed staring out over the grasslands. "Oh, hello, Mr. Spencer."

She sounded almost bored. Pain exploded behind his eyes. His heart had crawled damned near up to his mouth, and she said, "Hello," as if she were on the brink of yawning. He no longer had any doubt. He wanted to blister her fanny. Hand to bare ass, blister her until she couldn't sit down for a month.

Swallowing back curses, he bore down on her. "*What* in the *world* do you think you're *doin'*?" he yelled, grabbing hold of her arm. "If there's one thing I don't need it's to be standin' over another grave today, feelin' like my guts is bein' tore out."

He jerked her to her feet, intending to jar her teeth. He was a bit more successful in the attempt than he set out to be. She didn't weigh much and parted company with the ground more easily than he expected, slamming against his chest, bouncing off, and staggering backward. He caught her by the shoulders to keep her from sprawling, his anger losing its steam. As soon as he determined that he hadn't hurt her, he started rebuilding pressure.

"You crazy little *fool!* You gotta death wish, or somethin'? Them plug-uglies would kill you without turnin" a hair!"

She gazed up at him with a calm, completely unruffled expression that sent a chill down his spine. "I hope they do it quickly. Do you suppose there's any chance of that?"

The icy feeling that danced up his spine radiated outward as if he'd been caught squarely in the back with five gallons of cold water, dousing his anger, blanking his mind for an instant. He stood there, hands clamped on her limp arms, staring down at her white face in stunned disbelief. In that moment, Race couldn't remember the last time he'd really looked at her and registered what he saw. At some point yesterday, he guessed. Last night, the light hadn't been that good for the most part, and later in the wagon, he'd been preoccupied with getting her settled.

What he saw now scared the ever-loving hell right out of him. Her small face was so white that a corpse would have had better color. The dark smudges he'd noticed yesterday under her eyes had turned bluish-gray. With the bruise along her cheek from where the ruffian had struck her, she looked as if she'd been beaten.

"Come on, sweetheart," he said softly. "Let me take you back to camp."

She tried to peel one of his hands from her arm. "Please, Mr. Spencer, you don't understand. I have to do this now."

"Do what now?" He was almost afraid to hear her answer.

"Let it happen," she said, her voice barely more than a whisper. "Before someone else gets hurt. If I put it off, I'll lose my nerve."

Race was starting to get a really bad feeling. "Rebecca, what are you—"

As if he wasn't speaking, she turned her head to gaze out over the flatland. "It's not going to stop. Don't you see that? Not until I make it stop."

When she tried to pull away, he released her arms, then trailed behind her, leaning around to watch her face as she wandered along the crown of the slope, the overlong hém of her skirt snagging on the grass. "I'm not supposed to be here. You can't change the way things are meant to be. That's what I did. I ran and escaped it. And now it has come for me."

The hair stood up at the back of Race's neck and he shot a wary glance around. "What's come for you, honey?"

"Death," she said dispassionately. "You can't cheat death. I was supposed to die in the arroyo."

The bad feeling Race had been starting to get was quickly becoming an awful understanding. "Sweetheart," he said, injecting a reasoning tone into his voice, "if you was supposed to die in the arroyo, you'd be gone coon."

"No. I ran." She glanced up at him, her eyes haunted. "I never told you all about that, did I?" A muscle near her mouth began to jerk. "Little wonder. What I did was—it was shameful."

"Running, you mean?" Race ran a hand over his hair. "Rebecca, running is all that saved your life!"

"Yes."

Just that one word. Hollow, yet filled with a world of heartache. He circled it cautiously, trying to make sense of what she was trying to say. "And now you think you're bein' punished?"

"No. Gathered. Or perhaps collected is a better word. Death always takes its due."

Gathered?

She looked up at him. "I was marked to die. Don't you see? Everyone else. All of them. I'm the only one who survived. Why would I be chosen as the lucky one?"

Gazing down at her, Race could think of a thousand reasons, none of which he felt he should share with her at that moment. He thought of Tag and imagined her lying in a hole next to him. He wanted to slap her. Shake her. Grab hold of her and never let go. What in God's name was she thinking?

"The fact is, I wasn't chosen," she continued, her mouth beginning to quiver again as she formed each word. "I'm alive only because I'm the worst kind of a coward."

His guts clenched at the look on her face. "Rebecca," he whispered, "you ain't no coward." He recalled how she'd walked out to warn him about the ruffians, how afraid she'd been to tell him the truth. "Trust me on that. I know better."

She held up a hand. "No. You weren't there. I'm a coward. You've no idea." Tears filled her eyes. "They were all screaming, begging for help. My mother . . ." She gulped, and her face seemed to dissolve, like wax melting in the sun, before she gathered herself together again. "And . . . and I ran. I hid in some bushes. Shut my eyes. Covered my ears. While they all faced death, I hid from it. Don't you see? Death won't be cheated."

A horrible urge to laugh came over him. Only this wasn't funny. She was serious. "Rebecca, death don't take potshots, then say, 'Oh, shit, I missed and got the wrong fella!' That's what you're sayin', ain't it? That death is huntin' you down and has bad aim."

She closed her eyes, and her face twisted as sobs began to jerk her shoulders. "It's me. Don't you see? That boy. He's dead because of me. All because of me." She bent slightly at the waist and pressed a fist between her breasts. Her sobs were horrible. "I can't *bear* it. It'll happen again. It will. I have to make it stop!"

Race grabbed her by the shoulders and gave her a hard shake. Her eyes snapped wide and she stared up at him in stunned bewilderment.

"Tag is dead because some lowdown, heartless son of a bitch shot him. *That's* why Tag is dead! Because the world's full of snakes pretendin' to be men. *That's* why he's dead. It don't have nothin' to do with you. You ain't marked, for God's sake! And you're not a coward. What was you s'posed to do, Rebecca? One small woman against sixteen men. Run out into the thick of it so the bastards could rape you? So they could slit your throat?"

"I should have *helped* my parents!" she cried, knotting her hands into fists at her sides. "I should have *tried*!"

"How?" Race knew he was yelling. But he couldn't

seem to stop. She'd come out here to die. Making a target of herself. Hoping those bastards would come for her. And it was nothing short of a miracle that they hadn't. "Listen to yourself! How could you have helped them? Name me one way!" He gave her another little shake. "You think you can take on a grown man? That's plumb silly. You don't even have the know-how to shoot a gun. What was you gonna do, take after 'em with a switch?"

"I could've"—she brought up a fist and thumped his chest—"*hit* them! I should've *hit* them! Bit them! Kicked them! *Fought* them! With everything I had! With all my *strength*!" She drew back and struck his chest again. "My mother! Oh, God! My *mother*! She *screamed*! She screamed and screamed." With a broken sob, she pummeled his chest and shoulders frenziedly, delivering a rash of punches. "She screamed my *name*! God forgive me. Oh, God! She screamed my *name*! And I covered my ears!"

Race scarcely felt her blows. But what she was saying nearly took him to his knees, every word breaking his heart. He understood now. Why she had come to this knoll. Why she looked as if someone had blacked both of her eyes. Why she'd been in shock when he found her. God help them both, he understood, and wished he didn't.

"Honey, listen to me. Listen, all right? There was nothin' you could've done. Nothin'! Save die beside her. You did what came natural. It's instinct to run if stayin' means you're gonna die! You think I wouldn't? Think again. I woulda left you to eat my dust."

"You *liar*!" She punched his shoulder again. "*You* wouldn't have run! You would have *fought*! If she'd screamed *your* name, you would have tried to save her!"

"If I was armed, damned straight! But you wasn't."

"Don't!" She held up her hands as if to block out the sound of his voice. "Even without guns, you would have fought them. Tried, anyway. With your *fists* if nothing else!"

"And you think you should've? That just plain don't make sense. With your fists, Rebecca? You really think you can belly up to a man? No way. He'd knock you into next week. Turn you every which way but loose!''

"You don't know that. Not for sure! I could've *tried*! I could've done *something*!''

Race could see she wasn't registering anything he said to her. In one ear and out the other. *Christ Almighty.* The guilt was tearing her apart, eating her alive. *She screamed my name, and I covered my ears!*

He bent and caught her behind the knees with one arm. When he tossed her over his shoulder, she shrieked. That was fine. He meant to startle her. Meant to scare the hell out of her, in fact.

"*What*!—You put me *down*! What're you—''

He jostled her to get a better hold. "Be still! Start throwin' yourself, and I'll drop you on your fool head!''

As he struck off toward camp, she made fists over the back of his belt to lever herself up. "Where—? *What* do you think you're *doing*?''

That was a damned good question. He was tempted to stop and put her down. Just because she'd gone loco didn't mean he had to go with her. But if he put her down, then what? The first time he turned his back, would she be here again, hoping to die? Hell, yes. As long as she had those crazy thoughts in her head, she wouldn't feel she deserved to live, and he couldn't say he'd blame her.

He had to do something—even if it was wrong.

"Where are you going?''

Lengthening his strides to carry them closer to camp where he at least knew he had men riding guard, he said, "I'm lookin' for a patch of soft grass.''

Her voice breaking with every bounce of his stride, she said, "So-o-ft gra-aa-ass?''

"I gotta a bad knee. When I rape a woman, I gotta do it on soft grass.''

Silence. Then a shrill, "*What?*''

At least he had her undivided attention. He saw Preach in the distance, riding circle, and lifted a hand. Preach swung his Stetson above his head to return the greeting. Race veered in that direction, Rebecca swinging back and forth over his shoulder like a burlap bag filled with hissing and spitting cats.

Preach, seeing that Race was heading toward him, wheeled his sorrel and rode to meet him. Race waited until horse and rider were nearly upon him, then gave his hired hand an exaggerated wink, after which he reached up and gave Rebecca's upturned fanny a friendly pat and squeeze. She made a sound that sounded like a cross between the bray of a jackass and one of Cookie's snorts.

"Hey, there, Preach!" *Pat, squeeze.* "I gotta favor to ask. You reckon you can ride circle for a bit, right around this here spot? Off a ways, of course, to give us some privacy?"

"You put me *down!*" she shrieked. She shoved harder on his belt and swung up, trying to see Preach. "This man has lost his mind! Tell him to put me down this *instant!*"

Preach gave Race a long, hard look. Then he smiled slightly. "Well, now, ma'am. Him bein' the boss, he don't take orders from me any too good." He turned a twinkling eye on Rebecca, who'd lost her grip on Race's belt and was back to dangling upside down again. In a lower voice, he said, "What'n hell are you up to, boss?"

Race patted her on the fanny again. "Well, it appears I gotta prove a point to this young lady. She's from Missouri. One of them mule-headed folks that's gotta learn every damned thing the hard way."

One of Preach's eyebrows shot up. "You don't say."

"Mr. Spencer! You—put—me—down—this—*instant!* If you don't, mark my words, you shall live to regret it!"

"Darlin', I told you, I gotta bad knee. First I gotta find soft grass." Race gave Preach another wink, then started walking again. Rebecca thumped him on the hip. When that didn't get his attention, she made another awful sound, and then he felt her trying her damnedest to bite the small of his back. He whacked her on the rump, putting enough force into the swat to make it sting. "Don't you dare bite me."

"*Ouch!*" She twisted and swung. "You let me down! I swear, if you don't end this foolishness this minute, I'll—"

"You'll what?"

"I'll report you!"

"When you reach Denver, you be sure to do just that very thing!"

She hung limp for several seconds, saying nothing. Then he heard her release a long-suffering sigh. "I know what you're trying to do, Mr. Spencer," she informed him, her voice jiggling with his every step. "And I appreciate the thought behind the gesture, even though I disapprove of your tactics. But it won't work. You're not a ruffian, first of all. So you see, the correlation you hope to draw isn't—"

"The what?"

"The—oh, never *mind!* Truly, this is *very* sweet. I don't think anyone has ever gone to such lengths to make me feel better before, but I'm telling you, it won't work."

She had stopped sobbing. That was a leg up. "It ain't like I'm goin' to a lot of bother. Makin' love to you might be a hair more taxin'. A man's gotta put some effort into that. It ain't like that with rape, though. Lot of fun for him, not much for her."

She sighed again, loudly, the sound stuttering with each bounce. "I'm not in the least afraid of you, Mr. Spencer. Yesterday morning, this may have worked. But I assure you, it shan't today! You're nothing if not kind and caring, and I know it. You'd never harm me. Not in a hundred years."

"Horny as a three-pronged goat. That's what I am. *Damn.* If I don't find a soft spot soon, I'm gonna be plumb tuckered before I get to the fun part."

"Oh, *bother!*"

He chuckled. "You don't think I mean to do it, do ya?"

"Well, of *course* not! Which is why this won't work. I know very well you're not about to hurt me, which means I shan't be afraid of you no matter how fiercely you snarl, which means that I shan't fight you as I would a ruffian. Which brings us back to my point, no correlation!"

Race slung her off of his shoulder, angling an arm up her back to break her fall just enough that she wouldn't be hurt, but not enough to prevent a landing that gave her a good hard jolt. She blinked in startlement. He followed her down, vising her hips between his knees.

As he captured both of her wrists in the grip of one hand and reached to unbuckle his belt, he said, "Honey, you got it all wrong. You ain't gonna fight me at all. In case you ain't noticed, I'm a hell of a lot bigger than you."

"Exactly," she said, looking up at him as if he weren't too smart. "I shan't fight you. So what is the point?"

Race gazed deeply into her blue eyes, almost as pleased by the trust in him that he saw there as he was surprised by it. Unfortunately, it didn't exactly serve him well at the moment. "You ain't real savvy, are you, darlin'?"

Belt unbuckled, he sat back and gazed down at her with what he prayed was a lecherous grin pasted on his mouth. Her eyes widened when he reached to unbutton her bodice. "Mr. Spencer, it *is* possible to carry this too far."

"Not a chance. I done it enough times to know when I'm finished." Two buttons, three. He thanked God she had so many buttons. "Now this is what we're gonna do," he said, looking deeply into her eyes again. "I'm gonna hold you down and have myself a real fine time, and you pretty much won't. And when you figure that out and start tryin' to get away, that's when you learn a hard fact. Which is there ain't a goddamned thing on this green earth you can do to stop me. You understand how it's gonna go now?"

The clear blue of her eyes darkened slightly as he unfastened the fourth button. They darkened considerably more with the fifth and sixth. By the eighth, she was beginning to look a little panicked.

A little panicked wouldn't quite get the job done. He avoided looking into her eyes again. Everything in him rebelled against doing this. But, damn it, he had to. At this point, he didn't care if she hated his guts for it. Anything to get that pain out of her eyes. And talking sense to her sure as hell wasn't going to do that.

Race parted the front plackets of her dress. "You sure are a pretty little piece of baggage. I think I'm gonna have more fun doin' this than I thought." He trailed his fingertips along the neckline of her exposed chemise. ''Oh, yeah.''

She bucked. And he had to hand it to her, she put more strength into it than he would have given her credit for, almost unseating him. Then she surprised him yet again by twisting a hand free from his grasp. *Slash*. She caught him with her fingernails at the corner of his eye and ripped her way along his jaw.

''Ouch!'' Race reared back and grabbed for his face. Bad mistake. In the process, he relaxed his grip on her other wrist. She jerked that arm free as well. ''You got me in the eye! Damn it, Rebec—!'' Her fist landed in his other eye socket—not *on*, but *in*, the size of her knotted hand a perfect fit. Race felt as if his eyeball jammed into his brain. *''Jesus!''*

Blind. He couldn't see anything but a blur, that being a totally pissed-off, panicked female. He cupped both his hands over his eyes, leaving only his nose exposed, and she went for that next, shoving hard with the heel of her hand. *Pain*. It slammed up the bridge of his nose, and, lo and behold, he could see something again.

Stars.

''Son of a-aa-a *bitch!*'' He grabbed his nose, felt the unmistakable warm wetness of blood on his palm, and threw up his other arm to shield his face from further attack. ''You broke my goddamned nose!''

She went suddenly still. Race swung off of her to kneel hunched over. ''Rest period!'' he cried. ''No fair hittin' a man when he can't see!''

Pain. He couldn't believe this. He hadn't even touched her anyplace important. *Damn*. She *had* broken his nose. Right at the weak spot. Slicker than shit.

He heard her slither away from him, her breath coming in fast pants. Then he heard her get up. The sound of little feet pattering across the grass to escape him brought no joy to his heart. He wanted to roar at her to get her little butt back there, that he wasn't finished with her yet. Not by half.

He twisted to sit cross-legged, elbows braced on his knees, face cupped in his hands. Instead of teaching her a lesson, he'd learned a couple, the first being not to tangle with a female unless he was willing to hurt her, which he wasn't, the second that he couldn't count on her to give him the same quarter.

Oh . . . damn. His nose! Crooked as the Allegheny. He pictured her running into camp, screaming, "Rape!" with her dress half-unbuttoned and her hair going every which way. He groaned. Pete would probably come out and finish what she had started. Race doubted he could defend himself. *Blind.* He stood corrected. The girl never should have run and hidden in the bushes. She should have waded right in and kicked ruffian ass.

"Mr. Spencer?"

He almost parted company with his skin. "Jesus H. Christ! Don't sneak up on me like that!"

"Oh, Mr. Spencer!" she said in a faint, shaky voice.

"I thought you ran off!"

"Well . . ." Catch of breath and a squeaky mewling noise. "I did run off a ways. Oh, lands! I just had to come back."

"Why? To drop kick me?" He wiggled his nose and cursed under his breath. "You'd best haul ass while you can. I'm gonna be damned mad as soon as I can see!"

He gave his nose another wiggle, then clenched his teeth and made a humming sound at the back of his throat to keep from cursing to turn the air blue.

"Mr. Spencer?"

"*What!*"

"Are you going to be all right, do you think?" she asked in a worried little voice.

He jerked his head up to gape at her blurry outline over his bent thumb. "Hell, no, I'm not gonna be all right! You broke my *nose!*"

"Oh, dear. Do you truly think it's *broken?*"

She'd damned near shoved his gristle into his brain, and now she sounded remorseful? He heard a rustling sound and the blur of her face came closer. The next instant her small hands were trying to pull his away from his face. "Oh, Mr. Spencer, I'm so sorry. May I look?"

He jerked away. "You stay away from me. *Christ!* I thought you was a cheek turner!"

"A what?"

Race realized he was talking through his wrist. He wrenched his mouth to one side and blinked to bring her into focus. That sweet little face. All those golden curls. She looked like an angel. What an illusion.

"A cheek turner! One of them Bible thumpers that don't believe in violence!"

"Well, I was. I've—it would seem I've fallen from grace."

He glared at her for a moment. No question. He outweighed her by at least a hundred and ten pounds. "Fallen from *grace*?"

"I asked you very politely to desist."

Race had no idea what "desist" meant, but judging by the context of the sentence, he got the nub of it. "I thought you said you wouldn't fight me. Next thing I know, you're clawin' and spittin' like a she-cat."

He heard her make a muffled sound of distress. Then she tried to pull his hand away again.

"Leave me alone, I said! Go nettle the plug-uglies!"

"Oh, Mr. Spencer, I'm so sorry!" Her voice went all quavery. "You *frightened* me!"

He shot her a glare. "Don't you dare."

"Dare what?" she asked shakily.

"Start cryin'. I mean it. Not one tear." He saw tears welling, and he narrowed his eyes.

"I'm sorry. It's just—oh, lands, I don't know what came over me." She bent forward at the waist, a hand pressed to her throat as she tried to see behind his fist. "I didn't mean to *hurt* you! Honestly I didn't."

"Could've fooled me."

"Are you positive it's actually broken?"

Race felt fairly certain. The bridge was leaning toward his right eye. "You know, this ain't the least bit fair. Puckerin' up. Makin' *me* feel bad. I didn't hurt a hair on your head, and didn't plan to!"

"Oh, mercy, I know. That's why I came back. You were a little too convincing there for a moment, I'm afraid. I lost my head.'' She tugged on his wrist. ''Let me look.''

''Rebecca, keep pesterin' me, and you're fixin' to get swatted on your other cheek.''

''Oh, you're such a meany. Come on. Move your hand. I won't hurt you, I promise.''

Race had made grown men turn tail with a glare. How was it that this half-swatch of muslin had absolutely no fear of him? ''I *am* mean. Meaner'n a sidewinder with a nasty disposition!''

''I know.'' She drew his hand slightly away from his face and her breath caught. ''Oh, merciful heaven, what have I done?''

''Is it that bad?'' He crossed his eyes trying to see.

She touched her fingers to her mouth, and tears spilled over her lashes onto her pale cheeks. ''Oh, Mr. Spencer, it really *is* broken! Oh, lands! What have I done? You were so handsome, and now just *look* at you!''

He flopped on his back and stared at the sky, thinking he'd rather have a bad case of bawdy-house itch than deal with her tears. ''Don't get all worked up. It's got a weak spot and breaks kinda easy. I know you didn't mean to.'' Angling one arm over his eyes, he sighed. He knew by tonight he'd have two prize-winning shiners. A busted nose usually brought black eyes with it. The pain had eased up, at least. ''Aw, hell. I had it comin'. Of all the damned fool things I ever done, that takes the prize. I wanted to make you feel better, and that was all I could think to do.''

From under his sleeve, he saw her crouch next to him and loop her arms around her knees. ''I know that,'' she said shakily. ''And it *was* foolish. But for some strange reason, it did make me feel better.''

He let his arm drop onto the grass above his head. ''It did?''

Still hugging her knees, she rocked forward onto her toes to look down at him with the biggest, prettiest, most shimmery blue eyes he'd ever seen. ''Just knowing you care that much makes me feel a bit better. After what happened to Tag, I'm amazed you don't detest me.''

For a few brief minutes, he'd nearly forgotten about Tag. Now the guilt slammed into him again. "What happened to Tag wasn't your fault," he said huskily. "It was mine. For not lookin' after him good enough."

A tear clung to one of her bottom lashes. Just hung there, glistening like a tiny prism. "I'd tell you how wrong you are to think that," she said, "but I know it wouldn't help. It's going to hurt no matter what."

Just as she was going to hurt, no matter what. *She screamed my name* ... He'd never forget the pain in her voice when she'd said that. "I reckon that's true," he admitted. "And that bein' the case, there ain't much point in you tryin' to elbow in and take some of my blame. You got enough of your own."

She gazed at the horizon for a long moment. "We're a fine pair." She released a weary sigh. "Oh, what a miserable day. I'd like to wish some of my life away— anything to put this far behind me."

Race could have gone for that himself. "Rebecca," he whispered huskily. "You gotta promise me, darlin'. Give me your word that you won't do somethin' loco like this again. No matter how bad you feel."

She drew her gaze back to his. "I feel as if I'm destroying your life."

"Then you oughta stay around to help me put it back together again."

Her mouth quivered at the corners. "Do you really want me to?"

In that moment, Race knew he wanted nothing more, and that it would probably end up being the biggest heartache of his life. "I really do," he whispered.

She smiled at him through her tears. "Maybe we can help each other. My life's in a pretty horrible mess, too."

"You got a bargain." He wiped his right hand clean on his shirt and held it out to her. "Shake on it?"

She laid her slender fingers across his palm. "A bargain, Mr. Spencer." She tipped her head to one side again. "I think the first thing we should put back together is your nose."

Chapter 13

"This here will have you feelin' better in no time!" Mr. Grigsley announced as he crawled back into the wagon, two brown corked bottles under one arm and another two clutched in one fist. "Fact is, it'll do us all a world of good."

Pete Standish, who sat with his back to the front end of the wagon, stretched out one leg, the leather of his chaps fanning over the top of his dusty boots. "You must be high on Cookie's list, Miss Rebecca. He don't share his elixir with just any old body."

"I brung some for everyone," Mr. Grigsley protested as he handed a bottle down to Johnny, who sat near Rebecca on the pallet. "I even brung one for you!" he said as he tossed a second bottle to Pete. "Here you go, missy."

Rebecca took her bottle, eyeing it curiously. "What is it?"

"My magic elixir."

"A medicine, you mean?" Rebecca glanced over at the cook as he sat across from her, leaning his plump shoulders against a cross board. "What is it supposed to cure?"

"Every damned thing," Pete said with a chuckle. "Includin' my good aim." He squinted at Mr. Grigsley. "I get to feelin' too good, Cookie, and the boss'll have my head when he gets back."

"Mine, too," Johnny agreed. "We're supposed to be guardin' Miss Rebecca."

"Such hogwash!" Mr. Grigsley said, uncorking his bottle. "You can't feel too good." He raised his bottle to Rebecca. "Pull your cork, honey, and bottoms up!"

With that, Mr. Grigsley tipped the container to his mouth and fairly guzzled the contents, whistling and shuddering when he finally stopped to breathe. Rebecca watched him, fascinated. "I've always taken elixir by the spoonful."

"That'd take all night!" Mr. Grigsley leaned forward and grabbed her bottle, removing the cork and then handing it back to her. "Drink! You see how easy I'm movin'? Hardly feel my cracked ribs. It's a magic cure, for sure."

"But, Mr. Grigsley, I'm not ill. I'm just worried about Mr. Spencer."

Johnny chuckled. "Cookie's elixir is especially good for worrying. Or jangled nerves. A few belts of that, and you'll feel as slick as butter on a flapjack."

"Really?" Rebecca took a small sip. A horrible, fiery taste washed over her tongue, and she shuddered, holding the bottle well away. "Oh, lands! That's—tasty."

"Ain't it?" Mr. Grigsley watched her. "Go on. Have a belt."

Rebecca was afraid she might toss up if she took more. But Mr. Grigsley was watching her, and she hated to hurt his feelings. She took a big gulp. The fire took her breath. She clapped a hand to her throat and sprang to her knees, trying frantically to inflate her lungs. Johnny rescued her bottle, snatching it from her hand so she didn't spill it. Pete leaned over to thump her between the shoulder blades.

"Everything okay in there?" Mr. McNaught called from outside where he stood guard at one side of the wagon. From the other side of the conveyance, Corey said, "Is Miss Rebecca all right?"

"She's fine as a frog's hair," Pete called. "And she'll be even finer here shortly. Cookie's treatin' her nerves."

"Oh, boy."

Rebecca finally caught her breath. As she sank down on the pallet, Johnny handed the bottle back to her. She took it between her thumb and forefinger. "I've heard of bitter medicine."

Mr. Grigsley smacked his lips. "It tastes better with every swallow. That's part of the magic."

Rebecca noticed that Pete had set his bottle of elixir aside untouched. Noticing her look, he said, "I ain't got a nerve problem, honey. Especially not worryin' over the boss. He'll be back from that arroyo before you know it, and the others with him, not a hair outta place on any of 'em."

Rebecca drew up her knees, wedged her skirt between them, and tucked her bottle in the depression of muslin. "His nose must be hurting terribly, riding horseback so soon after getting it packed."

Pete chuckled. "He'll live. Ain't the first time he's got that honker broke."

She sighed. "I'll be worried until they get back. I just can't help but think his going to the arroyo to get that money is extremely risky. What if those awful men shoot him?" Realizing how that sounded, she added, "Not that I'm not equally concerned for the welfare of the other three men who went with him."

"Another swig!" Mr. Grigsley ordered. "Come on. Trust me. You'll feel a whole lot better with some of my magic elixir under your belt."

A warm feeling was already spreading through Rebecca's middle. Blue, who lay on her left between her and Pete, whined. She scratched him behind the ears. "Perhaps I should dose you, poor old fellow." She saw Mr. Grigsley watching her and dutifully took another swallow of medicine. "It's not as breathtaking the second time. You're correct. It does taste better with each swallow."

Pete chuckled. "It'll cure what ails ya, no question."

Rebecca doubted that anything would ease her mind until she saw Race Spencer returning to camp, hale and hearty. But she took another swallow of medicine, nonetheless.

"Camptown ladies sing dis song, Doodah! doodah! Camptown racetrack five miles long, Oh! doodah day!"

Race heard Rebecca singing as he was unsaddling Dusty, and her voice, interspersed with gay laughter, kept ringing out the entire time he rubbed down the horse. Preach, who'd ridden with him to the arroyo, glanced at Race over the back of his gelding and shook his head. "Sounds like they're havin' a high ol' time."

Race grinned in spite of himself. He heard Rebecca cry, "Oh, lands!" Then she giggled. He gave Dusty a final pat, slung the saddlebags full of money over his shoulder, and struck off for camp. Trevor McNaught inclined his head to Race in greeting when he walked into the light of the fire.

"Howdy, boss."

Race gazed past McNaught at the wagon. Rebecca's shrill giggles drifted to him. "I never heard her laugh before," he told the grizzled cowhand. "Didn't figure I would, considerin'. Not for a spell, at least."

McNaught pulled a face. "Cookie dosed her with his magic cure."

"Oh, shit."

When Race threw up the rear flap and climbed into the wagon, Rebecca didn't notice him for going on a minute. She was too intent on Cookie. "How does it go?"

"Jimmy crack corn, and I don't care! My master's gone away!" Cookie belted out.

Rebecca chimed in behind him, swinging a brown bottle in time to the melody. Pete met Race's gaze the length of the wagon. "She was a little nerved up, worryin' about you. What with all else that's happened to the poor girl, Cookie decided to dose her."

Race settled his gaze on his charge, who'd been pale and hollow-eyed when he left her two hours ago. She now had some color in her cheeks and, despite the dark circles that still remained under them, her eyes had a pretty sparkle. Her braid had come loose from her head and hung in a raveling loop to one side, the end all that was still attached to her crown.

"He dose her or drown her?" Race asked.

"Mr. Spencer!" She shot up from the pallet, took two running steps, and launched herself at him, knocking him up alongside the head with the bottle as she threw her arms around his neck. "You're all right! Oh, lands! I'm so relieved."

If she'd been any more relieved, she wouldn't have been standing. Race lowered his shoulder to let the saddle-bags drop and caught her close within the circle of one arm. Her feet left the floor, and she hung there from his neck like an oversize necklace. "I told you I'd be fine, darlin'."

She pressed her face against his throat. "I was so-oo-o apprehensive!"

He narrowed an eye at Cookie. "If she gets sick, I'll wring your neck." He jerked when he felt her lips part and the tip of her tongue touch his skin. He tucked in his chin to look down. "Rebecca?"

"Mmm. You taste so nice."

Pete shot to his feet. "I gotta go see a dog about a man."

"A man about a dog," Johnny corrected as he fell in behind the foreman. "You ain't leavin' me here. Nossir!"

Cookie wasn't quite so agile, but he gained his feet with amazing speed, nonetheless. "I'm flat tuckered, all sudden like! Reckon I'll head for my bedroll."

Race leaned his head far to one side, trying to escape velvety lips. "Don't leave!" He turned in time to see Johnny dive over the wagon gate, Cookie not far behind him. "Hey, fellas!"

Cookie looked back over his shoulder at Rebecca, who was nibbling under Race's ear. "I heard tell some gals get real friendly. Sure am glad it's your trouble and not mine."

Race watched his cook swing out. The next second the flap dropped. He stood there, stretching his neck, trying to evade the sweetest mouth on God's earth as it latched onto his earlobe. "Rebecca?"

"You taste salty," she said with a giggle. The next instant, she sang, "Swing low, sweet chariot!" and damned near busted his eardrum.

Race had a feeling it was going to be a very long night and an even longer journey home.

*   *   *

After laying out a nightgown for Rebecca, Race left the wagon while she dressed for bed. Sitting with his back braced against the wagon wheel, he listened with growing alarm to the rustles, creaks and thumps coming from inside the conveyance. Trevor McNaught, relieved now of standing guard and warming himself by the fire, threw Race a questioning glance when Rebecca let loose with a peal of laughter. Lifting his gaze, the cowhand began staring at a point well above Race's head. Wondering what the man found so damned interesting up there, Race finally turned to look himself.

He immediately shot to his feet. The light of the lamp threw Rebecca's silhouette against the canvas. Her swaying figure was outlined in magnified detail. It looked as if she'd gotten her dress tugged halfway down her arms and become stuck. Wiggling and twisting to free herself, she was unknowingly putting on the equivalent of a hurdy-gurdy dancing show for McNaught, her small breasts, covered with only the tease of her wash-worn cotton chemise, clearly defined on the canvas in all their jiggling glory.

"Go find somethin' to do," Race ordered his hired hand in a silky voice. "And tell the other men to stay the hell away from here till I tell 'em different."

McNaught jerked erect, his expression wary. "Don't get pissed. I didn't do nothin'."

Race had an unholy urge to smash his fist into the other man's face, a feeling he knew was as unjustified as it was irrational. "Put your eyes back in your head, and get the hell outta here!"

As McNaught made fast tracks to do just that, Race rejoined Rebecca inside the wagon. Compliments of Cookie's elixir, she didn't even blink when she saw him.

"Hello!" she said cheerfully.

This from the young lady who'd never taken an unchaperoned walk with a man until last night? Trying to follow the advice he had just snarled at McNaught, Race made a valiant attempt to keep his gaze averted as he turned the lamp down so it cast only a feeble glow over the interior of the wagon. Then he grasped Rebecca's bare shoulders and pressed her down onto her knees so only the silhouette of her head would be revealed against the canvas. As he knelt before her, she smiled, her expression bemused.

"I find myself faced with an unprecedented difficulty, Mr. Spencer."

He had no idea what "unprecedented" meant, but she sure as hell had the difficult part right. "What's that?" he asked, his voice sounding as if he had a tight noose around his neck.

She wiggled and jerked one slender arm. "It would seem that I am ensnared. I do believe my dress shrank." In her attempt to extract her arm from the sleeve, she lost her balance and toppled sideways. "Oops!"

Race grabbed her at the waist. She giggled and swayed forward, colliding with his chest. She pressed her face against him. "Oh, my! I feel a bit dizzy-headed."

A bit? Race set her slightly away from him. The problem was that she had only unbuttoned the dress partway, leaving an inadequate opening to draw it down her arms. He reached for the buttons. The instant he no longer steadied her, she reeled to one side again. He caught her from falling. She giggled again, letting her head fall back. His gaze became riveted to her creamy throat. *Christ.* He was going to strangle Cookie for this piece of work.

"How about if you lay down on your back, honey?" he suggested.

She brought her head up to gaze at him with big, laughing blue eyes. "You may lay me, Mr. Spencer. Or I may lie. But I shan't *lay.* Unless, of course, you give me something to lay." She attempted to shake a finger under his nose. Able to reach only so high with her arms trapped, she shook it at his belly button instead. "Improper usage!"

"There ain't gonna be no usage, improper or otherwise. I just want you to lay down before you fall down."

She leaned toward him and whispered, "*Lie!* Lay is incorrect."

Race caught her behind the knees and flipped her over

onto her back. On the way down, she squeaked in startlement. As he settled her on the pallet, he found himself almost nose to nose with her, and damn him to hell for a bastard, he almost stayed there. Her sweet mouth was a few scant inches from his lips. All her inhibitions had gone the way of Cookie's elixir. He looked into her trusting, luminous eyes and knew he could make love to her if he wanted to—and God help him, he'd never wanted anything so much.

She gazed up at him. The sound of their breathing seemed loud against his eardrums. Her breasts nudged his chest, and the tips, abraded by their movements, were thrusting against the thin cloth of her undergarment, the hardened peaks burning holes in his shirt.

"Oh, my," she said softly, pressing a hand to her waist.

"You feelin' sick?"

Race wouldn't have been surprised if she'd said yes. But she shook her head. "No, I just—" Her breath caught. "Oh, my," she whispered again.

"What?"

She blinked and refocused on his face. "I have the funniest feeling in my tummy."

Damn. She was getting sick. He envisioned himself holding her head while she heaved until her toes curled.

"Funny little flutters."

Race's gaze sharpened on her face. "Little what?"

"Flutters. You make me feel funny."

He shot a glance at the pulse point at the base of her throat. Her heartbeat was racing. He dragged his gaze back to her face, took in her dreamy expression, and decided strangling Cookie would be too merciful a death.

"Rebecca," he said, his voice grating, "you shouldn't tell a man things like that. It's liable to get you into trouble."

"Things like what?"

He found himself grinning in spite of himself. Gazing down at her, it occurred to him that he'd been wrong to voice the warning. One of the things he found most special about Rebecca was her sweetness. Did he really want her to change? The answer was no. Angels were mighty rare. When a man came across one, he should cherish her just as she was. As for her getting into trouble, it was up to him to see that she didn't.

"Nothin'," he said huskily. "Forget I said anything."

He drew back and attacked the buttons on her dress. Once he'd slipped them all free from their holes, he sat her up, peeled the dress sleeves down her arms, and then reached for her nightgown, which he drew over her head without removing any of her other clothing. He would take off her shoes. That was as far as this unveiling was going to progress. She could sleep in her chemise, petticoat and drawers.

The tug of the nightgown finished loosening her raveling braid from its mooring. Her golden hair fell forward like a heavy rope over her slender shoulder, the silken strands brushing his knuckles as he buttoned the front of her gown. He sat back and noticed his hat lying at the head of the pallet near Blue. He guessed the Stetson had been knocked from his head when he had laid her down. That he hadn't noticed the loss gave testimony to the fact that his thoughts had been centered on other things.

She gnawed on her lip. "Are you going to go outside now?"

The way she asked told him she didn't want him to leave. He nearly groaned. Staying in here with her tonight, with Cookie's elixir numbing her inhibitions, was not a good idea. He counted himself to be a decent man, but he was sure as hell no saint.

"I'll sleep under the wagon. You'll be fine, honey."

She looked slightly panicked. He averted his gaze, not trusting himself to stand fast if she fixed those big blue eyes on him and pleaded for him to stay. Clenching his teeth, he seized her by one ankle and attacked the laces on her shoe. When both shoes were removed, he tucked her stocking feet under the quilts.

"Lay down, darlin'. Let's get you tucked in for the night."

She wrinkled her nose. "Lie," she said as she slumped over onto her back.

"Lie," he echoed, drawing the quilts up to her chin.

She turned her cheek against the back of his hand, her

lashes drooping as her eyes drifted closed. "Oh, Mr. Spencer . . ." she said on a dreamy sigh.

Race nearly said, "What?" But on second thought, he decided he might not want to know. If she said anything more about having a fluttery feeling in her tummy, she could end up with uninvited company in her bed. He would hate himself come morning if he took advantage of her that way. Besides, he'd given her his word that she could trust him, and a promise was a promise.

"G'night, sweetheart," he whispered.

"Good night, Mr. Spencer."

Race leaned over her to retrieve his hat. As he straightened and returned the hat to his head, she murmured something more, her lashes fluttering as if she were attempting to open her eyes. "What?" he asked softly.

"Please don't leave camp while I'm asleep." Her voice was breathy, her pronunciation slightly slurred. "Promise? I get scared when you're not with me."

Race felt as if a fist were squeezing something inside his chest. For as long as he could remember, most females had found him fearsome. It was quite a switch to have this girl trust him so completely, a compliment of the highest order. It made him feel unaccountably good about himself, as if he were a gentleman instead of a no-account. He just hoped he could live up to her expectations.

"I won't leave you, honey. I promise."

Race turned out the lamp before he left the wagon. When the darkness swooped down over him, he stood there for a long moment, listening to the soft huff of her breathing. A wry smile touched his mouth. Staying with the girl would be the easiest chore he had ever tackled.

Leaving her . . . or letting her leave him . . . might prove to be the problem.

Chapter 14

A long journey home. *Those words became a litany in* Race's mind during the endless days of northward travel that followed. A fair number of the cattle had sustained injuries during the stampede, which slowed their pace, forcing Race to stop more frequently to let them rest, which doubled the length of time it should have taken to make the trip. The trail for the wagons was usually little more than a cow path, every bump, rut, and chuck hole jarring the unsprung frame of Rebecca's wagon, and her as well. No matter how Race tried, he couldn't avoid all the rough spots. To make the trip less jarring for Blue, Race and Pete fashioned a canvas hammock for the dog, which they suspended from the underside of the wagon. There Blue received fewer jostles, was shaded from the sun, and seemed to travel in relative comfort until he began to heal.

Unfortunately, the same sort of comfort couldn't be provided for Rebecca. Race told himself that she was undoubtedly accustomed to the hardships of the trail, that she'd come through it all right. But with each passing day, she grew thinner and looked more exhausted, her fragile body strung so taut with tension, he could have plucked notes. He got to a point where he worried about her ceaselessly.

Two days into the journey, the endless flatland gave way to piñon juniper woodlands, a welcome change from the desertlike terrain they left behind. After that, Race lost

track of the days, the journey becoming a blur, the juniper
woodlands reverting back to flatland again, which in turn
gave way to thick stands of salt cedar as they passed
through the drainage lands of the Arkansas River and the
Rio Grande. More grassland, more juniper woodlands. It
seemed to him that they traveled in an endless circle and
never made much headway.

He needed to get Rebecca to his ranch, fast. Someplace
quiet and restful, where every minute of the day wasn't
spent on that bone-jarring torture rack called a wagon seat.
He didn't dare allow her to walk to give her a rest from
the jiggling, nor could he let her ride a horse. By his
count, there were seven ruffians still alive, and he knew
they were riding drag on his back trail. Nearly every day,
Race or one of the men spotted the tracks of their horses.

Race wasn't surprised. He had what the bastards
wanted, after all: the money. With that to lure them, there
was little chance they would lose interest and give up.
That suited Race just fine. No way in hell did he intend
to let Tag's death go unavenged, and having the ruffians
on his tail just saved him the trouble of having to hunt
them down later. With Rebecca and a herd to take care
of, he couldn't go after them right then, not without risk-
ing further financial losses or harm to the girl who had
come to mean more to him than he cared to admit.

Pete and Race frequently powwowed, trying to determine when the ruffians might make their move. Race believed the outlaws meant to follow them to wherever they
were going, let them get settled in, and wait to launch an
attack when they thought Race and his men had their
guard down. Pete agreed with that determination.

Race sincerely hoped the ruffians were that stupid.
Their waiting to attack him and his men on their home
ground would be their last mistake. Meanwhile, though,
the constant threat of trouble made it necessary to exercise
every precaution, and Rebecca, being defenseless, paid the
dearest price. The poor girl couldn't even seek privacy in
the bushes without Race dogging her footsteps, a loaded
rifle cocked and at the ready in the crook of his arm. As

a consequence, Rebecca's nerves seemed to become more frayed with each passing day.

She needed to put this hellish experience behind her and start over. Instead, fear had become her constant companion. Judging by her pallor and the circles under her eyes, she wasn't sleeping well, even with him bedded down under her wagon. Race had also noticed that she seldom let him out of her sight, her need to be near him almost frantic. When he had absolutely no choice but to leave her so he might tend his herd, he brought Pete and Johnny in from riding flank to guard her. But even then, he couldn't miss the desperate appeal in her eyes. Every second he was away from her, he felt guilty as hell.

From the start, Race had planned to take Rebecca to Denver at first opportunity, which would be soon if the weather held. But the few times he'd made mention of his plans, she had shown no enthusiasm for the idea, not even when he pointed out that her church friends in Santa Fe would probably come to fetch her if she telegraphed them from there. She clearly didn't want to leave Race, the devil take going to Denver and contacting her people down south.

Race guessed he could understand that. She'd been in the company of cheek turners when this whole mess started, and they had reacted to the danger like lambs awaiting slaughter. Rebecca wasn't stupid. She'd seen a lot of bloodshed, and she knew the trek to Santa Fe would be filled with peril. Her instinct for survival dictated that she remain with someone she knew would protect her. Oh, yes. Race understood. But her feelings also put him in a hell of a spot, a fact that became glaringly apparent to him toward the end of their journey.

As had become her habit each night, Rebecca was assisting Cookie in preparing the evening meal when she accidentally lost her grip on the container of salt and spilled the lot in the stew. Supper for over thirty hungry cattlemen was rendered inedible, which was no small catastrophe, and Cookie made matters even worse by ranting and raving.

"You just ruint hours of work!" he cried, stomping

angrily over to the cooking fire. "If I'd knowed you was so clumsy, I woulda salted it myself! Now, just look what you went and done! Help me? Some help you are, ruinin' the whole meal! I shoulda knowed better than to let a gol-durned female in my kitchen!"

Alerted by Cookie's cursing and hollering, Race hurried over to the chuck wagon. He found Rebecca frantically trying to salvage the stew by dipping away the oversalted surface with a large spoon, a feat made almost impossible because the concoction was boiling so rapidly. Taking quick stock of the situation, Race was alarmed by her pallor. Never having been a target of one of Cookie's tirades, she had never seen the little man lose his temper and was obviously taking every word he said to heart.

"Cookie, calm down," Race interjected. "There ain't no need to be nasty. She didn't mean to spill the damned salt, after all. It ain't that big a thing!"

"It ain't a big thing? Over thirty hardworkin' men to feed, and now they ain't got no supper!" Cookie cried. "If this ain't a fine mess, you takin' up for her, and here I am with nothin' to feed all them men! Well, it's your worry, not mine!" He glared up at Race. "I don't gotta take this off'n nobody. I quit!"

Knowing as he did that Cookie "quit" every time the wind blew wrong, Race wasn't overly alarmed by the proclamation, but Rebecca looked frantic. "Oh, no! Please, Mr. Grigsley, don't *quit*!"

As she whirled to plead with the cook, she held onto the spoon, flinging stew in a wide arc that splattered the front of Race's shirt and pants. He leaped at the burn and swatted at the searing clumps of carrots and potatoes that clung to his clothing. "Jesus H. Christ!" he cried. "Be careful with that damned spoon, Rebecca!"

Her expression horrified, Rebecca dropped the spoon in the dirt and hurried over to help swipe at his clothing, using her hands, a fold of her skirt, and even her sleeve to dab at the mess, her movements so frenzied that only a blind man could have failed to see how upset she was. Race immediately regretted his outburst.

"See there? *Clumsy!*" Cookie cried. "Ain't no place

for a female, bein' on a drive. Or on a ranch, for that matter!''

"Cookie!" Race said in a warning tone. "That'll be enough. She didn't mean to ruin your goddamned stew. We'll just have to whip up somethin' else, is all.''

Cookie stomped away. "You got a mouse in your pocket? *You'll* have to whip up somethin' else. Not me. I done cooked supper once, and I ain't about to again!''

Race turned to find Rebecca with a hand clamped over her mouth, her eyes swimming with tears. He settled a hand on her shoulder. "Honey, don't let him upset you so. Cookie just gets that way sometimes. He don't mean nothin' by it.''

Behind her cupped hand, she cried, "But he quit! What'll you do without a cook?'' She cast a glance at the stew pot. "He's right. I am clumsy. Supper is ruined! What will everyone eat?''

"Biscuits and gravy will do everyone for tonight. Quit lookin' so upset, darlin'. Some ruined stew ain't the end of the world.''

But as Race stirred up some biscuits, he began to suspect that to Rebecca, it seemed like the end of the world. She darted around him, attempting to do all of the work herself and apologizing profusely with every breath. Then after the makeshift meal was finally prepared, she ate nothing herself. Instead she hurried around the camp, solicitously offering each man coffee and asking if she could get him anything else, clearly trying to atone for having ruined the evening meal. To make matters worse, she was shaking so badly that each time she refilled a coffee cup, the unlucky recipient of her services nearly took a scalding bath.

Observing Rebecca's behavior, Race's concern mounted. This went beyond mere regret. The girl was frantic. It was almost as if she were afraid she might be banished from camp unless she regained everyone's favor.

When her efforts to appease became concentrated on Race, his concern for her became full-fledged worry. There was a feverish brightness in her blue eyes as she flitted around him.

Developing a headache from the tension, Race reached back to rub his neck, only to have Rebecca take over the ministrations. A few minutes later when he started toward the fire to get himself more coffee, she prised the cup from his hand to refill it for him. When she noticed him yawning, she crawled under the wagon to spread out his bedroll.

When she emerged from under the wagon, Race was waiting for her. "Rebecca, darlin', we gotta have a talk."

Already so pale she looked sick, she lost even more color as he led her to the edge of camp where they might have some privacy. Wringing her hands, she turned to face him as they drew to a stop, her big eyes resembling drenched blue velvet in the twilight. "I-I didn't mean to ruin the stew. It'll never happen again. I promise! And whatever I can do to make up for it, I will. Just name it."

That was Race's worry—that she'd do just about anything to mend her fences. Since he wasn't even angry with her and hadn't behaved as if he were, that struck him as an abnormal reaction. "Rebecca, things like this just happen."

Almost as if his words didn't register, she rushed to say, "I'm clumsy. I know I am. But from now on, I'll be extra careful. Truly!" Her eyes shimmered with tears. "Please, Mr. Spencer, don't be angry. It'll never happen again."

Her agitation was so great that an awful suspicion crept into his mind. "Rebecca, you ain't afraid I'll leave you behind, are you?"

At the question, her expression went stricken, as if she knew he might grow furious if she admitted to her feelings. She averted her gaze, staring off into the trees.

He had his answer. The realization hung there in his mind like an icicle. How could she believe that of him, even for an instant? It was a crazy notion and completely unwarranted. If he left her out here, she would die, either at the hands of the plug-uglies or from exposure and starvation. How in God's name could she think him capable of doing that to her?

Anger flared inside him. He barely managed to tamp it

down. That she was terrified was obvious, and terror blocked out reason. Her fears weren't an affront to him. They were simply a reaction to her situation, which apparently seemed dangerously unstable to her. And idiot that he was, he'd seen all the signs of that, realized something was wrong, and allowed the problem to fester.

Thinking back, he recalled all the times she had seemed frantic when he left her in camp, all the times when he'd turned to find that she had followed him somewhere, as if she was afraid to be separated from him by more than a few feet. It hit him then, like a fist between the eyes, just how completely dependent on him she had actually become. He was, quite simply, the only security that she had—the one person she felt she could count on to keep her safe.

And right now, she feared that he might abandon her.

Race couldn't imagine how awful that must make her feel. He rubbed his throbbing temple, struggling to get his thoughts clear. As he stood there gazing down at her, he tried his damnedest to put himself in her place—to understand how she must be thinking. But doing that was nigh unto impossible. At some point in his life, he knew that he'd been as slight of build as she was and as helpless to care for himself, but it had been so long ago, he couldn't really associate. Constantly threatened. Entirely dependent upon his goodwill. How long had she been feeling like that? For way too long, if the circles under her eyes were any indication.

He lowered his gaze to where she clasped her hands at her waist. Her tense fingers toyed with a button, twisting it, tugging on it, the pressure of her grip making her knuckles turn white. Lifting his gaze to study her taut features, he could see this wasn't a rational response. Her nerves were raw. She was exhausted. To survive, she needed him, and given all that had befallen her, he couldn't really blame her for feeling as if he too might be snatched away from her. Everything else had been, after all. Her home, her loved ones, her faith. Hell, even the clothes she wore weren't her own.

"Sweetheart, come here."

Since the night that Cookie had treated her nerves with his magic elixir, Race had avoided any close physical contact with her, fearing that his desire for her might get the best of his good judgment. Now he regretted that decision. If not him, who else was going to hug her? Right now, she needed the reassurance, but because it was easier and safer, he had kept his distance.

When he drew her into his arms, she pressed her trembling body against him and clung to his shirt, her face hidden against his shoulder. Race yearned to carry her to a private spot to sit with her cradled on his lap, as he had that long-ago afternoon in the bedroll wagon after the ruffian attack. But no. It was best to stay right where they were, standing so that their embrace couldn't become too intimate. The long and short of it was, he didn't dare trust himself.

"There's no way I'd ever leave you behind out here, darlin'," he whispered huskily, stroking her hair. "Deep down, you know that, don't you?"

"Yes," she said faintly. "It's just—oh, I don't know. Thoughts get in my head, and I can't shove them away." Her voice went thin and high-pitched. "I feel all mixed up inside, and all I can think about is doing everything I can to make sure you won't want to get rid of me."

Race thought of how attentive and ingratiating she'd been over the course of their journey. Rebecca, mending his shirt when he ripped it or replacing a button for him. Rebecca, shaking out his bedding each morning and neatly folding it. Rebecca, heating him shaving water and washing his clothes. Rebecca, fetching him refills of coffee and bringing him a supper plate each night, then going back to get him second servings if he wanted them. For nearly a month, she'd been trying desperately to please him in every way she could, and he had allowed it, being waited on for the first time in his life and relishing every minute of it.

Guilt swamped him. In her present emotional state, she would probably do almost anything for him. All he had to do was ask. And damn his insensitive hide, he'd just let it go. He'd known she felt insecure, of course, but he'd believed her fears stemmed from the massacre and that the problem would correct itself in time. Never once had he stopped to think there might be more to this than met the eye, or that some of her insecurities might have to do with him.

He closed his eyes and rested his jaw against her silken hair, acutely conscious of the feel of her beneath his hands. The fragile ladder of her ribs. The slender span of her waist and the soft flare of her hips. The curves of her body fit into the dips and hollows of his as if she'd been fashioned especially for him.

Damn. He wanted her as he'd never wanted any other woman—with a burning need that made him ache.

As he stood there, holding her close and struggling to control his physical reaction to her, Race began to entertain thoughts no decent man should, namely that she was his for the taking. All he had to do was press her, and she would accommodate him. In her present state, she'd be terrified of losing favor with him if she didn't. *His.* Dark images crept into his mind. Tantalizing images of Rebecca, acquiescent and desperately eager to please, peeling away her clothing, offering herself to him in whatever fashion he desired.

He clenched his teeth, trying to shove the thoughts away, but they weren't so easily dispatched. In fact, he could even justify them. If he made love to her, she would remain with him. He envisioned long winter evenings of holding her in his arms, exploring every sweet curve of her body. In return, he would see to it she was fed and cared for, and he would protect her from harm. Was that really such a bad trade? She was alone in the world. He was available and willing. She could do a hell of a lot worse. Why should he let her slip through his fingers when she could be his? Oh, yes. It would be so easy to convince himself there was nothing wrong with his taking her.

What man hadn't fantasized at least once about having a beautiful woman at his beck and call who would gratify his every desire? It was a heady feeling to know that if he placed demands on her right now, she would do whatever he asked. He could almost see her, kneeling before him and opening the bodice of her dress to bare her breasts, then pressing close to let him take her into his mouth. And for an awful moment, he was tempted almost beyond bearing to make the fantasy become a reality.

Then sanity returned, not because he was noble, but because he imagined the expression that would undoubtedly enter her eyes if he were to betray her that way. He wanted her, yes. But he didn't want to destroy all that she was in the taking, which was exactly what would happen if he took advantage of this situation.

Never in his life had Race suspected he had such a black side to his nature, that deep in the dark recesses of his mind there lurked a man who could even consider doing such a lowdown thing. Coming face to face with it left him feeling shaken and no longer sure he even knew himself. While he battled with his demons, Rebecca continued to cling to him, her trust in him so complete and unconditional that it terrified him. He nearly shoved her away and ordered her to get the hell away from him before he showed her what a bastard he really was.

Only he couldn't. God help him, he couldn't. She needed him right now, not as a lover but as a friend. Someone she could trust and count on, someone to support her while she healed.

He drew back to frame her small face between his hands. "You know, don't you, that nothin' you ever do will make me so mad that I'll ride off and leave you to fend for yourself?"

She nodded, but even so, he could still see shadows lurking in her eyes.

She needed time. All in all, it had been only a month since the attack in the arroyo. Pressing an avuncular kiss to her forehead, he led her back to camp, vowing with every step that from now on, he would be more attuned to her feelings and make more of an effort to reassure her.

That night after Race bedded down under the wagon, he lay there long into the night, trying to come to terms with the contradictory emotions warring for supremacy within him. During the month of travel, he had come to care about Rebecca more deeply with each passing day, and after their embrace earlier, he could no longer delude himself about how badly he wanted her. Nor could he completely banish from his mind the fact that she was his for the taking. All he had to do was play out his hand of cards, a royal flush, dealt to him by fate. By the time Rebecca came to her senses—which he feared she eventually would—he'd have her snubbed to a post and hobbled. He'd be happy. The only problem was, would she?

The question circled endlessly in his mind and stayed with him as he fell asleep, to trouble him even in his dreams.

By the time they entered Cutter Canyon, a relatively short distance from Race's ranch at the canyon's north end, Rebecca's dependency on Race had become so glaringly apparent that he could think of little else. *Damn.* He was only human, and his resolve was growing weaker with each passing day. She was beautiful and sweet, the kind of woman a man like him could usually only dream of possessing. How much longer was he going to be able to resist this kind of temptation?

The first evening in Cutter Canyon when Race left camp and walked down to the creek to fetch himself some shaving water, that question was circling in his mind like a dog chasing its tail. Confident that Rebecca was being closely guarded during his absence from camp by Johnny and Pete, he slowed his pace as he entered the woodland, letting the beauty of his surroundings soothe him.

The fallen leaves of cottonwood, willow, and box elder lay over the earth like a variegated carpet of yellow green, the thick stands of trees, their trunks ranging in color from white to gray brown, interspersed with wild grape, pin cherry, choke berry, and wild plum. Hunkering to fill the bucket from Gulch Creek, Race feasted his eyes, his hunger to once again be surrounded by trees and steep slopes finally appeased. Soon he'd be home, back on the ranch that he loved. Even with so many financial concerns awaiting him there, he was relieved to have this trip nearly over.

Somehow he'd make it through the winter, he felt sure. Most of his men had assured him they meant to stick with him, even if he was unable to cut them their pay. With their help, he'd be able to keep his base herd through the winter, then get a loan come spring to cover expenses and get his stock built back up. By next fall, he'd be back on his feet, something that wouldn't have been possible without the unswerving loyalty of his cowhands.

The only unsolvable problem Race felt he had was Rebecca.

"What're you lookin' so low in the lip about?"

Still crouched next to the stream, Race glanced over his shoulder to see Pete hunkered on the slight incline directly behind him. Hat tipped back, Pete eyed the trees on the opposite side of the creek, then trailed his gaze up the north slope of the canyon to the abundance of gamble oak and mountain mahogany that grew there.

"Who's guardin' Rebecca?" Race demanded to know.

"McNaught's fillin' in for me." Pete shifted his light blue gaze to his employer. "Thought I'd mosey down here and talk at ya for a couple."

"What about?" Race cocked an ear to listen to the lowing of the cattle. "Cows restive?"

"Ain't no problem with the cows," Pete assured him. "I just been noticin' you're in a stew about somethin'. Thought maybe you'd like to chew the fat with me."

Race averted his face and trailed his fingers in the water. "I appreciate that, Pete. But for once, I got a problem you ain't exactly an expert on, that bein' a female."

Pete chuckled. "I never said I weren't no expert on females. I said I didn't want too much truck with 'em. I was married once, a lotta years back. Even had me a son."

"You was?" Race was surprised. "That what turned you off women?"

"Yep. But prob'ly not in the way you think. Never seen another woman to hold a candle. I'm one of them one-woman men, I reckon, and she up and died on me. Her and my boy, both."

"Sickness?"

"Injuns." Seeing Race's startled look, Pete waved a

hand. "I don't hold your blood ag'in you. Don't even think it. Fact is, there's times I look at you and wish my boy had lived and turned out just like ya. I got enough years on you to be your father."

Race felt heat sliding up his neck. "That's a fine recommend, Pete. Thank you." Race let the water run from the bucket, then caught the handle on the crook of his fingers to let the pail float against the current. "I've often wished my pa had been like you. But he wasn't. So I count myself lucky to have you as my foreman instead."

"I take that as a real high recommend too." The slashes at each corner of Pete's mouth deepened. "Me feelin' sort of fatherly is what brung me out here, I reckon. You got yourself a hell of a problem with that girl. Don't you?"

Race threw him another startled look. "You noticed?"

Pete chuckled. "Well, I got to thinkin' it was sort of peculiar, her stickin' so close to your heels that she walks on your spur shanks. The poor girl's nose is gettin' flat at the tip. You're sorta unpredictable about your startin' and stoppin'."

Race grinned in spite of himself. "She does stick kinda close, don't she?"

"Closer than I reckon you know."

"How's that?" Race asked.

Pete got a distant look in his eyes as he gazed across the creek. "I don't rightly know if it's my beeswax to tell you. But a problem can't get fixed till it's pointed out. Ain't you noticed them circles under her eyes? The poor thing can't sleep at night."

Race sighed. "Yeah, I figured she wasn't restin' real good."

"You got it wrong. The girl ain't restin' at all."

"What?"

Pete sniffed. "I ain't the one who told you, all right? I don't want her mad at me. After you drift off and start snorin', she sneaks out with a quilt draped over her shoulders and sits near you with her back propped against the wheel spokes. Stays till almost daylight, then slips back into the wagon."

"What?" Race pushed to his feet, streaming water from the bucket. "Why didn't she—"

"Get back down here!" Pete jabbed a finger at the dirt. "Don't you dare go stormin' up there and givin' her what-for. The poor child can't help it!"

Race hunkered back down and set the bucket on the ground with a thunk. "I won't give her what-for. I just—" He raked his fingers through his hair. "Now, how come do you suppose she never came to me? I offered to sleep in there with her, damn it!"

"I reckon there's your answer," Pete said with a wink.

"What?"

"You slow, son? Most unbroke fillies is a little balky at first. She's got more reason than most, after seein' all she seen. I reckon as safe as you make her feel, the same feelin's don't hold true for sparkin' atwixt the blankets."

"Now how does that make sense? I make her feel safe, but she's afraid of me? That's what you're sayin'."

"It ain't so much her bein' afraid of *you*. It's more avoidin' your manly inclinations, which she can do leanin' against the wagon spokes but can't if you're spoonin' with her under the quilts."

"Of all the damned fool things." Race recalled all the times he'd noticed how worn out she looked. "Sittin' up all night? I've a good mind to give her a shake. You sure?"

"Well, of course. I wouldn't say it otherwise. I gotta go see a man about a dog about three every mornin', and I see her sittin' out there every blessed time. I started losin' sleep myself just to see when she went back to bed. I'd have come to you sooner, but I was hopin' the problem would cure itself. It ain't, and I don't think it's gonna."

Race flipped the bucket handle back and forth. "Jesus, Pete. What am I gonna do with her?" He propped his elbows on his knees, letting his wrists dangle. "If I sit by the fire, she sits nearby. If I go to visit a bush, she lingers where she thinks I'll come back into camp, pretendin' to be busy doin' somethin' so I won't know she's waitin' on me." He met Pete's gaze. "And that's not the worst of it. Practically the whole trip, she's been bendin' over backward tryin' to please me, and there's somethin' almost frantic about it.''

"I've seen," Pete admitted. "If you sit your coffee down, she gets you fresh or starts frettin' that it's too strong. If you look at her cross-eyed, she gets worried you're mad.''

"Sometimes I get the feelin' she'll heel if I snap my fingers." Race passed a hand over his eyes, taking care not to bump his still-tender nose. "I had me a—" He broke off and cocked an eyebrow. "Don't take this as no insult to her. I know it's a bad comparison. But I had me this dog once that was whupped all the time by its other owner. Took up with me, I reckon 'cause I wasn't mean to it, and until the day it died, that dog'd do anything for me, always rollin' belly up at my feet and waggin' to beat the band, like it thought I might haul off and kick it if the mood struck. I get that feelin' with Rebecca, like she's waggin' and tryin' to please me so I won't leave her.''

Pete nodded. "You got yourself a real beaut of a problem, I'm afeared.''

"You don't know the half of it." Race grabbed the bucket and slapped it into the water again. "Bastard that I am, I've been thinkin' real serious about snappin' my fingers and bringin' her to heel.''

Silence. Finally Pete said, "I ain't so sure that'd be a bad thing.''

Race fixed him with an incredulous look. "I'd be a lowdown skunk, and you know it. Just look at me, Pete.''

The foreman did as requested. "Except for some blue lingerin' on the honker, I reckon you look fine.''

"That ain't it, and you know it. I'm talkin' about me bein' such a dumb jackass. She's smart as a whip and has book learnin'. With all the big words she throws at me, I'd be one highfalutin talker if I could figure out what the hell half of 'em mean. I gotta get my 'X' witnessed! What in hell do I got to offer a lady like her?''

"A good night's sleep? And you ain't a dumb jackass. You're right smart about things you know. It don't take book learnin' to love a woman.''

"Do you think I don't know it? And much to my regret. She's had my tail tied in a knot ever since I first clapped eyes on her."

"Well, then?"

"It ain't that simple. I think she's lost her beliefs. I don't never see her pray. Don't trust in God no more. She's taken to trustin' in me for every damned thing instead. That's fine, to a point. But I ain't up to wearin' His moccasins, that's for damned sure. Her feelin's toward me ain't healthy! And I feel bad for wantin' to take advantage."

Pete drew his tobacco plug from his back pocket and tore off a piece. After returning the plug to his pocket, he settled back on his boot heels to enjoy the ritual of savoring and spitting. "Takin' advantage? That's an interestin' way of lookin' at it."

"How else is there?"

"Takin' what's offered, what's yours to take."

"She's mine to take only because she's got nothin' else and no one else! Her folks, her people, even her faith! I'm all she's got. The girl's scared of her own shadow."

"Then teach her not to be." Pete leaned forward and nailed a nearby rock dead center with a stream of tobacco juice. "If you want the girl, don't be a damned fool and lose her. If she's lost her own faith, then teach her how you believe. I reckon it's not so bad a way to think. You're a good man. As for the other, you can't give her back her parents, and if you send her back to her people, you ain't just a damned fool, you're a goddamned fool."

Race drew the bucket through the ripples, catching water only to toss it out again. "You don't think she'd be happy with 'em?"

"Happy? After she got over losin' you, maybe. She might marry up and have babies. But what happens when a plug-ugly comes along? You sit there, tellin' me how you got nothin' to offer her? You love her. You'd do all in your power to make her happy. And you'll fight for her. It don't sound to me like such a shabby deal."

Race stared at the water, his thoughts in a tangle. "You

make it sound so reasonable,'' he muttered, knowing it was anything but.

Pete sighed and pushed to his feet. ''You gotta do what you feel in your heart. If takin' her to Denver is it, then do it. But you'd best do it lickety-split. The way it is now, she's droppin' weight and off her food. You either gotta be her world, or you gotta wire her church folks to come take her back to her old'un. She can't go on like she is.''

At the thought of leaving her in Denver, Race felt as if a brutal hand had grabbed hold of his guts and was giving them a twist. Even worse was the thought of some ruffian harming her while grown men stood aside and did nothing to protect her. ''I don't know if I can let her go.''

Pete scuffed the heel of his boot through the leaves, digging a trench. ''Well, then, I reckon your decision's made, ain't it?''

Chapter 15

Light from the fire played on the canvas, casting a soft amber glow over the dark interior of the wagon. Almost afraid to breathe for fear of making a noise, Rebecca rose from the pallet and tiptoed the length of the wagon floor. One step. Two. She had become very good at this, making scarcely any sound as she touched her feet to the rickety planks. Since Race awoke at the least little noise, maintaining absolute silence was crucial. In a pattern that was now as familiar as the shape of her own hand, she stopped for a moment to hold her breath and listen.

Very good, she thought, slowly exhaling. He was still snoring.

Once she reached the wagon gate, she paused again, her senses attuned and alert for the least sign of danger. Noting none, she carefully unfastened one side of the flap. Light from the full moon bathed her face and turned the world outside to silver.

As she swung over the wood partition, she moved with agonizing slowness for fear of making the frame squeak. *Whew!* Bare feet finally touching solid ground, she allowed herself to relax a little.

After turning the corner, she crept in a half-crouch along the side of the wagon that faced away from the fire. Once at the right front wheel, she pulled the quilt more snugly around her shoulders and carefully lowered herself to the ground, taking care not to stir the dirt with the trailing quilt corners. After getting comfortably situated, she peeked beneath the wagon at the men presently gathered at the fire for hot coffee and a much-deserved break from riding guard on the herd.

Relief flooded through her when she saw that all of them were still talking, none looking in her direction. It wouldn't do for any of them to see her sitting out here. They'd tell their employer immediately, which would get her into something of a pickle. If Race learned she was having difficulty sleeping, he would insist on joining her in the wagon at night, and propriety aside, she simply wasn't certain she could feel comfortable with such an arrangement.

It wasn't that she didn't trust him. Far from it. While in his company, she felt absolutely safe. Just the opposite was true when he left her, even for short periods of time. For no reason she could pinpoint, she felt frantic. It was like being locked in a chest with a dozen venomous snakes slithering over her skin. Mindless terror, her body pouring sweat, her heart slamming, her lungs grabbing desperately for oxygen.

The fear always disappeared the instant Race returned. The mere sound of his voice worked on her raw nerve endings like a soothing balm. Unfortunately, she sensed that he had feelings for her that went far deeper than just friendship. Sometimes, she'd turn toward him when he didn't expect it, and she would catch him watching her, his dark gaze lambent with yearning and searing her everywhere it touched. It was a proprietary look, and it concerned her.

Unlike the brethren in her church, whose ardent inclinations were held in check by religious strictures, Race Spencer was a rugged, earthy man who answered to nothing and no one, not even God. As kindly and considerate as he was in all other ways, she feared he was the kind of man who would give his woman no quarter behind closed doors, the devil take her modesty, her beliefs, and her inhibitions.

Thus came into play her reluctance to sleep in the wagon with him, even though she would have trusted him with her life in every other way. According to Rebecca's ma, rest her dear soul, even the kindest and most caring man suffered from primitive physical yearnings—yearnings that could overpower his good sense if a woman he desired was foolish enough to tempt him. In light of that, it struck Rebecca that sleeping with Race in a small enclosure, barely wide enough for them to turn over without bumping into each other, might be foolhardy indeed. He was a very large and frighteningly strong man. If his passions overcame him, her goose would be cooked.

Crazy, so crazy. She was afraid to sleep near the man, yet she clung to him like an insecure child.

As she settled her back against the wagon spokes, the frantic feeling that always came over her at night when she was alone in the wagon dissipated. The sound of his snoring—so deep and close she could almost feel the vibrations—curled around her like an embrace. Blue, who slept next to him on a pad of wool blankets, chimed in with softer snores of his own, making her smile. What a pair they were, the big tough cowboy and the convalescing hound. Blue was able to walk without assistance now, albeit painfully and with a limp. Rebecca felt sure he would soon be recovered enough to chase rabbits again.

She angled her head to peer through the wheel spokes at Race. Flickering light played over his long muscular body, splashing gold patterns over his black shirt sleeve and the gray wool blanket that covered him. He lay on his side, the arm closest to the ground stretched toward her.

Sighing, she fixed her gaze on the stars above her, prepared for yet another long night of sitting alone in the darkness with only her thoughts for company. It was better than lying awake in the wagon, though. At least out here she felt a sense of calm that, despite the cold, was more restful than being tense with fear all night.

What a beautiful place, she thought dreamily, shifting her gaze to the treetops that rose in black silhouette against the moon-silvered night sky. She loved the smells and sounds—the pungency of autumn leaves moldering on the woodland floor, the crisp coolness of the air, the scent of the trees, slightly sharp with a wildwood muskiness, and the clean moistness that seemed to hover over everything, compliments of the nearby stream, which filled the night with the constant rushing sound of water cascading over rocks.

Race said it was even prettier at his ranch in the foothills of the Rockies southwest of Denver, that there were thick stands of lofty ponderosa pine and green meadowlands tucked among the trees. After the first snow, he said it always looked like a wonderland there, with white drifts in places, a blanket of white over everything.

Oh, how she hoped it would snow soon. *Before* he got a chance to take her to Denver. Just the thought of his riding away and leaving her in a strange place made her breathing get shallow. Hundreds of people she didn't know. Drunken men on the boardwalks. Streets going every which way in a confusing maze. Having no one to turn to. She wasn't ready for that, not yet. She closed her eyes, trying ward off the panic, but it was like a fist closing around her throat.

If it would just snow, he wouldn't be able to take her anywhere, and she'd be with him until spring. Surely his cabin would be large enough to accommodate them both comfortably, without forcing them into such close proximity that her presence would be a temptation for him. It would be a simple enough thing for her to make a pallet on the floor at the opposite side of the room, well away from his bed.

"Countin' the stars, darlin'?"

Rebecca jumped so violently at the unexpected sound of his voice that she lost her hold on the quilt. Pressing a hand to her throat, she turned to squint through the wagon spokes at him.

"Mr. Spencer?"

"Who else'd be under your wagon?"

He hooked a big hand over the wheel rim and crawled out. As he settled to sit beside her, he seemed to loom, his breadth of shoulder and length of leg making her feel dwarfed. Drawing up the knee opposite her to rest his arm, he turned slightly toward her, his ebony hair glistening in the silvery moonlight, his chiseled features etched with shadows, the collar of his black shirt open to reveal a V of muscular chest. As he studied her, his coffee-dark eyes seemed to take on a satisfied gleam, his firm yet mobile mouth tipping up at one corner, as if he were secretly amused by something. She had an uncomfortable feeling it had something to do with her.

She expected him to ask what she was doing out there, and she searched her mind for a believable lie. She had just decided to say she had come out for a breath of fresh air, when he said, ''You gettin' anxious to go to Denver?''

Her heart caught. Keeping her expression carefully blank, she replied, ''I've tried not to count too heavily on it, actually. It could snow, and then I couldn't go until spring.''

''Nah.'' He tipped his head back to study the sky. ''Now that we're this close to home, I can take that worry off your mind. We got a good month before the snows'll hit.'' He settled his gaze back on her face, his eyes still gleaming. ''In three days, we'll reach my ranch, and we'll head out straightaway. I'll have you in Denver within five days.''

''I'm not in that great a hurry. I'm sure you'll want to get your herd settled in and see to business that's been neglected in your absence. After all you've done for me, being patient is the least I can do.''

He shrugged her off. ''Pete can handle the herd and anything else that comes up. Gettin' you settled somewhere is my first concern.''

Rebecca gulped, struggled to breathe. *Stay calm. Don't panic.* But it was easier said than done. She dug her nails into the quilt, applying so much pressure they felt as if they were pulling from the quick. *Inhale, exhale. Don't think about his leaving you.* But it was there in her head, a vivid tableau, Race riding away from her on his buckskin, his black outline getting smaller and smaller until he disappeared from sight. She started to shake.

In a thin voice, she said, ''Mr. Spencer, what if I were to tell you I don't wish to go to Denver?''

He didn't look in the least surprised. ''I'd offer you two other choices.'' He searched her gaze. ''One of 'em would be permanent, though.'' His shifted his bent leg to better support his arm, then began clenching and relaxing his hand as he turned his head to stare into the darkness. ''So you probably wouldn't be interested in that one. Which'd leave you with just one choice, livin' in Cutter Gulch until you decide you wanna contact your people in Santa Fe and tell them to come fetch you.''

''In Cutter Gulch?'' Her voice sounded as shrill as a reed whistle.

She swallowed and grabbed for breath. *Cutter Gulch?* That sounded nearly as bad as Denver. And she didn't *want* to contact her church family. Why couldn't he understand that? Why should she go to live in Santa Fe with misguided fools who believed a benevolent heavenly Father would protect them from all harm? She knew better. And now that she no longer believed as they did, how could she possibly live where she'd be expected to get on her knees countless times each day?

She was going to be sick. Violently sick. Sweat filmed her face, and tears burned at the backs of her eyes. She *needed* him. And he was thrusting her away from him. She wanted to grab handfuls of his shirt and shake him, plead with him. Instead she just sat there, hugging her knees and swallowing down her gorge. She felt him return his gaze to her, and she feared he could probably see her trembling.

He released a weary sigh, and from the corner of her eye, she saw him bend his head and rub his brow. Then he suddenly laughed, the sound coming from deep in his chest and laced with self-deprecation.

''Christ,'' he said, his voice pitched to barely more than a whisper. ''It's a damned good thing I never had to stay permanent with my mother's people. I'd have been a sorry excuse for an Apache brave.'' He glanced up, his mouth tipping into a crooked grin that flashed white teeth. ''Every time I captured me a pretty little white gal, I'd have been turnin' around and takin' her home within a week. I would've spent all my time comin' and goin'.''

Rebecca couldn't see how the observation related to their conversation. She was just relieved to see the calculating gleam vanish from his dark eyes, to be replaced by the tender warmth she had grown to expect. He drew up his other knee to rest his other arm, both wrists dangling. "Well, hell . . ." he said with another sigh. "So you ain't too fond of the idea of me takin' you to Denver, huh?"

"No," she replied shakily.

He puffed air into his cheeks. "You know, darlin', livin' in Cutter Gulch wouldn't be so awful bad. It's only about ten miles from my place, and you just might like it there. And it ain't like you'd be all alone, with no friends. All us fellas, we'd be close. If you needed us, there we'd be." He leaned forward to pluck a blade of grass and twirl it between his fingers. "If you wanna send the church money on to Santa Fe, I'll help you make arrangements for transport and pay your livin' costs until you find work. I could probably even help you find a job, as far as that goes, by givin' you a high recommend around town. You wouldn't make fancy wages, but probably enough to get by."

Ten miles? That was a very long way in terms of how often a person might make the trip. "Do you go to town frequently?"

"Every few months." He flashed her a smile. "I'd step it up to once a month if you was there."

Once a month? Rebecca leaned over her knees and pretended to be fascinated with her big toe. "Mr. Spencer . . ." Her heart came up in her throat. "I—you wouldn't happen to—to have a position of employment for me on y-your ranch, would you?"

He dug the heels of his boots into the dirt, raising the toes, then lowering them. Silence. She was dying, praying to a nonexistent God for him to say yes, quivering inside with a horrible, clawing panic. She sneaked a glance at him. He was studying the trees, a distant expression on his face. She hoped he was thinking of different jobs she might perform for him.

He sighed again. Spread his knees. Bent his head to stare down at the earth between his boots. Took to staring off again. Finally he said, "You know, darlin', we got us a helluva problem here." He turned his gaze on her, his expression solemn. "I'm gonna be straight-out honest with you. And I hope you'll not hold it against me. But I reckon you might." He stuck the blade of grass in the corner of his mouth and directed his gaze straight ahead again. "I know you feel frantic when I talk about leavin' you in Denver," he said, his voice turning husky. "And I know you ain't got no big itch to go to Santa Fe and live with a bunch of faint hearts who wouldn't lift a hand to save themselves, let alone you.

"To my credit, I got to feelin' guilty and tried to make Cutter Gulch sound good, but it don't look like you're real high on that idea, either." He took a fast breath and huffed on the exhale. "I know you been sittin' here by this wheel every night to be near me because you're afraid and can't sleep. I also think I know why you was afraid to ask me to sleep with you in the wagon. And I know that you get real frantic other times if I leave camp, even with Johnny and Pete here to watch over you." He paused. "It also ain't escaped my notice that you been tryin' real hard to please me, like maybe that'll make me less likely to wanna be rid of you."

Rebecca couldn't bear to look at him. So she stared through a blur of tears at the wedding ring pattern of the quilt. She felt stripped naked. Ashamed. It was all true. Every word. The worst part was, she couldn't even explain it to him. She didn't understand it herself.

"That's what I know about you. Now let me tell you some things about me, which is the part you'll probably hold against me." He leaned back against the wheel and straightened one leg. "First off, knowin' all that I do about how you're feelin', and knowin' you got no control over it, that gives me a damned good hold on your lead rope. You followin' me?"

She wasn't, quite, but she nodded, aware that he was studying her even though she didn't look up.

"Secondly, I—" He broke off and groaned. "Christ." Seconds ticked by. "I gotta real deep fondness for you," he finally said, "and it ain't a plain friendship sort of feelin'. It's the kind of fondness that's got powerful-strong yearnin's ridin' double behind. It started the first time I clapped eyes on you, it's been growin' ever since, and now it's startin' to get the best of me. I reckon maybe you guessed that. I don't know. But, anyhow, that's how it is. I was waitin' for you to come out here tonight. I wasn't asleep. And I set out from the start when I mentioned takin' you to Denver to herd you into my brandin' chute and lock the gate.''

Another heavy silence fell. In her peripheral vision she could see that he was gazing into the trees again, so she sneaked a glance at him. As if he sensed her perusal, he turned to look at her.

''The long and short of it is,'' he went on huskily, ''that you can stay with me. No goin' to Denver, no goin' to Santa Fe, no livin' in Cutter Gulch. But you gotta pay a mighty steep price. You either marry me, or you gotta go. Where you go is up to you.''

She hugged her knees more tightly and closed her eyes.

''I'm sorry it's that way. I know you have a real big need for me to be your friend right now.'' His voice went thick and gravelly. ''I feel like I'm failin' you, and I suppose I am. But try to understand it ain't by choice. The sad truth is, I can't have you live with me, Rebecca. Sleepin' a few feet away, always close at hand. I want you too much to handle it for months on end, and my cabin's the only place I can put you. Me, tryin' to steer clear of you. It'd just never work. And I'll be damned if I'll have you in my bed without marryin' you, even if it would leave you free to go later. My feelin's for you run too deep to do you that way, for one, and to be honest, I'd probably love you so much by the time you got a hankerin' to leave, I'd hobble you and snub you to the bedpost.''

She nodded, her throat closed off so tightly she wasn't sure she could speak.

He swore under his breath and threw the blade of grass away. After a long moment, he said, ''If you do some thinkin' about marryin' me, you need to know that your leery feelin's about sharin' my bed is groundless. I'd never hurt you, honey. I'd write it in blood for you, but

I can't write a lick, so you just gotta trust my word. If it's any comfort, I gotta a load of failin's, but breakin' my word ain't one of 'em.''

Rebecca propped an elbow on her knee and rested her forehead on her upturned palm. "Oh, Mr. Spencer, what am I going to do?" she asked in a taut voice.

"Whatever it is, I'll help you all I can. I hope you know that."

"I know you will."

"Well, that's somethin'." He gave a low, bitter laugh. "At least you don't think I'm rotten all the way through."

"I don't think you're rotten at all." She raised her head to fix a tear-filled gaze on him. "You're the best friend I've ever had."

A suspicious brightness came into his eyes as well, and he blinked. "Thank you for that. It means more'n you know." He ran a hand over his hair. "I gotta ask, though. Does that mean you got no deeper feelin's for me?"

Rebecca nearly said no. But that wasn't being entirely honest, and she felt he deserved at least that from her. "I'm not sure," she said shakily. "I have difficulty breathing when you're not with me. What's that mean?"

He chuckled softly. "I reckon it means you gotta lung problem." He held up an arm. "Come here, darlin'."

Remembering his admission about having "powerful-strong yearnings" for her, she stiffened. "I, um . . . probably shouldn't."

A twinkle of mischief warmed his eyes. "I ain't hoverin' that close to the edge. Come here." He snaked his outstretched arm behind her, catching her at the waist, and then ran his other arm under her bent knees. The next instant, she was on his lap, the quilt hanging off one of her shoulders. He pressed her head to his chest and rested his cheek against her hair, his strong arms cradling her close. "I been wantin' to do this for damned near a month."

Rebecca looped an arm around his strong neck. "Oh, Race."

"Race? Did I hear you right? I'll be damned. The lady

finally calls me by my first name! We're flat makin' progress.''

She smiled against his shirt. "You must think I'm such a silly goose," she said wearily.

"Nope. Not a bit of it." He rubbed his jaw back and forth over her braid. "You're gonna get over this, honey. Trust me on that."

"I'm not so sure anymore. If anything, it seems as if it's worse."

He gave her shoulder a comforting squeeze. "Hey, now, you listen up." His hand stilled on her arm. "You ever done diggin' that loosened the dirt around the roots of a big tree?"

Rebecca closed her eyes. This man—this impossible man. What did trees have to do with anything? "No, I can't say that I have."

"Well, I have. There on the knoll where my cabin sits, there's this here fir tree. One big son'buck. Must be hundreds of years old. That tree's seen storms and drought and every other damned thing, but it's grown big and strong anyhow." He pressed his lips to her temple, a feathery, comforting kiss, as a father might give a beloved child. "Would you say that tree's a silly goose?"

Oh, God. She wanted a chain and padlock to bind his arms around her. "No, I don't suppose I would."

"Well, I ran water to my cabin and put me in a pump at the dry sink. Took some diggin' and pipe layin' to do it, and that big old tree was square in my way. I dug around its roots. Had to take an ax to a couple. But damned if that tree didn't bounce right back. Got a little sickly-lookin' for a month or so that summer is all."

Rebecca found herself smiling in spite of herself. It didn't matter if he made sense. He meant well. And knowing he cared about her feelings—it made her heart ache. The very best kind of ache, of course.

"Anyhow, I was flat impressed by that tree's grit. I really thought it'd probably die, or maybe never be quite the same. But it fooled me. Before that, I never paid much mind to that tree. There's hundreds on my ranch a lot like it. It was a real pretty tree, to be sure. Prettier than most.

But it was still just another tree.'' He squeezed her shoulder again. "After all that happened to it, though? Seein' it go through that and gettin' strong again? Well, I gotta tell you, I developed a real special regard for that damned old tree.''

"Is there a point to this story?''

He chuckled. "You ain't real patient, are you? Hell, yes, there's a point.'' He moved his hand to her back, lightly massaging the tense muscles his fingertips unerringly found. "Like I said, I got a real high regard for that tree. And one night, not long after it started lookin' healthier, along came a windstorm. A real bad'un. Took part of my barn roof, blew down fences. I was all het up over the damage. That evenin' when I come in from workin', I noticed that old tree was leanin' funny. I went over to look and seen that the side where the roots was damaged had lost hold in the wind. That tree was about to fall over.

"It flat made me feel sad, I'll tell you. So I rounded up all the men from the bunkhouse, and we set to work with ropes and horses, pullin' and heavin' on that damned old tree until we got it standin' straight again. Then we tied off to other trees with the ropes to give the poor thing some ballast where its roots was all in a stir. Then we filled in around the injured ones with fresh dirt and packed it down.''

"Did it recover?''

"I been there two years, and that was the first summer. I kept the ropes on that old tree pulled tight, replacin' the ones that got weak from rot, until this last summer. So it took nigh onto two years. But that old tree has put itself down some new roots now, and it's as strong as it ever was. Had us a windstorm a few months back. Never bothered it a whit.''

Rebecca traced her fingertip over one of his shirt buttons. "And I'll recover, like your tree. Is that what you're saying?''

"I'm the one tellin' this here story.''

She smiled in spite of herself.

"Real recent like, I happened upon a little gal in an arroyo,'' he said huskily. "Kneelin' like a little golden-

haired angel, smack in the middle of a bloodbath. Starin'
off, pale as cream. I took me a look around, and I figured
all the terrible things she must've seen. And I gotta tell
you, I worried that she might never come right again.''

''She hasn't.''

''Would you let me tell my story?'' He pressed a kiss
to her temple again. ''Anyhow . . . she was a real pretty
little thing. But females is kinda like trees—you find 'em
every which way you look. She was prettier than most,
but she was still just another female. No offense intended,
you understand.''

''None taken,'' she whispered, her mouth trembling in
a smile.

''Like my tree, that little gal surprised me. She not only
come right. She damned near shot me!''

''I did not!''

''Well, part of you was wantin' to draw my blood.''
He made a sound that was half-laugh and half-sigh.
''Hissin' and spittin' and raisin' all kinds of sand. I was
flat impressed, and in that moment, that little gal stopped
bein' just another female to me. I developed me a real
high regard for her grit.'' He moved his jaw to make room
as he settled a hand over her hair. His voice when he
spoke again rang with regret. ''Then I took off and left
her, worryin' about my goddamned cattle. And while I
was gone, a windstorm come along, and by the time I got
back to her again, she was leanin' sort of funny. Ever
since then, I been tryin' to give her some ballast on her
weak side to keep her standin' straight, but there's been
some high winds that came 'long to shake her off balance
again. I reckon that'd be enough to make anybody lose
faith and not trust her roots to hold.''

Rebecca made a fist on his shirt. ''Oh, Race . . .''

''You're just leanin' hard on me right now, darlin'.
That's all. You need time to heal and get some strength
back in your legs. I got every confidence you're gonna
be fine. You just gotta believe in yourself as much as I
do.'' She felt his arms tighten around her. ''Even harder,
sweetheart, you gotta try to believe in me. I ain't gonna
walk off and leave you without tyin' off with ropes to

give you ballast. Be it in Denver or Cutter Gulch. I'll see to it you'll have someone to lean on.''

She wanted to lean on him. No one else.

Silence settled. After a long while, he said, "So, what d'ya think?''

"About what?''

"About trustin' me to tie off with rope,'' he said with a chuckle.

Rebecca had never trusted anyone quite as much. "I do. I trust you.''

"Well, then? Should I be plannin' on that trip to Denver? Or do you wanna give Cutter Gulch a go for a while.'' He leaned around to try and see her face. Then he rested his jaw atop her head again. "Uh-huh. That's a real interestin' answer.'' He sighed. "I'll tell you what let's do. Let's give Cutter Gulch a try. All right? I'll get you all lined up out there, make sure you're with real fine folks who'll watch after you and get word to me straight-away if you need me. And on top of that, I'll come see you once a week, without fail. There's a nice place to eat there. You can dress up pretty as a picture, and I'll slick up, and I'll take you out to a fancy supper. Won't that be fun?''

She kept her face hidden against his chest. "I can't.''

"You can't? Go to supper, you mean? It ain't against your religion, I hope.''

"Anywhere. I can't go.'' She started to shake and pressed closer to him. "I can't leave you. I'm afraid to be someplace where I can't see you. I know it's crazy. I know it's stupid. I'm afraid of things that aren't even there! But knowing that doesn't help.''

He moved a hand to her hair. "Ah, sweetheart.''

"I'll marry you. I have no choice. I can't go away from you. Please, Race, I just *can't*!''

The frantic note in her voice was Race's undoing. God, how he loved her. On the other hand, as much as he wanted her, as desperately as he needed her, he wasn't willing to take her any way he could get her. There had to be a line drawn at some point that a man didn't allow himself to step over.

"All right," he said gruffly. "You win, darlin'. You can stay with me until spring. We'll make out some way. Maybe by then you'll be feelin' better about things. You reckon?"

"But you said—"

"Oh, hell. I know what I said. I was just goin' on."

"No, you weren't! You're just saying that to make me feel better."

He chuckled. "If that ain't just like a woman. Not happy with the fish when she's got him hooked. But in a snit if he ain't interested in her bait."

She made an exasperated sound.

"I'll get you learned up on handlin' a Colt," he told her, laughter lacing his voice. "If I take after you, you can shoot me and put me outta my misery." He drew the quilt around her shoulders, then set her off his lap. "Come on, darlin'. Let's go to bed. You gotta get some rest. Could be lack of sleep is half your problem."

"In the wagon, you mean?" She sounded none too certain about that being a good idea.

Race pushed to his feet and drew her up beside him. "Why not? We're gonna be keepin' close company for the next six months, anyhow. We may as well start tonight."

An hour later, Race was nearly asleep when Rebecca called softly to him from the pallet at the opposite side of the wagon. Using the crook of his arm for a pillow, Race blinked awake and focused on the young woman across from him. In the rosy glow of the fire that filtered through the canvas, she was so beautiful lying there on the multi-patterned background of quilt blocks—even covered from chin to toe in her modest cotton nightgown. Just looking at her damned near broke his heart.

"Yo?" he said softly. "I'm awake."

She sat up, her eyes luminous in the dim light, her mussed coronet shining like a pink-gold halo at her crown. "I was just—Mr. Spencer, could I ask you an extremely personal and most embarrassing question?"

So they were back to "Mr. Spencer" again, were they?

Race raised up on an elbow. "I ain't the real bashful type, darlin'. Fire away."

"That's what worries me."

He could tell by her expression that it actually did worry her, which made him want to smile. "Don't let it worry you. It takes all different types to make the world interestin'. You and me—hell, we're so different, we're flat fascinatin'."

Looking faintly exasperated, she said, "Mr. Spencer, this is *very* difficult for me. Please don't tease."

He wasn't teasing. She was the most fascinating creature he'd ever met. "I'm sorry. What is it you wanna ask me?"

She flapped a hand. "Well, you know, if I were to marry you?"

His heart stuttered. "Yeah, what about it?"

"I, um . . . have some concerns in regard to your, um . . ." She leaned toward him and whispered, "In regard to your manly inclinations."

Since she'd whispered it, Race didn't think she was asking if he drank, smoked, or chewed tobacco. "My inclinations when I'm makin' love, you mean?"

She brushed at her cheek, her gaze skittering from his. "Is *that* what you call it?"

He bit back a grin, amused that she was still whispering. "That's one of the polite names for it. What d'you call it?" he whispered back.

She leaned toward him again. "When my mother spoke with me about what to expect on my marriage night, she referred to it as 'a man doing his business.' "

"Ah." Race nodded and shrugged. Then he whispered, "So what's your concerns?"

She wrapped a tuft of quilting yarn around her finger and drew it so tight that even in the dimness, he saw her fingertip go dark. By that alone, he knew how difficult it was for her to speak with him like this. "When my mother talked to me, she explained what I might expect from a man of my own religious persuasions. In our faith, physical unions take place solely for the purpose of procreation. How would you feel about that?"

Race was flat amazed. Somehow he hadn't pictured Bible thumpers as being that type. He and his men—well, now, that was another story. Every few months they headed north to a larger town for a little procreation to break up the boredom—betting on horse races, playing poker, drinking, and dancing. And enjoying some procreation was definitely all they had in mind when they headed to an upstairs room with a sporting woman.

"Why, honey, I'd be real pleased," Race replied. "To be honest, I figured we might come at that particular activity from two different directions and that it'd take us a spell to find us a happy meetin' ground."

She looked slightly bemused. "You mean—" She flapped her hand again. "You mean you're of the same mind?"

"Absolutely."

Her bemusement turned to unmistakable incredulity. "Truly? Somehow, you struck me as a man who—" She went to flapping her hand again, this time so hard he had cause to worry she might bust her wrist. "Are you certain, Mr. Spencer? It's terribly important to me, you understand. That my life partner share the same views, I mean."

Race had a bad feeling that maybe he couldn't see shit for all the manure. "Rebecca, what is it, exactly, that's worryin' you?"

She wound the yarn around her fingertip again. "Well . . . due to certain recent events in my life, it has come to my attention that not all men are governed by religious strictures when it comes to that sort of thing. That they have base, animalistic urges that I would find abhorrent."

Pete was a savvy old codger about females, after all. "You been worryin' about what you saw them bastards in the arroyo doin'."

She nodded, then let the yarn slip free from her fingertip and began wringing her hands. "I know, of course, that you'd never be cruel! I just mean—well, the tendencies to do those kinds of things—to a woman. Do you have those sorts of inclinations?"

"Honey, them ruffians is all a half-bubble off plumb. You know what I'm sayin'? They're loco. With normal men who ain't loco, there ain't a whole lot of difference between how one fella goes about things and how another one does.''

She sneaked a glance at him. "Are you saying you would go about it the same way my mother described? Like the brethren, I mean?''

He chuckled. He couldn't help himself. "Do they stand on their heads and drink water from a glass while they're at it, or what?''

She rewarded him with a startled giggle, which she stifled by biting her lip. "Ma never made mention of it, so I rather think not.''

"Well, then, since I got the same equipment as any other man, churchy or not, I think I'm safe in sayin' I do it pretty much like your people do it.''

She averted her gaze from his. "I have one other question.''

"Ask away. Like I said, there ain't a whole lot I'm bashful about.''

"Frequency," she said softly.

Race couldn't believe he'd heard her right. "Beg pardon?''

"How often? Ma told me what I might expect from Henry, but I—''

"Who the hell's Henry?" Race immediately wanted to kill the son of a bitch. Jealousy, white-hot and clawing, grabbed hold of him. "*Henry?*''

She fastened a startled gaze on him. "Henry Rusk. He's the brother the Council of Brethren selected to be my future husband. That's why Ma explained my wifely duties to me, because the council had chosen my life partner. She would have had no reason to prepare me, otherwise.''

"Do you got feelin's for him?''

"I respect and like him." As if she feared he would find that appalling, she rushed to add, "I'm sure I would have grown to love him in time, and he me. We were to become officially betrothed when I reached Santa Fe, where he and his family live now, and married sometime next summer, the precise date as yet undecided.''

Race pushed up to sit cross-legged. "So you and this here Henry ain't betrothed yet?"

"No, and even if we were, Henry and the others are bound to think I'm dead. Another wife will be selected for him, and he'll get on with his life. Happily, I'm sure." She sighed. "It's not as if ours would have been a love match."

"So how often did your ma say you could expect good old Henry to—" He cleared his throat and gestured with his hand. "Well, you know. How often?"

She wrinkled her nose and her pretty mouth tightened. "Once a week."

Race didn't blame her for looking disgusted. "Jesus, how old is Henry, anyway?"

"Twenty-two."

Race pictured a Nancy-boy fanatic with a protruding Adam's apple who wore horn-rimmed spectacles. "Sweetheart, with me as your husband, you could pretty much forget that once-a-week business. I can do a helluva lot better than that."

She fixed lustrous blue eyes on him. "Truly?"

For the first year, he'd have this girl for dessert after every meal, then love her senseless at night. She wouldn't have a problem sleeping anymore, that was for damned sure. "Honey, pleasin' you would be the most important thing in the world to me, I swear it. If you ever agreed to marry me, that is."

She searched his gaze, then bent her head to fiddle with the buttons on the front of her nightgown, which ran from chin to waist. "Well, I've been doing a great deal of thinking since we retired." She looked up and nibbled at her lip. "I, um . . . truly don't believe I'm ever going to wish to return to my church family in Santa Fe. Since the arroyo—" She broke off and glanced around, as if she sought answers in the shadows beyond the glow of the firelight. "I just don't have the same beliefs now, and I doubt I ever will again."

Race doubted it too. Not because he believed she'd never regain her faith. Without it, he feared she'd never have the ballast she needed to withstand the windstorms life had a way of blowing at a person. For that reason, he counted it as damned important to somehow restore her belief in her God. How he would manage that, he had no idea, the only certainty being that when he did, he'd encourage her to believe differently than she had before. To stand on her own two feet. To fight to defend herself. To trust in her God to give her the strength to fight her own battles, instead of counting on Him to fight them for her.

"I see," he said softly. "I reckon I can understand you not wantin' to go back. As much as I'm sure they love ya, they'd expect you to take up where you left off, and that'd be damned hard after all you been through."

She started to wring her hands again. "Yes, and that being the case, I am pretty much alone in the world now. You are my only close friend. There's Pete. And Johnny and Mr. Grigsley, of course. And I've become fond of them. But not like I am of you." She dragged in a deep breath, then exhaled with a lift of her shoulders. "Anyway, there's no one in Denver for me, no one in Cutter Gulch. There's only you.

"I, um, don't suppose that's a very good reason to marry a man. But on the other hand, I must say I am much fonder of you than I ever was of Henry, and I fully intended to marry him. I also feel convinced I would have come to love him in time. So why wouldn't the same hold true with you?"

Race had a lump in his throat the size of a hen egg. "Rebecca, are you sayin' you'll be my wife?"

"Are you absolutely sure you want me?"

He couldn't believe she was about to say yes. "Ah, honey. There's nothin' I want more in the whole damned world."

"Even though you know I don't have the same depth of feeling?"

Race felt positive he could make her love him, given a bit of time and half a chance. "Even though," he said softly. "I just got one question. I know how come I want you. But what do you figure to get out of this marriage? I offered to let you stay with me for the next six months."

She bent her head. "It's not that I don't trust your word

or anything. But it occurs to me that if you were to become truly miserable, rather than have me shoot you, you might elect to make me go to Cutter Gulch.''

"So this is kind of like a guarantee to you that I won't do that?''

"A guarantee that I can stay with you, yes.''

"Well, hang me for a fool, darlin', but I said six months, and I'll give you six months. I don't break my word.''

"And then?'' She lifted her shimmering gaze to his. "When the six months are up? You'll want to be rid of me. You'll take me someplace and leave me there.''

Race couldn't imagine leaving her anywhere. "You're liable to be feelin' a hair different in six months, honey. That gives you some healin' time. You'll be stronger and not feelin' so froggy. You sure you don't wanna wait and see how you feel then? Marriage is forever.''

"You're attempting to talk me out of it.'' There was a note of accusation in her tone. "You've changed your mind.''

"Nope. Get that outta your head.''

"It's true!'' Her voice went shrill. "You were all ready to do it, and now you're not.''

"Damn it, Rebecca, that ain't it!'' He raked his fingers through his hair. "I'm tryin' to do the decent thing instead of the rotten one, which is a helluva lot more appealin'. I haven't changed my mind. I just don't wanna take you as my wife unless you're sure.''

"I'm sure. This way I know you won't leave me. Not next month, not in six. Come spring, I'll still be all alone in the world except for you. What will change? Nothing!''

"Well, I sure as hell ain't gonna beat you off with a stick. If you're sure, you got yourself a deal.''

"Well, then?'' she said, her voice vibrant with anxiety. "It's decided?''

"It's decided.''

She smiled slightly. "Have you any plans for when?''

"When will we get married, you mean?'' Race flashed her a slow grin. "If you're sure you wanna do it, darlin',

I ain't a man to let the prettiest little trout I ever seen slip off my hook."

"I'm absolutely positive I want to do it," she assured him.

"Well, then, as far as I'm concerned, we can do it right now."

"Now?"

She looked so startled that he chuckled. "Actually, I reckon we'll probably marry twice. You'll be wantin' to say words in front of a preacher someday, I'm guessin'."

"Someday? Most assuredly, Mr. Spencer, no 'some-day' to it."

"Fine with me. As soon as we can arrange it, all you gotta do is say the word, and I'll be happy to marry you in front of a preacher." To Race's way of thinking, her kind of marriage wasn't really necessary, and until he got the ruffians off their backs, there was no telling when it could even be done. He wasn't about to wait that long. "Meanwhile, though—what with you bein' a lady and all—I reckon you'd feel easier about sharin' my bed if we had us a formal agreement. I'd be right proud to marry you in the way of my mother's people, that bein' the Apache way."

"The Apache way?" She blinked. "Um . . . Mr. Spencer, is there truly such urgency? We're only three days from your ranch. Correct? Why can't we simply wait to share a bed until then?"

"Because you ain't sleepin', and until we get settled at the ranch, which could take a spell, it'll be hard to get away to get married in town."

"But if you're in the wagon or the cabin with me, I'll sleep."

He bit back a smile. "Darlin', lookin' at you right now, I can't say, in all honesty, that you seem real relaxed."

She gave a shrill little laugh. "And you think my shar-ing your bed will relax me?"

"Uh-huh." He ran his gaze over her tense body, think-ing to himself that within an hour, he could have the girl feeling as if her bones had melted. "I guarant-ass-tee it."

"Actually, Mr. Spencer, I think I would prefer to wait

and have a conventional ceremony. I'll be fine for however long it takes to arrange it.''

"You'll get your preacher ceremony, Rebecca. I promise you that. But for now, we can't go that route, and I ain't inclined to let you go on like you are until we can. You ain't fine, darlin'. You got circles under your eyes, you're droppin' weight, and you're wound up like a watch spring. As your husband, I got a magic cure for all three problems.''

"The last time I partook of a magic cure, I couldn't walk.''

She wouldn't be able to walk this time, either. "Rebecca, among your church folks, ain't it an upheld rule that the man makes the important decisions and a woman does like she's told?''

"Yes,'' she said faintly.

Most times, Race felt that way of thinking was damned near as stupid as turning the other cheek. But he had no qualms about using it to his advantage in this instance. If she was too skittish to gentle break, he would at least be able to hold her, which was bound to make her feel safer. That way, maybe she would get some rest.

"Well, then, I've decided to marry you the way an Apache man would in an urgent situation.''

"Wh-what does that entail?''

He touched the tip of her nose and winked at her. "Rebecca Ann Morgan, from this moment and until I'm dust in the wind, you're my woman, my life, my heart. I have spoken it.''

"And that's all there would be to it?'' At his nod, she looked slightly appalled. "And what words would I say?''

"You don't get to say nothin'.''

"Why? Surely both people must make a vow.''

"Nope. It ain't necessary for the woman to make a vow. Just the man. And it's more like statin' his feelin's, actually.''

"Oh.'' She frowned. "What if the feeling isn't reciprocated?''

"Isn't what?''

"Returned. What if the girl isn't so inclined? Doesn't wish to marry him?"

"Well, a smart man usually tests the water first, I reckon. If he ain't so smart and he takes a girl who don't want him, she accepts it. Ain't a whole lot else she can do once she gets took. An Apache man is kinda bent on keepin' what's his when it comes to his woman."

"That seems rather barbaric."

Race smiled. "It ain't a whole lot different than the way your folks do things, from the sound of it, gettin' your husband picked for you instead of pickin' him yourself."

She wrinkled her nose, much as she had moments before. "Would you mind waiting until tomorrow, at least?"

"I can't see the point." He rose to his knees and reached to smooth her hair, smiling at the way the curls immediately popped back up and wondering how she might look with it down. His gut knotted at the thought of her coming to him, as if in a dream, wearing nothing but waves of gold falling over her shoulders. "Sweetheart, don't look so worried. I ain't gonna bite. Not hard, anyhow. You trust me, don't you?"

"Yes."

"You wantin' to do somethin' havin' to do with your religion to make it seem more right to you?"

She shook her head. "No. I just don't feel comfortable with that barbaric custom of being 'took,' is all. Just the thought gives me the shudders."

Race leaned down to look her in the eye, his nose scant inches from hers. "I didn't notice you shudderin'."

"When?"

"When you got took. Honey, I done did it."

"You done did what?" she asked, looking mildly alarmed.

"Took you."

She glanced around as if she'd missed something. "I didn't get 'took.' "

"You sure as hell did. I said the words, clear as rain."

She blinked. "I thought you were simply informing me of the way it was done."

"It was more showin' you, actually." Race noticed her eyes going dark. He knew from experience that wasn't a good sign. "Sweetheart, don't get all het up. I ain't gonna be all over you like dogs fightin' over a bone."

She fixed a frightened gaze on him. "Dogs fighting over a bone?"

"Bad choice of words. I got a talent for it." He settled a hand over her nape, his fingertips feathering through silken curls. "You gotta know I ain't gonna force you to do nothin' you're afraid to do, or that you feel real nervous about. Not straightaway, anyhow."

"Of course."

"Well, then? Think of the Apache thing as a handshake marriage. We'll get married again when the time is right, all fancy and proper to your way of thinkin'. Until then, we're married all fancy and proper to my way of thinkin'. What real difference does it make how we done it, as long as we're married?"

She hugged her waist. "None I guess." As her voice trailed away, the alarmed expression came back over her face. She pressed closer and whispered, "Does that mean this is our *wedding* night?"

Race wasn't sure why she was whispering, but given the fact that he'd just married the girl, he figured this was just one of the hundreds of times he'd probably do things that didn't make sense to him, simply to please her. Pitching his own voice to a whisper, he replied, "I reckon so. Why?"

"Oh, lands!" she cried, loud enough to scare snakes in six counties.

Chapter 16

It was obvious to Race the instant he touched his new bride that theirs had no chance of being the most satisfying wedding night on record. She knelt next to the pallet, gazing at the quilts. He touched his palm to the small of her back. *Her trembling back.* He wasn't sure if she was shaking from fear or from cold.

"Sweetheart?" On his knees and slightly behind her, he leaned around to see her face. "You gonna jump on in? You're gettin' chilled."

Judging by her less than enthusiastic expression, he might have just asked her to leap in a rattlesnake pit. He tossed the quilts back, then grasped her arm to guide her forward. With halting movements, she took it from there, twisting to sit and scooting to the far side of the makeshift bed. Race removed his guns, folded the gun belt around the holsters, and placed them carefully on the floor at the head of the pallet.

Acutely aware of Rebecca's gaze on him, he smiled slightly as he took off his shirt. She shot him one startled look, then immediately squeezed her eyes closed. He decided the old saying, "just keep your pants on," might be damned good advice for him to heed, at least until she settled down some and became more comfortable around him. He tossed the shirt near his guns, then sat at the edge of the pallet to pull off his boots and remove his thick leather belt.

Finally ready to join her in bed, Race drew up his knees

slightly to rest his arms and study her. There was something peculiar about the way she lay there, flat on her back, eyes squeezed closed, fine-boned hands folded beneath her breasts. *Christ.* She looked like a corpse laid out for burial.

"Rebecca, darlin', are you scared?" he asked softly.

A disgruntled frown passed over her delicate features. She cracked open one eye. "Mr. Spencer, if you . . . if it's your intention to consummate, I'd truly prefer to maintain a degree of separateness, which is difficult to do while conversing." Her mouth softened a hair. "As for your question, never having done my wifely duty before, I'm quite tense, but I wouldn't go so far as to say I feel afraid. My mother assured me it will be quick and involve only a tolerable amount of pain. I can't imagine why she would have lied to me about it."

Race reached up to stroke his chin, more to hide his grin than to check for stubble. He had a feeling he could go to bed tonight with a beard rough enough to sand wood and it wouldn't matter one hell of a lot. "I wish I could put your mind at ease, honey, but the honest truth is, I don't know no more about it than you probably do."

She opened both eyes and one of the sweetest smiles he'd ever seen curved her mouth. "Oh, I'm so pleased," she said softly. Then she wrinkled her nose and giggled. "I feared perhaps you had firsthand knowledge, and I was rather hesitant to come straight out and ask you." She took a deep breath and sighed. "To be honest, Mr. Spencer, I sorely misjudged you. I had you pegged as a—well, please don't be offended—but I rather suspected you were no stranger to fornication."

"Fornication?" Race had no idea in hell what that was.

"You have that look about you," she informed him apologetically. "To someone of my persuasions, a rather dangerous look. Very worldly and—well, earthy. But if you're as ignorant as I about bedroom matters I was obviously wrong."

Race drew his hand from his chin to hold up a staying finger. "Whoa, there, darlin'. Don't go barkin' up that rope."

"What rope?"

"The ignorant rope." He turned, lifted the quilts, and slipped in beside her. "I'm a dumb jackass about a lot of things, but makin' love ain't one of 'em." He propped his head on the heel of his hand to gaze down at her. "I was talkin' about the virgin pain and your ma sayin' it was tolerable. I don't know nothin' about that because I ain't never been with a first-time gal. The ladies I been with, and there's been a number of 'em, was all well broke to the saddle, if you know what I mean."

The puzzlement in her luminous eyes told him she didn't. "Well broke, Mr. Spencer?"

He traced the fragile line of her cheekbone with the back of a knuckle. "Never you mind. It ain't important."

Her expression grew troubled. "So you have considerable experience with . . . fornication?"

Race was beginning to glean the meaning of the word. Yet another highfalutin tongue waggler, compliments of his golden-haired angel. "I reckon I do."

He smiled slightly, noting the rapid pulse beat at her temple when he pressed the backs of his fingers over the spot. The girl hadn't lied. She wasn't scared; she was plumb terrified. He decided then and there that he needed to hold off on staking his claim. *Consummate,* she'd called it. She had big words for damned near everything, even screwing. Fornicating? Jesus H. Christ.

Given the fact that it didn't appear he'd be fornicating any time soon, Race decided he could send her off to sleep with something else that might comfort her in her dreams. "You disappointed in me, knowin' I been fornicatin' before I met you?"

She nibbled at her bottom lip as she considered the question. "Well, it is a sin, you know."

For a young woman who said she was flat done with God and all that Bible-thumping stuff, she sure had strong leanings in that direction. Doing his best to sound surprised, Race said, "Fornicatin' is a sin?"

Her eyes widened slightly. "Surely you know that."

"Well, I know you ain't supposed to do it outside marriage. Cookie explained that to me. But I can't see how much of anything, no matter how wrong, is a *sin*. What're you sayin'? That it's my fault I fornicated?''

''Well, of course, Mr. Spencer. If not your fault, whose might it be?''

''God's.''

That brought her to a sitting position. She whipped around to fix an incredulous gaze on him. ''God's? Where in heaven's name did you get that idea? The wrongs you commit are *your* doing, and they are therefore *your* fault. How on earth can you lay the blame at God's door?''

Race kept his expression carefully solemn. Looking stupid wasn't a problem. He seemed to have a talent for that. ''Well, because, darlin'. He's my Maker, ain't He? Accordin' to how you believe, anyhow. I'll tell you straightaway that I ain't real up on the Bible. Not bein' able to read, I just have to go by things I've heard, here and there.''

''God is your Maker, yes. But that doesn't make Him responsible for your actions.''

Race settled in for a long wait while she launched into an explanation of how things worked, telling him the story of Creation and about God's making man in His own image, but giving him free will and then a whole bunch of warnings about all kinds of things he shouldn't do. ''So you see, how you choose to live your life, and the things you decide to do while you're living it are entirely up to you,'' she concluded. ''If not for free will, man would have no choices. As it is, he does. Therefore if he elects to do something wrong or terrible, he alone is held accountable, not God.''

Race assumed a bewildered frown. ''Hm. That's purely amazin'. All this time I had me the idea that when people done really terrible, horrible things that it was all God's fault. And now you're tellin' me He don't got nothin' to do with it? That the folks who commit the act bear the whole blame? And I got black marks on my soul for all the wrong things I done?''

''Absolutely. We alone are responsible for our actions.''

Race gave her his best ''gotcha'' look. ''Then explain

me this one thing, darlin'. How come is it you're blamin' God for what them heartless bastards done to your people in the arroyo?''

Her face drained completely of color, and she stared at him for so long with a shocked, blank expression on her face that he almost wished he'd kept his mouth shut. He kept waiting for her to say something. Instead, little muscles in her face started to twitch, and it seemed to him her skin grew taut over the bones, making her look almost skeletal.

Then, before Race could anticipate what she meant to do, she leaped up, ran to the wagon gate, and jerked aside the flap. ''Rebecca, come back here!''

In a blur of white, she vanished into the darkness. Cursing, Race strapped on his guns, grabbed his wool blanket from the floor, and rushed after her, half-afraid she'd venture a dangerous distance from camp and encounter the ruffians, whom he knew were following them. He was relieved when he found her kneeling beneath a tree just beyond the edge of camp. Upset the girl might be, but stupid, she wasn't.

Tender of foot, he gimped his way to her over stickery evergreen needles, sharp stones, and twigs. As he drew up behind her, he heard her sobbing and saying in a broken voice, ''Oh, God . . . oh, God . . . oh, God . . .''

He went down on one knee behind her, draped the blanket over her shoulders, and then folded his arms around her. She was shaking so horribly that he wanted nothing more than to beg her forgiveness for hazing her into a trap like that, but truthfully he wasn't and never would be sorry. His little angel needed her God back, and if Race had to hurt her some to see that she found Him, he figured the end justified the means.

So he said nothing. Offered no apology or words of comfort. He just held her so she wouldn't get cold and felt his heart breaking a little more with each one of the sobs that racked her slender body. When she had cried herself nearly out, she began to lean more heavily into him, turning slightly to press a damp cheek against his bare chest. *Silence.* Rubbing her arm through the blanket,

Race gazed up through the pine boughs at the moon-silvery sky and the clouds that drifted overhead, like wispy layers of gauze between him and the twinkling stars.

God. Race had determined long ago that He had many different faces and as many different names, and that He showed Himself to people in different ways. Race believed—deeply. And he supposed that the God he did believe in was the same one Rebecca knew. But, by the same token, a lot of her ideas and convictions struck him as totally loco. He might be wrong, but it seemed to him there was little joy in her way of believing, that it was mostly trying to be impossibly good and following so many rules they were hard to keep track of.

Maybe it was the Indian in him, but Race wasn't much on rules. To him, God was moonlight coming through pine boughs, the birth of a new fawn, the drift of a snow-flake, the innocence in an angel's blue eyes. His God was all beautiful. No hellfire and damnation. No lightning-bolt vengeance. Just love and goodness. To Race's way of thinking, the only rule his God probably wanted him to follow, hard and fast, was to try his best to be a decent man. It made sense that if Race and everyone else would only work hard at being decent that all those other lists of rules would be unnecessary. Being decent sort of came with its own rule book.

"My parents, the others, they trusted in Him to protect them," Rebecca whispered, her voice weighted with weariness. "They believed in free will, just as I explained it to you. Yet they also believed God was their shield. How is it that you can cut your way through all the intricacies of it, seeing so easily that it can't be both ways, but well-educated Bible scholars like my papa and the other brethren could not?"

Race continued to massage her arm, his gaze fixed on the moonbeams. "Honey, I ain't the one to answer religion questions for you. I ain't got a lick of Christian learnin' under my belt, and to tell ya the truth, the parts of the Bible I have heard tell of sound sorta farfetched."

She followed his gaze to the silvery light coming down through the trees.

"I can tell you this, though, it bein' somethin' I've seen and noted." He tightened his hand over her arm. "There's men like me, who can't read a word or write a lick, and we're dumb jackasses, no arguin' the point. But there's also men that can read and write, who spend so damned much time doin' both that they're dumb jackasses in their own right."

She stiffened and threw him an incredulous look. "Are you saying my papa was a dumb jackass?"

She sounded so indignant, Race chuckled. "Well, bein's I call myself one, I reckon he's in good company. I don't mean dumb, I don't guess. Ignorant, in my case. Confused, in his."

"I'm amazed you know a word like 'ignorant.' "

He sighed. "Now, see there? Start talkin' religion, and you're pissed off."

"Your referring to my father as a 'dumb jackass' has nothing to do with religion. I would appreciate it if you would concede the point and retract the statement."

Race met her gaze, which was fairly snapping. Her moods swung as violently as a sapling in a high wind. "Rebecca Ann, you wantin' to fight with me?"

"If you're going to besmirch my father's memory, yes, indeed!"

"Then talk so's I can understand you."

Her small nose moved closer to his. "Say you're sorry. Do you understand *that*?"

He chuckled. "I sure as hell do." Then in a softer voice, he said, "I'm sorry. I only meant that it sounds to me like your papa read the whole damned Bible, and it's a thick bugger. I don't know what parts of the Good Book he found his beliefs in, but it stands to reason there was a helluva lot of readin' betwixt one point and another. I think he plumb forgot readin' about 'free will' by the time he read the part about God protectin' him from all harm. The two don't mix real good, and it'd be easy to get your facts muddled, takin' them, one by one, from such a big book. You hear what I'm sayin'?"

"That my father didn't have good sense."

Race chuckled again. "That ain't what I said. Your papa probably made great sense most of the time. He raised you, didn't he? I gotta tell ya, that gives him a real high recommend in my books."

She looked slightly mollified. "Thank you."

"Ain't nothin' you gotta thank me for. I'm just statin' the facts. As for your papa, I just believe he got his thinkin' crossed on a couple of things and come up with some ideas that didn't make much sense at all.

"I ain't sayin' all his thinkin' was dumb. Take me, for instance. I think I'm a sensible man, most times. But here I am, kneelin' under a tree with no shirt on and stickers in my big toe. That might make sense if I had me a lovin' woman in my arms, but instead, I'm out here arguin' with one."

She smiled and rested her cheek against his chest again. "You know . . . having seen the things I've seen—those ruffians and the terrible things they did—and knowing heartless men like that have free will, I don't know how I could have expected God to protect us from them. He can't give free will to only the good people."

"Do you feel some better, knowin' He didn't break a promise to you?"

"I feel bad for blaming Him," she said softly. "And afraid, knowing He can't protect me."

"I ain't sayin' that. He can and He does. He can give you the strength you need to get through the windstorms, sweetheart. And sometimes, if you listen close, He can steer you clear of danger. I remember one time, gettin' a crawly feelin' on my neck and stoppin' my horse. Two seconds later, a rock slide broke loose and hit right where I would've been if I hadn't stopped. I reckon He protects us in all kinds of other ways, too. I'm just sayin' I don't believe he can stay a cruel man's hand, that's all."

She lifted her gaze to the moonlit sky once more and didn't speak for a while. When she finally did, she sighed. "This makes twice."

"Twice for what?"

"The two worst weeping spells of my life, and both

times you've somehow made me want to laugh instead of cry. You're a good man, Mr. Spencer. For a fornicator.''

He grinned. ''You make it sound like I done it every day and twice on Sunday. In truth, it wasn't all that often that I went to town, and it's a damned good thing, or I'd be broke.''

''Broke?''

He kept forgetting he needed to watch his tongue. He sighed and resumed gazing at the stars.

''What have you been studying up there?''

Race stared up through the pine boughs for a long while before replying.

''God,'' he finally whispered.

Race.

His name became a gentle whisper in Rebecca's mind over the next three days.

Since he spent most of each day driving the oxen with her on the wagon seat beside him, he decided to put the time to good use, and Rebecca found herself attending school, Race Spencer style. He spent hours patiently sharing with her his wealth of knowledge—teaching her how to tell her directions, showing her how to find water, telling her what to do if she became lost. He frequently stopped the wagon with no warning, tied off the leads, set the brake, and lifted her down from her perch for an impromptu walk.

''That there's a wild onion,'' he would point out one time.

When next he stopped the wagon, he would stand beside the trail, booted feet spread, hands at his hips, his black Stetson cocked to shade his eyes, and say, ''Find me a wild onion, darlin'.'' As Rebecca set off to do that, Race and Blue heeled behind her like a pair of faithful hounds. Unless, of course, she happened to point out the incorrect species of plant, whereupon the very tall hound nudged back his hat, jutted his squared chin, and said, ''Rebecca Ann, *that* ain't no wild onion!''

He didn't seem to realize she was teasing him if she popped back and said, ''It ain't?'' Instead of hearing the echo, he would get an exasperated expression on his burnished face, roll his eyes, and say, "No, it *ain't*!" So much for her progress in cleaning up Race Spencer's English.

He was quite successful in teaching her, however. Throughout most of the first day, he showed her edible plants that grew wild in that country and how to find them. On the second day, he made her collect those plants without his assistance, and that evening, he set himself to the task of teaching her how to make "starvin' man's stew," a watery and not very tasty concoction that he claimed would keep her alive for days in the wilderness until she found better food or ran across people.

It didn't take Rebecca long to determine that her "handshake" husband was trying, in the only way he knew, to shore up her self-confidence, which he had so eloquently likened to the roots of his injured fir tree. Though not entirely certain that knowing how to make "starvin' man's stew" was going to result in her feeling any less fearful, Rebecca appreciated the thought nonetheless. And since she enjoyed being with him so much, she decided the lessons couldn't hurt.

Race. With each moment that passed, it became clearer to her that it wasn't so much all the things that he tried to give her, but the man himself, that was the sweetest gift. His strong hand clasping hers. The ring of his laughter in the crisp fall air. The shine of sunlight on his hair. The comfort of his arms around her at night. The knowledge that, even though he desired her, he held back from taking her. A man could stand fast against his primitive urges if he had Race Spencer's sense of honor and strength of character. Her mother had been very wrong to believe otherwise.

On the night of their "handshake" marriage, Race had asked her if she had no deeper feelings for him than friendship, and Rebecca had floundered in the tangle of her own emotions, uncertain how to reply. She had considered him her best friend, she'd told him, as if that bond somehow precluded a deeper, more meaningful one from developing. Not so, she was beginning to suspect now. It wasn't impossible for a woman to fall in love with her best friend. It was simply rare that two such strong bonds might develop in tandem.

Their last evening on the trail before reaching his ranch, Race approached Rebecca where she sat by the fire and dropped some clothing on her lap. "Go put them on," he told her.

Rebecca's eyes filled with tears when she held up the jeans and small shirt, for she knew they had belonged to Tag. She threw Race an incredulous look. "I can't wear these."

"That's pure silly, darlin'. He'd want you to get some use out of 'em." He hooked a thumb over his broad shoulder toward her wagon. "Go on. Get 'em on. If the pants is too big, come back out and I'll cinch the waist with rope."

"May I ask why?" Rebecca had never worn britches in her life, nor any clothing that wasn't solid black. She glanced at Pete, Johnny, Preach, and Trevor McNaught, who sat with her at the fire, sipping coffee. "It's not a very appropriate ensemble for a lady."

Race leaned down, the edge of his hat brim nearly touching her forehead, his twinkling brown eyes holding her gaze. In a whisper for her ears only, he said, "Rebecca Ann, mind your husband and do as you're told before I warm your backside."

She drew back to regard him with a narrowed eye. "Are you lookin' to get your nose broken again, mister?"

"Only if you'll let me have some fun first," he whispered back.

Rebecca was still blushing when she returned to the fire a few minutes later, holding up the jeans around her waist so they wouldn't fall in a puddle around her ankles. She was relieved to note that the other men around the fire were gone.

"Where is everyone?" she asked.

"Mindin' their business."

From that reply, Rebecca deduced that her husband had ordered the men to make themselves scarce. True to his word, Race cut a length of rope and fashioned her a belt.

Then he bent down to roll up the pant legs so she wouldn't trip.

"There just ain't a helluva lot to you, is there, darlin'?" he said, nudging his hat back to lazily peruse her body. By the time his gaze locked with hers, a smoldering shimmer had begun to warm his. "Mm-mm," he declared with a wolfish grin. "You're sure put together nice, though."

Rebecca's face went hot. She glanced up to make sure no one had heard him. Mr. Grigsley was the only person in sight, and he was quite some distance away, doing something by the chuck wagon. "If you think I'm going to simply stand here and display myself, you're wrong."

"That ain't my plan." He pushed to his feet to tower over her, his mouth kicked up at one corner in the crooked grin she'd come to love so much. "You ready?"

"For what?" she asked suspiciously.

"Well, now, there's a question." He grasped her elbow to tug her along beside him and led her to the edge of camp where he released her arm to face her in a half-crouch, his hands splayed on his thighs. He thrust his jaw at her. "Take your best shot, darlin'. Try to break my nose."

"Have you lost your mind?"

"Nope. It's part of the lesson. Take a swing at me. Then I'll teach you how to do it right."

Rebecca gaped at him, completely incredulous. "What is the purpose of this lesson?"

"I'm gonna learn you how to kick my ass, that's the purpose." He pointed to the bridge of his nose, which still sported a faint trace of blue. "Come on. Don't be bashful. Swing at me."

"No! I might hurt you. I'm going back and change into my own clothes. This is silly."

A determined glint came into his eyes. "It ain't silly. Bein' in so close to the herd, we can't start practicin' with guns yet. We gotta save that for when we reach the ranch. But I can start teachin' you how to defend yourself in other ways. If you can learn to kick my ass, honey, you'll be able to kick just about anybody's."

Rebecca leaned toward him and whispered, "I am not

going to practice with guns when we reach your ranch. And I am not going to learn how to beat you up, end of subject. If you will recall, sir, I believe in only passive forms of resistance.''

"In *what*?''

"A cheek turner, I believe you call it.''

"No, you ain't. Not no more.''

"I beg your pardon? Says who?''

"Says me. Them cheeks of yours is mine now, darlin'. Every sweet inch. And you're gonna learn how to keep other men's hands off of 'em.'' He pointed to his nose. "Come on. Swing.''

"No. I want no part of this.''

He flashed her a devilish grin. "Let me put it to you this way then. Either you try to kick my ass, or I'm gonna carry you back to the fire, jerk them jeans off, and have myself a fine time playin' ticktacktoe on them cute little cheeks of yours in broad daylight.''

Put to her like that, Rebecca decided to take her best shot. Luckily for him, he ducked.

Late that same night, Rebecca was nearly asleep when Race, who lay on the pallet beside her, suddenly jack-knifed upright and threw himself on her. Before she could even cry out, she was pinned, her arms anchored above her head, a heavy, muscular thigh angled across hers to keep her from kicking. For a horrible moment, she thought he meant to rape her.

"Guess what?'' he said huskily.

"You've been overcome by your ungodly urges?'' she said thinly.

His face cast into shadow, he grinned, his straight, white teeth gleaming eerily in the dim firelight. "I was gonna say, 'I gotcha,' but I reckon that's close enough.''

Her heart started to pound. Until this moment, she hadn't believed she could feel truly afraid of him ever again.

"I got at least a hundred pounds on you. You ain't gonna get your hands loose. I got a firm grip. And you can't kick. What're you gonna do to keep me from goin' after you like you're a plump little pigeon and I'm a starvin' man?''

Rebecca strained to get her wrists free from his grip, remembering once before how she'd twisted free. This time, however, his hands were like iron manacles. "Race, you're frightening me.''

"That's plumb silly. You know I ain't gonna hurt you. But if it was another man, you'd flat be in trouble. Right?''

She conceded the point with a mute nod. It felt to her as if she were flat in trouble now.

"Reactin' fast is everything," he said softly. "Give me an edge at all, and the first thing I'll do is"—he caught both her wrists in the grip of one hand—"that, which leaves you helpless and me with a hand free to play or slap you senseless. You don't wanna let that happen." He took one of her wrists in each hand again. "So . . . pretendin' I just now jumped you and knowin' you gotta strike at me while you got a chance, what've you got left to get at me with?''

When she only lay there, gazing up at him, nonplussed, he sighed and said, "Your teeth, honey." He showed her the different positions a man might assume as he wrestled her into a body pin. "In this position, go for the arm," he said. "Bite to take a hunk, and he'll let go of at least one hand to knock you loose.''

"Lovely. Bite him, and then he gets to beat on me?''

He chuckled. "The second he turns loose of one of your hands, go for his eyes." He showed her how. "No scratchin'. Jab with your finger at the inside corner with all your strength.''

"What will that do? Put his eye out?''

"Onto his cheek.''

"Oh, mercy.''

"You can't be fainthearted, darlin'. Not if you're fightin' for your life. You go for the bastard's eyes.''

He glared down at her so fiercely that Rebecca smiled. "Yessir.''

He went on to show her other places to bite, one being the shoulder, after which he said, "He'll rear back. Only for a second, so you gotta be ready. As soon as he does, he'll let go of a hand, like before, so go for his eyes. And if he lifts his hips, knife up with your knee and get him in the balls.''

She closed her eyes. "Race, must you be vulgar?"

"What d'you call 'em?"

She slitted one eye open. "His manly parts?"

He rolled off of her onto his back and angled an arm over his eyes, his chest jerking with silent laughter.

"What is so funny about that, may I ask?"

He finally caught his breath and said, "Sweetheart, if you wanna call 'em my 'manly parts' when you're talkin' with me, that's fine. But if you're ever facin' down a man, say with a gun? It just loses somethin' if you say, 'Not one step closer, mister, or I'll blow off your manly parts!' " He began to laugh again, this time until tears ran from the corners of his eyes. When at last his mirth subsided, he sighed and said, "You gotta say balls. Ain't no two ways about it. Otherwise he'll take the gun away from you, sure as shit.''

Rebecca rolled onto her side facing him with her arm tucked under her head. "I think the whole point is silly, anyway. If I were going to shoot a man, I'd never shoot him there. I'd aim for something vital.''

Race laughed until he was weak. Then, after explaining that "manly parts" were "pretty damned vital," he took Rebecca into his arms.

"Do you know," she whispered, tracing light patterns on his bare chest with a fingertip, "that almost from the first, I've always loved to have your arms around me?"

He trailed warm, silken lips over her forehead. "That's because this is where you was always meant to be," he whispered.

Chapter 17

This is where you was always meant to be.

Those words that Race had whispered to Rebecca came back to her the following afternoon when she finally got her first glimpse of his ranch. *Home.* That was her first thought. She had finally come home.

Situated in the foothills of the Rockies, his land stretched to the horizon, encompassing countless grassy meadows bordered by steep, forested slopes. As the small caravan of wagons and the slow-moving herd traversed the winding, rutted trail that led to the central part of the ranch, Race kept up an almost continuous monologue, familiarizing Rebecca with the terrain. Directing her gaze to towering stands of fir and pine, he rattled off the names of the different trees, the only two of which she managed to recall being the ponderosa and lodge pole pine. He also called her attention to some of the wildlife he spotted, a mountain chickadee, a mule deer, a bounding cottontail, a marmot, and a cougar on a distant ridge.

Upon spying the cougar, Race slowed the wagon to a stop and slipped his arm around her shoulder. Following his gaze, she stared in amazement at the huge cat. Never had she seen anything like that—a fiercely wild predator, outlined against the powder-blue sky like an animated carving limned in gold. Even at a distance, the creature's great size, power and grace of movement, and sheer beauty were absolutely stunning.

Next to her ear, Race whispered, "Now, darlin', you

know why I don't question the existence of God.''

She turned to look up at Race's burnished face, thinking that if she needed proof of God's existence, she need only to look at this man. In the space of a few violent minutes, she had been stripped of everything that truly mattered to her except life itself—her parents, her relatives, her friends, her self-confidence, her world. Even her God. There had been absolutely nothing left. On that fateful evening in the arroyo, it might have been anyone who found her, kneeling in the middle of that bloodbath, mindless with shock. But by some wondrous twist of fate—or perhaps by the hand of God Himself—it had been Race Spencer, a man who was, in every way, a consolation for all that had been taken from her.

Looking at him, she knew she would eventually heal, and until she did, he would provide her with the support she needed to stand. He was also offering her a world to replace the one lost to her, as well as a chance to love and to be loved. He had given her so very much, this man. And he was still giving, trying to make her believe in God again, trying to restore her self-confidence, making his home her home. Thus far, all she'd done was take from him. Taking and taking, giving nothing in return.

With her gaze, she traced the features of his face—the high forehead, the bladelike nose, the high cheekbones, the strong line of jaw and chin, those eyes that always seemed to see to her soul, and the firm yet mobile mouth that fascinated her so. He was so very like the mountain lion, big and intimidatingly powerful, his body roped with muscle. There was also a wild, savage aura about him— an indefinable something that marked him as different, possibly the Apache blood that ran in his veins. Yet for all of that, he was beautiful in a raw, purely masculine sort of way, as rugged and dauntless as the landscape around them.

Needing to touch him, she reached up to stroke the strands of ebony that fell like glistening silk threads over his collar, then she trailed trembling fingertips to his cheek. He had touched her just like this, so many times, almost reverently, as if he were trying to commit every angle of her features to memory.

His were already carved upon her heart.

"What?" he asked softly.

Rebecca realized she was looking up at him through tears. Over the course of the month-long journey to this pocket of paradise, how many times had she sat in the back of her wagon, her gaze fixed on the lumbering cattle behind the caravan of wagons, trying to spot this man at the edge of the undulating herd? For all their leathery ruggedness, the other cattlemen fell short by comparison, failing to sit a horse with his ease of movement, all of them smaller in stature, none of them possessing his lethal edge. Race, swinging a rope with the same precision that he handled his guns. Race, singing out to the cows, his deep, resonant voice drifting to her on the afternoon air. Race, whistling and waving his black Stetson, as he cut his horse back and forth through the herd.

How many times had the mere sight of this man soothed her—slowing the frantic beat of her heart, easing the constriction of her windpipe, a balm to her frayed nerves. Countless times. So very many times, in fact, that the incidences were a confusing jumble of images in her mind, the only clear detail about any of them being that *this* man, and this man only, had the power to set her tilting, spiraling emotions back on their axis. *This* man's smile, and *only* his, could reach across a distance and embrace her in warmth. How could she have sought him out so frantically, needed him so desperately, and basked in the comfort of his presence so completely without sensing deep within herself that she loved him with all her heart?

"Oh, Race," she whispered shakily.

"Sweetheart, what?" He glanced out over the rolling hills around them, looking for all the world as though he was ready to do battle with whatever might be distressing her.

"I'm just thinking how very much I love you."

His face went utterly still, as if the muscles beneath his skin had turned to granite. His gaze held hers, his dark eyes taking on a suspicious brightness. After a long moment, he said in a gruff voice, "Rebecca Ann, don't tell me that unless you mean it. It means too much to me for you to say it lightly."

In that moment, Rebecca knew how very much he loved her in return, and that he was almost afraid to believe she cared for him in the same way. "I mean it from the bottom of my heart," she assured him. "I love you, Race Spencer."

Switching the leather leads into the grip of his left hand, he reached over to thumb a tear from beneath her eye. Then he tipped his hat back and bent his head to lightly brush his lips over hers, the contact so airy she wondered if she had imagined it. When he drew back, she followed him as if attached to him by invisible strings, her heart slugging in her chest like a labored piston.

Glancing at Pete and Corey, who were just then riding past the wagon on their horses, he grinned and nudged her erect. "Behave yourself. You know what I do with wantin' women, don't ya? I leave 'em wantin' more."

" 'Wantin' women?' " Rebecca repeated. "As in *'wanting'*?"

He arched an eyebrow. "Ain't you ever heard of wantin' women?"

Rebecca started giggling.

"What's so funny?"

She hugged his arm and rested her head on his shoulder. "Nothing! Just take me to my new home, Mr. Spencer. I have a feeling I'm going to love it there."

For the remainder of the ride into the main part of the ranch, Rebecca was breathless with wonder. She'd never seen such a beautiful place. Dense thickets of Gambel oak wove between the stands of trees, splashing the hillsides with red and orange, forming a brilliant contrast to the azure Colorado sky. Race pointed out occasional wild roses on the lower slopes, from which he said she could collect petals to make medicinal teas. He also assured her that the creeks and narrow streams that ribboned the meadows were plentiful with fish, just in case she tired of eating beef and wild game. It seemed to Rebecca that even the air smelled different there—fresher and more invigorating.

She hauled in deep breaths, feeling almost giddy. "Oh, Race, I love it!" she said, letting her head fall back and closing her eyes. "It's absolutely divine."

"The cabin ain't much," he warned her. "Next spring and summer I'll start the house, but you'll have to make do where we're at for at least a year, maybe even two."

Rebecca braced her hands on her knees, so excited she was unable to settle her gaze on any one spot. "I don't need a fancy house to be happy. Especially not with so much beauty around me."

When she glanced at him, his gaze snagged hers, and for several long seconds they stared into each other's eyes. Then his mouth tipped into one of those grins that always made her heart catch. "Darlin', any time you wanna see somethin' that's truly beautiful, take a gander in the mirror."

Just as he said that the wagon crested the hill, and before them lay the small valley where the main part of his ranch was situated. Off to the right, nestled among tall pine and fir, a log cabin perched on a gentle rise, below which lay a smattering of outbuildings and a large log barn. Beyond that stretched velvety green pastures, tidily fenced with split rails. Two creeks, sparkling in the sunshine like silvery satin ribbons, ran the length of the bowl, one of them trailing over the slope where the cabin sat, the water a stone's throw from the dwelling's front stoop.

"Like I said, it ain't much," he said.

"It's beautiful. More beautiful than I imagined, by far."

"It's nowhere near as beautiful as you," he said softly. "Once we get down there, I'll be busy till almost dark."

Her gaze fixed on her new home, Rebecca curled her hands over the edge of the wagon seat. It was well past time that she begin performing her wifely duty. The fact that he'd postponed the consummation of their union for this long was probably nothing short of a miracle. In as matter-of-fact a tone as she could manage, she said, "I'll still be a wantin' woman when you get back, Mr. Spencer. There's no need to hurry."

He drove the wagon off into a deep rut. The conveyance lurched and tipped sharply to the left. Cursing, he grabbed hold of her arm to keep her from pitching off the seat. As he loosened his grip and turned his attention to getting the wheel out of the hole, he said, "Jesus H. Christ, Rebecca Ann! Are you *tryin'* to make me have a wreck?"

Bent forward over her knees before the cheerful blaze in the stone fireplace, Rebecca ran the brush through her long hair, lifting as she reached the ends to separate the nearly dry strands. From outside, she heard the muted sound of men's voices, a reassurance that Johnny and Corey were still standing guard over her. Race had given them orders not to leave her alone for even a second while he was away.

Their presence should have made her feel safe. Should have, but didn't. If the cabin creaked, as all houses often did, her heart would skitter with alarm. She also found that she couldn't resist glancing over her shoulder constantly. Somehow, she had to stop this. It was like a sickness had taken root in her mind, and nothing could eradicate it.

In the time she'd been alone, she had gotten down on her hands and knees three times to check under the bed. As if someone might have slipped into the cabin through a hairline crack? There couldn't possibly be an intruder. Rationally, she knew that. Yet she found herself pacing, looking in the trunk next to the wall, peering behind the wood stove, and then returning to the bed again to look underneath it.

The funny part was, she had no idea what she might do if she actually found someone. A fair-size man could hide under the bed, she supposed. But if she were to look under there and see one, her heart would stop from sheer shock. So why bother?

As for the trunk, it might have been large enough to accommodate a smallish midget. That wasn't to mention that the space behind the wood stove wasn't exactly roomy either. Her fear made no sense. She *knew* that. So why wasn't she able to put it from her mind?

Despite Race's reassurances that her nervousness was normal and would pass, Rebecca was beginning to think she might never get over it. Even here, in the cabin, she'd become breathless several times. It was the most horrible sensation, suddenly suffocating as if the air had been stripped of oxygen, her heart slamming so violently that she felt as if she might faint. She could sense it coming on—a strange, fluttery feeling in her chest, sweat filming her skin, her breath beginning to come more quickly. And then, wham, it would hit her. So far, she hadn't passed out, but she'd seen black spots a few times and felt as if her legs had turned to water.

Was she going mad? The thought terrified her almost as much as the spells.

The heat from the fire bathed her in warmth, making the cotton of her gown feel almost hot against her shins. She wished she could take a nap. After soaking in a hot tub of water for nearly an hour, she should feel deliciously relaxed, but she didn't.

She pushed up from the chair, tossing her hair away from her face as she took a turn around the room. She held the hairbrush clenched in her fist like a club as she leaned around to peek behind the wood stove one more time. If a man jumped out, she would brush him to death.

A hysterical laugh came up her throat, and tears filled her eyes. She spun away from the stove, determined to make herself stop this. *Insane*. It was insane. And if she knew that, why did she allow herself to do it?

Intending to return to the rocker, her bare feet seemed to stick to the floor planks. She stared at the trunk along the opposite wall. Inside it, Race stored clothing, an extra pair of boots, some handguns and ammunition. There were perhaps six inches of empty space beneath the closed lid. In addition to that, the length of the trunk was no more than four feet. No man could possibly hide in there. A half-grown boy wouldn't fit in there. She was *not* going to lift the lid again. She absolutely was not. To do so would be absurd.

All her life, she'd been "so levelheaded." Everyone had commented on it, from the time she was small. *"Have Rebecca go with the other children. She'll watch after them."* Or, *"That Rebecca is so mature for her age."* Or, *"That daughter of yours is such a responsible child."* Or, *"That Rebecca! She hasn't a flighty bone in her whole body."*

She'd never been one to snivel, as so many young girls and women were given to do. Tears, Papa had always told her, were a waste of time. Better to tackle the problem and correct it than to whine. Crying only made one's head ache. And it was true. Rebecca had no patience with weepers. Never had and never would. But now she'd become one.

Since the massacre in the arroyo, she had wept bathtubs full of tears. Not only because she was grieving. She might have made more allowances for herself if that had been the case. But, oh, no. She got tears in her eyes if the wind blew the wrong way or the leaves of a tree rustled suddenly. In fact, she had tears in her eyes right now. It was as if a dam had burst inside of her, releasing all her emotions. Self-pity, anger, fear.

Foolishness!

She strode angrily to the trunk, her breath coming in short pants, tears streaming down her cheeks. For an endless moment, she simply stood there, shaking violently, telling herself that this time she would maintain control. This time she would *not* indulge her idiotic imaginings. Then, despite her resolve, she sobbed and jerked the trunk open.

Rebecca, the levelheaded one, was dead. The sniveling coward she had become closed the trunk and went to look under the bed, even though she knew she would find only Race's saddlebags, stuffed to bursting with the church's money.

When she returned to the fire, she felt immensely better. That she was disgusted with herself seemed beside the point. She could relax now. Feel safe for a few minutes.

When she felt the need, she would circle the cabin again, peeking in all the hidey-holes. As long as no one actually saw her doing it, perhaps she could go quietly mad without anyone else realizing it.

The sturdy, store-bought rocking chair she'd been surprised to find in the cramped cabin creaked as she sat back. She rested her elbows on the chair arms, the hairbrush dangling from one hand. Leaning her head against the back rail, she trailed her gaze over that end of the room, taking in the stone fireplace, the laden gun rack above the mantel, the log walls, the exposed ceiling rafters, and the bare plank floors. It was a sturdily built house. By all rights, she should have felt secure.

Perhaps, in time, she would.

Race had done nothing to pretty the place up, but considering that he had lived alone and probably worked long hours outdoors, the one-room cabin was remarkably clean. So as not to interfere with the window shutters, isinglass had been stretched over wooden frames and fitted inside all of the window casings, each frame secured with only wing locks for easy removal. On warm days next summer, she would be able to let in fresh air—if she weren't crazier than a loon by then and hiding in that trunk.

Stop it, Rebecca. Think cheerful thoughts.

Pushing to her feet, she turned to trail her gaze over the rest of the room, trying to imagine herself in the kitchen area, bustling about as she did household chores, kneading bread or baking a pie. She pictured Race coming in of an evening to sit at a table laden with good food she had prepared.

Just behind the rocker, Blue lay sprawled on the floor, loose jowls resting on his front paws. As if sensing her gaze, he opened his droopy eyes to look at her, then sighed and went back to sleep. Even the dog thought she was crazy.

She began brushing her hair again, her attention drifting from the handmade plank table at the center of the room to the antiquated wood stove on its left, which flanked a long section of work counter, over which were suspended open shelves, some filled with dishes and cooking pans, others with food. In Rebecca's opinion, the water pump, which Race had mounted over the dry sink, was the nicest feature in the cabin, a luxury she was unaccustomed to and hadn't expected. It had been incredibly easy to heat water for her bath. Having water at hand inside the house would also save her from having to venture outdoors to the well when Race was gone.

Hating herself for doing it, she circled the cabin once more, wishing he would come back soon.

A misty twilight blanketed the forested hillside in a blue-gray gloaming. Wind whipped over the ridge, swaying the evergreen boughs and making the huge trees creak. Crouching to see in the poor light, Race touched his fingertips to the dead ash and embers of the abandoned campfire, then glanced up at Pete, still astride his bay.

"They was here a couple of days. Broke camp this mornin'."

Race pushed to his feet to gaze across the valley. At the opposite end of the bowl sat the cabin. He imagined the men who had gathered by this fire twelve hours before, could picture them standing exactly where he did, seeing exactly what he saw.

"They'll strike soon," Race said. "Warn all the men. I want 'em pullin' shifts to watch the cabin tonight."

"Should we ride guard as best we can to watch over the cows, too?"

Race shook his head. "With 'em loose on open range? The ones we brought in today will be broke up into large bunches now, some here, some there. If someone wants to do 'em mischief, we can't protect 'em all. We gotta concentrate on the house, to hell with the cows."

The leather of Pete's saddle protested as he swung his weight onto one stirrup to follow Race's gaze. "How'n hell you reckon they knew we was headin' here?"

Race unfastened his holster tabs, curled a finger under the handle of each Colt, and lifted to check for leather grab. If the moment came when he had to draw, he wanted no surprises. In the past, only his life had depended on his speed. Now Rebecca's would as well.

"They probably scouted up ahead of us," Race replied. "Ain't that many ranches in these parts. The trail we was on led here. Stands to reason."

"At best, they was still just guessin', though."

Race clenched his teeth. They were smart bastards. "Good guess." He angled a look at his foreman. "You can bet they know the lay of the land around here now like the backs of their hands, and that the sons of bitches went through every buildin' down there, includin' the house. When they strike, their every move'll be figured to a gnat's ass."

Pete sighed. "You gonna warn Miss Rebecca to be expectin' trouble?"

Race walked to his horse. "I ain't sayin' a word to her, and I don't want any of the men to either. She's got enough on her mind."

"That's true enough."

Race swung up into the saddle and unwrapped Dusty's reins from around the pommel. "Nothin' she can do but worry, and I ain't too sure she can handle that right now. The poor girl's froggy enough as it is."

"I can't much blame her. If anybody ever had call, she does."

Race met his foreman's gaze. "This time, Pete, no matter what happens, I want every man to put her safety first, to hell with everything else."

"You think they know we got the money?"

Race gave a bitter laugh. "They always thought that, even at first, when we really didn't. That's why I went and got it." He shrugged. "Nothin' to lose. With them already thinkin' Rebecca had it with her, actually goin' to get it didn't put her in any more danger. They'll still figure she's got it. That's why I say she's our first concern. They'll try to draw us away from her again, like they done last time. No matter what happens, we can't fall for it and leave her unguarded."

"They gotta realize some of the rest of us know where it's at by now."

Race smiled. "Pete, that's the difference atwixt us. I think like an outlaw and you ain't got it in you. You gotta figure the kind of men they are. One word says it. Greedy. If one of them had that money, you reckon he'd tell anybody else? Hell, no. He'd keep it hid for himself. It's beyond them that Rebecca might've handed that money over to me. In their wildest imaginin's, they'd never do it. They're thinkin' she's kept it a secret, that it's either still in the wagon, or that she's got it with her, or maybe that she hid it somewhere down south. In their minds, she's the only one who can lead 'em to it.''

"So when they strike, they'll go after her for sure."

"That's right." Race nudged Dusty into a walk down the decline. "When they try to draw us away from her, we gotta make it look like we fell for it, then circle back."

Clicking his tongue to his bay, Pete fell in to ride abreast of his employer. "That's damned risky, ain't it? What if they get to her while we're circlin'?"

Race's chest went cold. "Never knowin' how or when they might strike is lot riskier, Pete. I'd just go after the bastards, but I'm afraid to leave her to do it for fear some of 'em might double back and get to her. My only other choice is to lure 'em in and kill the sons of bitches."

"Usin' her and the money as bait?"

"That's right."

Rebecca jumped with a start at a loud thumping sound on the front step. Then loud knocks shook the door. A wave of relief washed over her. She ran the length of the room, grabbed the bolt to lift it, and then froze. She was assuming it was Race. But what if it wasn't?

"Wh-who's there?"

"It's me, darlin'. Open up! It's colder than a well digger's ass out here."

She tucked the brush under her arm, quickly swiped at her cheeks, and lifted the bolt. The cabin door swung open and Race stepped inside, accompanied by a rush of cold evening air.

"Damn, it's nippy out there tonight!" he said as he dropped the bolt and leaned his Henry against the wall.

Even with the brim of his black Stetson shadowing his face, she saw him run his gaze from her unruly cloud of hair to the tips of her toes, which peeked from beneath the hem of her nightgown. She turned and walked back to the fire, where she stood facing the room to finish brushing her hair dry.

Still regarding her, Race removed his hat, hung it on a hook near the door, then bent to loosen his holster ties. After collecting his Henry, he crossed the room to the bed, leaning the rifle against the wall next to the headboard before unbuckling his gun belt and draping it around the bedpost. As he turned back toward her, he settled his hands at his hips, his gaze trailing the length of her as slowly as warm honey dripping from a spoon. In the flickering fire shine, his freshly shaved jaw glistened like polished teak, and it looked to her as if his hair was slightly damp. She glanced at the tub propped against the wall near the stove.

"It looks as if I'm not the only one who took a bath."

He raked his fingers through his hair. "Had to get the trail dust off. Cookie had water heated over in the bunkhouse, so I scrubbed up there." He trailed his gaze the length of her again. "How'd it go, bein' alone here all afternoon?"

Rebecca began brushing her hair with renewed vigor. "Oh, it went fine! I wasn't nervous at all."

He watched her closely. Too closely. She had the awful feeling he knew she was lying. The way she saw it, she had no choice. He had a ranch to run. He couldn't stay with her constantly, and with men watching the house, there was no reason for him to feel that he should. She wouldn't tell him how nervous she'd been. The truth would just make him worry the entire time he was away from her, and she didn't want that. Besides, how could she possibly explain that she'd opened his trunk four times, prepared to bludgeon a midget with her hairbrush?

"Not nervous at all? That's an improvement."

"Yes, isn't it?" She hit a tangle and nearly jerked her hair out by the roots. "I'm much better, and I'm sure I'll continue to improve. I feel much more secure here than I did out on the trail." She flashed what she hoped was a convincing smile, even while she heard herself chattering like a magpie. "Having sturdy walls around me makes all the difference, I suppose."

His mouth twitched. He moved to sit at the end of the plank table, his long, black-clad legs extended and crossed at the ankle, his dark gaze still fixed on her. Unnerved by the way he watched her, Rebecca avoided his gaze and continued brushing her hair.

"Hungry?" he asked, his voice warm and seeming to trail around her like tendrils of smoke.

"I had a bit of the stew Mr. Grigsley gave us." She'd actually taken only one bite, been unable to swallow it, and given the remainder of the serving to Blue. "Would you care for some?"

"I'm not hungry right now. At least not for food." He ran his gaze the length of her again, his eyes twinkling warmly as though at some private jest. "Enjoy your bath?"

"It was wonderful." She truly wished he'd stop looking at her like that. It was starting to give her the whim-whams. "I filled the tub next to the wood stove so I didn't have to get out to keep adding hot water, and I soaked for nearly an hour." She deliberately failed to mention that she'd left the tub once to pad around the room, peeking under and behind things, dripping water every step of the way. She'd had to mop the floor with her towel after she finished bathing. "What a luxury a deep tub is. I'd nearly forgotten."

"So every inch of you is fresh-scrubbed and sweet as the petals of a rosebud."

It was more an observation than a question, so she gave no rejoinder.

"I really like that nightgown," he said huskily.

She glanced down. "It's just like the other one."

"Hmm. I never got to enjoy the other one."

Rebecca ran her fingertips over the buttons to make sure they were all fastened. His mouth twitched again. He drew his watch from his pocket and flipped it open. Smiling slightly, he returned the timepiece to its place and pushed erect.

"I guess I'll build up the fire before we call it a night."

He snapped his fingers at Blue and went to the front door to let the hound out for a run. "At this altitude, it gets mighty cold before dawn, even at this time of year."

Rebecca glanced at the nearest window. The twilight was only just now giving way to complete darkness. "It's awfully early for bed. Isn't it?"

He moved toward her, his pace slow and soundless. Looking up into his gleaming eyes, she thought of the powerfully muscled mountain lion they had seen on the ridge that afternoon. "It'll be late before we finally get to sleep," he told her.

"It's certainly going to take me a while," she agreed. "I'm not really tired."

Instead of stepping around her to get wood from the box next to the hearth, he stopped in front of her, took the brush from her, and began to run the bristles through her long hair. "Your hair shines like spun gold." With every stroke of the brush, he lifted, releasing the lengthy strands from the bristles with a flick of his wrist so they fell forward in wavy curtains over her shoulders. "Have I ever told you that you're the prettiest thing I ever clapped eyes on?"

He ran the brush through the drape of hair that lay over her left shoulder. She jerked slightly when the brush bristles grazed her breast. She glanced at him suspiciously, but he'd already moved around to brush another section. She decided the contact must have been accidental. He circled to stand behind her, brushing the back of her hair and running it through his fingers. Then he brought the brush forward to brush the hair lying over her right breast, the bristles once again grazing the peak of her nipple. She stiffened and glanced back at him. He lifted a dark eyebrow.

"What? Am I doin' it wrong?"

"No." She swallowed a sudden thickness. "No," she said again, softer this time.

"You just tell me if you don't like somethin', darlin', and I'll stop."

Untangling curly tresses with his fingertips as he wielded the brush, he trailed his knuckles lightly over her left shoulder blade and down the small of her back. Then, moving over a bit, he traced another path downward with the backs of his fingers, his touch so insubstantial she couldn't believe it was deliberate. She relaxed and closed her eyes.

"No one's brushed my hair for me since I was a little girl. It feels nice." Her bones felt as if they were melting. The bristles flicked over her left nipple again, making her flesh harden. "Mmm. This is lovely."

"Feel good?" he asked softly.

"Mmm." It felt *so* good. She wanted to melt and run through the cracks in the floor. His chest pressed against her back. She leaned against him, enjoying his solidness and warmth. The brush bristles made a light pass over her nipple again, sending shocks of sensation from there to a place low in her abdomen. "I could let you do this every night."

"At your service."

Another pass over her breast. Her nipples hardened and started to ache. The brush bristles dragged over a sensitive tip yet again, sending jolts of feeling through her. She jerked erect and stepped away. "Thank you. That was nice."

He smiled slightly and set the brush on the fireplace mantel. "I'll tend to the fire. Why don't you get into bed. I'll be right along."

While he placed three large logs in the grate, Rebecca went to stand by the bed, which rested against the wall in one corner. "Which side is yours?"

He glanced over at her, the heightened brightness of the flames playing over his face. "I'll take the outside," he said, his eyes once again seeming to gleam from within as he ran his gaze over her. "That way I'm between you and the door."

Staring down at the two pillows, Rebecca was assailed by a feeling very like the one that had come over her earlier as she regarded the trunk, her feet glued to the floor, her heart pounding. Only this time, the urge that came over her was to retreat, not advance. Behind her, she heard Race circling the room to close and secure all the shutters. At the door, he stopped to let Blue back in, then dropped the bolt.

Rebecca bent to turn down the covers, fussing unnecessarily with the flannel sheet and fluffing the down pillows in their linen cases. "I'm surprised you have two pillows on your bed."

"I used one, and Blue used the other one."

"Oh." Rebecca leaned closer to peruse the cases.

"I changed the beddin' just before I left," he informed her, his voice laced with laughter. "And he used the outside pillow. Tomorrow, I reckon I'll have to find a couple of old saddle blankets for him to use as a bed. He's gonna be rousted out of his sleepin' spot now that you're here."

Rebecca considered offering to let him and the dog have the bed while she slept happily unpestered on the floor, but somehow she doubted Race would go for that idea.

A rasp of metal and a loud click came from behind her. She turned to see Race working the lever action of another rifle, which he'd evidently taken from the rack above the fireplace. He stepped past her to prop the gun against the wall next to the Henry.

"Are you expecting trouble tonight?"

"Nah." He went to the trunk. As he threw up the lid, he said, "I always have weaponry and plenty of cartridges near at hand while I sleep. In this country, it ain't smart not to be ready. Indians, grizzlies, cougars, and two-legged polecats."

Her skin prickled, and she glanced anxiously at the door.

He chuckled as he drew three boxes of cartridges from the stash of ammunition she'd seen inside the trunk. "Honey, don't feel nervous. I take precautions just in case." He closed the trunk and moved back toward her. "We ain't had trouble of any kind around here in so long, I plumb forget when. I just got me a habit of figurin' on the highly unlikely. That's all. Keeps me from gettin' unpleasant surprises."

After stacking the ammunition boxes on the floor near the two rifles, he began unbuttoning his shirt. The front plackets fell open to reveal a wealth of burnished chest, his breast muscles bunching with every movement of his arms, horizontal ridges striating his flat belly. When he started to peel the shirt off, she averted her face.

"Not tonight, Blue," he said when the dog walked over to gaze at the bed.

The hound huffed and returned to lie down in front of the fire.

Rebecca's pulse skittered and her throat went suddenly dry. This afternoon, she had invited Race to consummate their marriage tonight, and her reasons for doing so were still valid. He had given her so very much, never asking for anything in return. It was her obligation—her wifely duty—to make her body available to him.

In the brightness of the afternoon, she hadn't felt nervous. And by all rights, she shouldn't have felt nervous now. But for reasons beyond her, she was.

She pressed a hand to the stand-up collar of her cotton nightgown, her palm smashing the two top buttons against her larynx. Her legs were quivering, giving her reason to fear she might collapse. Her heart felt as if it were going to pound its way through the wall of her chest. She gulped and closed her eyes.

This was absurd. What was there to feel nervous about?

"You gonna stand there all night?" he asked.

Dragging in a huge breath that made her feel slightly dizzy, Rebecca drew back the quilts and slipped into the bed. Scooting over to the far side of the mattress, she lay on her back, covers drawn to her chin, hands folded beneath her breasts, eyes closed. *Nothing to it.* Ma had never lied to her—not once in her whole life—and she'd promised that this wedding night business was uneventful, simple, and quite quick.

She had nothing at all to worry about. Not one thing. Except for the firelight that played over the room, of course. She could see the golden glow through her closed eyelids. She would have greatly preferred total darkness. But it was a woman's lot, a necessary part of becoming a wife—and someday, a mother.

The bed suddenly lurched, the frame creaking and

groaning as her husband sat on the edge of the mattress. Rebecca hauled in another deep breath, determined to be serene. *Thump.* His boot? She heard him moving, his breath hitching. *Thump.* Then came a whisper of sound. She kept her eyes squeezed closed. She hoped he would leave his trousers on as he had the other nights.

The quilts vanished.

Her eyes flew open. He smiled and shifted himself over her, the breadth of his bronzed chest eclipsing much of the light and shadowing her face. The gleam in his coffee-brown eyes had become a determined and slightly mischievous glint. She groped with her right hand for the quilts he'd pulled off her, almost simultaneously felt cool air on her upturned toes, and realized he'd thrown the blankets clear to the foot of the bed. This was *not* the way Ma had promised the brethren did it.

"Howdy," he said in a low, husky voice that made her nerve endings trill.

Chapter 18

"Race?" Rebecca said in a twangy voice. "You, um . . .
removed the quilts." She realized he'd braced a hand on
her opposite side so he might lean over her, which trapped
her between a muscular arm and his bare chest. "May I
have them back, please?"

He leaned closer. "Chilly? I'll take care of that in short
order, darlin'."

He already was. His chest was nearly touching hers,
and the heat of him radiated over her. She swallowed
again. "Race, you don't happen to own a nightshirt, do
you?"

"A what?"

She glanced down and immediately wished she hadn't.
"A nightshirt. If you have one in your trunk, I would
greatly appreciate your wearing it."

His white teeth gleamed at her in a slow grin. "Honey,
I don't own a nightshirt. The closest I come to that is
wearin' my long handles in the winter, and now that I got
you to keep me warm, I won't wear them."

"Wh-what on earth shall you wear then?"

His grin deepened. "You, I reckon."

Rebecca was still trying to digest that when he suddenly
straightened, grasped her by the shoulders, and bodily
lifted her with unnerving ease to sit her up. She was
greatly relieved to see that he still wore his black trousers.

His hands went to her hair. Running his fingers through
it as though it were the finest silk, he whispered in a deep,

raspy voice, "The first time I ever seen you, I imagined you comin' to me wearin' nothin' but your beautiful hair."

His eyes caught light from the fire and glinted as though shot through with flecks of gold dust. He lifted her hair to drape it forward over her breasts, then arranged the wavy tresses so they fell apart to reveal only the very tips of her breasts. Glancing down, Rebecca felt fire flood into her cheeks. Even though she wore her nightgown, it was a suggestive thing for him to do.

"That's how I imagined you," he murmured. "Peekin' out at me, sweet as little rosebuds and beggin' to be kissed."

The fiery feeling spread from her face down the back of her throat to pool, molten and swirling, in the pit of her stomach. He chuckled.

"From the way you're blushin', I got this feelin' I'm flat outta luck." His gleaming gaze held hers. He drew back slightly to regard her. "My God, you are so sweet." He cupped a hand to the side of her face and feathered his thumb back and forth over her cheek, his touch light and tantalizing. "Sweetheart, are you that nervous?"

Rebecca's tongue felt stuck to the roof of her mouth. "I would probably feel some better if you were wearing a nightshirt."

"I reckon maybe I'd best keep my pants on then?"

She would hope!

"Anything else botherin' you?"

"Well, I'd really like for you to simply get on with it, if you wouldn't mind. Afterward we can talk. All right? I'm rather anxious to get the first time behind me."

His smile faltered, and his thumb stilled on her cheekbone. "Ah, honey. I'm sorry. I need my ass kicked between my shoulder blades." He leaned forward to touch his forehead to hers, his much larger nose pressing the wishy-washy tip of hers to one side. He lightly trailed his fingertips from her cheek into her hair. "Here I am takin' my time, and you're all tense. I should be workin' on makin' you forget what you're nervous about."

Rebecca's eyes crossed trying to look into his, so she let her lashes fall closed.

Thrusting both of his big hands into her hair, his hard palms cupping the sides of her head, he lifted his forehead from hers to kiss the tip of her nose. Rebecca grabbed hold of his broad wrists as he tipped her back ever so gently onto the bed and followed her down, bracing his forearms at each side of her shoulders.

His chest grazed the tips of her breasts as he bent toward her. "Don't be afraid, sweetheart," he whispered, his silken lips brushing so lightly over hers that the touch was more part of his whisper than actual contact. "I'll make it nice for you. And I'll do my damnedest not to hurt you, I swear it."

"Oh, Race . . ."

His mouth settled over hers while her lips were parted to speak. She sucked breath—his breath—which was sweet and warm and tasted slightly of coffee. Silken lips, the tip of his tongue tracing the shape of her mouth, then pressing forward. Rebecca jerked, horrified. He was sticking his tongue in her mouth?

That was the last thought she had for several drugging seconds. *Race.* He teased the sensitive roof of her mouth, then dipped low to flick the thread of sensitive tissue under her tongue. Her head swirled. She forgot to breathe. She ran her hands over the bulging strength of his upper arms to cling to his broad shoulders. Lands, what was he doing to her?

Suddenly she wanted to melt and run into him, lose herself in his heat and strength. Something low in her belly went tight and achy, making her feel warm all through her nether regions. As he kissed her, he brushed his chest lightly back and forth over hers, dragging her cotton gown with him. Her nipples sprang taut, the tips poking against the cloth, shocks of sensation shooting into them with his every movement.

Kissing was frowned upon by the brethren before marriage, so Rebecca had never tried it. It was *lovely*. She hoped he did this part of his business rather often. Oh, yes. This was truly lovely. His mouth. She'd watched his lips quirk a hundred times, watched their movements as he spoke. They were as silken and warm as they looked, feeling so wonderful against hers that she never, never wanted him to quit. Firm, yet molten.

He caught her bottom lip lightly between his teeth, rolling the tender inner side toward his tongue, then began to tease the sensitive surface. *Oh, yes.* She definitely liked kissing.

Back and forth, ever so lightly, his broad chest grazed hers. Her breasts seemed to swell, and her blood seemed to surge into the tips, each beat of her heart making them throb and get harder. Her spine arched. She dug her nails into his shoulders, a yearning, urgent feeling building inside her that quickly became a horrible need, only she didn't know for what. She arched higher to press the burning points of her nipples more firmly against him.

He drew one hand from her hair and stopped kissing her to nibble his way along her cheek, his mouth teasing and making her skin tingle. To her temple, back down to her eyelids, then—oh, dear heaven—to her ear, his breath whispering to her, echoing as he nipped her earlobe and then lightly trailed the tip of his tongue over the sensitive hollow beneath. Then he kissed his way along the side of her neck, making her shiver, causing her breath to hitch.

Oh, yes . . . oh, yes. She truly, truly *loved* kissing. His clever mouth. He caressed her with it, drew her skin tight to lave it with his tongue, making the yearning inside her sharpen. A wall of hot muscle. His strength all around her. His hips pressing hers against the quilts, each slow undulation adding to the strange ache.

Only dimly aware, Rebecca felt his hands shake slightly as they worked the small buttons of her gown, then gently drew the material open. Cool air brushed her breasts, making her shiver. But it was a strangely lovely feeling. A coiled, warm inner tension that expanded and thrummed.

"Lordy, darlin', I can't breathe for wantin'."

Her collarbone . . . he was tracing its shape, licking the V. A vague sense of alarm nudged at the corners of her mind, but she couldn't concentrate on it. The sensations. So many, all at once, high, low, and in between. Her mind flitted from one pleasurable shock of feeling to another.

Then his hot tongue dragged over her taut, aching nipple. A spine-snapping jolt coursed through her, jerking her body taut, stealing her breath, making her heartbeat skitter and hesitate. His mouth closed on her and drew sharply. Rebecca felt the pull clear to her toes. Her eyes flew open. She looked down. She saw his dark face nuzzling her pale fullness. He inched back, tugging her nipple forward, his teeth catching the throbbing tip as he drew it out as far as it would go, then released it.

For a horrified moment, she gaped. Then he sucked her into his mouth again. Reality slammed into her brain.

She shrieked. Shoved. Shrieked again. What was he *doing*? Angels above. Oh, mercy! He'd lied. *Lied!* Bald-faced lies, every word!

The man was rife with ungodly urges.

Rebecca's first scream raked through Race's head like sharp talons. The second one had him springing to his knees.

"What?" he cried, grabbing her by the shoulders. "Sweetheart? What? Did I hurt you?"

Her answer was to shriek again and scramble away, frantically trying to tug the front of her nightgown closed. "Leave me alone! Don't *touch* me! You lied. *Lied!*"

Blue lumbered to his feet and started to bark. Then he started to bay. The next second Race heard running footsteps and shouts. His men descended on the cabin like a colony of ants on a bread crumb. The front door shook in its frame as fists pounded on the thick wood.

"Boss!" Pete yelled. "Hey, boss!" A commotion. "Get back!" Pete roared. "I'm gonna kick the son of a bitch down."

"No!" Race yelled. "It's all right, Pete! Don't kick the door in!"

"Show yourself, goddamn it! How do I know somebody ain't holdin' a gun to your head?"

"I'll be right there!" Race turned a worried gaze on his bride who had wedged her shoulders into the corner between the log headboard and wall. "Sweetheart, I'm sorry. I'll be right back. All right?"

She looked as enthusiastic about that prospect as she might have been about a tooth extraction. Swearing under his breath, Race paced to the door, lifted the bolt, and cracked open the portal only enough for Pete to see him. "We're all right. Just a little misunderstanding."

"A misunderstanding?" Pete looked ready to skin live rattlers. "She near scared me to death!"

"I'm sorry. It's my doin', not hers." Race started inching the door closed. "Thanks for comin' so fast. I appreciate it."

He eased the door shut and dropped the bolt back into place. Moving back toward the bed, Race studied Rebecca, who clutched the front of her nightgown together, her eyes huge splashes of darkness in her pale face. She looked less afraid than she did scandalized.

"You lied!" she cried.

Race had no idea what she thought he'd lied to her about. "Sweetheart, I didn't lie to you. Can you talk to me? Tell me why you think I did?"

That seemed to horrify her even more. "No! I don't want to *talk* about it." She pressed her face against her up-drawn knees. "How could you! How *could* you? You lied and *tricked* me! I trusted you!"

Race knelt before her on the bed and spread his hands on his thighs. For the life of him, he couldn't think what he'd done. She'd been getting as hot as a fanned ember one second, then had started screaming and trying to get away from him the next.

"Honey, please. We have to talk about it. Otherwise I won't know what I did."

She crossed her upper chest with her arms, curling her fine-boned hands over her shoulders. "You *lied*! You gave me your *word*!"

Race twisted to sit Indian fashion and braced his elbows on his knees, leaning forward to search her face through the gloom. He could see she was horribly upset, that she truly did believe that he'd lied to her about something.

She jutted her small chin at him. "Why did you hide the truth?"

"What truth?" Race asked, striving to be calm. One of them had to be. "Sweetheart, what in hell do you think I lied about?"

"As if you don't know! Telling me you go about it like the brethren. Hah! None of the brethren would *ever* do that. You *lied*, out-and-out lied! And stupid me, I believed you!"

"I did *not* lie," Race retorted.

"You most certainly did! You said you had no ungodly inclinations!" Her voice rose to a shrill pitch on that last word.

Race went back over all he'd done. The only explanation he could think of was that he'd hurt her, though he couldn't think how. "Honey, is your nipples tender? Is that it? I never in the world meant to hurt you. Was I too rough?"

She shrieked and covered her face. "Don't speak to me of such! You're a vulgar, crude man, and I'm not married to you! Do you hear me? I am *not*!"

"Rebecca, you ain't talkin' good sense, here. People don't get married and unmarried over a little misunderstandin'. They talk it out."

"I didn't get married. I got *took*!"

Race sighed and thrust his fingers through his hair. "Took, married. We're gonna talk this out. Now you tell me, what did I do that upset you so bad?"

She persisted in keeping her hands over her face. Meanwhile, the unfastened front of her gown gaped open, giving him a perfect view of her right nipple over the tops of her knees. The same nipple he'd so recently been loving. Still distended, it looked rosy in the fire shine, giving him reason to believe maybe it was tender. Females got all out of sorts at certain times, mood-wise and otherwise, and their breasts tended to be sensitive then, too.

It wasn't usually something a man could determine by looking. Rebecca's, for instance. The tip thrust eagerly forward, as if begging for more attention, a request Race would have happily granted had the lady attached to it been a little more cooperative.

"You know very well why I'm upset," she accused in a muffled voice.

"No, I don't know." He rocked forward onto all fours. Upon closer inspection of her nipple, he concluded that his eyes hadn't deceived him. Pink as a little rosebud, it stood at attention and was pulsating with every beat of her heart. Tender, he decided. He'd been too rough, evidently. The ruffians in the arroyo had enjoyed inflicting pain, an inclination Race had promised her he didn't have, and now, in her inexperience, she believed he'd lied to her about it because he had hurt her.

Grasping her knees, he shoved downward to straighten her legs, then straddled them. Bracing a hand at each side of her thighs, he gazed at the backs of her hands. "Rebecca, take your hands down, darlin', and look at me."

"No!"

"Sweetheart, I won't do it again. All right? I'm real sorry. After this, you got the reins. How's that sound. However suits you is exactly how I'll do things, I promise. All you gotta do is tell me what's nice and what's not."

"Well, that *wasn't*! It was horrid!"

"It'll never be horrid again. You tell me how you want me to do it, and that's how I'll do it."

She jerked and sobbed. "How do I know you're not lying again?"

"I ain't never lied to you. Have I?"

"Yes."

He sighed. "Sweetheart, let me show you." He remembered how he'd tugged at her with his teeth. Up until then, she'd been melting in his arms like honey on a hot biscuit. "Was it nice at first?"

"Yes."

"Well, then? We'll just do what's nice for you. Nothing that isn't, I promise."

She parted the fingers of one hand to peer at him through the crack. "Do you swear?"

"I'll not only swear. Can I show you?"

"Well . . ."

Race decided that at times like this, actions might reassure her more than words. He bent his head and very gently drew on her nipple. She shrieked, jerked, and clobbered his ear with a hard whack of her elbow. He reared back, holding the side of his head.

"*Ouch!*" he roared. "Damn it, Rebecca Ann! I know I didn't hurt you that time!"

She was back to clutching the front of her nightgown. "You!"

Clearly beside herself, she twisted away from him and tried to crawl off, only her gown was caught under his knees. Race caught her arm and drew her around to face him. "What in tarnation's the matter with you?" he cried, still holding his ear.

She doubled up her fists. "Don't *touch* me! If you do, I won't be responsible. I'll fight the way you taught me and break your nose again! And this time, I'll mean to do it!"

Race reared back out of her reach. "*Why?*"

"Why?" she repeated incredulously. "You try to do things like that, and you ask me why?"

"Like what?" Race was beginning to get an inkling, though he couldn't quite believe he had it right. "Kissin' your breast, you mean?"

She clamped her hands back over her face and shuddered. "Stop *saying* things like that!"

"Like what? Breast?"

She made a keening sound. Blue took up the lament, throwing back his head and making a little circle with his mouth, going, *"How—oooo!"*

"Shut up!" Race yelled. Blue kept howling, but Rebecca jumped with a start and started holding her breath. "Not you, honey." Race shot the howling hound a murderous glare. "Blue! I don't need you stickin' your nose in this! Shut up!"

The hound broke off and whined.

Race figured he had his answer about the breast business. He rubbed a hand over his face and blinked. "Rebecca, do you got it in your head that me kissin' you there is ungodly?"

She drew her hands from her face to gape at him in amazement. "Of *course* it is! You promised to just do it the regular way, and you *lied!*"

"What's the reg'lar way, Rebecca Ann? I guess maybe I ain't real clear on that."

"You're just supposed to do your business!"

His business? "What, exactly, is that?"

"Just doing *that* and nothing else!"

He sat back on his heels, unable to believe his own ears. "Is that what your ma told you? Honey, I think you misunderstood."

"I did not. She was explicit and told me *exactly!*"

Race recalled all the tales he'd heard about some of the stricter Christian sects, the gloves in August, the downcast eyes. His gaze shot to her pile of black outer clothing and gray undergarments that lurked like a shadowy specter where she'd set them against the wall. A sinking sensation entered his belly.

"Rebecca Ann, are you sayin' that the brothers in your church don't touch a woman's body? That they just"—he swung a hand—"*do* it and that's it?"

She averted her face, her chin trembling. "I never got through one *line* of Keats!"

"Line of what?"

"Ma said I could pray or meditate and ignore the goings-on. I was going to think about my"—she shuddered—"my favorite poems by Keats!"

Race barked with laughter. She turned accusing blue eyes on him. He held up his hands. "Honey, I'm sorry! I ain't laughin', honest."

Pulling a straight face, he moved to sit with his back against the log footboard. Meditate and ignore the goings-on? He couldn't help himself. He began to laugh again, this time so hard he had to hold his stomach. Tears started to stream down his cheeks. "I ain't laughin' at you," he managed to gasp out. "I truly ain't, darlin'." He swiped at his cheeks, had nearly managed to get control of himself, and then pictured Henry with the horn-rimmed glasses making love in a three-piece suit and hat. He lost it all over again and laughed so hard, his spine went limp.

He slid down the footboard and rolled over onto his side.

When at last his mirth subsided, he sighed and said, "Shit," wondering why he'd started laughing in the first place. All in all, it wasn't funny. The girl he loved wanted to think about poems while he made love to her, and God forbid he should interrupt her train of thought. "Well, hell."

"Are you quite finished?" she asked primly.

Race angled his head up to look at her. She was buttoned to the chin again. "I reckon."

"Then I shall take this opportunity to inform you that I don't believe we suit. A marriage between us would be disastrous unless you can forgo your ungodly inclinations."

He sat up, swiped at his cheeks, and met her gaze dead-on. "That just ain't gonna happen, darlin'. What you think of as ungodly, I call beautiful."

She hugged her waist and bent her head. Race could tell by the way she held herself that she'd hoped he would come to heel if she gave him an ultimatum. An ache entered his chest, for he truly did love her. Just not so much that he was willing to kow-tow to a set of marital rules dreamed up by sick-minded people. There wasn't a spot on her that was ungodly, and there was nothing ungodly about his wanting to love every inch of her. If she believed that, she was as mixed up in her thinking as the rest of them, and she'd be a lot happier, not to mention a lot more satisfied, once he got her straightened out.

"Remember when I told you I was worried that maybe we was comin' at this from two different directions, and it might take us a spell to find a happy meetin' ground?"

"Yes."

"Well, I reckon I was more right about that than either of us thought. That don't mean we don't suit, darlin'. That means we don't suit *yet*. You give some ground, I give some ground. We'll get it worked out."

"I am *not* going to give ground on my principles."

"Honey, I ain't the least bit inclined to go messin' with your principles. It's your body I got my sights set on."

She threw him a horrified look.

He lifted his hands, doing his best to look harmless, which wasn't one of his talents. "We'll work this out. Trust me."

"How can we possibly? You have inclinations I find abhorrent!"

"Well, tell me what you expect, and let's work on it from there." He propped his arms on his bent knees, trying his damnedest not to think of Henry in his three-piece suit. "How does the brethren do it?"

She raised her small chin to look down her nose at him. "My mother said I was to lie still, on my back, and offer no protest. That my husband would come to me in the darkness, join me under the quilts, nudge my gown up to the area of my hips, and do his business, quickly and with every consideration for my refined sensibilities. That there was nothing much"—she gulped—"nothing much to it. And that if I so chose, I could ignore the goings-on, devoting my thoughts to prayer or meditation until he finished."

He would not laugh. If he did, she'd never forgive him. Race stroked his chin to hide his mouth. "Well, there, you see? We got it half-licked already. At least now I know what's allowed and what ain't."

Her blue eyes turned dark and bruised-looking as she searched his gaze. He truly had upset her apple cart, which was no laughing matter.

"You mean you might be willing to abide by those practices?"

"Well, now . . ." Race did some fast considering. "Is kissin' like we done before all hell broke loose—is that allowed?"

"Yes."

He kept stroking his chin. "Now do I got this right? From your buttoned-up collar to your hipbones—that's all no-tresspassin' territory."

"Correct."

"But everything from the hipbones on down is okay?"

"Correct."

"And in the okay area, is there rules?"

She looked bewildered. "Rules?"

"You said your ma explained it all exactly. What do the brethren do while they're goin' about their manly business? Give me exact instructions so I don't do it wrong."

She blinked and shook her head. "She didn't describe *that* part." She flapped her hand. "They just do it—however they do it."

Hallelujah. "So there ain't no rules on *how* I do my manly business."

"Not that I'm aware of. That is *your* business. The wife doesn't involve herself with that part."

Did she ever have a surprise coming. Race arched an eyebrow. "So I can go about my business however I want?"

She took a moment to answer. No one could ever accuse this girl of being slow-witted. She sensed the trap, but in her innocence, she apparently couldn't think what it might be. Race felt a little guilty about that, but in his experience, sometimes a conscience was a man's worst enemy, and if this wasn't one of those times, he'd eat his boots.

"I suppose you may," she finally replied. "It is your business, as I said."

"And no complaints from you, right? Barring me hurtin' you, of course, which I'll take care not to do. You'll just meditate on your poetry and not involve yourself?"

"That is my preference, yes."

Race nodded. "Do I got your word? No involvin' yourself. You'll do your poetry stuff and leave me to my business, however it suits me to do it?"

"Do I have your word you won't venture higher than my hips and subject me to vulgarities?"

"Unless you ask me to, I give you my word I won't."

"How can you even *think* I'd ever *ask*?"

"I'm just leavin' it open is all. Do I got your word on your part of the deal?"

"Yes, you have my word."

Race bit back a grin. "One other thing," he said, holding up a finger. "How much time do I get?"

She fixed big, bewildered eyes on him. "Well, I don't know. How long does it take?"

"Well, that there's just the thing. Sometimes longer than others. So do we agree I can have as much time as I feel like I need?"

"I—guess so."

Race lifted his hands. "Well, now. See there? A happy meetin' ground."

She glanced at the spot where she'd been lying, looking none too thrilled about returning to it. "And you promise me you'll abide by those rules?"

"I promise. How about you?"

"I promise." She looked dubious. "If you swear you'll be content with the brethren way of doing it forever."

"Unless you ask for something more, you bet. That'll suit me just fine."

"Swear it. On your honor."

He held up his right hand. "I swear on my honor I'll never lay hand or lip on you from your hipbones to your collarbone—unless you ask me to."

"Shall I lie back down then?"

"I reckon."

She scooted over to her spot and stretched out like a body ready for burial again, squeezing her eyes tightly closed. "Race?"

He smiled slightly. "What, darlin'?"

"Don't forget the quilts."

He reached behind him, grabbed the quilts, and rose to his knees to draw them back over her. "Clear to the chin?"

She snuggled all down, keeping her eyes closed as if her life depended on it. "Please."

Race tugged them clear to her chin, then slipped under with her. "I can lay my arm over you, can't I? I've done that lots of times before."

"Yes. That should be fine."

He curled a hand over her waist and pulled her close. "Come here, sweetheart. You're still upset." He reared up on an elbow to kiss her closed eyelids. "I'm sorry I went at it like that and shocked you. You gotta know I'd never do it on purpose.''

She turned her cheek toward his lips. ''I'm sorry I hurt your ear. Is it all right?''

''It's fine.'' Race moved his hand from her waist to smooth her hair back from her face. ''You are so beautiful, sweetheart. Just lookin' at you fair breaks my heart. Have I ever told you that?''

She lifted her lashes, her mouth curving in a smile. ''Oh, Race.'' She hugged his neck. ''I'm sorry for all the mean things I said.''

He gathered her close and pressed his face to her hair, feeling as if he held the riches of the world in his arms. ''Don't even think about it. I knew you was just beside yourself.''

She pressed her body closer, fitting her curves to his hollows. He smiled to himself, remembering the time that she'd told him she had fallen from grace. His little angel was about to take a mighty long tumble.

Chapter 19

Kissing. *Race's lips made Rebecca feel as if as if she'd* just died and gone to heaven. Floating. Filled with warmth. Eager to feel such bliss again, she willingly surrendered her mouth to him. He didn't disappoint her, slowly, thoroughly teasing every sensitive place, making her breathless. And once again, his chest grazed hers, the accidental abrading of her protuberances making her ache inside. But that was all right, she told herself hastily, because she felt certain he wasn't doing it on purpose.

With each kiss, each touch, her thoughts fragmented more. Unable to help herself, she dug her nails into his shoulders, possessed by a need to hold on to him and get closer that was overwhelming and fierce. Seemingly impervious to his raked flesh, he nipped his way down the column of her neck, setting her skin afire.

"Oh, Race . . . oh, Race . . ."

"What, darlin'? Am I wanderin' too close to your collar?"

At the question, tears burned at the backs of her eyes. He would stop. All she needed to do was ask. She could feel that in the sudden tension of his body. Why that made her want to cry, she didn't know. Only it did.

She lightly ran her fingertips over the ridges of raw power in his shoulder, and she knew, deep inside where reason couldn't reach, that every ounce of his strength was hers to command, that with a whispered plea, she could make him stop . . . or continue. She remembered last night—how he'd suddenly launched himself on top of her. The relentless vise of his grip, the weight of his hard body holding hers down. This man could do anything he chose to her. Anything. She would be helpless to stop him. Instead he touched her as if she were made of fragile glass.

She'd walloped him on the ear with her elbow, and he had reared away, keeping his distance, as if she were a threat to him. The most beautiful part about that, what made her want to cry, was that she *was* a threat. Bless his dear heart, he would have let her break his nose rather than slap her silly, which was probably what she had deserved. *Am I wanderin' too close to your collar?* Oh, God ... She loved him so much, so very, very much. The sound of his voice was a song bursting like a glorious sunrise inside of her.

She felt his hand tighten at her waist as he trailed his lips over her cheek and found the wetness of her tears. "Sweetheart, you're cryin'. What'd I do?" Rebecca couldn't reply. "Should I stop?" he asked.

"Oh, Race!"

He moved his hand from her waist, slipping it between her and the mattress to draw her close against him. "What, darlin'? Don't be scared. Is that it? I swear to God, I'll take care with you. Don't be afraid."

"I love you!" She clung to his neck, pressing herself as close to him as she could get. "I'm not afraid. I just— oh, Race, I love you so much it hurts."

He went still, as if he heard the words but was afraid to believe them.

"I love you," she repeated. "I love you so very much."

Something that felt like a shudder ran through his big body. He splayed his hand over her back—a hand so wide and leathery hard, she felt sure his fist could splinter wood. Yet when he touched her, he made her feel like a priceless treasure. "Ah, darlin'," he whispered shakily. "I love you, too. With all my heart and soul. With everything I got. But it ain't supposed to make you sad."

"I'm not! I'm happy!"

He trailed kisses to her other cheek, tasting her tears. "Well, hell . . ."

He sounded so thoroughly bewildered and frustrated that Rebecca giggled. She couldn't stop herself.

"Christ on crutches." She felt his lips curve in one of those crooked grins she loved so much as he trailed kisses to her ear. "Am I ever gonna understand you, Rebecca Ann? Cryin' because you're happy. Sometimes, darlin', you don't make a lick of sense."

She tipped her head to accommodate his mouth, the word "lick" making her yearn for him to tease her sensitive spots with the tip of his tongue again. As if he sensed her need, he granted the wish, finding a deliciously vulnerable place beneath her ear. Her breath snagged and her muscles felt as if they were melting. "Oh, yes," she whispered throatily. "Oh, yes, *there*. Like that. Oh, yes . . ."

She felt him tugging her gown up, and for just an instant she felt afraid. But then his wide palm lightly caressed her thigh, and it felt so lovely. Butterfly touches, everywhere, until it made her feel as if her skin would turn inside out if she lay still. Her heart began to slug against her ribs like a fist, and her breath came in shaky rasps.

With feather-light fingertips, he trailed touches to the apex of her legs, dipping between her thighs to tease her sensitive skin, then leaving to trace tantalizing paths to her knees. He made her feel as if her insides were turning into hot syrup. She wanted to melt over his fingers. Just open herself to his touch and flow into him.

Suddenly she felt the quilts shift, and the next instant she felt his moist, silken lips on her thigh. Her eyes flew open and she stiffened.

So breathless she could scarcely speak, she managed to gasp out, "Race, wh-what are you—aa-aaa-ah!—wh-what are you doing?"

From under the quilts, his muffled baritone said, "My manly business, darlin'. It's all right."

Rebecca clamped her knees together. "Are you—sure it's—oh, my God, what—?"

He gently pried her knees apart, and then she felt his broad shoulders working in between her legs. She grabbed hold of the headboard, so shocked she couldn't speak for a moment. He wasn't going to—oh, lands, he was. The tingling nerves just beneath her skin sang with delight at every caress. Only her mind seemed able to comprehend how utterly base his kissing her legs was or that she should protest.

"I don't think this is the way—" He was tickling her inner thigh with the tip of his tongue. It was the most incredibly wonderful feeling. Better, even, than kissing. It was even better than chocolate, and that was her favorite thing in the whole world. "Race, are you—are you positive this is the way it's done?"

"Darlin', think about Keats. This is my business down here, not yours. Right?"

She closed her eyes. "Keats?" she said shrilly.

He pressed closer, forcing his shoulders higher. "It's all right, sweetheart. Remember what your ma said. You just lie still and don't pay me no nevermind." He tickled his way straight up. She jerked and held on to the headboard, staring at the ceiling. "I'll tell you when I'm finished, all right?"

When he was finished? Rebecca felt a thrum of raw yearning thread through her middle. Her eyes. She was supposed to close her eyes. Only . . . oh, dear heaven. Keats? "Will you—will you be long, do you think?"

"Only as"—he ran the tip of his tongue down her inner thigh toward the mattress, finding skin that was so tender, her nerves leaped at every teasing flick—"only as long as it takes, swee—oh, darlin', you are so sweet. The taste of you . . . I feel like I'm lappin' honey."

She felt his big hands cup her rump. Her eyes went wide. Oh, lands. Honey? He didn't mean to—oh, merciful angels. He lifted her, and the white-hot wetness of his mouth surrounded her. She grabbed for breath, her lungs whistling, her arms jerking as she dug her nails into the log of the headboard. He wasn't really doing this.

She was dreaming it, surely. No one would actually—oh, dear God, Race would.

In the next heartbeat, his tongue curled around something there. She jumped, recalling a small flange of flesh in that area that had always been so supersensitive that she'd taken care never to touch it. Race had no such compunction. He settled in there like a bee on honeysuckle. A jolt went through her whole body. "R-Race?"

His voice, when it came, felt as if it sent vibrations clear to her tonsils. "Sweetheart, this ain't none of your concern down here. You're just supposed to lie still and let me do my business, remember?"

"I—I can't!"

He chuckled. This time, she was positive. The vibration went clear through her. "That's the rule." His tone brooked no argument. "This down here is mine to do with, however which way I want, right?"

"Y-yes."

"Well, then? You lie still and don't concern yourself."

After issuing that edict, he settled back in, lapping lightly at that place. She arched up. She couldn't stop herself. Shrill little bleeps erupted from her. She clung to the log for dear life. Arched higher. Higher. "Oh, lands . . . oh, lands . . . ohhh, *mercy*!"

"There's a girl. Give it to me, darlin'."

"Yes. Oh, yes." Somehow—she wasn't sure how— she suddenly had handfuls of his hair. "Oh, my God! Oh, dear heaven. I'm sorry! I'm interfering."

He chuckled again and then splintered every rational thought in her head by drawing her into his mouth, capturing her flesh to drag it with his tongue. White-hot fire darted from his mouth into her. She dug into the mattress with her heels and pushed up, surrendering that part of herself completely, her hips moving with every draw of his mouth, her muscles jerking in rhythm to his teasing flicks. Faster and faster. Drawing harder and harder. A frightening pressure built within her, the ache growing sharper and sharper. Then, just when she felt sure she could no longer bear it, he drove harder against her, taking her with fierce pulls of his mouth, until she felt as if she shattered like a mirror, the fragments catching and reflecting multicolored light like prisms as they rained through her mind.

She was so precious. All his life, Race had heard the word ''cherish,'' but until now he'd never loved anyone so much that he'd understood the meaning. She *was* his angel—a girl made up of sunbeams and cloudy lace, with eyes like the summer sky. She was warmth and light— the tender new blossoms of spring flowers—a beautiful, perfect gift. As she experienced passion for the first time, it was as if he was experiencing it for the first time as well. And perhaps, in a way, it was his first time. Race Spencer—a hard man with an untouched heart.

Until now. This girl held his heart in her hands. She could make it sing with gladness—or bleed with sorrow. Or leap with joy with one little convulsive arch of her spine and a lift of her slender hips—as she gave herself to him.

He worshipped her.

He nearly wept at her guileless urgency and the utter trust she was giving him. No holding back. Just sweet and total vulnerability. And then he felt her shatter, her entire body convulsing, her surrender to him absolute. As she shuddered in climax, he could taste every beat of her heart in the sweet throbbing of her flesh.

Afterward, he gently soothed her sweetness with light strokes and kisses, easing her into a limp calmness, caressing her tortured nerve endings to chase away the ache. When her breathing began to even out, he rose over her. She looked up at him with her lashes drooping low, a dreamy smile on her mouth. ''Are you finished?''

Race bent to kiss her. ''No, darlin'. I'm just lettin' you rest a minute before I do it again.''

Her eyes widened. ''Again?''

He smiled and shifted to lie beside her, one arm holding him up so he might watch her face. He ran his hand down to the joining of her legs, delved deep with a fingertip into her hot sweetness. She gasped and grabbed his shoulders, her head falling back as she arched toward him, her breasts only inches from his mouth, the overlay of worn cotton more tease than covering, the only question being which of them it tormented most. Even through the cloth, he could see the swollen tips of her nipples, throbbing and thrusting up, begging for his attention. His little Bible thumper's body had turned traitor against her.

Race worked her with his hand, loving every expression that crossed her small face. The startlement. The wonder. The strain of building need. He backed off. Brought her back up. The second time when she arched her back and he glanced down to see her nipple thrusting against the thin cotton, he rubbed it with his chin. She gasped and trembled.

"Oh, yes!" she cried.

He gave her another rub. His promise not to touch or kiss her there hadn't included his chin, after all.

She sobbed and pushed up for more. "Oh, Race, please. My protuberances!"

Her *what?* The girl had a tongue tangler for every damned thing. Fortunately, he was growing accustomed to all her highfalutin words. *Protuberances.* That worked. Beautiful little gems like that deserved a fancy name.

"Darlin', do you want me to love 'em?"

"Oh, yes! Please . . ."

Race bent his head, caught her nightgown in his teeth, and dragged it up her slender body to bare her breasts.

"You gotta say it. Otherwise I'm breakin' my word. Ask me to kiss 'em."

The cool air turned the swollen tips as hard as little spikes. He smiled as she pushed them up at him.

"Sweetheart, you gotta ask."

She made a frustrated sound, grabbed him by the hair of the head, and jerked him down to her. "Just *do* it!"

He figured that had "please" beat all to hell. He also figured he had a right to tease her unmercifully before he gave her what she wanted. He circled, laving all around each crest with his tongue, moving in so close he could feel the throbbing heat. Then a quick drag. Then back to circling. When he finally was aching himself for a real taste of her, he nibbled and began to suckle. To his surprise, he felt her body begin to jerk, and he realized the little minx was climaxing. He felt the rush of hot sweetness against his hand. Damn. She was starved for loving. Twenty-one years old, and never been kissed. She was coming apart in his arms.

Race decided that anyone who had waited over twenty years for this had a right. He took her twice more with his mouth, glorying in the sweet way she trembled and gave herself to him.

When the moment finally came for him to either take her or explode from the waiting, Race rose over her, caught her behind the knees, and pressed his hardness against her slick heat. She opened heavy-lidded eyes to gaze up at him, clearly too sated and exhausted to even realize he was about to hurt her. The coward in him wanted to just drive it home and get it over with, but the man who loved her with every beat of his heart couldn't break her trust like that.

"Sweetheart," he whispered, his voice throbbing with regret, "I'm gonna hurt you this one time. I'm sorry."

She blinked and focused on his face, her eyes shimmering in the firelight. "I know," she said softly. "Would you just hold me while you do it, Race? It won't hurt so bad and I won't be scared if you're holding me."

Tears scalded his eyes. He lowered himself over her to scoop her up in one arm. She wrapped both hers around his neck and clung to him. "I'm not afraid now," she whispered.

He could tell by the tension that had entered her small body that in spite of her brave words, she *was* afraid, and in that moment, he would have given everything he owned not to cause her pain. The truth was, he had no idea how bad it might hurt her when he entered her. It wasn't only that she was a virgin, but she was a delicately made woman, and he was a large man.

He nudged into her opening, and she jerked taut. *Christ.* He had barely started, and already it was killing her. He heard her drag in a sharp breath and hold it. He buried his face in her beautiful hair, wondering why God had decided it should be like this, forcing a man to hurt the one person in the world who was his soul.

"Do it," she whispered fiercely. "It's not that bad. Really."

He inched farther in, and her insides convulsed, calling her a liar. Alarm coursed through him. "Oh, Jesus. Darlin', I can't. It's hurtin' you."

He started to draw out. He'd never felt a woman so small and tight. If he forced his way in, he was afraid he'd tear her. "Sweetheart, I'm afraid you're too small."

Before he sensed what she meant to do, she drove upward with her hips and impaled herself. Race's heart stuttered in his chest and felt as if it stopped beating. He felt her channel give way and was terrified she'd torn herself. She clung to him, shaking violently.

"It's all right," she cried. "It's all right."

Feeling the wet heat of her all around him nearly made him lose it. In a heartbeat, he was trembling as violently as she was. "Oh, damn."

She gave a weak little laugh, and the tension started to ebb from her. She pressed a wet cheek against his neck. "It truly is all right," she whispered. "The hurting isn't as bad."

"It isn't? Honey, are you sure?" At her nod, Race drew back and carefully nudged forward again. "How's that?"

"Oh, my!" she said, sounding startled.

"What? Is it bad?"

She sighed. "Oh, Race, why didn't you tell me?" She bumped her hips against him, slightly off with her aim. "Oh, my! It's—oh, it's extraordinary! You're phenomenal—it's so *wonderful*!"

Phenomenal. He kind of liked that one. A great, huge tongue tangler of a word.

Carefully he began a slow rhythm. When she began to buck and sob, he knew it really was all right. He increased the force of his thrusts, still holding himself in check, his thoughts so centered on her that his own need was held at bay. Then she convulsed around him, the walls of her channel grabbing at his shaft as her orgasm rocked her.

That was it for him. He drove home, hard, his own release so explosive that he felt as if the top of his head blew off. Heaven—hell. He spiraled through a maze o brightness, his body locked in violent stiffness, his muscles knotted, his seed bursting forth from him with each squeeze of his heart.

Afterward he collapsed, rolling with Rebecca in his arms to drape her on top of him so his weight wouldn't crush her. She sprawled across him like a silken drape that was a little too short, her toes hitting low on his shins. His heart slogging in his chest like a laboring train engine on a steep incline, Race stroked her beautiful hair, his eyes closed, feeling as though he were floating with her on a cloud.

His last thought as he drifted with her into slumber was that she must truly be an angel, after all. He knew because she'd just taken him with her to see the glory of heaven.

Chapter 20

It was a good hour since dawn had burst over the valley.
The ranch was alive. His men were out and about, tending
to the routine and never-ending tasks of a working spread.
Race was no exception. After jawing over plans for the
day with Pete, he'd headed for the barn to get a start on
his own work.

His mouth tipping in a dreamy smile, he forked some
straw, thinking as he tossed it toward the horse stall that
when the sunlight struck it right, the color shimmered like
Rebecca's hair. *Last night.* His heart caught, and he
glanced up the aisle toward the open barn doors. Through
the opening, he could see the cabin.

A half hour ago, she had been snuggled down asleep
when he sneaked out to do chores, a little, golden-haired
angel with her nightgown still rucked up under her arms,
one petal-pink *protuberance* peeking out over the quilt at
him.

Damn. His rod went rock-hard, and the pitchfork
slipped from his hands to fall forgotten in the straw. She
needed at least a couple of days to recover. A decent man
would leave the poor girl alone and let her sleep. But he
wasn't feeling very decent at the moment.

He struck off for the house, calling himself a bastard
with every slap of his boot soles on the packed dirt. But,
hey . . . it wasn't like he had to actually *do* anything.
Right? Just kiss her awake and love on her for a while.
That was all. Maybe throw open the shutters near the head

314

of the bed to catch the sunlight pouring in from the eastern sky.

The thought of her, bathed in sunlight, made his blood pound in his ears. Those slender legs, opened for him, her nightgown arranged precisely over her hipbones so his territory was clearly marked. Oh, yeah . . . Those cheek-turning brethren were smart men, making up rules like that. *Just don't pay me no nevermind, darlin'. Read your poetry.* Howdy-do!

Next trip to town, he was buying the girl a book. Hell, he'd buy her a dozen. Thick ones. This winter after the snow fell, he'd wake her up of a morning with a sip of coffee, then lay her on her back, open the book, and stick her cute little nose in it. She could read poems while he started his day out right.

He stepped softly onto the stoop. As he pushed open the cabin door, he lifted up on the crossbar so the leather hinges wouldn't creak. *Still asleep.* Silently, he slipped inside, closed the door behind him, and eased the bolt down into its niche. Leaning back against the log wall, he hiked up one foot to remove his boot, then set it carefully on the floor and took off the other boot. After tugging his holster ties loose and unbuckling his gun belt, he carried it with him as he tiptoed across the room.

She was so precious, lying twisted slightly at the waist, a fine-boned hand palm up next to her face on the pillow, her dainty fingers loosely curled, her hair fanned out around her in a tangled mass of spun gold. Her pink nipple peeked out at him through the shimmering strands, just as he'd once imagined. He locked his gaze on it as he bent to set his guns on the floor. Carefully, quietly, he moved to the window and lifted the shutter bolt to open the panels wide. Soft sunlight poured over her like melted butter.

Race moved back to the bed and sank onto one knee beside her. She moaned and stretched, arching toward him like a kitten that wanted petting. He bent his head and caught that vulnerable tip of pink between his teeth to tease it ever so lightly with his tongue, his gaze on her face to gauge her reaction. Her fair brows puckered in a frown. Her nipple, however, woke up straightaway and bade him good morning in the sweetest way possible, by swelling and turning instantly hard.

He loved on it gently, granting what it begged for, content to let Rebecca frown bewilderedly in her sleep while he and her sweet little protuberance struck up a fast friendship. While he provided it with attention, he inched the quilts away from her body. Then taking care not to startle her awake, he ran a hand under her rump to shift her hips. Relaxed in sleep, she offered no resistance as he positioned her slender legs.

Abandoning her breast, Race moved down on her and parted that nest of gold curls to reveal the pink folds of sweetness. Restlessly she shifted her legs, then moaned in her sleep. At any moment, she would awaken. He didn't mind. He would have her halfway to heaven again before she ever opened her eyes.

Over the next three days, Rebecca silently revealed to every man on the ranch who ventured within ten feet of her *exactly* what her husband had done to her in bed. No question about it. The girl might as well have gone out and painted pictures on the side of the barn, three feet tall and in full color. Every single time Race looked at her, she turned an alarming shade of brilliant red. No matter who was around, no matter how serious or unrelated the topic of conversation, one glance from him in her direction, and it was as if he'd touched a lighted match to her lamp wick.

To their credit, the fellows were perfect gentlemen about it in Rebecca's presence, none of them letting on that they noticed anything strange. Well . . . Pete did choke on his coffee the first time he witnessed it, but Race didn't hold that against him. A man couldn't really help it when something startled him and he sucked fluid down his windpipe. But beyond that, none of the men let on by word or look in front of Rebecca that they knew anything had taken place between the newlyweds.

Unfortunately the same courtesy was not extended to Race outside his bride's company. Catcalls, hootin, laughter, off-color inquiries about how he liked married life. Race got a rash of teasing, the worst part being that it was dished out in such a way that he couldn't, in good conscience, get angry. Nothing ever was said that could be construed as being disrespectful to Rebecca. Just the opposite. There wasn't a man on the crew who didn't hold "the little missus" in high regard. The only time they actually mentioned her name, in fact, was when they were giving Race a hard time about treating her right, the general message being that she was a fine lady, and if they discovered he wasn't being good to her, they would stand in line to kick his ass.

Race was hopeful that her blushing would subside as the days passed. For one thing, since that morning when he'd awakened her with kisses, he had done nothing more than cuddle her at night to give her body time to recover. It seemed to him that three days was a mighty long time for her to still be so painfully embarrassed. Hell, for him, it seemed like six months since he'd touched her.

Not so for her. On the third evening when Race came in from working, all he did was glance her way as he hung up his hat, and she started to glow. He wondered then if he shouldn't have a talk with her. By the time supper was over, he was convinced of it.

She'd fixed him a meal fit for a king—fried chicken, mashed potatoes, gravy, fresh biscuits, and snap beans. He ate like a horse. As near as he could count, she had four bites, chewing each a fair hundred times and chasing it down with milk. She'd dropped weight out on the trail, and if this kept up, she was going to drop even more. Since arriving at the ranch, the circles under her eyes were gone, which was a good sign. He couldn't honestly tell if she'd gotten some color back in her cheeks, though, because lately, whenever he looked at her, all of her turned red.

After helping her clean up the kitchen, Race battened down the shutters, built up the fire, and sat in the rocker, angling glances over his shoulder at his wife, who seemed unaccountably busy doing nothing at the work counter. As near as he could tell, it was her goal to scrub a hole through the wood with his one and only dishrag, which was fast wearing out.

"Rebecca? Can you leave that go for a while?" he asked. "I'd like to talk at you for a minute."

As she made her way toward him, Race vowed that as soon as he deemed it safe to take her to Cutter Gulch, he was going to buy her a whole new wardrobe from the skin out and burn those damned black dresses. How she managed to look so beautiful in such an ugly, somber sack, he'd never know.

Clasping her hands behind her, she came to stand before him on the hearth. Her posture and flushed face made her look very like a guilty twelve-year-old who had reason to believe she was about to get her fanny warmed with the razor strop. Resting his elbows on the chair arms, he leaned forward to search her big, blue eyes. No doubt about it, she had her tail tied in a knot about something.

"Sweetheart . . ." Race wasn't exactly sure how to start. After quick consideration, he decided there wasn't a good way. He just needed to plunge in and see where the current took him. "Are you embarrassed about all we done the other night?"

That was a fine start. He couldn't believe he'd asked such a stupid question.

Her face went from mere red to a throbbing scarlet, and her gaze skittered off to a point at the opposite side of the room. Race noticed her slender arms elbowing out, then straightening, which gave him reason to believe she was wringing her hands behind her back. She was obviously embarrassed. Painfully so. And damned if he knew how to ease her feelings about it. He had really hoped that he might make love to her again tonight, but if she turned this red just talking about it, he was afraid she might go up in flames if he touched her.

"Rebecca, we gotta talk this out, you know. This ain't gonna work."

She closed her eyes. Race saw her chin start to quiver and realized she was battling against tears. His heart caught, and a wave of guilt swamped him. Here she was, suffering untold agony about some damned thing, and all he wanted to do was strip that black rag off her and give her something more to stew about.

"I understand," she said shakily. "We don't need to talk about it."

He was glad one of them understood something. "I think we do need to talk about it. Until we iron this out, we kinda got us a wrinkle."

She still had her eyes closed. Instead of answering, she was busy chewing on her lower lip.

"Honey, I don't wanna make it hard on you, layin' things out on the table. I can see it ain't easy for you to talk about. But we gotta come to some kinda agreement about how we're gonna go on from here. Don't you think? Maybe reach an understandin', so both of us can move past this and get on with our—"

She whirled from the hearth and went back to the work counter, where she grabbed up the rag and started scrubbing as if she were possessed again. "I'll go to Cutter Gulch tomorrow," she informed him in a squeaky voice. "Maybe Pete will agree to take me."

Race pushed up from the rocker. "What'n hell are you gonna do in Cutter Gulch?"

"I'll—I don't know. Get a job, I guess! At least I won't be here."

"You mean you wanna leave? Ain't that kinda like shootin' the horse to smooth out the ride?"

She turned to face him, and for the first time in three days, she wasn't red. Instead her face had turned deathly white. He had a bad feeling he was getting his first glimpse of Rebecca in high dudgeon. Or maybe killing mad was a better description.

"You know, Race, I don't blame you. All right?" she said in a taut voice. "But by the same token, you must admit that you basically got what you asked for! If that wasn't—" She broke off and held up her hands, as if words eluded her. Her eyes filled with tears. "If it was going to give you such a disgust of me, why did you do it?"

A disgust of her? Race stepped toward her, not quite

able to believe his ears. "You think I got a disgust of you?"

She hauled back her arm and let fly with the dishrag. It went *splat* on the center of his face, clingy and wet, and clung for a moment. Then, as it slid off, it caught on his nose. He blinked and slowly reached up to pluck it away. For a young woman who hadn't had a clue how to have a good fight when he first met her, she was proving to be a damned fast study.

"Do you truly want to know what I think?" she asked. "I think you are a hypocritical jackass. That's what I think!"

She had the jackass part right. He wasn't sure about the rest. So what else was new? "Rebecca Ann, if you wanna argue, talk plain English. What'n hell does 'hypocritical' mean?"

"It means you have one set of rules for me and another for yourself." She presented him with her back. "You wanted me to want you," she cried in a shrill voice, "but then as soon as I did, you no longer wanted me!"

"That ain't true." Race fell into step behind her, leaning around to try and see her face as she turned this way and that. It was like trying to herd a duck. "You ain't thinkin' what I think you're thinkin'?"

"I have concluded that you don't think," she replied waspishly. "I believe you have sawdust between your ears. I was perfectly content to be a lady beyond reproach! Only because *you* pressed me, did I engage in lewd behavior! If you were going to have a disgust of me afterward"—she whirled to face him, her big blue eyes filled with a world of hurt—"why didn't you leave me as I was?"

Race grabbed her shoulders before she could go wheeling off again. "I don't have a disgust of you. I think you're the sweetest thing that ever walked! And I do want you."

"You don't! You haven't touched me since."

Race could see that had been a big mistake, one which he could rectify in short order. Before she could guess his intent, he swept her up into his arms. "I didn't touch you because you was new broke.'' He strode toward the corner of the room. When his knees bumped the mattress, he dropped her and had joined her on the bed before her startled squeak trailed away. ''I didn't wanna hurt you by makin' love to you again before you healed up. *That's* how come I didn't touch you.''

She fixed incredulous blue eyes on his. ''Truly?''

Race set himself to the task of unbuttoning her dress as he laid out the facts. ''I think you're beautiful. I think you're still a lady, no matter what we do in bed. It don't matter! And I want you more now than I did before.''

''Even though I was so abandoned?''

He bent to trail kisses along her fragile jaw. ''I didn't mean to abandon you, darlin'. I was tryin' to be thoughtful. I promise I'll never be thoughtful again, startin' now. When I get done, you're gonna feel like you been rode hard and put away wet.'' He kissed her, long and deep. When he came up for breath, he said, ''And one more thing, just so we're clear on it. If you ever—and I do mean *ever*—try to leave me, I'm goin' with you.''

Over the next few days, Race worried ceaselessly about when the ruffians would make their move. He had expected them to do it right away, and the waiting wore on his nerves. Staying close to the cabin, leaving work undone, constantly afraid for Rebecca's safety. It made him a little crazy.

He finally decided that enough was enough. Just because his usual work had been pretty much curtailed didn't mean he couldn't put this time to good use. He had a wife whose self-confidence had taken a beating and who was afraid of her own shadow. Teaching her how to take care of herself and fight back might go a long ways toward making her feel less vulnerable.

Overriding Rebecca's objections, Race forced her to learn how to handle guns, starting with his rifles, then working on her aim with a pistol after she became fairly proficient with the larger weapons. She didn't like it. Given her upbringing, firearms represented evil, their only permissible use for hunting game, and that being a man's pursuit. But Race insisted, making her target practice for several hours each afternoon out by the barn, relentless and exacting in his role of teacher. Taught to mindlessly obey her husband, Rebecca acquiesced, albeit unenthusiastically. Race didn't care. She was becoming a fair marksman, and he was convinced that, sooner or later, the ability would not only bolster her confidence, but might even save her life.

On the evening of the fifth day of weaponry instruction, Race sat her on the rocker, handed her a screwdriver, a rifle, and a Colt .45, and said, "Take 'em apart, clean 'em, and put 'em back together."

She gaped at him. "Surely you jest!"

He crouched next to her to supervise. "Get after it. You ain't goin' to bed until they're clean as a whistle, completely reassembled, and reloaded."

"I can't!"

"There ain't no such word. Do it."

It took her three hours, but she did it, and he saw to it that she did it well. Race rewarded himself for a lesson well taught and her for a lesson well learned by steering her over to stand by the bed and removing every stitch of her clothing.

When he started unlacing her chemise, her cheeks turned a pretty pink. "Race, the lanterns. You forgot to turn them out. It's like broad daylight in here."

He smiled and grasped her wrist to turn her arm inner side up. Tracing the network of blue veins beneath her skin with a fingertip, he said, "The first time I ever noticed those little squiggly lines, they reminded me of the lines on a trail map, and I wondered if they was all over you." Reaching the bend of her arm, he bent to kiss the tender skin there. "I've noticed since that they ain't everywhere, but what ones you got, they lead to some real interestin' places. And guess what?"

"What?" she asked faintly, shivering at the way he kissed and tasted her sensitive skin.

"I love to follow new trails and see where they take me." Straightening, he resumed his attack on her chemise lacings. "I gotta leave the lamps lit to see where I'm goin'."

"Oh, no . . ."

He touched a fingertip to her lips. "You just lay back and close your eyes, darlin'. You got a bad habit of interferin' in my manly business. It ain't wifely."

"Race, it's embarrassing. I'm not going to—" She sucked breath as he opened the chemise. "I'm not going to display myself with the lamps all burning."

"Sure you are."

"It's unseemly."

"Not to please your husband."

"It's unladylike."

"You're the finest of ladies the rest of the time. But I don't want you to be one in my arms, darlin'. I just want you to be all mine."

He leaned slightly to see as he touched the outside swell of one breast. "See there?" he whispered. "Followin' this trail"—he traced the faint blue line of a vein—"just look where it's gonna take me."

She gasped and closed her eyes. "I can't."

"Darlin', there ain't no such word. I thought we just went through that."

Grasping her by the shoulders, he pressed her down onto the bed and joined her there, then proceeded to follow every trail on her. At the end of each, they both found paradise.

Peace. Race lay with his disgustingly unladylike and very nude wife wrapped around him like a baby opossum. Occasionally Blue snorted in his sleep or the fire embers popped. Otherwise, the cabin was silent, the sense of contentment that surrounded him as warm as a down-filled quilt. It was so easy to forget at moments like this that a threat to Rebecca's safety lay beyond these sturdy walls, or to believe that anything unpleasant could touch them. Yet lingering at the back of his mind, Race never completely forgot. He didn't dare, for this precious girl he held in his arms counted on him to protect her.

A sudden pounding on the door made Race jerk. Usually when he was summoned unexpectedly from bed, the only person Race had to worry about dressing was himself. But this time, he had only just grabbed his pants when he flung them back on the floor and started tearing through the bedding to find Rebecca's chemise. Blinking like a little barn owl, she was sitting up in all her barebreasted glory. For reasons beyond him, he didn't want anyone to come in, see her hiding under the quilts, and guess she was lying there, stripped stark-naked. That was silly, of course. It wasn't as if every man out there didn't know he had made love to her. Rebecca's three-day blushing spell had pretty much erased any doubts about that they might have had.

"Just a minute, Pete!" he yelled.

Out of necessity, Race had long since developed the ability to wake up clearheaded and alert. Grogginess could get a gunslinger killed faster than you could spit and yell howdy. But the same couldn't be said for Rebecca. She just sat there, looking a little limp in the spine, with a confused expression on her face. Race grabbed one of her boneless arms and stuffed it through the armhole of her chemise. By the time he got the garment completely on her and drew the front together, she was beginning to come more awake.

"Can you lace yourself?"

"Who is it?" she asked dazedly as she bent her head and applied herself to the task. "Is that Pete hollering?"

Race threw on his trousers, kicked the rest of Rebecca's clothing under the bed, and rushed to the door, raking his fingers through his hair en route. Pete and Trevor McNaught stood outside.

"The bastards is slaughterin' the cattle," Pete bit out. "You best hurry."

Race nodded, pushed the door closed, and wheeled back the way he had come. As he hurriedly finished dressing, Rebecca pelted him with questions, the last of which put him on the spot.

"It's them, isn't it?"

Race met her gaze as he bent to tie down his holsters.

"They won't get to you this time, darlin'. I give you my word."

Her face drained of color. "Pete said for you to hurry. You're leaving me?"

She looked so panicked that Race crouched and cupped her face in his hands. "Rebecca, darlin', listen to me. All right?" She clutched his wrists and nodded, her eyes dark with fear. "I ain't really gonna leave you. You understand? It's you they're after. They figure you've got that money stashed away somewheres. I had a choice of leavin' you here to go after the bastards, or waitin' 'em out and lurin' 'em in. I picked this way because it's the least risky for you. You understand? We'll make it look like we're leavin' you alone—to get 'em to move in where we can take 'em. But I won't ever be far off. No matter what happens, I don't want you gettin' real scared. God as my witness, I'll die before I let one of 'em touch you."

"You're using m-me as b-bait?"

He truly hated the way that sounded. "Sweetheart, you gotta know I'd never do it if I wasn't sure I could keep you safe."

She nodded, but the terror in her eyes told him she feared he might fail.

"Trust me," he whispered. He pushed up and went to take the newly cleaned Colt .45 from the gun rack above the mantle. When he returned to her, he laid the gun beside her on the bed. "For just in case. If one of 'em gets close to you, shoot him."

She looked as if he'd just asked her to fornicate with him in the barnyard while everyone watched. "Oh, Race. I-I don't think—"

"That's the trick, not thinkin'. It ain't like you'd ever harm anyone by choice. But you gotta right to defend you and yours. Them men are mean snakes, darlin'. Your God knows that, and He ain't gonna hold it against you if you protect your sweet self."

As far as Race was concerned, that ended the conversation. He kissed the tip of her nose. "Come bolt the door after me. All right? Then finish gettin' dressed. I'll be back as soon as it's over. And after that, you ain't never gonna have to feel afraid like this again.''

If ever Race had doubted she had grit, she proved him wrong then. Never a word of protest. No pleading with him not to leave her. He knew damned well she'd been having a tough time during the day when he left her alone in the cabin. This had to be one of the most frightening moments of her life. But she followed him to the door as he had asked, and when he turned to kiss her, she stood with her shoulders back and her small chin lifted, clearly determined not to fall apart.

"I love you, darlin'," he whispered as he kissed her.

She caught his sleeve just as he started to slip out the door. "Please, don't get hurt," she cried shakily. "Promise me."

That was a promise he might not be able to keep. "I'll do my best."

Deathly quiet . . . Somewhere way off in the distance, rifle shots echoed in the darkness, but in the vicinity of the cabin, there was no sound. Rebecca found the silence more terrifying than if she'd been able to detect some sort of noise. No wind. No creaking of Race's fir tree just outside the kitchen window. Nothing. It was an unnatural silence—eerie and spine-chilling. Knees drawn to her chest, she held the Colt .45 wedged in the crease of her lap, her thighs pressing it against her abdomen, the hammer spur poking her in the navel.

There was a certain irony in the hiding place she'd chosen. She was huddled behind the wood stove. The fire still smoldered in the grate, making her uncomfortably warm. It seemed better than sitting out in the open, though, or hiding under the bed. No one would think to look behind a hot stove. Would they?

She had no idea how long Race had been gone. An hour? The fire in the fireplace had been burning brightly when they'd been awakened by Pete's pounding on the door. Now it was nearly out. That was the only means she had of gauging how much time had passed, and since she'd never paid much attention to how long the fire lasted, it didn't give her much to measure by.

Every once in a while, an ember in the wood stove's firebox would pop, nearly scaring her out of her skin. When she jumped, Blue would lift his head from his paws and peer up at her. Even though the heat was nearly unbearable where he lay beside her, he stayed, panting occasionally to cool himself. He thought he was overly warm? He lay beside the stove, not behind it. She was the one who was about to cook.

Silly hound. He probably looked at her and thought, *Silly woman.* And she had to concede the point. Sitting behind a wood stove on the floor and partially baking her knees wasn't exactly intelligent.

More rifle shots. Rebecca leaned her head back against the log wall behind her and counted the reports. *Seven.* Pete had told Race the ruffians were slaughtering cattle. Was a steer going down with every one of those shots? The thought made her feel sick. She had done nothing but bring Race Spencer bad luck since he'd first clapped eyes on her.

She made tight fists, thinking of the money stashed under his bed. Whether he liked it or not, she was going to insist on paying him back for all of this. It was only right. What was left of the church money she'd send on to Santa Fe. There would still be plenty for the brethren to buy their livestock, equipment, and the necessary seed to put in their crops next spring. In the letter she sent with the money, she would explain all that Race had done in their behalf and all that he'd suffered in the process, and they would understand why she'd felt it necessary to make restitution.

A sudden crashing sound made Rebecca leap. Blue shot up onto his haunches and snarled. She grabbed him by the ruff. *Oh, God.* She wasn't sure from what direction the noise had come, but it sounded as if someone was trying to break in. Terror constricted her chest. More beads of sweat popped out all over her body. She flattened herself against the wall, her staring eyes bugging from their sockets.

Crash! This time she heard wood splintering. Someone

was trying to break in a window or the front door. The sound came from the front section of the cabin. The stove blocked her view. Were they inside? *Oh, God, please . . . not again.* Race had promised. *Promised!* Where was he? They were going to get to her! Where was he?

The *kaboom* of a gun exploded in the night. Immediately thereafter she heard gunfire all around the cabin. Running footsteps. Shouts. *Kaboom—kaboom!* Blue started to bark and tried to lunge away from her. She clung frantically to his ruff, afraid he'd attack someone and get shot again.

"Quiet, Blue! Shhh. They'll hear. Shhh."

The dog settled back, snarling low in his chest. Rebecca had started to shake so badly that she could barely hold on to him. More gunfire. She closed her eyes. Tried to pray. The words that had once come so naturally to her were now beyond her reach, as was the faith that had once sustained her. Race said there was a God. If so, where was He? Why wasn't He protecting her? She'd been good. All her life, she'd been so good. Doing for others. Praying every day, on her knees more times than not. Avoiding evil. Reading the Bible. Where was God? Where was Race? Why, when she needed help, was there never anyone?

Her breath started to come in shrill little pants. The veins in her temples felt as if they might rupture from pressure. *Suffocating.* Race wasn't going to come. Where was he? Where was he? Please, Race. Come back. I need you! They're going to get me.

Images of the blond ruffian's knife flashed in her mind. She imagined one of his cohorts creeping toward her, even now, a knife clutched in his hand, the blade glinting like dark death in the faint glow from the fireplace. Something creaked. A board? Shrill whistling sounds erupted from her as she fought frantically to breathe.

A sudden pounding echoed through the cabin. She jerked and nearly lost control of her bladder. *Pounding, pounding.* The stove seemed to tilt. The room started to rotate. *Gunfire.* Whistle, whistle. Pant, pant. *Screams.* Her mother screaming, screaming. *Rebecca! Rebecca! Rebecca!*

She closed her eyes and clamped her hands over her ears. *No, no, no.* Her ma. Oh, dear God in heaven. Please, please, please! She couldn't bear it. *Can't do anything. They'll kill me. Hide. Have to hide. Right here. In the bushes. Stop, Ma! Please, God, make it stop!* But it didn't stop.

Nothing could block out the sound of her mother screaming her name . . .

Chapter 21

Three days. *Sitting on a stool beside the bed, Race held* his wife's hand, his thumb circling continuously over its back to trace the network of fragile bones. Pete stood beside him, his hat held at his waist, his leathery face drawn as he gazed down at the girl who stared so sightlessly back at him.

"I'm sorry, boss."

Race could only nod. Speaking was beyond him. The doctor had just left, and with him, the man had taken the last of Race's hope. His prognosis was merciless, frightening, and heartbreaking. *She may never snap out of it, Mr. Spencer. I hate having to tell you that, but the sad truth is, some people don't have the constitutions to live in a harsh land like this. It ends up breaking them.*

Rebecca wasn't just broken. She was shattered like fragile china, and according to the doctor, there was nothing Race could do to piece her back together. He wanted to throw back his head and scream. Shake his fist at God. Rip things apart. He'd kept his promise to her. He and his men had killed the ruffians before they managed to enter the cabin. But all the ruckus they'd raised while getting the job done had scared Rebecca so badly that she'd gone back into shock.

The doctor said that often happened with shock victims. *A similar incident can cause patients like this to have a relapse. And the second time is usually far worse than the first. I'm so very sorry, Mr. Spencer, but it isn't a good*

*sign when a patient remains in a stupor for so long. With
each passing day, it becomes less likely that she will recover.*

Not Rebecca. He would have happily died rather than
lose her, especially like this. *Living death.* Her heart was
beating. She was breathing. But her body had become
nothing but a shell. She would drink for him. He had
cooked up some soupy broth and he was forcing some
down her every couple of hours. But how long was that
going to keep her alive? A month or two, the doctor said.
Race imagined watching her waste away, each passing
day leeching more of the life from her body.

He hunched his shoulders and brought her hand to his
lips. A sob shook his shoulders. Then another. He felt
Pete's hand on his back. Race knew he should feel embarrassed. Crying like a baby. *Christ.* He hadn't cried,
really cried, since his mother died. Maybe it was fitting
that he should weep again now. For the second time in
his life, he was losing his world.

He loved this girl so much. Cherished everything about
her—her shyness, her funny ideas, her innocence, her
sweetness. She'd been like a song in his life after years
of silence, making him laugh again, making him dream
again, giving him hope again. He wanted to give her babies. He wanted to see her hold one of his babies to her
breast, to see her dainty little hand curl over its head, her
slender fingers stroking its ebony hair as it nursed. He
wanted to build a home on this knoll, with the old fir to
stand sentinel over their children while they ran and
played in the yard. He wanted to carve a cattle empire
from this land that he could pass on to them. God help
him, he wanted to hear Rebecca laugh, just one more time.
See her smile, just one more time. Hold her in his arms
and make love to her, just one more time.

"God, Pete, I can't lose her like this. I can't."

"I know it's hard, son. But all you can do is pray and
leave it to God."

Race remembered how he'd tried to teach Rebecca how
wrong it was to count on God for every damned thing.
Stand on your own two feet. Pray to Him for the strength

to fight your own battles, not for Him to fight them for you. Now, here he was, praying with every breath he took for God to save her because he couldn't. There was no way to fight this fight. Nothing he could do. His only option was to put it into God's hands and trust in Him to bring her back to him.

Hoarsely, Race said, "Her papa was right, after all. In the end, the only real hope any of us have is that God will save us." He squeezed her hand, horribly conscious of how small it felt beneath his fingers. "Maybe this is my lesson. I was so damned convinced it was always up to me. You know? So cocky. Gonna take on the world. He's showin' me I can't. By takin' her, He's gonna take me to my knees."

Pete squeezed his shoulder. "That's crazy thinkin', Race Spencer."

"Is it? I don't think so."

"It's true that in the end, we only got one hope, and we all gotta know that as we live our lives. But it's also true that we got two feet to stand on, and we got it in us to fight when we have to. In the end, when you can't fight no more, you put it into God's hands, but until then, you use the strength He gave you and the brains He gave you to defend yourself as best you can. He wouldn't take her from you 'cause you done that or tried to teach her to do that. It's crazy to think He might."

Race closed his eyes, remembering how he'd felt three nights ago when he had found her huddling behind the wood stove, her body drenched with sweat, her hair singed, her knees pressed against the metal and blistered from the heat. To be that afraid . . . He'd never been that afraid in his life. He kept picturing her, huddled back there, so scared she stayed, despite the pain. The thought of it. Oh, God, it made him sick. He'd called her name, growing more and more frantic, never thinking to look behind the stove until Blue had led him to her.

"Maybe I should've just let her alone," he thought aloud. "Maybe by messin' with her beliefs, I just made it worse. I tried to make her over. It ain't right to do that to somebody. You love 'em like they are, or you walk away. You don't go tryin' to change who they are. I done that to her. About every damned thing. Maybe if I would've just let her be, she would've gotten better on her own and would still be all right. Instead I stripped all she was away and tried to make her like me."

"You're flat bent on takin' the blame for this, I see," Pete said grimly. "Guilt's a terrible thing, son. It'll tear you apart if you hang onto it."

"Like it tore her apart? I'm in good company then." Race kissed the backs of her fingers, his gaze on her expressionless face. He'd never known anyone more pure of heart. "I should've let her be. As soon as we got the herd here, I should've taken her to her folks down south. They're her people, not me. They would've understood her and loved her like she was, instead of tryin' to change everything about her. I told myself they wouldn't keep her safe. But the truth is, there around Santa Fe, on a big farm, what real harm could've come to her? But I kept her with me. Pure-dee old selfishness, wantin' her for myself. She would've been safe with them. Look at her now. By keepin' her, I killed her."

"She wanted to stay with you," Pete reminded him.

"She didn't know what was good for her. I should have been thinkin' clear for both of us. All them folks love her. They've loved her all her life. They're bound to understand her better than I do. I knew she was troubled. Why didn't I take her to 'em, let them try to heal her?"

Pete sighed. "You don't know that they could have."

Race straightened and took a deep breath. "Maybe I should take her to them now."

"What?"

Now that the idea had struck him, Race couldn't set it aside. "Take her home. To her people, Pete." He glanced up. "Ain't it worth a try? Maybe if she sensed them around her, felt safe. Maybe she'd come right."

"To Santa Fe? You can't take her to Santa Fe in this shape."

"Why not? I can hold her in front of me. Ride hard. Except for the two plug-uglies that hightailed it, they're all dead. I don't gotta worry about any trouble on that front. There's no threat anymore. Why can't I take her home? Her own people might be able to help her. Do you deny there's a chance of that?''

Pete rubbed his jaw. ''I ain't denyin' nothin'. It might help her. Then again, it might not. But she'll die afore you get her there. How you gonna feed her? Here you can keep broth cooked up. You can't on the trail.''

''I could carry it in jugs. Cook some up each night. Take dried meat for the fixin's. I could get her there. I have a good month yet before the first heavy snow comes. And it's bound to storm up this way first. It'll be warmer down south until deeper into winter. I can make it.''

Pete sighed and whacked his hat against his leg. ''I think it's a crazy risk to take. Better to just stick here, see how she comes along.''

''And watch her die.'' In that moment, Race knew he couldn't do that. ''Damn it, Pete, I been a fighter all my life. It ain't in me to flop over on my back. Not if there might be a way to save her. I'd rather lose her that way, fightin' for her life with everything I got, than to just sit here and watch her fade away.''

Pete looked at Rebecca, long and hard. ''I told you once that you gotta do what's in your heart. If that's what you feel is right, then all the talkin' in the world ain't gonna change your mind.''

''You think I shouldn't do it.''

Pete shook his head. ''I think it's a mighty big risk. That's all.''

A mighty big risk. Those words haunted Race as he journeyed south. It seemed to him that each second that passed was measured by the continuous and rhythmic clop of Dusty's hooves on the sun-baked earth of the grass-lands south of Denver. The sun hung like a yellow orb in the blue sky, searing even in the cool, autumn weather. He wrapped Rebecca in quilts and held her cradled in his arms, her golden head resting on his shoulder, one hand curled lifelessly in her lap, her other arm dangling more times than not, as if she were dead.

God knew she was as still as death. He wanted to urge

Dusty into a trot, to drive the horse relentlessly forward to reach Santa Fe in time. Before his world died in his arms. Each day he broke camp before first light and rode, hour after endless hour. Then the sun would sink behind the mountains to the west and the moon would rise, bathing everything in silver, and still he rode, pushing the horse and himself beyond endurance. *Clippety-clop, please, God. Clippety-clop, please God.* That was his constant prayer, the only one he knew. *Please, God.*

Doubts tormented him. Should he turn back? What if he wasn't getting enough water down her? What if the broth he made each night when he stopped to rest wasn't nourishment enough to sustain her? Maybe she would have gotten well back at the cabin, and by heading south, he'd consigned her to certain death. What if he got her to her people in Santa Fe, and they couldn't help her? What if nothing could help her? What if this was all just a bitterly cruel lesson, to teach him he couldn't always fight his own battles, that sometimes the only thing he could do was get on his knees?

Sometimes he imagined he saw a spark of recognition in her beautiful blue eyes. His imagination? A desperate hope? He spent hours, riding along, his head bent, letting Dusty have rein, to stare into those endlessly deep, sightless blue eyes. He spoke to her. Softly, tearfully, cajolingly, angrily. Hour after hour, saying her name, pointing out things in front of them, remembering aloud the times they'd shared and telling her how dearly he cherished the memories.

I love you, Rebecca Ann. Come back to me. Please, come back to me. If it'll make you happy, darlin', I'll hang up my guns. We'll live on the farm with your church folks. Would you like that? I can be a farmer. I'd make a damned good farmer. Don't you think? Just don't die on me, honey. Please, don't die on me. I'll never leave the lamps burnin' again and embarrass you. And I won't never build up the fire, either. I'll do it the brethren way. I swear, I will. Do you hear me, Rebecca Ann? I'll learn how to read, and I'll get to be like your papa, a Bible scholar. Smart as a tack, that's what. I'll learn highfalutin words. I'll get me horn-rimmed glasses and make love to you in a three-piece suit. I'll do anything to make you happy. Just don't go away from me like this, darlin'. Please, don't leave me.

Nothing. No answer. No flicker of life in her eyes. Sometimes he got so frantic, he wanted to shake her.

Goddamn it, wake up! I'm your husband, and I'm orderin' you to stop this. Say somethin' to me. You can't just crawl away inside of yourself and hide! That's what you're doin', damn it! Hidin' from life. Wherever you are, darlin', you gotta come out. Stand up to it. Fight back, for God's sake. You won't be alone. I'll be there, right beside you. I swear it. But you gotta make a stand. You can't just curl up and die. You're leavin' me. Leavin' me all alone. I'd never do it to you. Please, don't do it to me. You think I'm strong. You think I'm never afraid. Well, think again. I'm not strong, and I'm scared to death! I can't live without you. Do you hear me? If you won't fight for yourself, then, damn it, love me enough to fight for me.

At night after cooking and bottling the broth he poured down her each day, Race heated water to bathe her and put her in a fresh gown. Then he washed the soiled gown and the flannel pads he had to keep under her all day, hanging the lot near the fire to dry overnight. He slept with Rebecca in his arms, his body so exhausted that he ached, his heart stripped of hope, his mind clamoring with fear.

Race Spencer had finally come up against an enemy he couldn't defeat. Its name was Death.

Broth. Water. Rebecca floated in the grayness. It was like being inside a blanket that had been sewn shut, so soft and nice. She wasn't afraid of anything in there. Nobody could get her. She needed no one. And nothing could hurt. *Rebecca.* Race kept calling her name from a long way off, kept talking to her. She couldn't see him. Couldn't feel him. Sometimes he sounded so sad. So afraid. She wanted to tell him to come inside the gray blanket with her. No sadness, no fear. The only time anything felt sort of real was when she choked on the water and broth he kept forcing into her mouth.

He talked to her. Sometimes she couldn't make out the words. They were just a faraway sound that didn't bother her. But every once in a while, they came closer and made a bit of sense. *Come out of there. Come back to me. Fight for me.* The words tugged at her, made her want to reach through and touch him. *I love you, Rebecca Ann. Do you hear me, darlin'? I worship the ground you walk on. I cherish the air you breathe. I love you with my whole heart and soul. Fight for me. If you can't for yourself, do it for me.* When the words reached through to her, she could sometimes turn around and around inside the blanket until she found a little, tiny hole. If she moved close and peeked out, she could see him. Just his face. And only for a few seconds. Then the hole would start to shrink, growing smaller and smaller, until it was tinier than a pinprick.

Race drew Dusty to a stop on a slight rise and stared down at the white farmhouses and outbuildings below. The houses were situated in a large circle around a common, the barns and outbuildings extending out onto the surrounding grassland from behind the dwellings. Race saw a few oxen in one fenced field, three horses in another. No other stock was visible. The people he saw outside wore all black garments, as drab and lifeless-looking as the farming community they were trying to start.

Race remembered Rebecca telling him that the brethren couldn't buy stock, crop seed, or farming implements until they had received the proceeds from the land sale in Pennsylvania. These folks had come here with only the money to erect their homes and farm buildings, with enough left over to survive the winter. Without the money in Race's saddlebags, they would lose their shirts come spring.

Well, their wait was over. He'd brought them their money. He'd also brought them his woman.

Even if he hadn't seen the black-garbed people moving about the community common, Race would have known he'd come to the right place by the farming community's layout, the houses built in a perfect circle, each one exactly alike. It obviously wasn't acceptable for a man to slap red paint on his barn or to build a bigger house than his neighbors had. One for all, all for one.

A sinking sensation entered his stomach. He had to agree with the sheriff in Santa Fe. A bunch of real strange folks lived here. Race had gone into town first to get directions so he could find this place. He'd ended up getting a lot more from the sheriff than just that. An earful, more like. The Bible thumpers out this way, according to the sheriff, weren't exactly neighborly. They stuck to themselves, and they didn't want to be bothered. Real straitlaced people, the women covered chin to toe and painfully shy in manner, the men stern and unsmiling.

Race would stay here if Rebecca got well. He would hang up his guns, and he'd eat dust, walking behind a plow from dawn to dark. He'd wear a sacklike suit and a funny-looking hat. He'd even try to grow a beard, though his Apache blood made his whiskers come in thinner than most with only a few stray hairs where others had sideburns. He'd pray and read from the Bible. He'd go to meetings. In short, he'd go to hell and back every day and twice on Sunday if it would make her happy.

But that didn't mean he was going to like it.

Nudging Dusty's flanks, Race started down the slope. As he rode near the farm, two men who worked together installing fence posts stopped to stare at him. Then a woman in the common caught sight of him and cupped a hand to her forehead to shade her eyes. After a moment, he saw her stiffen and take a faltering step forward. Race suspected the woman had recognized the girl he held cradled in his arms.

The woman shouted something. A moment later, other black-clad figures began emerging from the houses to gather in the common. Race headed straight for them, praying with every breath he took that their familiar faces and voices would reach Rebecca and bring her out of the stupor.

None of them offered to speak when Race drew up in front of them. Their faces all looked the same to him. The women all wore their hair in braided coronets atop their heads, as Rebecca did, except that they looked sturdy, drab, and plain, while she looked delicate, golden, and beautiful. The men seemed shapeless in their loose black suits. Their beards covered their faces to such a degree that Race was mostly aware of only their staring eyes.

"My name is Race Spencer," he informed them in a hoarse voice. "My wife is dyin', and I've brought her home to you in hopes your love and prayers can save her."

Race swung his right leg over Dusty's head and slid off the horse with Rebecca still clutched to his chest. He shifted his gaze from one unreadable face to the next, his eyes burning with tears. Why were they just standing there? She was dying, and all they could do was gape at him?

"Her folks was all massacred. I'm the one who found her. She was in shock. She got better for a time, and durin' that time, I took her to wife, thinkin' I could keep her safe and make her happy. But the men who killed all her folks came back, and she went like this again. You gotta take her. Please. She's in shock again. The doctor says she's dyin'. And I can't save her." He found himself staring into a thin young man's gray eyes. "Please, take her. Help her, if you can. Pray your words over her. Tell her she's home."

The young man stepped forward and took Rebecca's limp body into his arms. Her golden head lolled on his shoulder. Her blue eyes stared blankly from her pale face. Her arm dangled limply from her shoulder. Race gazed at her through a blur of tears, his own arms hanging like lead weights at his sides.

He had gotten her here. She was still alive. Maybe these people who knew her and loved her would know what to do for her. He sure as hell didn't.

That was Race's last thought. The next instant, he pitched forward in a dead faint.

"Oh, mercy!" Sarah Miller cried. "Zachariah, help me!" She knelt by the unconscious man, reached to turn him over, and froze when she saw his sidearms. "Oh, dear heaven . . ." She glanced up at her husband. "Father, I believe this man is a gunslinger."

Zachariah knelt on the other side of the stranger. "Many men wear a gun, Mother. It doesn't necessarily mean—"

"He's wearing two," Sarah said softly. She glanced up at Henry Rusk, who was gazing down at the girl he held in his arms, his expression stricken. "God have mercy. What kind of man has our Rebecca gotten herself tied up with?"

Nessa Patterson, a woman of considerable girth, hurried over to Henry, her hands fluttering as she checked Rebecca for injuries. "Whatever on earth is wrong with her? Oh, my, Henry. Take her to our place. She's in a very bad way."

George Hess had just settled back with his boots propped on the corner of his desk to enjoy his afternoon brandy and an expensive Cuban cigar when a loud knock sounded on his closed study door.

"Who is it?" he barked, displeased that someone would choose this moment to disturb him. If it was that stupid Mexican housekeeper he'd recently hired, he was going to fire her on the spot. The damned woman was about to drive him crazy.

"It's Gib," a muffled, masculine voice replied.

George sighed. "Come on in."

When Gib stepped through the doorway, George couldn't help but note how incongruous the hired gun looked in the well-appointed room. Gleaming knotty pine, leather-bound books lining the shelves, expensive furnishings, and an imported Tibetan rug. In his filthy, stained buckskins, Gib looked as out of place in here as a turd on a fine china plate.

George lifted his snifter. "May as well pour yourself a drink."

The slender hired gun stepped over to the mahogany sideboard, pulled the stopper on the brandy decanter, and sloshed a measure of liquor into a snifter. As Gib turned toward the chair in front of the desk, George ran his gaze over the younger man's leather garments, barely able to control his sneer. The gunslinger looked like a cross between a vaquero and a redskin, the stench that came off him so sharp it stung George's nostrils.

Following George's example, Gib threw up his legs to settle his dusty boots on the desk, his spur shanks scarring the polished oak. The hired gun's arrogant disregard for his possessions made George's blood boil, but the smile he pasted on his face revealed no trace of his anger. One of the problems with employing sidewinders was that you didn't dare antagonize them for fear they might bite.

"I thought you went to town for a little slap and tickle." George meant that literally. In the year since he had hired Gib, he'd had to bail the man's ass out of jail three times for beating whores. The little bastard couldn't get his rocks off unless he hurt a woman first. "What happened. All the ladies run when they saw you coming?"

Gib smiled and took a slug of brandy. The man was too unrefined to sip the stuff. George figured he could pour Gib a jigger of bull piss, and the son of a bitch would never know the difference.

"We got us a problem," Gib said. "Race Spencer just paid a visit to our local sheriff."

George had been about to take a puff from his cigar. He froze and swore under his breath. "Spencer? You sure? He's in Colorado. Or so you said. What in the hell would he be doing here?"

"I followed the man for a month. I reckon I know him when I see him. As for why he's here, who knows?" Gib twisted in the chair to expel gas, the sound disgusting, the resultant stink even worse. "Had the little blond with him. Appeared to me she was ailin' with something. Judging by the bulge of the man's saddlebags, he brought the church folks their goddamned money."

"Christ!" George slapped his brandy glass onto the desk, slopping liquor onto the blotter. "I told you this would happen if you didn't get that money. I goddamned told you, didn't I?"

Gib's blue eyes went cold and threatening. "You dissatisfied with my work, boss man? I got plenty of job offers."

George gripped his chair arms with such force his knuckles ached. "I know you did the best you could. It's just so damned infuriating. I sent sixteen men to take some money from a bunch of religious fanatics who wouldn't piss on their own pant legs if they were afire, and only two of you came back. Empty-handed, I might add! Now you tell me Spencer is here with the damned money. Do you know what that means? Do you?"

Gib's eyes began to glitter. "Don't raise your voice at me. I don't take that kind of shit off nobody, old man. No matter how much you pay me."

George sat back, struggling to calm down. "I don't mean to raise my voice. It's simply that this will cause me no end of difficulty. I told you, under no circumstances did I want that goddamned money to reach Santa Fe. Now those Bible thumpers will be able to buy their mules and farming equipment. Unless I drive them out, they'll plant crops come spring. And they will undoubtedly have enough capital left over to make their payment to the bank as well. If you had done your job, they would have gone broke and pulled out come spring instead of breaking ground. I could have gotten their land dirt cheap after they left, no one the wiser."

"Calm down. You'll get your goddamned land. Then you'll be the largest landholder and richest cattle rancher in this territory."

"If we make a mistake—just one—I could end up being the richest rancher ever to shake a hoof for a hemp committee."

"No mistakes." Gib smiled and shrugged. "We can burn the church folks out just like we did so many of the Mexicans. Make it look like a comanchero attack. It doesn't have to be a situation that casts suspicion on you. A few unshod horses in with the shod. A little rapin' and scalpin' tossed in for looks. The law here will never think you were behind it. Hell, if that little blond doesn't have somethin' catching, maybe we'll even steal her. Comancheroes do that, you know. She'd bring a fine price across the border."

"Not after you had your fun with her, she wouldn't."

Gib laughed. "True. But she'd be a nice little reward for all my trouble."

George recalled the staggering sums of money he had paid this man and his ragtag bunch of hired guns to either drive out or murder the Mexicans who had recently owned parcels of land all around his ranch. "I pay you handsomely for your services."

"Yeah. But it's all relative, right? You've gained a hell of a lot more than you've paid, old man. Thanks to me, you own tons of land you had no hope of buying otherwise. Land you had no moral right to take, and once it was abandoned, you got your hands on it for a fraction of its worth. Every dime you've ever paid me was money well spent, and you know it."

George huffed. "Don't talk to me about moral rights. As if those Mexicans' stupid land grants meant anything?"

Gib chuckled. "I reckon they meant something to the Mexes. And there are a lot of folks who'd disagree with you. According to treaty, the Mexicans had every right to own that land."

"This is U.S. territory now, and I don't give a shit how the Treaty of Guadalupe Hidalgo reads. Why should I let a bunch of stinking greasers stand in the way of accomplishing my dreams?"

Gib held up his hands. "I'm not saying you should. I'm just saying you've paid me to get the job done, and I've done it. You've gotten their land, extended your boundaries, and have one of the biggest spreads in northern New Mexico. All thanks to me."

"With one big exception, the Lunas' parcels, which just happen to have the water I need."

"Hey, it's not my fault they were smarter than you gave them credit for!" Gib said with a laugh.

George couldn't argue the point. The Lunas had seen what was happening to all their neighbors and had decided to get out while the getting was still good, selling their parcels for a decent market price to that religious sect back east. Now George had a group of fanatics to contend with, a stickier problem, by far, than no-account greasers. The sheriff might get a little more upset when it was a passel of white U.S. citizens who were murdered.

And murdered, the fanatics would be. George couldn't risk being linked to any of this church business. A dozen of the sect members had already died in Colorado, and he had orchestrated their deaths. If he sent in men to attack that farm and allowed anyone there to live, that person might start putting the facts together, realize the two attacks were related, and then figure out who stood to gain from the results. George Hess wasn't about to dance at the end of a hangman's rope.

"I want that land," he told Gib gruffly. "No loose ends, no problems rearing up to bite me in the ass later. You understand?"

"Spencer is a mean son of a bitch, and he's one of the fastest I've ever seen. I don't risk dying cheap, Hess. You want me to take him, you're gonna increase my pay substantially."

"Maybe I don't want you to take him. Be simpler to just wait until he rides out and then settle our business with the Bible thumpers."

"And have him get wind of it, then come back here after my ass? No way! Right now, he thinks the attack in that arroyo was random—just some no-account skunks who got wind of the money those folks were carrying. But the minute something happens here, he'll put it all together. When he does, you're a dead man. I'm not going to be buried with you."

George thrummed his fingers on the chair arm. For the most part, he seldom felt intimidated by only one man, no matter how fast with a gun. But Race Spencer wasn't your average leather slapper. Judging by his reputation, the man had two traits that made him far more dangerous than most, intelligence and ethics. Gib was right. Spencer would be the type to return to Santa Fe to right a wrong, and George wanted no loose ends.

"He's real taken with that blond gal," Gib pointed out,

still arguing his case. "Watches over her like a mother hen. Even if he doesn't leave her behind, we'll be killing all her church folks. That isn't going to make her very happy. I don't want the bastard gunnin' for me later to avenge her people, and that's exactly what he'd do."

"All right!" George cried. "Just shut up. I'm trying to think."

"Excuse me all to hell."

George sighed and met Gib's gaze. "I understand your concerns. Now try to understand mine, that being *can* you take him? He got the best of you and a goodly number of men up in Colorado. And judging by his reputation, he's one fast son of a bitch. In a fair fight, I'm not sure you can take him."

Gib chuckled. "Pardon me, boss, but do I have 'dunce' printed in red across my forehead? Who mentioned fair? I'm not gonna pace it off with the bastard. He's too good. He'll be one man against eight. None of those church people are going to lift a hand against us! We'll lure Spencer out to face us, put a couple of slugs each in his hide, then do our business with the fanatics. Trust me. I know what I'm doing."

"So does he. That's what worries me. You're used to outsmarting dumb leather slappers, and it's made you arrogant. Spencer is not dumb."

Gib grinned. "Spencer has a loyal streak a mile wide. In the gunslinging business, that isn't a real smart way to be. In his case, it's going to get him killed." Gib finished off his brandy. "He's the kind who'll walk straight into flying lead rather than stand aside while his woman is being roughed up, and I know how to make a skirt sing out real pretty. He'll come to me, and when he does, he's a dead man."

Chapter 22

Race smiled to himself as he ran the currycomb over Dusty's flank. Seventeen and eighteen years old respectively, Matthew and John Patterson, the sons of Race's host and hostess, were bantering back and forth in the center aisle of the barn as they forked straw into the barn stalls. As young men everywhere often do, they were boasting to each other of their physical prowess, their claims growing more and more unbelievable with each exchange. If it got much deeper, Race was going to holler for a shovel.

"You call that impressive?" John cried. "I can chop three cords of wood without resting and never break a sweat."

Gazing over the top rail of the enclosure, Race studied John's face, noted the sheen of perspiration on the young man's forehead, and nearly chuckled aloud as he resumed currying his horse. If the young man broke a sweat pitching straw, it stood to reason that he probably poured sweat while chopping wood.

"Oh, yeah?" Matthew retorted. "Well, I once chopped five cords of wood without stopping to rest. And when I finished, I wasn't even tired. If you don't believe me, go ask Pa."

Race shook his head. Rebecca's church folks looked strange, and when you first got to know them, they seemed strange. But after being around them for five days, Race was starting to realize they really weren't so differ-

346

ent, after all. Young men everywhere had to flex their muscles, and their most used muscle was usually their tongue.

As Race recalled, he'd never engaged in boasting matches, not so much because he'd been above it, but because his life hadn't allowed him the luxury. At John's age, he'd been eighteen going on fifty, already making his living by hiring out his gun, a profession that, by its very nature, precluded bragging. Sooner or later, a boastful gunslinger found himself having to back up his brag with fact.

"Hey, Mr. Spencer," John called. "How many cords of wood can you chop without resting?"

Race straightened to look over the stall partition at the young men. "If I'm feelin' my oats when I start, maybe a half-cord. You fellas flat have me beat, hands down." Both youths had the good grace to look shamefaced, their beardless cheeks turning pink with embarrassment. Race turned back to comb out Dusty's mane. "I reckon it's all the good cookin' you growed up on. Bound to make a difference, don't you think? My ma died when I was a tyke, so I never got good grub in my growin' up years. Made me kinda puny, I reckon."

"I wouldn't go so far as to say you're puny. But you are right about one thing." Matthew came to fold his arms atop the closed stall door. "Our ma is a fine cook, isn't she? That dessert she made last night was so good I went back for thirds."

"It was mighty good," Race said in all sincerity, a smile tugging at his mouth as he recalled how much more responsively Rebecca had swallowed last night when he had poked a spoonful of the milk-thinned chocolate pudding in her mouth. "Even Rebecca liked it."

"That's why Ma made it, I think," John observed, joining his brother at the stall door. "Rebecca always has loved her chocolate."

Matthew grinned. "You remember the time she sneaked the spoonful of cocoa powder?"

John threw back his head and laughed. "She thought it would taste good, and of course, it didn't. Tasted so bad, in fact, she gasped, got it up her nose and down her throat. She almost strangled.''

Race left off currying the horse to lean against the stall partition. He enjoyed hearing stories of Rebecca's life before he'd met her. ''I never knew she loved chocolate so much.''

''Oh,'' Matthew said, ''she's the worst! Anything with chocolate in it, and that girl lays back her ears and dives right in.''

''You just wait and see, Mr. Spencer,'' John inserted. ''Ma will have her set to rights in no time.''

Race believed John might be right about that. Nessa Patterson, a plump, rosy-cheeked woman with twinkling brown eyes and hair nearly as dark as Race's own, had been working tirelessly these last five days to prepare nourishing meals for Rebecca. Meat and vegetables ground to a paste consistency and thinned with broth. Mashed fruits thinned with juice. So far, Race could detect no improvement in his wife's emotional state, but there was no question that she had benefitted physically. Thanks to Sister Nessa's efforts, Rebecca had gotten some color back in her cheeks and was regaining some of the weight she'd lost, which gave Race reason to feel far less worried. As long as his wife got all the food her body required, she wasn't likely to weaken and die, as the doctor from Cutter Gulch had predicted. And where there was life, there was hope.

For that reason alone, Race thanked God that he'd brought Rebecca here. Never having cared for a baby, Race hadn't thought about grinding and mashing foods. Nessa Patterson had fed Rebecca a full meal the very first night and had been preparing her three full meals a day ever since, with all kinds of snacks in between.

As if he read Race's thoughts, Matthew said, ''Set to rights? Poor Rebecca's going to wake up with two chins just like Ma.''

Race chuckled in spite of himself. Nessa was a well rounded figure of a woman, no question about it. ''I don' care if Rebecca wakes up with *three* chins.'' Race's throat went suddenly tight, for he meant that with all his heart

He didn't care if Rebecca was fat or skinny. Hell, he didn't care if she developed warts. Just as long as she *was*, he'd take her any way he could get her. "Thanks to your ma, Rebecca's not gonna sicken and die now before she has a chance to get well. She's quite a woman, your ma. You best be glad you got her."

John grinned and elbowed his brother, who was a tad plump. "Look who's talking about two chins. You're about there yourself."

Matthew straightened suddenly. "Ma's hollering for us."

John turned to listen as well, his smile slowly fading. After a moment, he frowned slightly. "That's not Ma. It sounds like—" He shoved away from the stall door. "Something's wrong!"

Race heard it then as well. Faint shouts, then screaming. He burst out of the stall to run after the boys up the aisle. As the three of them spilled from the barn into the bright morning sunlight, the sounds became more audible. Angry shouts, frightened screams. As Race ran toward the back door of the Pattersons' house, he saw smoke spiraling into the sky. A fire? The Patterson house looked fine. But something was burning. It looked to Race as if the smoke were coming from the opposite side of the common.

Just as Race and the boys reached the Pattersons' back porch, several gunshots cracked in the crisp morning air. At the sounds, Race's skin prickled. The Brothers in Christ owned rifles but used them only for hunting game. They wouldn't be firing weapons out in the common.

John struggled to open the back door, his shaking hands fumbling with the knob. Once in the kitchen, the young man staggered to a halt, his face turning white. Race's stomach dropped as he reeled to a stop beside him. The kitchen bore signs of a struggle, two chairs tipped sideways, a china plate lying shattered on the floor.

"Ma? Pa?" Matthew came to a stop next to his brother, his face draining of color. "Dear God, what happened in here?"

Rebecca. His ears ringing with the report of more gunfire out in the common, Race rushed through the house toward the front bedroom where he and Rebecca had been sleeping since their arrival at the farm. As he passed through the dining room and sitting room, Race saw more signs of a struggle, a lamp, surrounded by spilled oil, lying broken on the floor, furniture tipped over, the front door hanging ajar by one hinge. Out in the common, he saw horsemen riding past, firing their guns into the air, the dust of churning hooves drifting into the room, interspersed with screams and the gunfire.

Since coming to the farm, Race had removed his guns and hadn't worn them since. They were in the bedroom closet with his saddlebags, the gun belt hanging on a wall hook, his Henry propped in the corner.

Even as Race hurried across the sitting room to the bedroom, his legs went watery with alarm. The door stood open. In and of itself, that wasn't strange because Nessa kept an eye on Rebecca whenever Race left the house. No, what struck terror into Race was the chaotic disarray that he saw beyond the doorway—the quilts that had covered Rebecca jerked partly off the bed and trailing onto the floor, the lamp and clock on the bedside table knocked over, the water glass that Nessa kept filled and handily positioned beside the bed lying overturned near Rebecca's pillow.

"Angels above," John whispered shakily, "where is she?"

Once inside the bedroom, Race skidded to a stop and cast a frantic look around. *Rebecca?* She was gone. Since he knew damned well that she hadn't left on her own and doubted that Nessa or Gerald Patterson would have moved her for any reason, the only possible explanation was that someone had come in here and taken her.

Race ran to the window and swept aside the curtains to look out. Beyond the glass he saw church members, men, women, and children, running this way and that like a flock of panicked black sheep, two men on horseback herding them into groups. Scanning the houses that encircled the common, Race saw other men kicking open doors, still others emerging from yawning doorways with the terrified occupants of the houses scurrying before them at gunpoint. *Sweet Jesus.* Race saw another man galloping his horse around the edge of the yard. In one hand he held several burning torches, which he was tossing, one at a time, onto the shingled roofs of the houses.

Race whirled away from the window and advanced on the closet, half afraid he'd find his weapons gone. When he jerked open the door, relief flooded through him. He grabbed his gun belt from the wall hook and strapped it around his hips. *Rebecca.* Oh, sweet Lord in heaven. She was out there somewhere. If she was aware on any level, she had to be terrified. This would be enough to ensure she never recovered, that she'd remain an empty shell for the rest of her life.

"What are you doing?" Matthew called from the doorway that opened into the sitting room. "Mr. Spencer, what have you in mind to do?"

Race made no reply, figuring it was fairly obvious what he meant to do. As he frantically rifled through his saddlebags for his extra ammunition, he kept seeing the men outside in his mind's eye, their tan leather clothing, the fringe, and the tarnished conchae. *Idiot!* Never once had he stopped to consider the possibility that the ruffians who had attacked Rebecca's wagon train might have been hired guns, sent by someone from Santa Fe to prevent that church money from reaching the members here. *Papa and the other brethren were so very careful to keep the money we were transporting a secret,* Rebecca had told him. *They installed the fake floor in the Petersens' wagon by dark of night. I can't think how the ruffians learned that we were carrying church funds.*

"You boys know who those men work for?" Race asked Matthew as he checked his Henry to be sure it was loaded.

"The big man—the one wearing the buckskin jacket and mounted on the bay—his name is George Hess. He's a cattle rancher in these parts."

Race nearly groaned aloud. He knew of Hess. Growing up on the streets of Santa Fe as a kid, he'd hated the man, in fact. George Hess, a big auger, one of the richest ranchers in the territory. The night his mother had died and

Race had run to the saloon for help, it had been Hess and some of his hired hands who refused to stir themselves from their drinks and poker games to help a half-breed Apache squaw who was bleeding to death out in the alley. The man was a racially prejudiced bastard.

Oh, God, Race thought. *Why didn't I stop to think?* It was so apparent to him now—so horribly apparent. *Land.* Granted, the disputes over grazing land in the northern New Mexico territory were, in his opinion, still in their infancy. Race expected to see the grasslands here run red with blood before it was all over. But it certainly wasn't as if the land grabbing hadn't already begun. The Treaty of Guadalupe Hidalgo that granted certain Mexican families parcels of prime ranch land in New Mexico was a sore point with many of the Anglo cattlemen, and some of them were already taking matters into their own hands to drive the Mexicans out.

"Did the church buy all this land from Mexicans?" Race demanded to know.

Matthew raked a hand through his hair. "I don't—yes, come to think of it, yes. A family named Luna owned all of these parcels. I never met them, but that's a Spanish name, isn't it?"

Race was so furious with himself that he wanted to put his fist through something. *If the money doesn't reach the church members in Santa Fe by early spring, the church will go bankrupt. The brethren won't be able to plant crops or make their land payment to the bank. They'll lose everything.*

Race was shaking as he returned to the window. *They'll lose everything.* Everything . . . the tracts of land. Without that money, the brethren would have been forced to pull up stakes in the spring, leaving all of these parcels abandoned. Some ambitious, greedy rancher could have come in after they pulled out and purchased these parcels for a little bit of nothing, increasing his holdings, nicely, tidily, and legally. Only Race had unwittingly foiled that plan by beating the ruffians at their own game up in Colorado and then bringing the money south before spring, thereby preventing the church from going bankrupt. By doing so, he had sealed these people's fates.

After ripping the curtains from the rod with a furious sweep of his hand, Race broke out the windowpane with the butt of his Henry. The cacophony of screams and shooting in the common drowned out the sound of shattering glass.

One thing George Hess hadn't counted on if he attacked this farm was to encounter a godless, gun-toting visitor who might fight back. And fight back, Race would. They had his *wife* out there, damn them, not to mention a horde of innocent, harmless people. *Children*, for Christ's sake.

"What are you doing?" John cried from the bedroom doorway. "We don't believe in violence, Mr. Spencer. You can't use that rifle."

"The hell I can't."

Matthew's voice was low and almost expressionless when he spoke. "Mr. Spencer, we've made you welcome here, accepted you into our fold, treated you like one of our family. Is this how you're going to thank my parents for their goodness?"

Saving their lives was exactly how Race intended to thank them.

"You won't be welcome here anymore if you do this!" John cried. "You'll have to leave! Stop and think, Mr. Spencer! Of Rebecca, if nothing else. She may die if you take her away from here!"

Rebecca was going to die out there in the common unless Race did something. Race aimed his rifle at the man on horseback who was riding around the enclosure, setting fire to the rooftops with burning torches. "Matthew, those men out there are gonna kill everyone. Not just the adults, but the children."

"You don't know that. You can't know that for certain."

"Oh, yes, I do."

Race squeezed back on the trigger. The sudden explosion of sound in the room made both young men squeak in fright.

"Father in heaven, what have you done?" John cried.

He ran to look out over Race's shoulder. "Dear God, you *killed* him! Are you mad?"

Race jacked another cartridge into the chamber. "John, either go find a rifle and help me, or take your brother and go hide. I'm one man against several. My chances—"

"Spencer!" a man outside yelled. "Throw down your weapons and come out with your hands up! Do it! Do it right now or she dies!"

Race froze with the rifle butt not quite to his shoulder. *Oh, Jesus, God.* The bastard had Rebecca.

The gray blanket had ripped wide open, and Rebecca had been dumped out into a waking nightmare. Sunlight, blue sky, grass-scented wind cutting through her clothes to chill her skin. Gunshots, screams, people whom she knew and loved being herded into groups, the men apart from the women, the children apart from their mothers. It was like what had happened in the arroyo, all over again, only worse. Far worse. This time, it wasn't just older men and women who might die. One young woman held an infant in her arms. There were toddlers, screaming for their mothers. Older children, sobbing and moaning.

In the past, Rebecca had awakened a few times not recognizing where she was, but it had never been like this, in broad daylight, with a man's arm clutching her around the ribs and a huge, curved knife held to her throat. A dream? Reality? Her legs and arms felt rubbery. She had a sense of having been deeply asleep and being suddenly awakened by a noise—a blank, disoriented, fuzzy-headed feeling.

It didn't stay with her for long. A gleaming knife held to one's throat had a way of jerking a person awake fast—as effectively, if not far more so, than a splash of ice-cold water in the face.

Despite the explosion of terror in her mind, Rebecca held herself perfectly still, convinced that her throat would be slit if she so much as stiffened. The man who held her—she couldn't see his face—was tall, and her bare feet dangled above the ground, her heels bumping against the insteps of his boots. Without moving her head, she angled her gaze downward and glimpsed white, which told her she was wearing a nightgown, the only kind of white clothing she owned.

She *had* been asleep then. *Madness.* She didn't know where she was or how she'd come to be there. With a sweep of her gaze, she once again took in the faces of the people who huddled, sobbing and chuffing, in groups around her. Beloved friends, one and all. Members of her church family—those who had preceded Rebecca and her traveling party to New Mexico. Was she at the new farm in Santa Fe?

A wild glance at the buildings told Rebecca she must be. Dreaming. She had to be dreaming. She had no recollection of coming here. None. The last thing she remembered was— Horror grabbed her by the throat. Oh, God . . . the last thing she recalled was hiding behind the wood stove in Race's cabin and being so afraid that her mind began going black. Shock? Had she gone back into shock? If so, how had she gotten here?

"I'll kill her, Spencer! So help me, God! On the count of ten! Either you drop your guns and come out with your hands up, or she's dead! One, two, three, fou—"

"You bastard! She's in shock. She doesn't even know what's happening!"

Race's voice. Rebecca followed the sound to the window of a house. She glimpsed a flash of blue-black hair. *Race.* Shock. She'd been unconscious? Oh, God. What was going on? Who was this man? There were houses burning.

"Four!" the man who held her yelled. "Five! Come out, Spencer. You gonna let her die in your place? Six!"

"You'll kill her anyway, you son of a bitch! Do you think I don't know that?"

"If you come out, we'll give her and the others until morning to clear out," the man who pressed the knife to Rebecca's throat cried. "It's your ass I want, Spencer. Fourteen of my men! You killed fourteen of them! And you're gonna pay. You hear me? It's you I want! You and me, we got unfinished business. Come out, and we'll give the others a period of grace to get out of here! Seven! Eight!''

''Hess!'' Race roared from inside the house. ''Give me your word, goddamn it. Swear that you won't harm any of 'em or allow any of 'em to be harmed. Otherwise I'll open fire, and you're gonna take the first bullet, you bastard!''

''You have my word!'' a man yelled from somewhere behind Rebecca. ''My word of honor. None of them will be hurt if they leave before morning.''

Rebecca felt the knife pressing against her throat and a horrible, watery sensation trickled through her. *Fear. Race. Her gaze clung to the window. Come out. Save me. Please, don't let him kill me. Please, please, please* . . .

His rifle appeared in the window. Rebecca nearly dissolved with relief when he tossed it outside. The Henry hit the dirt, butt first, then thudded onto the patchy grass. He was going to come out. He wasn't going to let her die. *Thank you . . . thank you. Oh, Race . . . thank you.* His dark arm appeared in the window opening again, his gun belt clutched in his fist, the pearl handles of his Colts gleaming like creamy wedges of cheese against the dull black metal and dark leather.

''I'm comin' out!'' Race called as he chunked out the side arms. ''Stop countin', you murderin' bastard. Harm a hair on her head, and I'll see you in hell.''

Rebecca felt the man's chest jerk with laughter against her back. ''That's big talk for an unarmed man, Spencer! Get your ass out here. I gave you my word. Hess gave you his. I ain't gonna harm the woman.''

Within seconds, Race's tall, black-clad frame appeared in the open doorway. As he stepped out onto the porch, he raised his empty hands, his palms forward, his long fingers slightly curled. The wind caught his black hair, whipping the strands across his dark face. Rebecca stared at him. So glad. So very glad. The knife wasn't going to slice into her jugular. She wasn't going to die. Race would always keep her safe. Always. He'd promised. And he never broke his word.

He looked so big and strong and formidable. As he

stepped off the porch, the thick ropes of muscle in his thighs snapped the black denim of his jeans taut. That long-legged, loose-hipped stride. The hard, relentless cut of his features. The grim set of his mouth. He made all other men look like pathetic near-misses. He would always keep her safe. Always.

His dark gaze cut to her face. Their eyes met. She saw his stride falter and knew he'd just now realized she was aware. He kept coming, his gaze locked on hers now, as if he were trying to tell her something. *Run, darlin'. You hear me? Run.* Rebecca swallowed, horribly conscious of the sharp blade pressed against her throat. She couldn't run until this filthy animal turned her loose. His stench rose around her, acrid and searing.

When Race was about five feet away, the man drew the knife from Rebecca's throat and tossed her aside. She saw the ground coming at her, tried to break her fall, but her arms and legs didn't react well to the messages from her brain. *Shock.* She recalled the last time she'd awakened from a stupor and how her body had refused to work. It seemed a dozen times worse now. Numb, weak, disconnected. She hit the dirt like a boneless rag doll, the side of her head cracking against the earth. For an instant, she saw stars. Oddly, she felt no pain, even though she knew hitting the ground so hard would normally hurt.

"You bastard," she heard Race say. "You got feelin's for nothin' and no one, do you?"

She managed to get an arm under her to push up. *Run, darlin'. Run.* Oh, God. How could she possibly? Her body felt like a mass of half-set jelly. Nothing worked. She doubted she could get to her feet, let alone run anywhere. Only somehow she had to. If Race had to worry about her, he'd be distracted. He might get hurt if he wasn't completely focused on those men.

Rump on the ground, Rebecca dug in with her elbows and pushed with her heels to drag herself away. A few inches. Then a foot. *Pain.* She was beginning to feel some sensation now. Along her side, where she had struck the dirt. And in her elbows, where she shoved them repeatedly against the ground.

As she pulled and pushed herself away from the men, she fixed her gaze on Race, who seemed even taller and more powerfully strapped with muscle from her prone position than he had when she'd been upright. He was a head taller than the man with the knife. Rebecca cast the thinner, leather-clad man a look of sheer aversion. Filthy, horrible crea—

She froze and stared, her heart starting to slam violently against her ribs. It was *him*. The monster who had raped and tortured her mother.

The man smiled and sheathed his knife. Her gaze followed the weapon to his hip. The knife that had slit her mother's throat. *Oh, dear God.* It all came back to her in a rush, the faces of the men who'd slaughtered her loved ones no longer featureless. Her mother's killer . . .

In a blur of tan leather, he moved forward and began to pummel Race with his fists. Rebecca shoved frantically with her feet to get farther away. None of the strangers seemed aware of her. She was just another Bible thumper to them—and a barely conscious one, at that. They were paying her absolutely no heed. *Oh, God. Oh, God.* Her mother's killer. It was *he*. She remembered now. All of it. *Oh, dear God. Merciful Lord.* Run, hide, get away from him. Away!

She slithered backward between two horses. Glancing up, she saw that both animals were riderless. Horses? Riderless horses? She couldn't believe her luck. She could get on one of the animals. Before any of these men realized what she was about, she could ride away. Later, when it was all over, she'd come back for Race. *A horse. Oh, thank you, God.*

Keeping her terrified gaze fixed on her mother's killer, it took Rebecca a moment to realize that Race was doing nothing to defend himself. That horrible sound of fists striking flesh. *Thud. Thud. Thud.* That murdering monster was battering Race's face, and he was just standing there, with his booted feet braced wide apart to keep from reeling backward under the blows.

Rebecca blinked. This wasn't right. Race? He was her warrior. The one who would always wade in, fighting

The one who would always, always win. Why was he just standing there, doing nothing to defend himself? He could break that horrible man into little pieces. Smash his face to a bloody pulp with a few blows from his massive fists. Why wasn't he fighting back?

The smaller man started burying his fists in Race's abdomen, the force of the blows knocking Race backward with such force that he staggered to stay on his feet. Yet still he made no move to defend himself. He just stood there and took it. Rebecca couldn't believe it. *If she had screamed your name, you would have tried to help her. You would have fought them with your fists, if nothing else!* As clearly as though it had happened yesterday, Rebecca remembered telling Race that, and to this day, she believed it with all her heart. He was a fighter. Nothing frightened him. He was the kind of man who would walk right up to death, stare it directly in the eye, and spit in its face with his last breath.

It hit Rebecca then, with the force of a blow to her own midriff, that Race was doing exactly that right now—engaging in a stare-down with death. He hadn't come out here to fight for her.

He had come out here to *die* for her.

She dug her fingernails into the grass and dirt, staring at him. Watching him take the punishment of the other man's fists. Her Race. Her heart. He had made a trade with these murderous animals—his life in exchange for hers. *No!* She wanted to scream it, but her throat wouldn't work. He couldn't *die!* He couldn't. How would she live without him?

Like the giant tree with injured roots that grew beside his cabin, Race suddenly went down. Over two hundred pounds of muscle-hardened flesh and bone. He fell unimpeded, the dull impact of his body as it hit the ground seeming to resound in the air. Other men wearing tan leather descended upon him, seemingly from out of nowhere, to grab him by the arms and lift him between them like the Savior on the Cross. Her mother's killer laughed. The sound slithered through Rebecca like a legion of scorpions, a horrible, despicable sound, in part a memory, in part reality, that made her shudder. While his murderous cohorts held Race slumped between them, the monster pummeled him. His face, his midriff. Blow after blow. *Thud. Thud. Thud.*

She had to do something. Oh, God. Someone had to do something. She turned an imploring gaze on the group of church brethren who stood nearby. They merely gaped, their horrified expressions nightmarishly reminiscent of the looks on the brethren's faces that evening in the arroyo as her father had been shot down in cold blood. Dazed, uncomprehending, incredulous. They weren't going to do anything, she realized. Not to help Race or to help themselves. It simply wasn't in the brethren to resort to violence, not even in self-defense, and it never would be.

"Rebecca!"

Race's hoarse cry jerked her gaze back to him. He had fallen to his knees. Blood streaked his dark face. His dark eyes burned into hers.

"Run, darlin'!" he cried. "Run!"

A dizzying sensation of tumbling backward came over Rebecca. As if separated from her own body, she saw herself in the arroyo, huddling in the bushes with her hands over her ears. *Rebecca!* her mother had screamed. *Rebecca! Run, sweetheart, run! Save yourself. Run, baby. Run!* Only she hadn't been able to move. Terror had held her in its grip. So she had huddled in the bushes, and soon, all her mother had screamed was her name. Over and over and over. *Rebecca!*

"Run!" came Race's broken cry again. "Get out of here, damn it! Run!"

Rebecca lay there, frozen, her gaze darting from the brethren to the sisters to their weeping children, then back to Race—her husband, her life, her very heart. He was going to die. He could have stayed in the house and battled his way out of this. But to save her, he'd thrown down his guns and walked out here, knowing with every step he took that they would kill him.

In her mind's eye, she saw herself, clasped to that monster's chest with his knife at her throat, her gaze clinging to the window. *Please, Race. Save me. Please, don't le me die.* And he'd loved her so much that he'd come out to trade his own life to save hers. Now, here she lay—a quivering, sniveling coward.

I should have done something! I should have fought them—bit them, kicked them, hit them with all my strength! She screamed my name, and I covered my ears!

Rebecca pushed to a sitting position. Not again. She wasn't hiding, not ever again. She'd rather die.

If you won't fight for yourself, love me enough to fight for me. She staggered to her feet. *Dizzy. Legs like rubber.* She couldn't help Race, she thought frantically. God help her, she could barely stand up. *Shock.* The horrible trembling assailed her body. A marionette, controlled by a prankster. She was too weak. Horribly weak. Her bones seemed to have no substance.

She grabbed hold of the horse's saddle to hold herself up. *Don't ask God to fight your battles. Ask Him to give you the strength to fight them yourself.* Strength. She needed strength. *Love me enough to fight for me.* She couldn't remember when Race had said that to her, she only knew that he had. And she did love him. If she couldn't save him, then she would die beside him. Better that than to crawl away like a whipped dog. Never again. Never. She couldn't live with it.

Please, God. Give me strength. Just for a few minutes. Help me to think. To stop shaking. Help me, please. So I can help him!

Still clinging to the saddle to hold herself erect, Rebecca found herself staring at a rifle. Seconds ticked past as she gaped at it. A rifle? An insane urge to giggle came over her. There was a rifle in the saddle boot, just inches from her nose. A *rifle!* Pictures flashed in her mind—of Race, of the barn, of the haystacks. *Take a steady bead, sweetheart. Now breathe in and breathe completely out. That's it. Now, squeeze slowly on the trigger. Don't pull your shot. Good girl, Rebecca Ann! That's a bull's-eye, darlin'!*

Rebecca glanced at the horse's dangling reins. With a trembling hand, she reached to grab them. Going up on her tiptoes, she brought them back over the horse's head and wrapped them around the pommel to maintain tension on the bridle bit. She hoped the horse would feel the constant tension and stand still, just as it might if a rider drew back on its reins. Her hands seemed to become less shaky as she secured the strips of leather. *Thud. Thud. Thud.* She blocked out the sound. To help Race, she had to stay focused.

With any luck, this horse had been conditioned not to panic at the sound of gunfire, just as Dusty, Race's stallion, had. If the animal would only stand fast while she was shooting, she could use its massive body as a shield so she wouldn't be felled immediately by return fire. Knowing these men and their ignoble traits, imperviousness to gunshots would be an important trait in one of their mounts. *Please, God.* She would fight this battle by herself. She just needed a little luck and the strength to do it.

She unfastened the strap on the saddle boot and withdrew the rifle. It was a lever-action, rapid-fire weapon, similar to Race's Henry. After shoving hard against the horse's haunch to bring it around broadside to the killers, she brought the rifle to her shoulder and sighted in, just to see if she would be able to hold the weapon steady enough to shoot it. A sense of calm settled over her as she recalled Race's telling her there was no such word as "can't." She could do this. *All you have to do is believe in yourself as much as I do.*

One nice thing about being slight in stature was that she could lean against the horse and fire the rifle under its head, using the animal's front shoulders as a barricade to protect her from being hit by return bullets.

Bracing herself against the horse's sturdy body, she worked the lever action of the rifle to jack a cartridge into the barrel. She could do this. Leaning forward, she brought the rifle to her shoulder and sighted in on her mother's murderer. Her heart froze when she saw the flash of his knife in the sunlight. She stared, caught in the clutches of horror. That monster had grabbed Race by the hair of the head, and he was about to cut his throat.

Oh, God. Please, God. Give me strength. Keep my aim

steady. Rebecca got a bead on the ruffian. He stood in front of Race, who was still held half-erect by the other two men. A head shot was her only safe recourse. If she aimed lower and missed, she'd hit her husband.

Breathe in. Now breathe out. Slowly squeeze the trigger. Don't pull your shot.

The blast of the rifle jolted through Rebecca, forcing her back a step. For a nightmarish instant that seemed to last an eternity, the huge, curved blade of the knife hung there under Race's chin. She had missed! The ruffian was still going to kill him.

Then, as if time had missed a gear and suddenly grabbed hold again, the knife fell to the ground, followed an instant later by the ruffian, who collapsed in a huddle at Race's feet.

From that moment on, everything went crazy. The two men holding Race let go of his arms and dove for the dirt. She heard cursing. Rebecca jacked another cartridge into the chamber, took a deep breath, and stepped out from behind the horse. Keeping her gaze fixed on the men who'd been behind her and out of her range of sight while the ruffian held the knife to her throat, she yelled at the top of her voice, "Hess!"

At her shout, all the men stopped searching for the sniper who'd just shot one of them and whipped their heads toward her, their movements almost simultaneous. Almost, but not quite. One large, gray-haired man in a buckskin jacket turned at her shout just a beat faster than all the others. Rebecca aimed her gun directly at him.

"Call them off, Hess!" she screamed. "Or you're a dead man!"

All the men froze, their startled gazes fixed on her. She knew what they were thinking. A cheek-turning Bible thumper?

Their first reaction was incredulity. The dead ruffian had tossed her aside, and none of them had given her another thought. A cheek turner, shooting at them? Even now that they saw her standing there with the rifle, they couldn't quite believe it had been she who'd shot one of them.

When they could no longer deny the evidence of their own eyes, they all got smug, half-amused looks on their faces. She knew exactly what was going through their minds. Driven by desperation to save her husband, she'd gotten off one lucky shot. But they didn't believe for an instant that she was good enough with a gun to be that lucky twice, especially not against such stiff odds.

And God help her, they were right. Five of them? Oh, merciful angels. They were going to fill her so full of holes, she'd look like a colander.

"I mean it, Hess! Twitch a muscle, and I'll blow your goddamned balls off!" In her side vision, Rebecca saw the men who had dived for cover near Race beginning to stir. "You men, over by my husband! Move another hair, and Hess is dead!" Rebecca snugged her finger over the trigger. "Your men can take me, Hess! But not before I kill you, you bastard! Call them off, now! Or come dance with me in the fires of hell! Your choice!"

Hess's face lost color. "Calm down, little lady. I'm just gonna lift my hands. Lay down your guns, boys."

"Slowly!" she shouted. "One sudden move, by any-one, and I'll kill you, Mr. Hess. Don't test me! You other men! Don't make the mistake of pointing a gun barrel toward me as you're laying down your weapons. I'm a real nervous Bible thumper right now, and if I see the nose of a gun, I'm gonna kill your boss!"

Hess went a shade whiter in the face. "Easy, boys. Do what the lady says. There's always another day."

"Another day? Don't count on it. Has he already paid you for this day's work? I thought not. If I kill your boss, you'll receive no pay! It's a very simple thing! You want to die for nothing? I'm fast. I'll kill Hess and one more of you before you get me. While you're taking those guns out of your holsters, you'd better be asking yourselves if you want my bullet to find you as a target!"

A raspy, slightly shaky voice called out, "I got these two covered, darlin'."

Tears stung Rebecca's eyes. Race. He had evidently regained his senses enough to grab a gun from the dead man's holster. She had him to back her up now. A tremo of weakness ran through her, and she wanted to lower the gun and sob in relief. But, no. Race was hurt. Badly hurt, possibly. She couldn't count on him. Not this time.

She had to fight this battle all by herself.

Rebecca could scarcely believe it when all of Hess's men slowly drew their guns from their holsters, grabbed the revolvers by their barrels, and bent to lay them on the ground.

"Back up! Five paces, hands in the air." She stepped farther out from the horse, moving the rifle barrel back and forth. "I'll shoot the first man who holds his mouth wrong! Keep backing up. That's it. Away from your weapons!"

When the men had put a safe distance between themselves and the dropped revolvers, Rebecca thought her legs were going to buckle.

"John! Matthew!" Race yelled. "Get out here and collect these weapons!"

Pain lanced across Race's belly as he pushed to his feet. "You other men! Get some rope to tie the bastards up!"

Black figures began to rush in all directions, the men leaping to do as Race asked. John and Matthew Patterson came running from the house and began scrambling to pick up the guns. Many of the other brethren were heading for their barns to get rope. Race kept the gun he'd confiscated from the dead man's holster trained on the two ruffians who had held him up while he received one of the worst beatings of his life. But even as he kept the bastards covered, most of his attention was focused on one person—a fragilely built blond in a wind-tossed white nightgown whose eyes had turned a fiery blue.

Race had never been so proud of anyone in his life, and he doubted he would ever be again. He couldn't get enough of looking at her. Pale as wax. Swaying with weakness and looking as if she might lose her grip on the rifle at any second. How she had found the strength to do what she'd just done, he would never in a hundred years know. But somehow she had.

When the brethren returned with rope and began binding Hess and his men's hands behind their backs, Race made his way toward his wife. He felt none too steady on his feet himself, but she looked as if she might collapse.

When he reached her, he had to pry the rifle from her clenched hands. Tears formed at the backs of his eyes. A lump the size of a goose egg lodged in his throat. He wanted to weep, tell her how much he loved her, and drop to his knees, right then and there, to thank God for bringing her back to him. Instead, he just stood there, so weak his legs threatened to fold as he bent to let the rifle fall to the dirt.

As he straightened, instead of telling her how very much he loved her, he said, "Rebecca Ann Spencer, I can't believe I heard you tell George Hess you were going to blow his balls off."

Her mouth twisted and her narrow shoulders started to jerk. Race couldn't tell if she was about to laugh or cry. Then a sob tore up from her, answering his question. He hooked an arm around her and pulled her against him.

"Oh, Race, I love you."

His voice throbbing with tenderness, he cupped a hand over her beautiful hair and whispered, "I love you, too, darlin'. You'll never know how much. And I've never been so proud of anybody in all my born days."

"Be careful," she cried. "Don't hug me too close. You're h-hurt!"

That he was. He couldn't remember when he'd last ached in so many places all at once. And judging by the way she trembled, he doubted she was feeling any too good herself. As soon as it truly sank in that she'd just killed a man, she would probably feel even worse. Most people spent a goodly long while on their hands and knees in the bushes after their first gun battle, and she would be no exception. In fact, given her upbringing, it might hit her even harder.

All of that aside though, Race had a sense of certainty and rightness. He'd told her once that they needed to find a happy meeting ground, and today he believed with all his heart that they'd finally found it, not in each other's arms as he'd once thought they might, but standing side by side, shoulder to shoulder. Somehow, by loving her with all his heart, he'd helped her to heal and had taught her to stand on her own two feet. In turn, she'd taught him how to do the one thing that came hardest for him— how to surrender and get on his knees.

As he rocked her in his arms, Race couldn't help but think that on his knees was exactly where he should be. It wasn't every day a hopeless, hard-bitten, played-out gunslinger was sent his very own angel. This girl truly was heaven-sent, a precious gift to cherish. He meant to do just that, with every beat of his heart and with every breath he drew, for the rest of his life.

Epilogue

Cutter Gulch, Colorado
1876—nearly eight years later

Folding the letter into its envelope and stowing it in the reticule that dangled from her wrist, Rebecca Ann Spencer smiled over the news she'd just received from the church farm in Santa Fe. All was well with the Brothers in Christ, according to Nessa Patterson. George Hess and his ruthless hired guns were still in prison. The farm had shown a profit again this last year, which was good, and Samuel Stevens, one of Rebecca's dearest lifelong friends, had finally gotten married last June to Molly Parker, a lovely girl who Rebecca felt sure would make him a wonderful life partner. Nessa had also sent word that Henry Rusk's wife, Arlene, had recently presented him with a third child, a beautiful baby girl. Rebecca would always feel a special fondness for Henry, who might have become her husband if things had gone differently. It was so good to know that he was as happy with his life as she was and that all the people who had once made up her world were doing so well.

Firmly taking each of her sons by the hand, Rebecca walked briskly along, the hem of her specially made, doeskin riding skirt snapping saucily with each tap of her boot heels on the boardwalk. She was running late for a luncheon date with a very handsome and extremely important man, her husband of exactly eight years. To mark the occasion, they would celebrate with Pete and the children over lunch, and then tonight they would have a private candlelight supper for just the two of them.

"Ma, what's an annie versey?" seven-year-old Zachariah Spencer asked. "Am I gonna have one when I grow up?"

Rebecca was about to answer when five-year-old Abe piped in and said, "You get ever' darned thing, Zachariah. I'm gonna get the annie versey. Pa said!"

"Huh-uh! He never!"

Smiling, Rebecca glanced down at each of her long-legged, sable-haired sons. By some odd quirk of Mother Nature, they had inherited only one physical trait from their mother, her sky-blue eyes, which were almost startling in contrast to their dark skin. Otherwise, they greatly resembled their father, both possessing his strong, chiseled features, sturdy build, and lazy, loose-hipped stride. The little stinkers even had Race Spencer's crooked grin, which still made Rebecca's pulse quicken when he flashed it in her direction. They were both going to be devastatingly attractive men, just like their pa.

"I have a feeling you will both celebrate many an anniversary," she said with a chuckle. "If you don't grow up so wild and ornery that you scare all the girls off, that is. Keep on as you are, and to find a wife, you'll both have to hogtie a girl and pack her back to the ranch across the rump of your horse!"

"A girl?" Zachariah pretended to retch. "Havin' Rachel and Sarah underfoot is bad enough! I ain't packin' home no wife! I'll let you have the annie versey, Abe. If there's a female attached, I'm runnin' the other way." Zachariah glanced up. "Except for you, Ma. For a female, you aren't too bad."

"Well, thank you. I think." Rebecca laughed as she stepped down off the boardwalk to cross the alley. "I'll remind you of your present sentiment about females in about twenty years, young man. We'll see how you feel—"

A muffled scream from somewhere in the alley brought Rebecca reeling to a halt. Releasing the boys' hands, she cupped a palm over her eyes to peer into the gloom between the buildings. What she saw made her heart stutter in her chest. Two very rough-looking men had an Indian woman on the ground, and though Rebecca couldn't see clearly, it appeared to her that they were trying to rape her. Her chest went cold. She threw a frightened glance up the street, then glanced back over her shoulder. It being Sunday, the shops were closed, and there wasn't another soul on the boardwalk in either direction.

"Zachariah, listen to me," she said in a low, no-nonsense voice. "I want you to take Abe by the hand and run like the very devil to the hotel restaurant. Tell your pa and grandpa Pete where I am and that I'm in trouble. Can you do that?"

Zachariah stared, wide-eyed, into the gloom. "Ma, what're those men doin'?"

"A very bad thing." She caught her elder son's face between her hands. "Zachariah, *go!* Tell your pa I need him, faster than fast! Hurry, sweetie."

Zachariah jutted his chin, looking very like his father when he turned stubborn about something. "No! I ain't leavin' you!" He leaned around to look at his smaller brother. "Abe, you run for Pa! He's at the restaurant! You tell him to come quick. I'm stayin' here to watch after Ma!"

Rebecca grabbed her son's arm and gave him a shake. "You'll do as I say, young man!" Even as she spoke, she heard Abe's small feet beating a rapid tattoo down the boardwalk toward the hotel. "Oh, lands! Zachariah, I swow, you're Spencer stubborn and twice as ornery!" She pointed at the ground. "Don't you move from this spot. Do you hear me? Not one inch. If I holler out, you start yelling at the top of your lungs for help. But you stay put!"

"All right, Ma."

Rebecca straightened, wiping her suddenly damp palms on her riding skirt. *Oh, God.* As she started into the alley, the sudden lack of sunlight made her blood run cold. She wanted nothing more than to turn and run to get Race herself. Going down there, empty-handed, to confront two possibly drunk, mean-natured men wasn't very smart. But just as her footsteps faltered, Rebecca heard a child crying. Her heart caught, and she broke into a run.

She'd covered only a few feet when she saw several two-by-fours of varying lengths leaning against the building, scrap wood, she guessed, from recent repairs that had been done to the boardwalk. She paused just long enough to grab one of the boards, then proceeded down the alley.

Stopping about six feet shy of the struggling trio, Rebecca straightened her shoulders, lifted her chin, hid the two-by-four behind her back, and cried, "Gentlemen, desist this *instant!*"

The two would-be rapists whirled in startlement to stare at her. Rebecca could smell the whiskey on them even at a distance. The terrified squaw tried to jerk down her skirt and wriggle away, but one of the men had a firm grip on her ankles and was holding her legs spread wide. The sight made Rebecca want to vomit. Standing a few feet farther down the alley, just beyond the adults, was a tiny Indian girl whom Rebecca guessed to be about four, her daughter Sarah's age. The child was so terrified, she had lost control of her bladder and drenched her little moccasins. Rivulets of urine had made tracks in the dust that filmed her skinny brown legs.

"Who'n hell are you?" one of the drunks demanded to know.

Rebecca stared at his unshaven face. Tobacco juice had run from the corners of his mouth and dried in the creases of his whiskery chin. She'd seen him trying to kiss the poor Indian woman. Rebecca wondered how the poor thing was keeping her gorge down. These two were filthy, vile excuses for men, if ever she had seen any.

"I, sir, am Mrs. Race Spencer! And I demand that you release that woman. Now!"

"Go away and mind your own business, lady. We just bought this here squaw, and we'll do what we damned well want with her!"

Over my dead body, Rebecca thought. She kept her vow to herself, however. If Race had stressed anything while teaching her to defend herself, it had been to employ the element of surprise to best advantage when she pitted her strength against men.

She tightened her grip on the two-by-four. If these no-accounts persisted in their activities, they were about to get a surprise, all right. Possibly the biggest surprise of their lives.

"Gentlemen, I shall ask you one more time. Do, please, desist!"

The men ignored her as if she hadn't spoken. Rebecca remembered Race once assuring her that he wasn't planning to tear into her like two dogs fighting over a bone. That was exactly how these two men were going after the poor Indian woman, as if she were a morsel to be fought over and devoured. They cared not a whit about the terrified little girl who watched them mistreating her mother. Knowing that Race had once witnessed a similar atrocity being inflicted upon his Indian mother, Rebecca grew more furious by the second, determined that this situation was going to end much more happily for both child and mother.

Rebecca drew the two-by-four from behind her, positioned her hands at one end for good swinging power, and waded in. *Never back off. Give no quarter. Go for blood, darlin'.* Rebecca's first swing, which she executed with all her strength and every ounce of her weight, caught the man nearest her alongside his head. He sprawled sideways, bawling like a castrated calf. On her backward swing, Rebecca caught the other man squarely on the chin. His eyes rolled back in his head and he toppled, finally granting her request and desisting, as she had so politely asked him to do, not just once, but twice.

Before Rebecca could execute another swing with the two-by-four, the first man regained his senses and dove at her legs, catching her around the knees. The board flew from her hands, she fell backward on the ground, and he crawled up her sprawled body, nearly suffocating her with his fetid breath.

"You want some of the same, you stupid bitch!" h roared, grabbing the lapels of her blouse. "I can have th squaw any old time. Ain't often I get to sample a fine thing like you!''

Just as the man's hands settled over Rebecca's breasts, something small and dark cannoned into him, knocking him backward. "You take your filthy hands off my ma!"

Zachariah! Rebecca scrambled to her feet, horrified. Her seven-year-old son was swinging his arms like a windmill in a high gale, his little fists pummeling the man in a hail of blows. Rebecca retrieved her board, terrified her child might be harmed. With all her might, she hit the man over the head. He didn't go down. She hit him again. And still he didn't go down. Just then, the other man revived and came to his knees. He would have tackled Rebecca, but the little Indian girl, taking her cue from Zachariah, leaped onto his back like a crazed little badger, reaching around to claw at his eyes and sinking her teeth into his ear. Rebecca went back to work on Zachariah's opponent. The fourth time she beaned the man, he went down like a felled pine tree, out cold.

Zachariah sat astraddle him, his small fists doubled, his lips snarled to show his teeth, his blue eyes fiery. He looked for all the world as if he'd whipped the man completely by himself.

Rebecca turned her attention to the other man, ordering the little girl to get out of the way. The instant the child leaped from the fellow's back, Rebecca swung with the board, nailing him along his jaw. He fell face first to the ground and didn't move.

Silence. Rebecca stood there for a moment, ready to bean both men if they so much as twitched. Neither did. When she deduced that they were unconscious, she leaned her club against the building and hunkered down beside the poor Indian woman, who had obviously endured some cuffing and rough handling. After helping her to sit up, Rebecca began checking her for injuries.

"Are you badly hurt, dear heart?" she asked.

The woman didn't reply. Rebecca guessed she spoke no English and, after studying her a moment, decided she must be a Cheyenne. Since the Sand Creek Massacre, the Cheyennes were a downtrodden lot. Rebecca wasn't at all surprised that some no-account white man had taken advantage of the Cheyenne people's misfortune to buy himself a squaw. The Indians believed the price paid for a woman to her family was her "bride price," the reverse of a dowry, and that a purchased girl was going to be a white man's honored wife. Unfortunately, most white men didn't see it quite that way and, after buying an Indian woman, treated her like chattel, working her like a slave and lending her to his friends. It was a horrible fate for any woman, and one that Rebecca sorely wished never occurred.

The child looked as if she might be a half-breed. Rebecca turned on the balls of her feet and held out an arm to her. "Come here, sweetness. It's all right now. Those mean men aren't going to hurt your ma anymore. I give you my solemn oath."

Some gestures were evidently universal, the offer of a hug being one of them. The little girl ran straight into Rebecca's arms and clung to her, still shaking with fear. Just then Race appeared at the end of the alley. He swung Sarah down from her perch on his shoulders and ran toward his wife and elder son. Pete arrived seconds later with Rachel and Abe in tow. Leaving all three children standing between the two sections of boardwalk, the wiry ranch foreman hurried to follow Race.

"What happened!" Race roared when he took in the scene. "My God, Rebecca Ann, are you all right?"

The poor squaw quailed in fright, flattening herself against the wall. Rebecca felt the child in her arms begin to shake more violently. "Race, sweetheart, please, don't yell. You're frightening them half to death." Choosing her words carefully out of regard for her son's innocence, Rebecca told Race and Pete the story. "I couldn't just walk away, so Abe ran for help."

Race glanced at the unconscious men. "Help? You wantin' me to haul 'em over to see Doc? Or should we just bury 'em?"

Zachariah chortled with laughter. "You should've seen her, Pa. She flat walloped the sand right out of 'em with that board!"

"Your son didn't make a bad showing of himself, either," Rebecca said proudly. Nodding toward one of the unconscious men, she said, "He knocked him off me and pounded his face. I didn't know he could take up for me like that."

After running his big hands over Rebecca to make certain she was unharmed, Race hunkered down and tousled Zachariah's hair. "Good work, son. I thank you for stayin' to watch after your ma. I guess you're growin' up, ain't you?"

Rebecca smiled when her husband's dark gaze turned back to her. He cupped her chin to tip her face and better examine it. "You sure you're okay, darlin'?"

The husky concern in his voice caught at Rebecca's heart. On this, their eighth anniversary, she would have expected their love for each other to have become complacent and less consuming. But if anything, their feelings ran deeper, their passion as easily kindled as it had been at the first, if not more so. He caught her gaze, and for a moment, they regarded each other, communicating without words, the warmth in his eyes telling her how very much he loved her. She thought her answering smile probably sent him the same message in return. He feathered his thumb over her cheek, then looked back at their son.

Rebecca returned her attention to the squaw and noticed how warily the woman was watching Race. Rebecca patted his broad shoulder, then pointed to her wedding ring. "Husband. My husband." She lightly stroked the woman's arm. "No harm. Don't be afraid."

"Don't she speak English?" Race asked.

"I don't think so. Could you try to communicate with her, Race?"

"What'll I tell her?"

Rebecca cupped a hand over the little girl's grimy hair. "Tell her she is coming home with us, and that she'll never have to be afraid again." She thought for a moment. "That she will be like a sister to us, and her daughter will be our niece. She can help me with the household chores, and she'll be very happy living with us."

Race shot her a questioning look. "Rebecca Ann, we

don't know if she wants a home. It's temptin' to do nice things for folks, but you gotta give 'em a choice. You know?''

"Very well, then. Phrase it as an invitation.''

Race spent several minutes speaking to the woman, using his limited knowledge of the Cheyenne tongue and Indian sign language to extend Rebecca's invitation. When he finally stopped gesturing and grunting, the squaw got tears in her eyes, nodded enthusiastically, and said, "Yes, please, thank you! Little Weasel, she like go.'' She motioned with her hand. "With you? Home to Spencer Valley. Little Weasel be big happy!''

Race narrowed an eye at Rebecca. "All of that, and she talks Anglo?'' He shook his head. "Women!''

Despite his gruff tone, Rebecca knew Race was touched. Her actions today could never undo the tragedy that had taken Race's mother, but in some small way, maybe it evened the score, if only by a small margin.

Race chuckled and pushed to his feet. "Well, Pete! Looks like we're gonna have some new faces at the ranch. What say we haul these stinkin' carcasses over to the sheriff and head home. It don't look like we're gonna make it for that lunch date.'' Scooping Zachariah off the unconscious man, Race said, "Is this the one that laid hands on your ma?''

Zachariah nodded.

"I figured.'' Race bent and grabbed the man by his hair. "Come on, you miserable son'buck.'' As he started to drag the man away, Race glanced back for his foreman. "Hey, Pete! You comin'?''

Pete was still staring at the squaw, apparently oblivious to all else. He had a rather dazed look on his weathered face.

"Pete!'' Race barked. "What'n tarnation's the matter with you. You goin' deef?''

Pete jerked and seemed to come back to himself. "I'm comin', boss.'' His pale blue eyes still locked on the Indian woman, he smiled slightly. The squaw lowered her lashes, clearly unnerved by his intent regard. Pete slanted a look at Rebecca. "I've heard of women bein' prettier than sunrise, sunset, and ever' damned thing in between. But I ain't run across a female that pretty in a nigh on thirty-five years." He seemed to focus and realize Rebecca might take offense. "Exceptin' for you, of course," he amended.

Rebecca glanced at the squaw, who looked rather ordinary in her estimation. Then she looked at Race, who arched an eyebrow, apparently as bewildered by Pete's behavior as she was. Then they both smiled. Pete never noticed the exchange. He had hunkered down in front of the frightened squaw and taken her hand.

Lightly caressing the backs of her fingers with his callused thumb, he said, "Ain't no need to be feelin' afraid no more, sweetness. Nobody'll lay a mean hand on you in Spencer Valley. You got Pete Standish's word on it. You hear?"

The little squaw smiled shyly and nodded. Pete started to stand up, then stopped to cup the little girl's tear-streaked face in a leathery palm. "Ain't nobody gonna hurt you neither, darlin'." He rubbed at her still wet cheeks. "I'll be. You're pert near as pretty as your ma! You know it?"

Pete swung the child up onto his hip. Rebecca's heart warmed at the gentle expression in the foreman's eyes. She had a feeling Pete's days as an ornery, cantankerous, aging bachelor had come to an abrupt halt. After a moment, the foreman set the child back down, patted her head, and smiled kindly at the squaw again.

"Yessir, two right beautiful females, them two are."

Rebecca pushed erect as Pete grabbed the other drunk and started dragging him toward the street. When the Indian woman stood, Rebecca linked elbows with her, called for Zachariah, and grabbed the little girl's hand.

"Let's go home," she said softly.

Ten minutes later, the Spencers left town, their buckboard a mite overcrowded, but every passenger smiling.

To this day, the folks in Cutter Gulch still tell the story of that long-ago Sunday afternoon when Rebecca Ann Spencer, once a cheek turner and a dyed-in-the-wool Bible thumper, beat the ever-loving hell out of two grown men in the alley next to the general store. Some people claim the poor girl had no choice but to turn ornery, living way to heck and gone out there in Spencer Valley with that ex-gunslinger husband of hers. A quarter-breed Apache, he was, and if rumor was true, meaner than a sidewinder. Kidnapped the poor girl, you know. Reverted back to his Apache ways, they say. When he finally got around to marrying the woman, right and proper, folks say she was eight months pregnant with their third child. Indecent, treating a God-fearing, Christian woman that way, but somehow, no one in Cutter Gulch could work up the courage to tell Race Spencer that to his face, not even the Baptist minister.

Other folks maintained it was the raising of her sons that turned Rebecca Ann Spencer so dad-blamed feisty. Could be true, for sure. Anybody who ever had truck with the Spencer boys could testify on a stack of Bibles that both of those young men had a wild streak a mile wide running through them. After all, how many young men have you known who would dare to kidnap and hogtie the Cutter Gulch schoolteacher, then carry her home on the back of his horse? Zachariah Spencer did exactly that, then married the poor girl the Apache way, giving her no say in the matter at all. Now, if that wasn't something? And, even worse, the black-hearted polecat got away with it!

CALLING ALL WOMEN TO THE WORLD OF AVON ROMANCE SUPERLEADERS!

Would you like to be romanced by a knight in shining armor? Rescued by an English earl with a touch of gypsy blood? Or perhaps you dream of an Indian warrior or a rugged rancher.

Then the heroes of Avon's Romance Superleaders are exactly what you're looking for! And our authors know just what kind of women these tough guys need to shake up their lives and fall in love.

So take a deep breath and let the romantic promise of Samantha James, the sexy magic of Christina Skye, the soul-kissed passion of Constance O'Day-Flannery, and the heart-stirring warmth of Catherine Anderson plunge you right in the midst of an explosive love story.

*What could be more romantic than an honest-to-goodness **Christmas Knight**, who lives and breathes to rescue damsels in distress? In her truly magical fashion, Christina Skye makes that fantasy come true for a '90's woman, just in time for the holiday season. See why Virginia Henley said, "Christina Skye is superb!" and why this romance should be on your holiday shopping list!*

Hope O'Hara's quaint new Scottish inn is falling down around her ears, but she's determined to get it in tip-top shape for the Christmas crowd. So when she's on the leaky roof one rainy evening, nearly falling off the slippery thatch, her cries for help conjure up a rescuer from across time—knight Ronan MacLeod.

CHRISTMAS KNIGHT
by Christina Skye

Hope screamed. Her fingers burned as she clawed at the roof edge, losing inches with each passing second.

Thank God the rider had come from the cliffs, answering her call.

He rocked forward into the wind while his anxious bay sidestepped nervously along the narrow trail. A branch swept past his head, and he ducked and called out at the same moment he saw Hope.

She did not understand, his words lost against the boom of thunder. Desperately, Hope clawed at the soggy reeds, which shredded at her touch. Her foot sank through a rotting beam and swept her out into cold, empty space.

She pitched down the wet reeds, a captive of the rope

lashing down the tarpaulin, her scream drowning out the man's angry shout. As if in a nightmare she plunged toward the ground, spinning blindly.

The great horse neighed shrilly as its rider kneed forward.

Instead of hard earth, Hope felt the impact of warm muscle halting her descent. Her breath shuddered as she toppled forward, clinging to the terrified horse. She was alive.

Breathless, she turned to study the man whom she had to thank for saving her life.

His long, black hair blew about his face, as wet as her own. Darkness veiled his features, permitting only a glimpse of piercing eyes and tense jaw. But the strength of his body was unmistakable. She blushed to feel his thighs strain where she straddled him.

He muttered a low phrase to the horse, the words snatched away by the wind. The sounds seemed to gentle the creature, and Hope, too, felt curiously calmed by the soft rhythm of his speech.

Above their heads the tarpaulin swept free and a four-foot section of packed reeds hurtled toward the ground. The rider cursed and kneed the horse away from the unstable roof, struggling to control the frightened mount.

Hope understood exactly how the horse was feeling. She sat rigid, aware of the stranger's locked thighs and the hard hands clenched around her waist. Dimly she felt the rider's hands circle her shoulders and explore her cheek. Hope swept his hand away, feeling consciousness blur. The cold ate into her, numbing body and mind.

Deeper she slid. Down and down again . . .

Finally, even the rider's callused hands could not hold her back from the darkness.

NOVEMBER

In a rough and tumble world, Catherine Anderson always manages to find a refuge of safety and calm, where love conquers all. Publishers Weekly *praised her as a "major voice in the romance genre." In Catherine's newest historical romance she shows us that even a former gunslinger can learn to love and* **Cherish** *a woman.*

On the trail to Santa Fe through New Mexico Territory beautiful, sheltered Rebecca Morgan loses everything and everyone she's ever had in the world. She is plucked from danger by rancher Race Spencer, a loner who reminds the young innocent of the wild land. Although she's not ready to trust anyone again, Rebecca is beginning to realize that in this life the love of a good man might be her only salvation.

CHERISH
by Catherine Anderson

"Countin' the stars, darlin'?"

Rebecca jumped so violently at the unexpected sound of his voice that she lost her hold on the quilt. Pressing a hand to her throat, she turned to squint through the wagon spokes at him.

"Mr. Spencer?"

"Who else'd be under your wagon?"

He hooked a big hand over the wheel rim and crawled out. As he settled to sit beside her, he seemed to loom, his breadth of shoulder and length of leg making her feel dwarfed. Drawing up his knee to rest his arm, he turned lightly toward her, his ebony hair glistening in the silvery moonlight, his chiseled features etched with shadows, the collar of his black shirt open to reveal a V of muscular chest. As he studied her his coffee-dark eyes seemed to take on a satisfied gleam, his firm yet mobile mouth tipping up at one corner as if he were secretly amused by something. She had an uncomfortable feeling it had something to do with her.

She expected him to ask what she was doing out there, and she searched her mind for a believable lie. She had just decided to say she had come out for a breath of fresh air, when he said, "You gettin' anxious to go to Denver?"

Her heart caught. Keeping her expression carefully blank, she replied, "I've tried not to count too heavily on it, actually. It could snow, and then I couldn't go until spring."

"Nah." He tipped his head back to study the sky. "Now that we're this close to home, I can take that worry off your mind. We got a good month before the snows'll hit." He settled his gaze back on her face, his eyes still gleaming. "In three days, we'll reach my ranch, and we'll head out straightaway. I'll have you in Denver within five days."

"I'm not in that great a hurry. I'm sure you'll want to get your herd settled in and see to business that's been neglected in your absence. After all you've done for me, being patient is the least I can do."

He shrugged her off. "Pete can handle the herd and anything else that comes up. Gettin' you settled somewhere is my first concern."

Rebecca gulped, struggled to breathe. *Stay calm. Don't panic.* But it was easier said than done. She dug her nails into the quilt, applying so much pressure they felt as if they were pulling from the quick. *Inhale, exhale. Don't think about his leaving you.* But it was there in her head, a vivid tableau: Race riding away from her on his buckskin, his black outline getting smaller and smaller until he disappeared from sight. She started to shake.

In a thin voice, she said, "Mr. Spencer, what if I were to tell you I don't wish to go to Denver?"

He didn't look in the least surprised. "I'd offer yo two other choices." He searched her gaze. "One of 'e

would be permanent, though.'' His shifted his bent leg to
better support his arm, then began clenching and relaxing
his hand as he turned his head to stare into the darkness.
''So you probably wouldn't be interested in that one.''

DECEMBER

The dark of night is full of romantic promise and during **One Moonlit Night** *a vicar's daughter has a run-in with a rakish earl. With heart-stopping excitement, Samantha James weaves a beautiful love story that is sure to enchant. As Romantic Times said, "Samantha James pulls out all the stops, taking readers on a spectacular roller coaster ride."*

The new Earl of Ravenwood has gypsy blood running through his veins. Half wild, half noble, and completely inscrutable, he is the subject of much speculation. So when the dark lord nearly runs down gently-reared Olivia Sherwood in a carriage accident, she can't help but feel trepidation. Surely there's no other reason for the racing of her heart?

ONE MOONLIT NIGHT
by Samantha James

" 'Tis midnight," he said softly. "You should not be about at this hour."

Olivia bristled. "I'm well aware of the hour, sir, and I assure you, I'm quite safe."

"You were not, else we would not be having this discussion."

Olivia blinked. What arrogance! Why, he was insufferable! Her spine straightened. "I am not a sniveling, helpless female, sir."

His only response was to pull a handkerchief from deep in his trouser pocket. Olivia stiffened when he pressed it to her right cheekbone.

386